# Get Over It

## A Steamy Rock Star Romance

### Cheryl Terra

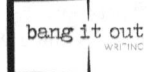

**Bang It Out Writing**

# Trigger + Content Warnings

While this book and the series it is part of are lighter romances, they do explore heavier topics that some readers may wish to be aware of prior to reading. I have tried to address those topics here without spoiling the story, however if you have concerns about any of the items listed and wish to know more, please reach out to me via email at **info@cherylterra.com**.

---

While not explicitly occurring within the text of the story or between the characters involved in Get Over It, there are discussions and descriptions of toxic relationships, emotional abuse, and non-graphic physical abuse.

This book also features mild scenes discussing trauma and therapy, parental death, assault, depression, cheating (not between characters featured in this book), and slut shaming.

As a steamy romance, this book is intended for mature adults. There are multiple sexually explicit scenes and profanity.

# Prologue

My name is Aspen Haws, and this is a love story, and if you're not into that, then fuck you.

I know it's pretentious to pretend that *my* love story is any more important than anyone else's. But it is to me.

Maybe I'm biased, but when it comes to love stories, I think ours is pretty fucking good. And I guess people like love stories because it means that there's a shred of hope for everyone to meet *The One* and have their own fairy tale. I mean, that's not the case. Not *everyone* gets a happily ever after. Statistically, some people are just going to die alone.

I guess that's supposed to be one of those things people don't say out loud, though.

Regardless, this is a love story, and it happened to me, which I suppose means it could happen to anyone. I'd like you to be advised, though, that I refuse to include any sappy descriptions of the sunset or refer to anyone's body parts as throbbing rods of passion. And hair flowing romantically in the wind is unrealistic, messy, and bad for your hair. It causes breakage.

So there will be none of that here, at least not from me. He's the romantic one, so I can't speak to what he might say. I know what I'm going to say, and it's going to involve a lot of sex, stubbornness, and the word "fuck." And if that's a problem, I urge you to refer to the first line of this story.

# Chapter One

*Aspen*

"Did you dream of doing this as a kid?"

Lac La Biche was the worst location to have a chatty office manager like Marina. The very picture of a walking, talking, ditzy blonde stereotype was the last thing I needed when in the middle of one of the most intense pre-audits I'd ever had to do. Why *anyone* thought it was a good idea to establish a manufacturing location for industrial green energy solutions in a place where generations of blue collared families had defined their entire personalities on a love of oil and gas—not to mention a place that was in the middle of fucking *nowhere*—was beyond me.

It probably had something to do with those Old Boys Clubs I kept hearing about and were never invited to, on account of my vagina.

Still, George—the Old Boy who oversaw this particular location—somehow got it off the ground, which meant letting it fail was not an option. My job was to perform an internal audit that mimicked the one the government would perform a year from now so they were ready. So, despite the aggravating annoyance that was Marina, I was supposed to be polite to her.

We were *technically* co-workers, after all, even if I was that villainous coworker that everyone hated because it was my job to tell them what they were doing wrong.

"This specific job?" My fingers paused on the keyboard as I referred to the notes beside me. "No. I didn't know pre-audits were a thing as a child. But I wanted to do something where I got to travel a lot."

"That's what I meant." Marina leaned back in her chair and stretched, thrusting her chest so far forward in the air that the buttons on her blouse threatened to pop. "I didn't even know what an office manager was, but here I am! And I love it, which is just so good, you know?"

"Well, if you love it so much, you need to do the job properly." I motioned at one of the many, many horrendously completed reports sitting on the desk. "This is a mess. If you don't correct this before your actual audit, they could shut your entire location down."

Instead of what I'd hoped for, which was the immediate acceptance of my word and resolution to correct her myriad of stupid-ass errors, Marina smiled flippantly. "I'm sure they wouldn't go *that* far."

"They absolutely would. This is one of the worst setups I've ever seen."

The dumb smile on her face faded. "Wow, you sure don't sugar coat it."

I regarded her carefully. Marina had the look of a woman who never had to work for much. Her hair was perfectly dyed, not a single split end or darkened root showing. Her nails were meticulously manicured, red paint sharply contrasting with her skin. And on her ring finger, a diamond far too big for someone who had to earn her keep working a boring office job.

It didn't take a rocket surgeon to figure out that the reason Marina had that gaudy ring and this cushy little title was because she was fucking George's son.

I closed my notebook and shut down the program on my computer. Straightening my shoulders, I looked at Marina without an ounce of humour on my face.

"I am telling you this both professionally and personally. Do the job properly. I know you're a year away from your real audit, but that's barely enough time to fix the mess you've made here. I've set up the programs we've discussed to help manage your paperwork load, but you are in for at least a few months of overtime to get this place up to company standards."

"A few months of *overtime*?" Marina looked incredulous. "There's no way George will approve that. He can't pay me for all those extra hours."

Turning, I started putting my things into my laptop bag. "You're on salary. It's expected of you to put in overtime when necessary."

"That's illegal."

Oh, to be that fucking naïve.

"It's not, and I suggest you make a plan to deal with it now. George will lose this location if you don't catch up. And let me be very, *very* clear: most of these issues? They're on you."

She closed her mouth, then opened it again, then frowned. "You're not going to put that in your report, are you?"

I paused with my hand resting on the zipper of my bag, closed my eyes for a moment as I attempted to rein in every ounce of patience I could possibly muster, then looked up at her.

"You cannot actually be serious," I replied, failing to muster up any patience whatsoever. "That is my job. To report on the status of the location, so that when your *actual* audit occurs, you're ready."

"Oh, come on!" The giggly girlishness of Marina's voice faded into a whine. "Help me out, please, Aspen? George trusts me and I hate to let him down."

I straightened the last of the papers on the desk and tucked them away before picking up my bag. "Look, I deal with this all the time. It's not hopeless, but I don't have time to sugar coat things just so you're less offended. If you want my honest opinion, quit. Let George hire somebody qualified for the role to fix it before the real audit occurs. Because if you don't have a job, and your father-in-law doesn't have a job, and your fiancé doesn't have a job, who exactly is going to take care of your kid?"

Her eyes seemed to pop. "How did you even know that?!"

I raised my eyes at her in what I hoped was a mysterious way and glanced at her belly, where there wasn't even a hint of a swell.

"I'm a *pre-auditor*," I said, as though it was some highly specialized job that involved far more badassery than it actually did. "It's my job to catch details." I started towards the door, my spine straight and heels clicking powerfully on the tile. "Please tell George I will be here at eight tomorrow, and I need to meet with him immediately. My flight is in Edmonton at two, so he can't be late."

Marina was still gaping at me, and I let her stand there as I marched down the hallway towards the elevator. I certainly wasn't going to tell her she talked loud enough while booking her appointment at the health center that the entire office knew her 'secret.' George would probably have another heart attack if he found out Marina and his son were acting like normal adults outside of wedlock. Not from the shock, but from the sputtering and screaming as he disowned yet another one of his children.

Not that I was supposed to know any of that, of course.

Just as I left the building, my phone rang.

"Haws," I answered.

"Stop answering like that. It sounds ridiculous," Darby said.

Behind every executive is someone like Darby: an executive secretary who was smarter than almost anyone else at head office. People saw her glowing tawny skin and thick, platinum-highlighted hair and assumed she was just a pretty face meant to sit there and... well, look pretty. Unfortunately for those people, Darby was Kevin Wu's right-hand person. He was the first to admit she knew the ins and outs of the business better than he did. It was an unusually honest admission from a CEO, certainly, but his self-awareness was part of why I enjoyed working for him.

Darby's competence and snark made her one of the few people I answered the phone for every time she called, and one of the few I enjoyed talking to. At work, I needed to be Big Scary Aspen, the person who forced everyone to get their shit together before regulatory came through and fucking obliterated them. I didn't have to be like that around Darby.

"Sounds less ridiculous than 'Aspen,'" I said. "Let me guess, you just got the results from Didsbury and you're calling to confirm I didn't make any mistakes because, oh fuck, that location is hemorrhaging money?"

"What? No. But that sounds awful. There's a change of plans. Kevin wants you back at the office as soon as possible. Your new flight is to Montreal at ten a.m. tomorrow."

That wasn't normal. I frowned as I reached my rental car. "Am I being fired?"

It took a few moments before Darby stopped laughing hard enough to answer me. "He can't afford to fire you, stupid. I can't tell you why right now. It's a good thing, though, so don't panic. But it's urgent, so Daniel's going to do the Fort St. John pre-audit."

I groaned. "Daniel's an idiot. He's going to fuck it up, Darb. This is a terrible idea."

"I know. But this is more important."

"More important than my actual job?"

"Mm-hmm."

I sighed. "Come on. We're friends. Not even a hint?"

"I don't like you that much," she said.

"Bitch."

She laughed. "We're on for drinks after, then?"

"Of course. See you tomorrow."

She hung up and I hesitated, looking back towards the building. I considered turning back, then got in the car and called Marina over Bluetooth. As suspected, it went to her voicemail.

"Marina, I can't make it tomorrow," I said. "Please give my regards to George and let him know a copy of the final report will be emailed to him within the week. I apologize I can't make it to discuss the results in person."

# Chapter Two

*Theo*

"... PRETEND TO LOVE him for that kind of money."

A swell of hoots and giggles blurred the conversation.

"For the rest of your life? What if he wants kids or something?"

"I can't believe you're actually sleeping with him. Like. Ew."

"It doesn't last that long. I just close my eyes and think of his bank account."

Another round of hollers filled the air, sounds that bit and stabbed and sickened me.

I wasn't meant to hear any of it.

It was girl's weekend, a getaway hosted at the cottage I'd bought at her insistence the previous year. I was spending *so* much money on real estate, she said, so why not buy something we'd actually use instead of just investing in it? She found the perfect place to get away from it all and relax, just a couple of hours away from Toronto in a particularly deserted area of cottage country. We could surround ourselves with nature, she said, nothing but trees and lakes and a starry sky to make love under while enjoying our secluded patio. And, of course, all the amenities one could think of: a hot tub, a pool, a steam shower, a full kitchen, a wine bar, a billiard room...

I'd been to the cottage three times and we'd try to fuck on the patio once, but Sheri complained that there were too many bugs and she was cold. It must have been pretty bad for her to even complain, given how long I apparently didn't last.

That was the patio they were on now, enjoying that sticky and humid evening under the pink-gold glow of the setting sun. Chilled jugs of sangria were being poured, gossip was flying like mosquitoes, and one of Sheri's friends was accidentally leaning against the intercom next to the door.

You know, the one she'd insisted we install, so if someone came to the front or if we needed something from the staff I was apparently hiring, we just had to press a button. I didn't protest; it did double-duty as a security system, which was good considering how fucking expensive the goddamn cottage was.

It was enabled with WiFi and connected to my phone, which is how I could see what was happening when I was in a city hours away. The first time my phone buzzed from the drawer I'd stored it in, I'd ignored it. I'd let it happen a few more times before I'd gotten annoyed enough to stop playing so I could turn my notifications off. Just as I opened the app to silence it for a few hours, one of Sheri's friends leaned against the goddamn button again.

"... pretend to love him for that kind of money."

Sheri's voice spilled out of the phone's speakers as an image half-blocked by a tanned shoulder appeared on the screen.

"*Close my eyes and think of his bank account.*"

Heat was rising in my cheeks.

"I don't blame you, Sher," came another voice out of the phone. It sounded like Betty Schultz, who had been the most shocked when Sheri and I began dating. "It's just funny that, of all people, Thtupid Theo is the one you're ending up with."

"Oh, come on, he doesn't lisp anymore. He's a rock star now."

They giggled.

I stared at the screen, my mind blank. The crystal-clear image on the screen showed Sheri tossing her head back as she shook her hair out. A hint of cleavage peeked from beneath her white sundress as she leaned forward to grab her wine glass. Her head tilted back, her neck long and elegant as she took a sip.

She looked beautiful.

And then there was me. Thtupid-Ath Theo with the fucking lithp. Sitting in another city, watching her tell her friends it was all a charade.

"I can't believe you're going through with this." I wasn't sure whose voice that was. "When do you think he'll propose?"

"Tomorrow night," Sheri said at the same moment the words shot through my mind. "After we get back. He's terrible at surprises. I've been practicing my shocked face all week."

I hesitated, then set the app to back up the video to the cloud before closing it. The studio seemed extra quiet.

Had I known? I asked myself.

She was different. That's what I'd thought, anyway. She wasn't in it for the clout or the exposure or for what I could do for her career. Sheri had known me when I was just a loser kid. Just Thimple Theo, with thick glasses and dirty jeans from being kicked around the playground.

Growing up, she wasn't the worst to me. That was about as much as I could say about anyone other than Rick. She hadn't been popular either and while she might not have, you know, stood up for me or whatever, she hadn't been an active participant in making my life hell. If she was shocked when my career took off, she had hidden it better than anyone else had. She didn't suddenly begin asking for handouts or reminiscing about the good old days as if I hadn't been teased and bullied mercilessly, like all the rest of them did. She cared about me... or so I thought.

Had I purposely missed the hints?

Had I realized early on that she was just playing with me like everyone thought?

No, I decided. And if I had, it was subconscious. I wanted things to work with her. I wanted to be with her, to marry her, to have my own little love story. What happened wasn't surprising, but that was because I just expected it. She was just the best actress in the line of women I had thought were The One.

Considering my last girlfriend was an actual actress, that was saying something.

I opened the desk drawer again and pulled out a black ring box before tapping the intercom button on the top.

"Rick," I called. "If you have a sec?"

"Coming, boss," Rick said.

I sighed. "Don't call me boss."

He opened the door a few minutes later. Blazing red hair was the only hint left of the lanky child who had been my best friend since we were both losers on the playground of that small town in northeastern

Ontario. Rick was the definition of puberty doing amazing things. With his height and his looks, he could have been anything—a model, an athlete, a businessman—and yet he was content working as my assistant. As many times as I'd asked him why, he shrugged it off. In his mind, he got paid to hang out with me all the time. And I had no complaints about that.

"Okay, but this better be good," he said. "I was in the middle of *Moulin Rouge.*"

Wordlessly, I put the ring box on the desk and slid it forwards. He glanced at it and then back at me, unusually silent.

"Return this, please," I said, my voice measured.

"What happened?"

"Nothing."

"Bullshit."

"I'm not going through with it. We're breaking up. But don't say anything. Sheri doesn't know yet."

"What happened?" he repeated.

"Nothing," I replied. "I'm over it."

"Don't give me that shit." He folded his arms. "Theo, come on. You've been planning this for weeks. There's no way you—"

"I don't want to get into it. Just please return the ring. Or keep it. Or go to the grocery store and hide it in a fucking cereal box. I don't care. I don't want it."

Rick sighed and picked up the ring box. "You're telling me what happened later. You can't hold shit like this in. Understand?"

I didn't respond.

# Chapter Three

*Aspen*

"No."

The room was silent. Kevin raised his eyebrows.

"What do you mean, no?"

Even Darby looked shocked. I paused another moment before speaking.

"I appreciate the offer, and it's very... nice, I suppose... to be considered for this position. But I don't want it."

"That's moronic. You're fucking crazy, Aspen."

Kevin Wu may have been uncommonly self-aware and easygoing for a CEO, but he was also smart as fuck and not known for beating around the bush. In general, I appreciated that, despite him calling me crazy. And I had to admit, I understood where he was coming from. There he was, offering me a promotion, a raise, living arrangements. Hell, he'd probably hire me a personal assistant and a chef, if I asked for it. Everything anyone could ever dream of, and yet...

"No," I repeated. "I like where I am and I don't want to give up the travel opportunities. What about Daniel?"

"Daniel's an idiot." He leaned back in his chair. "I thought you'd be happy about this. A chance to settle down for a while. Easier hours. You know, a way to have a life outside your job?"

"I like my job," I replied. "Are you saying I work too much, boss?"

"You know what I'm saying. You've been doing this for five years. Most of our people in these roles don't last more than two. You have over two months of built-up vacation time. You are aiming for a burn out, and as one of my top people, I can't allow that."

He wasn't wrong. I hadn't been on a vacation in years, but why would I? I had no one I wanted to visit for extended periods of time. Sure, I had friends all over the world, who I got to see regularly because of my job, and friends in Toronto for the occasional few days I spent in the city that I technically lived in, but settling down would mean boredom. It would mean facing time alone. It would mean having to grow up. And worse, it would mean facing the fact that having a family and kids wasn't on the table for me.

I didn't need a constant reminder of that.

"Aspen?" Kevin's voice was softer in tone as I snapped out of my thoughts.

"I like what I do now, Kev," I said quietly. My heart was pounding, but there was no outward sign of the emotional turmoil I was feeling.

Kevin looked sympathetic, but his eyes were hard. "Dean Bradford is off indefinitely for health issues. I don't have anyone else. Aspen, you're the only other person I trust to get this location set up."

He wasn't wrong about that, I thought. Wakeham was a small town, but in a key region of Ontario. Doing audits meant I knew exactly what to do and what not to do. It wasn't narcissistic to believe I would be good for the job, simply because I knew I was good at what I did.

"I just don't think it's a great fit," I said. "I know I can do the work. But you're asking me to give up something I love doing, and go live in a town of... what, like a hundred people?"

"It's got more than that," Darby interjected.

Kevin drummed his fingers on the table for a moment and put his pen to his mouth. "Okay. Here's my proposal. We can't keep you in the position you're in for much longer."

I opened my mouth to protest, but he shook his head.

"Aspen, it's a liability. If you don't take a proper break and end up getting sick like Dean is now, the company could be open to a lawsuit. So instead, what if we compromise?"

I raised my eyebrows. "What are you offering?"

"Same deal. Hell of a raise, living arrangements covered, company vehicle. You sign a one-year contract. After a year, if you want to stay, you can sign on permanently. If not, you can have your current position back." He looked at me sternly. "You've been doing pre-audits for years and you've saved the company billions. I need you to take that talent and start up a new location."

It was clear enough that he wasn't going to take no for an answer. For a moment, I thought I'd say it anyway. What was he going to do if I said no? Hire someone else? Send Daniel? Fire me?

More realistically, he'd still make me do it. There was something in my contract about being reassigned, and he knew as well as I did that he could simply force me to take the job. Then my options were simple: go to Wakeham, or quit.

And quitting would be just as bad.

"You know, most companies would just let me burn out if that's what I wanted to do," I grumbled.

"That's why you work for us. We're better than most companies." Darby snorted and he glared at her. "Quiet down, peanut gallery."

I pursed my lips and studied the offer in front of me. "Increase this by twenty percent, make the vehicle an Audi, and the living arrangements better be the nicest joint in town." I jotted it down and pushed the contract back to Kevin. "You're sending me to the middle of buttfuck nowhere to open a new location against my will. I don't think that's unreasonable."

"Ten percent, I can't guarantee an Audi but we'll do a luxury vehicle, and we'll arrange the nicest apartment money can rent," Kevin countered.

"Fifteen and I keep the raise when I come back to this role."

He hesitated for all of a millisecond, and I knew this would be his final offer. "Ten, and if you stay in the role, it gets bumped to fifteen after a year."

I didn't need to hesitate before agreeing. The money he was offering was already insanely good. At least I'd get to keep it. "Deal."

"Done." He noted the arrangements on the contract and passed it to Darby. "Take a few days off here in town so we can arrange everything. You'll be in Wakeham next week."

"It's not really buttfuck nowhere," Darby said as she straightened the papers. "My aunt lives near there. I think it's just over an hour away from Timmins. So it's like halfway between civilization and buttfuck nowhere."

"You're not helping," Kevin said as he rose to shake my hand.

I smiled politely, told Darby I'd meet her later to sign the contract and go for drinks, and swallowed the instinct to stamp my feet and scream.

# Chapter Four

*Theo*

SHE'D GOTTEN HER NAILS done.

It was the first thing I noticed. They were bright red and looked almost slick against her tanned skin. She'd probably gotten back into Toronto and gone straight to the salon for a full manicure, then charged it all to my card before coming home to find me sitting in the backyard, drinking a beer.

"I'm terrible at surprises," I said as she sat down with me.

"Hello to you too," Sheri said lightly. "And no, you aren't."

I sighed and leaned forward, putting my beer on the table before finally looking at her. "Well, you knew what I was going to do."

Sheri's face betrayed the slightest hint of confusion, but she said nothing.

"What do you think—was my bank account sexier before or after you told me to put an intercom on the patio?"

Her face stayed frozen. Even the breeze that had been making her hair dance across her shoulders seemed to stop.

"You've got nothing to say?" I pressed.

"No," she said, her voice flat.

I kept watching her. She wasn't looking at me. Her eyes were focused to the left, unblinking, her face like something carved of stone. Then, all at once, she reanimated.

"Actually yes." She folded her arms on her chest. "You were eavesdropping. Whatever we said or didn't say, that's creepy."

I almost laughed.

Almost.

I was so close to laughing that I felt the corners of my mouth lift, but I caught them before they turned to much more than a sad half-smile.

"You insisted on bringing your girlfriends out to my cottage," I started, my voice soft and then getting stronger. "You sat out there, drinking my wine and eating food I paid for. Someone leans on the intercom on my patio, an intercom you know damn well has video and speakers, because you *insisted* I put something like that in, and you claim that it's creepy that I overheard you saying you love my bank account but not me? That when we fuck, you close your eyes and think of how much money I have to get yourself off? Or were you faking that the whole time, too?"

Sheri's throat flexed as she swallowed.

"Did you ever love me?" I asked. "Or was it always about the money?"

Her eyes met mine for a brief moment before she resumed staring into the distance.

The fucking audacity.

She thought I was going to beg her to say it wasn't true. That I was such a fucking pushover, I would plead with her to give me another chance. That she was right, it was all my fault I'd overheard her say the things she'd said. That there had to be something, anything, I could do to make her love me because I was so hopelessly and irrevocably addicted to her I couldn't bear to think that she didn't love me back.

I stood up. "It's over, Sheri."

Finally, she seemed surprised. "What—wait, you—"

I picked my beer up. "I'm done with you."

Her arms uncrossed and she gripped the armrest of her chair. "Not... you're not... you *can't*."

"Done," I repeated as I started walking back to the house.

"What the fuck!?" She jumped out of her chair, her voice shrill. "Theo, are you serious? It was a girls' weekend. We were just talking shit."

"If you have any shit here, let Rick know and he'll bring it back to you."

"You're not. You're *not* doing this. You're letting me go because you can't get over being made fun of a little bit? You think you can do better than me, you ungrateful fucking—"

"That's enough." I was nearly at the back door when Rick came around the side of the house. "Miss Wilson, it's time to leave. I can drive you home if you need a ride."

"Miss Wilson?" Sheri made a sound like a snort. "*Miss Wilson*? I've known you since we were six, Rick. When did you get so goddamn formal?"

"When you pulled this shit," Rick said, just loud enough for me to hear. "That's my best friend and you've been playing games with him."

"I should have known the two of you losers were—"

I didn't hear any more. I shut the door and stepped into the kitchen, downed the rest of my beer, then pulled another out of the fridge. A few minutes later, Rick walked in through the front entrance. I passed him the beer I'd just opened and grabbed one more out of the fridge.

"Thank God she wasn't living here," he said.

"She didn't want a ride?"

"She'd rather walk across Toronto than accept a favour from a brown-nosing, ass-eating, shit-for-brains cocksucker like me," Rick said. "Oh, wait, I missed one. It was a *gay* brown-nosing, ass-eating, shit-for-brains cocksucker. Completely redundant, not to mention untrue, of course. I talk back to you way too much to be a brown-noser."

I managed a smile, but not much more than that. Rick's face went serious again.

"I know it sucks, man, but..."

"Don't." I took a swig of the beer.

"This was big, okay? You were together for almost two years. You can't just not deal with it."

"Can and will."

He raised his eyebrows but didn't argue, just picked at the label on his beer bottle as he waited for me to say something. When I didn't, he sighed again.

"You know you'll find someone else," he said. "You're a good guy, Theo. There's some hot, womanly babe out there just waiting for you, all... you know, all woman-like."

It was my turn to raise my eyebrows. "All woman-like?"

Rick took a sip of his beer as laugh lines appeared in the corners of his eyes. "Yeah, of course. Or, you know. Maybe she's not, like, sitting around waiting for you. She's probably doing whatever straight people do when they're not in relationships in the meantime."

"I have no idea what you're talking about."

"Well, what do you do when you're not in a relationship?"

I tilted my beer bottle at him in response and he rolled his eyes.

"Well, whatever the womanly version of that is, that's what your soulmate is up to right now. I'm sure of it."

I smirked, but still said nothing. He sighed again.

"Okay, well... I guess you should know, but Sheri's probably going to start the rumour that you broke up with her because we're secret lovers. She insinuated as much when she stormed off."

I made a non-committal noise.

"Does that bother you?"

"Nah," I said. "People have been saying that for years. Sorry you're getting dragged through it again."

"Don't be," Rick replied. "Guys love the story of my tragically closeted famous heart-breaker ex. A new version will put some life back into the flow of wanna-be lovers. Let me know when the rumours start up so I can hit the club and really capitalize on it this time."

"Happy to help."

We sat in silence for a bit, finishing our drinks. I pictured Sheri walking down the sidewalk. Maybe crying, but probably not. She probably had her face set, eyes straight ahead, hair blowing back behind her. Brushing against her shoulder.

The world had loved the idea of her just as much as I had. We were a fairytale, the rock star and his hometown sweetheart discovering their love years down the road. Of all the women I'd dated, Sheri was the one the media loved the most. I hadn't been with her because she was good for my career, nor did I care if our breakup affected it, but when the news got out it would be...

Messy wouldn't even begin to describe it. And that was without the implications she'd threatened to make that I was fucking my best friend. Most people would've thought it was nothing more than the rumour it was, but Rick's sexuality was common knowledge. I'd never asked him to hide who he was and he'd vowed he was done being in the closet after coming out when we were teenagers, so there was a good chance people might actually believe it.

I didn't give two shits about people thinking I might be gay, but I'd be fucking livid if I was painted as a cheater.

Then again, maybe she'd think it through a bit and not say anything. It wasn't like she was going to come out of it looking particularly good. The whole thing was on video, it wouldn't take much to refute any claims she might make.

Though that would mean the entire world would get to hear her tell her friends that I sucked in bed.

"I think I'm gonna take a break for a bit," I said suddenly. "Go back home. See my family."

Rick nodded and sipped his beer. "Sounds good. Okay if I tag along to see my parents, boss?"

"Don't call me boss."

"I'll book the tickets tomorrow."

# Chapter Five

*Aspen*

"HE'S CHECKING YOU OUT." Darby spun the straw around her glass in a lazy circle and looked pointedly behind me.

"Excellent." I tilted my head back, deliberately making it as clear as possible that I was taking the last swig of my beer before setting it down on the table with a clunk. "Let's see, is he going to notice I just finished my drink and get it for me, or saunter over here with a corny pickup line? Oh, or do you wanna take the underdog bet and see if he sends someone over to tell me about their shy friend who wants to say hello to me?"

"Don't be so harsh," cackled Darby. "He's pretty good looking."

"He probably spent more time on his hair tonight than I did."

"Which means he probably spent a lot of time grooming other stuff, too." She flicked an eyebrow up at me, then wrapped her lips around the straw in her drink.

She wasn't wrong about the guy in question. At first glance, he was muscular, clean-shaven, and dressed well. He was there with a small group that was loud and exuberant, but he didn't seem to be quite as obnoxious. When I looked over my shoulder at him, a dimpled smile flashed even, white teeth at me.

Yeah, he'd do.

I turned back to Darby just as the bartender was placing another beer in front of me. "Compliments—"

"—of the gentleman over there," I finished. "Thanks. Good job not taking the dark-horse bet, Darb." I turned again and raised the bottle at the man in thanks.

"So you're ditching me already?" Darby asked.

I shrugged unapologetically. "It's my last night in the big city before moving to a town where people probably turn a blind eye on kissing cousins because otherwise the dating pool runs dry. This is my last chance to get laid for the next year, Darb. You're really going to stop me before I ruin the wreath that is someone's family tree?"

Darby's laugh could be heard through the loud bar. "It's not *that* small of a town!"

I ignored her and glanced around. "Do you have your eye on anyone?"

"No." She sipped her drink. "I'm saving my energy to find a rich businessman husband at the conference Kevin's taking me to next weekend."

I checked my phone for the time. "It's only eleven. Does he look like the kind of guy who'd make me wait until a respectable time before fucking my brains out?"

"Nah, he looks like he'll take you home right away. If you go now, you can probably be back for another drink before the bar closes."

"Is that a challenge?"

"I'll expense a case of wine to Kevin's account if you get laid and come back before last call."

"You're on." I slid off the bar stool and straightened my shirt before patting down my wildly curly hair, hoping to tame any frizz that might have appeared.

"He's gotta make you come though!" she called as I started walking away, making more than one head turn in our direction. "Doesn't count if you don't!"

If he didn't make me come, losing out on a case of wine was the least of my worries.

Holding the beer he'd sent over, I made my way across the bar. There was a pleasant look of surprise on the man's face as I slipped past his friends and settled into the seat beside him, far closer than was strictly necessary.

"Thanks," I said. "I'm Aspen."

"No problem," he replied in a voice that was deliciously tinted with the hint of a French accent. "I'm Jerome. Nice to meet—"

"Look, Jerome." I leaned toward him. "Let me be honest with you. I'm a workaholic with a high sex drive and commitment issues who travels constantly. Well, I used to travel constantly, except now I've been promoted and tomorrow I'm moving to an hour away from the middle of nowhere. I'd invite you back to my place to fuck, but it's completely packed up."

"That... that is too bad," Jerome stuttered.

I waited, willing the gears in his head to turn just a little bit faster.

"Is your place available?" I asked once the pause became awkward.

"Oh! Uh. Yeah... yes." He nearly knocked his beer over as he straightened up in his seat. "Would... did... I mean, do..."

"You have such a way with words," I interrupted, my hand finding its way to his chest. "Well, you've talked me into it. Let's go back to your place, you suave casanova."

Was I a bit more forward than people were used to?

Yes.

Did it get me what I wanted, plus possibly a free case of wine?

Also yes.

I took Suave Jerome's hand and tugged him out of his seat. It took his friends a few moments to realize the incredulous look on his face wasn't because I was dragging him off to the dance floor but instead leading him out of the bar.

It was not lost on me in the slightest that if our roles were reversed, a gaggle of fiercely protective women in low-cut tops and mini-skirts would have surrounded us almost instantly, as they damn well should because I was well aware of how my actions looked. That type of forwardness from a man wouldn't fly with me, despite having perfected the technique myself. But it got me what I needed. Most of the time, at least. There were plenty of men who found the idea of a woman who just wanted to get laid and go home without any of the mating ritual bullshit both mythical and emasculating.

For the most part, though, I had a fairly good sense of who would be open to my particular brand of walking up to them and informing them I wanted to fuck, Jerome being one of them. And since our roles were what they were, instead of me being run out of the bar by strong, supportive women, the sounds of his friends' razzing rang in our ears as we walked towards the exit.

"Do you live close by?" I asked as we walked past the crowd of people waiting to get into what was apparently the place to be in downtown Montreal on a Thursday night.

"Uh... yes," he said. "Not too far. But..."

"But what?"

He flicked an eyebrow up as he glanced at me. "Is this some kind of trick? One of them told you to do this?"

I frowned, annoyed. "One of *who*?"

He had the decency to look embarrassed. "I guess not, then. I... you just seem too good to be true."

A decent enough recovery. I smiled. "Not used to women who know what they want?"

"I'm trying to figure out what the catch is. I bought you one beer, and you asked me to take you home."

"The catch is, I won't leave your house until you get me off, so you better know what you're doing."

He chuckled and relaxed, some of his confidence returning as he squeezed my hand. "Now, *that* I can do."

When we got to his place, some of his nervousness returned. He led me into an apartment that was small, but reasonably tidy. I removed my shoes as he turned the lights on and placed my purse on a side table near the door.

"Can I... would... maybe a beer?" Jerome stumbled.

I smiled at him, feeling very coy. "No. Unless you need one first."

His voice deepened a bit. "No."

I tried not to laugh as I started to remove some of my jewelry. I took a step towards Jerome. "Good. So, do you like things fast, or slow, or rough, or...?"

He swallowed hard. His eyes trailed down my body and back up, finally meeting my gaze when I was within arm's reach. He was tall, and I tilted my head up so I could make eye contact. His mouth opened to respond, but nothing came out. I smiled again.

"Why don't I start by undressing?" I said, my hands moving to the hem of my shirt.

"Here?"

"Is that a problem?"

"God, no."

My view was cut off as I lifted my shirt above my head, but once it was off, I looked back at him. His eyes were focused on my breasts, his mouth half-open. I took half a step towards him as I reached down to unbutton my jeans, but he finally closed the gap between us by beating me to the button first. I inhaled sharply as his fingers brushed my skin and reached up to remove my bra.

He undid my pants and pushed them down just past my hips, but Jerome seemed to be a boob man and lost focus on that task when I dropped my bra. He made a small noise and reached up, cupping a hand around each breast. After a couple of fumbling squeezes, he moved one hand up to my chin, tilting my face up and leaning in.

I responded to the kiss the same way I do every time a man kissed me: politely, but void of passion in the hopes that he would decide I was a terrible kisser and not bother with it anymore. Kissing and I had a complicated history. I didn't understand the appeal, but some guys couldn't get enough of it. And there were at least five other places on my body I would rather have Jerome's mouth than pressed against my own. So I let him kiss me, let him feel like we were connecting, then turned my head and gasped as though he had done something incredibly noteworthy somewhere else on my body even though he most definitely hadn't.

Unfortunately, Jerome was a kisser. He didn't notice my cold-fish method of kissing and turned my head towards his again. That meant it was time for my second kiss-aversion technique, which—while labour intensive—was far more effective.

I moved my hands to the waistband of his pants and deftly unbuttoned his jeans. My fingers trailed teasingly down the front of his boxers and Jerome groaned against my mouth. I pulled back and looked down at the bulge between us, then back up at him with another coy smile and traced the outline of his cock with the tips of my fingers.

"So hard already?"

"You have a magic touch," he said.

Infuriatingly, he leaned forward for another kiss. I pressed a finger against his lips before they could touch mine and Jerome dropped his hand away from my chin, looking at me questioningly. Biting my lip and looking up at him through my eyelashes, I pushed his jeans down his legs, then knelt in front of him as gracefully as I could. He murmured something along the lines of "Oh, God" as I guided his boxers down his hips and let his cock free.

Now is the part when I'm supposed to describe his dick.

Here's the thing.

It looked like a dick. It felt like a dick. It was the size of an average sized dick.

Even if it was a bigger dick, or a smaller dick, or a slightly thicker or thinner dick, it wouldn't have mattered. Dicks are dicks and they're great. They serve a purpose. So no, I did not reach into his boxers and pull out a *meaty member* or a *throbbing rod of velvet-wrapped iron*. I did not gasp in shocked awe at an appendage as thick as my wrist that I wouldn't be able to fit in my mouth.

Jerome had an average size dick, it looked like a normal dick, and when I put it in my mouth—where it fit quite neatly—it tasted just like any other dick would on a man with good hygiene.

And like many other men, hygienic or not, he groaned the second I had him in my mouth. I looked up at him and watched as he leaned against the wall, his head tilted up. One of his hands ended up resting on my head and I placed a hand on his thigh for support. I sucked slowly at first, teasing his length with my tongue and gently stroking, before increasing the speed of both my mouth and my hand and repeating the whole thing again. Tease him with my tongue, stroke a little more firmly, take a breath, repeat.

It wasn't long before I could taste Jerome's pre-cum dripping into my mouth. When his breathing began to get heavier and I heard that full-on groan again, I pulled back. He couldn't hold back a small whimper of disappointment as I gazed up at him and let the tip of his cock pop out of my mouth.

"Well, I can't let you finish already," I said teasingly.

He laughed and reached down to help me up. "Oh, trust me, I agree. There's a lot more I want to do to you before I'm done."

Thank God. That was promising.

Leaving his pants and my shirt in the front hallway, Jerome led me through the small apartment to the bedroom. Once we were there, he took his shirt off, then firmly grabbed my hips and pulled me towards him.

"These have to go," he murmured, the slight French accent thickening as he tugged at my jeans and buried his face in my neck.

He traced his tongue along my skin, leaving a trail that chilled me as it hit the air. I could feel my nipples hardening against his bare chest, and I reached down to shimmy out of my jeans. Once they were off, Jerome walked backwards to the bed, sat on the edge, and pulled me on top of him.

The only thing between us was the thin fabric of my panties, which were pretty much soaked. Rolling my hips, I felt his cock press against my slit through the fabric. One arm was wrapped firmly around my waist and he held my body close against him. The friction from shifting around in his lap was deliciously enticing and I gasped as he took my breast in his mouth, raking his teeth over my nipple.

The hand on my back slid lower, cupping my ass. He kept his face against my breasts, kissing and sucking and teasing my nipple with his tongue, then slowly making a trail to the other breast and repeating there. I ran my hands along his shoulders and back, while he used his to gently guide my hips in a rocking motion against him. Each movement simultaneously relieved some of the arousal that was pooling in my lower stomach while making me crave more, and more, and...

"Please," I gasped, my hands tapping against Jerome's shoulders.

His mouth left my nipple as he looked up at me, his eyes focused and dark.

"Can't take anymore. You got a condom?"

"Yep," he replied.

I moved off his lap, standing up while he reached to the other side of the bed, opening a nightstand. As he got the protection all sorted out, I peeled my panties off, dropping them unceremoniously on the floor. I moved my hand down to my pussy, touching myself lazily as Jerome finished up. He turned, took note of my hand, grinned, and started towards me.

"How do you—"

"Hands and knees," he said, his accent thicker than ever. The sudden directness was as amusing as it was telling; he was as eager to fuck me as

I was to have him inside of me. Grabbing my hips, he spun me around and pushed me down, barely giving me time to get into a comfortable position before he was behind me, the tip of his cock pressing against my wet entrance. He pushed forward, fumbling a bit as he tried to navigate the slickness of my pussy, but entered hard and fast once he got there.

I let out a loud, satisfied noise as he thrust inside me, only stopping once his hips met my ass. Groaning, he grabbed my hips again, pulling me close so his cock was as deep as possible. I pushed back against him, which seemed to kick start him into action.

I don't know how to phrase it more delicately, so I'll say it exactly the way I felt it: he began fucking the hell out of me. Like, legitimately, it was pretty impressive... at first. I gasped and moaned, urging him on—*harder, faster, yes, right there*—all that good stuff. As his intensity increased, I shifted on my arms so that I was just propped up on one elbow. That pushed my ass higher in the air, and he made a strangled noise as his cock burrowed even deeper inside of me. Snaking my hand down to my pussy, I fingered myself hard as he pounded me. It wasn't going to take long for either of us, not when he was fucking me like that, and that case of free wine Darby was going to expense for me was practically mine.

But when I heard Jerome panting just a few moments later, it was a little *too* soon.

"Don't you dare," I gasped. "I'm not done yet. Don't you dare come."

He didn't respond. Instead, he leaned forward, pressing harder against me, pumping his hips faster. The gravity of his body suddenly shifting caused my elbow to slip, and I let out a frustrated whine as I ended up face first on the mattress. The hand that had been bringing me closer and closer to the edge ended up trapped against my body, and I couldn't quite reach anymore. Infuriated, I pushed back against Jerome, ramming my ass against his stomach. Instead of making him move, that apparently did it for him, since he shuddered and cried out as he came.

"Fuck... sorry... fuck..." he panted, his hands tight on my hips.

That was fine. It was fine. I was close. It wouldn't take long.

He sat back so I could pull myself out from under him. He was kneeling on the edge of the bed, and just as I turned over, he made a move as if to lie down.

*That* was not fine.

I reached forward and grabbed one of his arms.

"You aren't done yet," I said, almost growling.

Still breathless, he looked shocked, his lips parted as if he was about to say something. Instead, he made the very wise choice to let me tug him forward, supporting himself on one arm while I guided his other hand between my legs. To the sound of him gasping for breath, he slid his fingers inside me, massaging my clit with his thumb.

My hips bucked towards him as his hand trying to match the speed his cock had just minutes before. I tilted my head back, toying with my nipple as my body responded to his fingers. Jerome's eyes were glued to me, his expression almost shocked, as though he couldn't believe I was touching my breasts while he fingered me. The sheer astonishment that he wasn't able to stop touching me until I told him I was done and the matching look on his face almost made me laugh.

As I suppressed a giggle, I felt it. A knot was coming undone in my stomach, the precursor to a release, and I let out a soft groan as I arched my back. He moved his hand faster, urging me along. Within a few quick, gasping breaths, I came, my pussy tightening around his fingers and legs clamping against his arm. I writhed, crying out, and felt my body tense as each wave of my orgasm made its way through me.

It eventually stopped, and my legs relaxed enough that Jerome was able to take his hand back. My eyes were closed as I worked to catch my breath and felt him lie down beside me. His eyes were on me and I could almost feel the self-satisfied energy rolling off him. Sure enough, when I opened my eyes, he was lying on his side, propped up on an elbow, and grinned as I made eye contact.

"Pretty good?" he asked.

I raised an eyebrow, and the smile faded off his face.

"Or... not?"

"I'd say... passable," I replied, sitting up and swinging my legs off the edge of the bed.

"Passable?!" He sat up as well.

I stood up and started dressing. "Well, I mean, I came, so that was good. That means I win a case of wine. But you lost points for thinking you could just lie down as soon as you were done."

"Wait, you won... what? And... well, okay, but I didn't actually lie down," he said.

"Yes, so it was passable. You got points back for that. And the actual fucking." I had my jeans on and turned to face him. "That was redeeming. Let's call it a B-, but we'll round it up to a B, since I *am* getting a whole case of wine if I get back to the bar before last call."

Jerome looked insulted. "A B? That's it? And... what the fuck, you're *grading* me?"

"That's still above average. I don't know what you're complaining about." I left his bedroom to search for my shirt and he followed me through the apartment.

"Oh, okay, of course. So what did I do wrong?"

"Don't take it personally." I did up my bra and put my shirt on. "You lost some credit for things that are just a preference, but a main point of feedback for future hookups? If she goes down on you, at least pretend to offer to eat her out, okay?"

He looked lost and at least a little embarrassed, which I did feel bad about. "I... well..."

"Jerome." I put my shoes on, then straightened up and looked at him. "Do the women you sleep with orgasm every time, or is it an unusual occurrence?"

He flushed pink and didn't respond.

"Okay, second tip for the future: aim for her to come every time, not just as a second thought, okay?"

"Jesus, if I'd known it was a fucking test, I would've studied," he replied sarcastically. "Anything else I was horrendous at? Kisses too sloppy? Dick too small?"

"Hey, you still got a good mark. I'm kind of a hoe, so take it as a compliment." I grabbed my purse and turned to the door. "Why don't you do some studying and when I'm back in town, you can do a retake and maybe earn some extra credit?"

"Are you actually for—"

"Thanks for the fuck, Jerome. Enjoy the rest of your night!"

"But—"

I didn't hear the rest as I left the apartment. Walking down the hallway, I checked my phone.

*So is Kevin buying your wine?* was the text message Darby had sent three minutes earlier.

*Our wine,* I replied. *Charge a nice shiraz to his card and I'll split the case with you. Be back at the bar in 5.*

# Chapter Six

*Theo*

"OH, THEODORE..."

Mom—the only person in the world I tolerated calling me *Theodore* even though it was her fault I was saddled with the name—started tearing up almost as soon as she'd opened the front door. Not that I'd knocked at my own parents' house; she must have been waiting nearby for me to arrive. But even as tears started streaming down her face and I braced myself for a surge of self-loathing and humiliation, she threw her arms out and pulled me in for one of those all-encompassing, unconditional hugs that a guy really only gets from his mom. I stiffened unintentionally, then relaxed as I hugged her back, needing it more than I'd even realized after spending a month pretending nothing was wrong.

Rick had talked me into staying in Toronto for a couple of weeks after it all went down.

"She'll stay quiet," he said about Sheri with a confidence I felt was unreasonable. "I know it, man. But if you drop everything and take off to Wakeham, everyone's gonna figure out what's going on."

I'd wanted to snap at him, but he was right.

"Just a couple of weeks," Rick said. "Finish up your press stuff, do the last couple of shows, then we go to Wakeham like it's just a short hiatus to relax instead of..."

Instead of hiding away from the prying minds and camera flashes as my life fell apart yet again, was what he was going to say and didn't have to.

But it was a good point. No one knew Sheri and I had broken up yet. Breakup rumours flew around, sure, but there were always breakup rumours. There'd been breakup rumours about me and women I'd never even met; Sheri hadn't been immune to that even before we'd officially announced we were dating. And she hadn't said anything about it either; my guess was since I had a record of the things she'd said, she knew she wouldn't come off well. That meant if I handled everything right, I could take some time for things to quiet down before dealing with the public fallout of yet another failed relationship.

So I'd spent a month building up walls, playing the role I'd thought was my dream: Theo Barker, rock star, someone who was confident and cool and collected. And maybe it should have been less of a role and more of a reality. I *was* a rock star. I *had* succeeded. I had a lot to be fucking proud of. But I'd also learned, time and time again, that I had to be careful where I put my trust and my heart.

Because there would always be people like Sheri. There would always be people who liked *what* I was, not *who* I was, and there seemed to be fewer and fewer of the latter every day.

But there was one place in the world I could count on to find those people, and I was finally there.

I was home.

I hugged my mom a little tighter. She always cried whenever I came home and she always hugged too tightly and for too long, but I was still sort of disappointed when she let go.

"What happened, honey?" she asked, her hands still on my shoulders as she looked up at me.

"Just didn't work out," I said.

She pressed her lips together. "Was there any particular reason?"

"Yep."

After waiting a moment, she sighed. "And are you going to share that reason?"

"He just got in. Leave him alone, Beth." My dad entered the front hallway and clapped me on the back. "Doing all right, Theo?"

"Thanks, Dad. Yeah," I said.

Mom sighed again, but apparently resigned herself to dropping it for the moment as she ushered me through the hallway. "Well, come on, come in. Dinner won't be for a bit but come grab something to drink. And are you sure you don't want to stay here with us? It's not a problem at all to make up a room and—"

"I've got my own place, Mom."

"I know, but I just hate the thought of you alone right now."

I might have run back to the small town I'd grown up in to get a hug from my mom and surround myself with family when my love life fell apart, but there were certain levels I wasn't willing to fall to—living with my parents being one of them. "I'm not alone. Rick's staying with me."

"Oh." She hesitated. "You're not worried about any... rumours?"

"It's a big place. He's got his own room and everything."

"Yes, but—"

I tried not to sound annoyed. "Would people thinking I'm gay seriously be the worst thing in the world?"

"You know damn well that it wouldn't matter to me or to anyone else who loves you," Mom said. "I just know how hard it is to keep your privacy these days and how much you value it."

Guilt surged through me at the hurt in her voice. "I value Rick's friendship more."

"And you know I adore Rick, I just—"

"He said it's fine, Beth," Dad chimed in.

"I'm his mother. I'm supposed to worry. It's what I'm for," she snapped back.

Dad raised his hands and looked at me, shrugging.

"It's fine. I just needed some time away from everything. If Sheri doesn't leak something to the press first, I'll release a statement in a few weeks, but I just wanted to..." My voice caught in my throat and I cleared it, my face burning. "Just wanted to get away and be around family for a bit."

"Oh, Theodore." Mom's voice wavered and she teared up again, unable to stop herself from putting an arm around me. "You know we'll always be here for you. No matter what."

I blinked hard as she hugged me again. As much as I was fighting it, the wall was coming down already, and as much as that was why I was *there*, part of me wasn't willing to let it go without a fight. My family was big on showing emotions—Dad teared up at animal shelter commercials and Mom had to talk him down from driving to the nearest rescue to take home all the dogs, and my brother James had cried more than his wife had when they'd finally gotten pregnant with their first kid—but the last few years had taught me to default to a poker face. Even though I knew there were no cameras around, that instinct was strong. I ran a hand across my chin, feeling the rough stubble under my fingers, and took a breath.

"It's fine," I said again. "I'm fine."

"Well, hi there, Fine—"

"Oh, *shit*," I groaned at the same time Mom shook her head in mock disappointment.

"—I'm Dad, and let's have a beer already." Dad went to the fridge and pulled out two bottles. "James and Lisa and the kids are coming for dinner. Kids are desperate to see you, apparently. We'll go sit out while we wait unless your mom wants a hand with—"

"Not a chance in hell do I want you getting in the way, Norman," Mom said.

"I can help you, Mom. What do you—"

"Theodore Barker, you set one foot in my kitchen and I'll let my grandbabies have at dessert before you even get to smell it." Gently, she guided me towards the back door. "You can help with the dishes after dinner."

No way I was going to risk missing out on dessert. Mom's devil's food cake was legendary. I squeezed her shoulders and kissed her cheek, then followed Dad out to the porch. He handed me a beer and settled into his usual spot, an old webbed folding lawn chair facing the backyard that he used instead of the more stylish Adirondack ones Mom preferred. I sat in one of those and took a swig from the bottle.

For a few long moments, I indulged in the noise. In Toronto or Montreal or any of the other places I frequented, silence was common. I had houses and hotel rooms and condos with thick walls to shut out the sounds of the world. In the studio, surrounded by soundproof walls and with headphones covering my ears, I heard nothing but the music I drew from my guitar. But Wakeham wasn't a place of silence: there were cars on the highway a few kilometers away, the gentle swoosh of their tires muffled only by the shivering rustle of leaves in the trees. There was no monotonous chatter to ignore, no plastic words or artfully insincere promises to acknowledge. Just the occasional chirp of a bird, a song in itself, sounds that were better than the pressure of silence.

"I know you don't want to talk about it," Dad finally said. "So I'm just going to say this quick and then we can talk sports."

Somehow, I'd been expecting that, so I nodded.

"Your mom liked Sheri because you liked Sheri, not because she had any particular attachment to the girl. She's upset things didn't work out, but she's more upset that she doesn't know what happened. I don't know who's in the wrong, or if you did something or she did something or what. It doesn't matter because you know we're always on your side. But when someone's entire opinion of a person rests on someone else's love of them, it's hard when you don't know why that love changed. And when you're... you know. *You*. Doing what you do and hiding from the world because you don't trust anyone, it makes Beth feel like you don't trust her."

He took a sip of beer before continuing.

"She'll get over it. She won't even tell you how she's feeling 'cause you're our son and she loves you. And I don't blame you for being quiet. Sheri's family still lives around here and things get around. For what it's worth, it sounds like they've been keeping their mouths shut too, if they know at all."

"I'm sure they know," I mumbled. "It's not some big conspiracy, Dad. I just—"

"—don't want to talk about it, sure."

He scratched at the edge of the label on his bottle. We were quiet for a few minutes, just drinking as birds flittered around the backyard and listening to the rush of cars that sounded like wind in the distance.

"I heard her tell a bunch of her friends she was only with me for the money." I didn't quite remember choosing to say the words out loud, but there they were, floating on the air as I stared down at my beer. "The only thing she loved about me was my bank account. I broke it off with her the next day."

My dad was an easy-going guy. He was known in Wakeham as the person who would help anyone with anything, whether they were fixing a lawn mower, chopping down a tree, or needed a friendly ear and a beer on the deck. Most people would have said he didn't have a mean bone in his body. He always had a kind word and a warm smile for everyone.

34

When I told him what Sheri had said, though, I swore his face darkened. He was silent, putting his beer bottle on the small wooden table beside him before gripping the arms of his worn-out old lawn chair as if to hold himself in the seat.

"Good call." His nostrils flared as he took in a deep breath. "Jesus, Theo, that pisses me right off."

"Makes two of us," I said, taking another swig of beer.

"Why aren't you telling anyone?"

I twisted the bottle in my hands. I knew the answer—the real answer—but I hadn't said it out loud. Not to Rick or myself or to anyone. It wasn't something I wanted to admit. But if anyone was going to understand, it was my dad.

"It's embarrassing." My face burned even as I said it. "After all this, I'm still Thtupid Thimple Theo to people. To her and all the... to everyone. I was dumb enough to think she really loved me."

"Trying to see the best in people isn't dumb." He took another sip of beer. "I'd say it's a pretty good quality to have with what you're doing for a living. Keeps you grounded."

"Keeps getting me hurt," I corrected. "And it's keeping me single, apparently."

"Someone's out there for you. You'll meet her when you least expect it."

I twisted the bottle in my hands again but didn't respond.

Neither of us had much more to say on the subject, so we sat on the deck, sipping our beers in comfortable silence until the sound of the birds and the leaves was broken by a vehicle crunching up the gravel driveway a short while later. There was no stopping the smile that started on my face as that sound reached my ears and I was full-on grinning as I heard two doors open and slam shut, followed by whooshing rattle of a sliding side door. Sounds of fighting siblings and my mom calling "They're in the back, dear, just go on around!" out the front kitchen window broke through the quiet afternoon. I took a last sip of beer, put the bottle in the bin near the door, and hopped off the deck just in time for a tornado of energetic children to sweep through the yard.

"Uncle Theo!" they screeched, almost in unison.

I knelt down and spread my arms, just barely keeping my balance as three kids tackled me.

"Guys, I missed you so much," I told them. "Look how big you're getting. You gotta stop growing so fast!"

They giggled and chattered in unison. I tried to keep up as each pulled me in a different direction. Grayson, Cole, and Anna made up a team of chaotic joy so intense that most in town said my sister-in-law Lisa was nothing short of a superhero. At seven, Grayson was the oldest, and Cole was only eleven months younger. Then Anna, who was four going on fourteen, was as rambunctious as both boys put together.

Grayson finally won the attention struggle. "Uncle Theo, I made the Legos you got me for my birthday and Dad took a picture and I brought a new set. Can you help me make it?"

"Of course, buddy," I said. "Go get your dad so I can see the picture!"

He raced off and Cole, still hugging me on the left side, took over.

"Uncle Theo, in school we started learning how to play the recorder and I said my uncle Theo knows how to play like twelve instruments and my teacher said that was a lot of instruments and I said you were gonna help me learn guitar one day and I know you didn't say you would but will you help me learn guitar?"

"Hell yes, man! I mean, heck. Don't tell your mom I said hell."

"Yeah! *Mom, Uncle Theo said he'd help me learn guitar!*" Cole was off and running.

"Uncle Theo, Mom said we're not supposed to ask why Auntie Sheri isn't here so I wanted to say I'm not going to ask you why Auntie Sheri isn't here," said Anna. "Do you like my princess dress?"

"And there goes that..." My older brother, James, was hauling a backpack full of kid supplies along with a cooler and a casserole dish. "We're, uhh... still working on some of these concepts with her."

"I love your princess dress, Anna," I said as cheerfully as I'd responded to her brothers. "Why don't you go say hi to Grandpa, okay?"

She ran across the lush green lawn, a trail of glitter flowing behind her. I stood up and took the casserole dish from James.

"It's all good," I said. "I appreciate the sentiment."

He rolled his eyes, put the cooler down, and grabbed the casserole dish back from me so he could put it on top of the cooler. "Nice try. If those little goblins all got a hug, I want one, too."

I laughed and pulled him in for a hug, which was thankfully less glitter-infested than the one I'd got from Anna.

"How's it going anyway, rock star?" he asked as we let go.

"It's good," I said, picking up the casserole dish again.

"You've always been a shitty liar." He clapped me on the shoulder. "But I'm glad to see you all the same."

"Hi, Theo," called Lisa.

James picked up the cooler and I jogged over to my sister-in-law, a pretty woman with olive-toned skin and straight, dark hair, and took the bag she was carrying.

"Do you guys leave anything at home when you go out?" I asked as she gave me a hug.

"Nope. Gotta prevent tantrums." Her hug was tight and comforting. "I'm so glad to see you. How are you doing?"

"Great." She raised her eyebrows at me and I forced a smile. "Right at this moment, I'm great. I'm happy to be home and to see you and James and the kids."

She regarded me for a moment, then nodded. "Fine, I'll accept it. For now. Did you bring anything for the kids? Because if you did, I swear, Theo, I'm going to hold you personally responsible for making them spoiled brats."

"I didn't. Not tonight, anyway. Mom didn't tell me you were coming over so it'll have to wait." Lisa gave me a *Look* and rolled her eyes. I wrapped an arm around her shoulders as we walked to the house. "What good is being an uncle if I can't spoil them a little?"

Seeing them was just what I needed. That whole dinner was just what I needed. Mom's cooking, as delicious as it was straightforward. Riveting tales of school and swimming lessons and the secret tree fort the kids had built in the woods behind their house. James's good-natured teasing and Lisa's brand of tell-it-like-it-is-ness. And, of course, Mom's devil's food cake, as rich and chocolatey and delicious as I'd remembered it.

After weeks of being lost in my feelings about Sheri and what had happened, I was surrounded by people who always had and always would care about me. After we ate, Lisa and I cleared up the dishes, then joined Mom, Dad, and James on the deck to enjoy another drink. The kids ran loose in the backyard, playing some game that seemed to involve throwing handfuls of the grass clippings Dad left on the lawn at each other.

"How's the new job going, Lisa?" my mom asked as Cole earned a significant grass streak down the back of his shirt.

"New job?" I asked, tearing my eyes away from my niece and nephews. "I didn't even know you were planning on going back to work. When did you... and what do you... you know. Do?"

Lisa beamed proudly. "Not too long ago. It's that big factory and office just outside town. Industrial manufacturing for green energy projects. With the kids in school, we figured it was a good time for me to go back."

I nodded slowly, trying to remember if I'd seen the factory she was talking about when Rick and I drove in and failing miserably. "You're enjoying it?"

She nodded. "So far. I'm the director's assistant. She's... well, different to work for, but that's okay."

"Different's one way of saying it," James snorted, turning to me. "Get this. Lisa's boss hasn't ever *run* a location before. She was doing auditing or something. So they send her to Wakeham, put her up in one of those nice apartments on Main Street, give her a sports car, and the woman seems to have no idea what to even do with herself."

"That's not nice," Lisa said. "She's a good boss. And she's working hard. I think she's just not used to having an assistant and working like... normal hours. She seemed surprised at how much I do for her. She was travelling constantly before this."

James scoffed.

"No really, I feel bad for her. I was thinking of inviting her for dinner one night. She doesn't know anyone here."

"You think there might be a reason for that?"

"James—"

"She told you that your skirt made your hips look lumpy," he said. "You came home and called her—well." He glanced at me and grinned. "Anna learned a few new words that day, let's just say that."

"Did she, now?" Mom asked steadily.

"Not from me." Lisa glared at James. "I believe I told you the story and *you* were the one who—"

"I think we can all agree that no one can truly be blamed," James said hurriedly. "But you *were* upset, babe."

"Yes, at the time, but maybe I've done some thinking about it since then. I think she's just very direct and not used to dealing with people. She's trying to get her feet under her. Wakeham isn't like other places, especially if she's used to always being on the road."

"You don't have to defend her. No one here knows her."

"Well, I feel bad for her. She doesn't know anyone here, and I don't think she knows how to make friends." Lisa folded her arms. "And she didn't just up and *say* that my hips looked lumpy. I asked her if she thought the skirt fit properly and she said 'it makes your hips look lumpy.'"

"Isn't that the same?"

"No," Mom answered. "I mean, she could have said it more tactfully, but you ask a loaded question..."

"Exactly." Lisa looked triumphantly at James. "I'm inviting her for dinner in the next couple weeks. And you *will* be nice to her. I think she just needs some friends, okay? She's... she's just a lonely stranger in a small town."

"That's kinda catchy," Dad said, tapping his hand against the arm of his lawn chair with zero rhythm or melody. "Theo, you need a hook for a new song?"

"Maybe if I was writing shitty country music," I said.

Mom gasped. "Theo*dore* Barker!"

James lost it, cackling as Mom looked at me, insulted. I couldn't hold back a laugh.

"Mom, I—"

"There is *nothing* wrong with country music. You were *raised* on country music. Garth and Johnny and Dolly and—"

"I was raised on *good* country," I argued. "What am I supposed to do with something like that? 'Oh, she was a lonely lil' stranger in a small, small town, tellin' folks they looked lumpy in their gown, gown, gown...'"

It was Lisa's turn to cackle, smacking my arm and cutting off my horribly stereotypical country song. For a while, none of us could stop laughing. With the sounds of the kids playing in the yard, a beer in my hand, and my family around me on a perfect mid-summer night, everything started feeling all right again. I grinned, sipping my beer as birds chirped and the leaves rustled. I might have hated living here when I was growing up, but there was no doubt about it now: I fucking loved being back in Wakeham.

# Chapter Seven

*Aspen*

I FUCKING HATED WAKEHAM.

Here are some of the things I hated about Wakeham:

There was no decent bar in Wakeham. Sure, there was a pub, but it was dark, dingy, and smelly, and I wouldn't even consider drinking anything that didn't come out of a bottle or a can. It was frequented by grabby old men and boys with fake IDs that the bartender turned a blind eye to. The windows appeared tinted, but at second glance, the darkened glass was likely decades-old nicotine-laden smoke that hadn't been cleaned off since before smoking was prohibited indoors.

Everyone in Wakeham stared at me. Everyone. Go to the grocery store? Little old ladies staring. Stop at the gas station? Gas attendant staring as if they'd never seen an outsider before. Walk down the street? Better hope you don't trip, because everyone is staring like you're a freak of nature. It hadn't happened yet, but I was counting the days until someone whipped out their phone and started recording as if I was a bear on the side of the highway.

Everything in Wakeham closed by nine, and most things by six. I hadn't adjusted to normal-people hours yet, and the idea of being at home and tucked in for the night by nine at night seemed outrageous. But there was nothing else to do. I couldn't even work. When I was doing audits, with travel time and the constant pressure I was under, twelve-hour days were the norm. But in Wakeham? I couldn't even work for ten hours. By five o'clock, the office was empty, and unlike when I was doing audits, there was only so much I could do without other people around.

I didn't know anyone in Wakeham, and *that* was saying something. How I, of all people, could be *lonely* was beyond me. I thrived on my own. But something about being stuck in one place without even having casual acquaintances was wearing on me. The few people I had met were all employees, and every single one of them seemed intimidated by me. In my old position, I wouldn't have minded. Intimidation was part of the game. But as a director, I wanted to seem at least approachable.

That was going to be a stretch, though. I didn't know if I could manage "friendly." I was still working on "polite." I had accidentally blurted out that my assistant's hips looked lumpy when she asked me if her skirt fit right, and that set me back a few points. Between that and the way half the employees seemed to avert their eyes when I walked by, I was barely ranking above ice queen.

Even worse, I *cared* about it.

I complained about all of this to Darby, who was sympathetic, but unmoved by my pleas to ask Kevin to reconsider.

"It's only been a few weeks, and you've already got that place running as if it'd been open for years," was her reasoning. "Stick it out a bit more. You'll settle in."

She also had other gems of wisdom. "Be more relatable. Stop talking to people like you're a robot."

"Try to act a bit more casual. Big Scary Auditor Aspen isn't the same as Director Aspen."

"Have you tried *not* telling your assistant her hips look lumpy? Or at least coming up with some softer phrasing for when people ask you questions?"

After hanging up the phone with her, I put my head on my desk and sighed. The absolute worst part about Wakeham was being bored. I knew I was doing well in the role and that Kevin would be hard-pressed to let me leave early. If I was being honest, the work itself wasn't horrible. It was repetitive, yes, and not especially interesting, and I spent more time in meetings than I ever had before in my life, but it wasn't horrible.

It's just that, at the end of the day, there was an end of the day. I had to leave the office, go to my apartment, and figure out what the hell people did between the hours of working and sleeping. Other than masturbating, which I was doing a lot of since I wasn't getting laid. But as it turned out, people did a lot of repetitive and pointless bullshit to fill their time. Watch TV, people suggested, but after one episode I was restless. Read a book, then, they would say, but apparently skimming page after page so I could get to the end faster wasn't "doing it right." Even walking—I mean, what the fuck was "walking"? Meandering aimlessly down the streets of Wakeham with no purpose, no goal, nowhere to go and nothing to do? What was the *point* of it?

What was the point of *any* of it?

Well, except for masturbating. I was very clear on the point of that.

A soft knocking at my office door snapped me out of my mopey reverie. I managed to sit up and throw my hands onto the keyboard so it looked like I'd been working before my assistant let herself in.

"Hello, Lisa," I said politely, pretending to type.

"Oh, sorry," she said. "Is it a bad time?"

"Not at all. I'm just finishing up this, uh, expense report." I typed one last line of gibberish and turned to her. "How can I..."

In my mind, Darby's voice screamed.

*"Casually!"* she shrieked above the imagined sounds of her gems of wisdom floating through my head.

I cleared my throat and looked at Lisa with what I hoped was a casual expression. "I mean, uh, what's... what's up?"

The moment the words left my mouth, I wanted to curl up in a hole and disappear. They sounded completely foreign and entirely out of character, like I was a corporation trying to relate to the youths these days or something. A look of amusement crossed Lisa's face and she glanced at my computer before taking a seat in the chair across from my desk.

"Well, two things, actually," she said. "First, I hope I'm not overstepping, but I... well. I've worked for you for a couple of weeks now. I know that's not long, but I feel like I know nothing about you. I know I'm just your assistant, but I was hoping maybe we could be friends, too." She glanced at my computer again, pressing her lips together as her eyes sparkled with laughter. "Second, that report might be easier if you, um... if you turn your computer screen on."

The wall didn't even consult me before putting itself up. I felt my face freeze as I glanced back at the computer, which was indeed completely dark, before looking back at Lisa and opening my mouth.

And then nothing came out.

I was at a loss for words, which was a new experience, and one I wasn't overly fond of. Lisa looked back at me with a sincere warmth in her eyes, something friendly and hopeful and kind. Still, trying to formulate a response took me a moment, and before I could say anything, her warm expression faded into a far more familiar one: straight up motherfucking terror.

"Or... I mean... I have definitely overstepped," she said, her voice shaking. "Damnit, James was right. I'm so... I am so sorry, Aspen. I didn't mean to sound, um—I'll uh, I'll just go back to my desk."

She started to get up and I panicked.

"No!"

She froze, eyes wide as she hunched half-out of her seat.

"Shit. I mean—" I cleared my throat again and took a deep breath, tapping into my Big Scary Aspen energy for what I hoped was even an iota of confidence, then looked back at Lisa. "Okay. Please sit down, Lisa."

She sat obediently, back straight and hands folded in her lap as if she was about to be scolded.

This was not off to a good start. I sighed.

"Look, Lisa. Here's... here's the thing." I stopped again, collected my thoughts, and then took another steadying breath. "I have worked primarily by myself for the past five years. I have one work friend, and I only see her when I go to head office. Otherwise, we just talk on the phone. I would not say I know anyone else I work with particularly well, and that also extends to my personal life. I'm usually in any given location for a couple of weeks at most, so I don't see my friends very often or for very long." Uncomfortably vulnerable, I looked at Lisa helplessly. "I am not good at this yet. And I think I might have resting bitch face."

Lisa startled herself with a laugh. "What do you mean?"

Laughter was good. I gestured at her. "Well, like right now. You caught me in a lie, which by all accounts, is hilarious. But I'm so... so *me* that I didn't know what to say. So I took a moment to think, and you started looking like I was a cat and you were some kind of threatened rodent."

"I looked like... a rodent?" she repeated.

Fuck. If there was a moment I *should* have paused to think, it was that. "No! Not... I mean you just looked like you were about to shit yourself or—"

Lisa raised her eyebrows. Grimacing, I sighed and put my head on my desk again.

"I swear to God I'm a fucking decent person. I just hate this place."

"You are a decent person," she said. "If not just a little... um..."

"Bitchy?" I mumbled against the desk.

"Blunt," she said, a gentle laugh in her voice. "As for hating this place..."

I groaned. "It's fucking awful and you know it."

"I mean, I understand why you're frustrated. It's hard to come to a small town. I'm not originally from Wakeham, either. It's kind of like walking into a club you aren't part of and everyone's staring at you."

I slowly lifted my head up from the desk. Lisa was looking at me sympathetically, though there was still laughter in her eyes.

"That's exactly what it's like," I said.

"And at least I moved here with my husband. You don't know anyone here, do you?"

I shook my head. "No one. I mean, I've met a couple of the managers before at other locations. Todd and Patrice and Hilda were all transferred here. But my job used to be telling them everything they were doing wrong, so they aren't my biggest fans."

Lisa smiled. "I don't think you're mean or anything, you know. I think it's just that people aren't used to you. But it's only been a couple of weeks."

"Everyone keeps saying that. It feels like forever." I leaned back in my chair. "I'm sorry I've been difficult to work with. And that I said your hips looked lumpy in that skirt. I could have found a better way to phrase it."

"Honestly, you were right. Sure, it came out a little..."

"Bitchy," I said.

"Blunt," she said again, laughing. "But you know, I don't mind that. Do you know how rare it is for someone to tell you the truth? I appreciate the honesty, Aspen. And, since I know you're not going to fire me for overstepping, I'm just going to start telling you about me and we'll become friends, okay?"

"Is that how it works?" I asked, amused.

Lisa shrugged. "I've been a stay at home mom for years. I have no idea how adults become friends so I'm just going to do it how my kids do."

That day, I learned a lot about how people filled their time. For the first time in—well, possibly for the first time ever—I got fuck all done at work. Instead, I spent my day getting to know Lisa—shooting the shit, if you will. She told me all about her three kids, who sounded adorably exhausting, and her husband, James. He was the one from Wakeham but had gone to Toronto for university, which is where he'd met Lisa. She wasn't from Toronto, but had decided to attend university there hoping to gain some independence from her family.

"Just typical teenager thinking," she said, laughing. "Could I have saved a ton of money and lived at home while going to UBC in Kelowna? Absolutely. Was I dead-set on getting as far away from the Okanagan as I could because I was so spoiled that I didn't realize that's where everyone else in Canada *wants* to live? Completely."

I laughed at that, sipping my coffee. "So you went to Toronto instead?"

"Yep. Thank God I met James my first month there, otherwise I might have dropped out that semester."

Lisa was sweet. Despite that, it turned out we had a fair bit in common. At least, as much as a single woman who was used to travelling the world and a mom-of-three from a small town could have in common. Lisa's hours between working and sleeping involved her family, of course, but she also liked to watch movies.

"James likes those stupid car shows, though," she said. "So usually I just end up reading."

"Anything good?" I asked. "I've been reading a bit more, but... well, I could use some recommendations."

Her cheeks turned red. "Um, it depends on what you like, I guess."

"Well, what do you suggest?"

It took a few minutes before she sighed and admitted why she was dodging the question.

"I like romance novels," she said.

"Oh," I said. "And you think I wouldn't because I don't seem like the type to believe in fairytales and happily ever afters?"

"Sure, let's go with that."

I folded my arms and raised my eyebrows. "Let's not. You can't just say that and then not actually tell me why."

Her face turned redder, but she started laughing. "HR's not going to come for me if I talk about steamy books, right?"

I rolled my eyes. "How are we supposed to be friends if we have to worry about HR?"

That got both of us laughing and I ended the day with a Post-It note list of books that she thought I might enjoy, though I had my doubts—romance wasn't exactly my particular brand of excitement. Still, I figured I might look up one or two of them. It would give me something to talk about with Lisa, which was good because I had no friends and having mutual hobbies would be a good way to get to know each other. And I liked dirty things, so maybe I could skim past the damsels in distress and heaving bosoms so I could get straight to the throbbing rods of passion and dampening lady gardens or whatever euphemisms the writers were using these days.

"Why don't you come by my place for dinner and a drink some night?" Lisa asked later that day when we were packing up to go home. "As long as you don't mind that my kids are hurricanes personified, we'd be happy to have you."

"You know, that'd be nice."

Lisa grinned as we walked out of the office. "Great. Why don't I drive you over Friday after work? We have that late meeting anyway, so by the time dinner's done, the kids'll be ready to go to bed and we can have a few drinks. With the kids back in school and James working half-days on Fridays, the house might even be reasonably clean."

I guess Lisa's kids were onto something, because it turns out, that was a great way to make friends.

# Chapter Eight

*Theo*

"No LUCK?" I CALLED as Rick tried to quietly close the door behind him.

"Oh, you're still up." The words slurred together and he stumbled a bit as he made his way into the kitchen. I heard the refrigerator door open, then a moment later he flopped on the other end of the couch with a bottle of water already dripping condensation. "What're you doing still up?"

"Watching a movie," I said. "Just finished about five minutes before you walked in."

"Oh yeah?" He cracked the water bottle open. "What kind of movie?"

"Horror. *Revenge of the Attacking Alien Whales* or something. It wasn't very good." I watched as Rick tilted his head back and slugged down some water. "How was the club?"

There was a pause as he finished chugging, then wiped his mouth on the back of his hand. "Far. Should have just gotten a room in the city. The cab driver thought I was joking when I told him where I was going but I made the tip worth it." He stopped and hiccupped. "Then again, I left like, an hour ago, maybe? And I'm still drunk. So good, I guess."

"Didn't meet anyone?"

He half-shrugged. "Made out with some guy for a while. Think he drank too much though. Pretty sure he puked."

"Before or after?"

Rick twisted his mouth in disgust, then chugged the rest of his water and got up to get another bottle. I heard him stumble, then open a drawer and rustle through it. When he came back to the couch, he had two beers and a bottle opener.

I raised my eyebrow at him. "You can barely walk. Should you really be having another?"

"Nope, so you better get to the point quick otherwise I might succumb to alcohol poisoning." He cracked both beers and shoved one in my hand. "It's been like two months. We're talking about Sheri."

I groaned. "Man, I was about to go to bed. And I don't want to talk about Sheri."

"You need to."

"I don't—"

"I know for a fact that the movie you watched tonight wasn't called *The Attacking Alien Whale Massacre* because that's not a real name and you hate horror movies. And you weren't paying attention because you were thinking about Sheri." He crossed his legs and sat back against the couch. "I've seen the fucking video. I know what she did. And you haven't said fuck all about it since then. It's time to unpack this shit."

"Rick, it's three a.m. I need sleep."

"Bullshit. You need to talk to me."

Ignoring him, I started to get back, only to end up falling back in surprise as Rick leaned forward and pushed me back onto the couch. Glaring at him, I tried to stand again.

"I can do this all night," he slurred, pushing me onto the couch again.

That was true, and there wasn't a ton I could do about it. I was an average-sized guy, but the only reason Rick would have seemed out of place on a Viking ship was because he was in the wrong era. "Drop it. I don't want to talk right now."

"You've said that every time I've tried to bring it up." He put his beer on the coffee table, his face uncharacteristically serious. "Theo, man, I know you better than anyone. You *need* to talk this out and I know damn fucking well that if you're not talking to *me* about it, you're not talking to *anyone* about it. And if you don't talk this through, you're going to make yourself crazy." He motioned at the TV. "You couldn't even think of a better excuse than *Return of the Whale Eating Aliens 3*. This shit's gone on too long."

I glared at him, my jaw tense. He stared back, holding my gaze with a stoic seriousness that shouldn't have been possible with the amount of alcohol he'd likely consumed. I could keep fighting him and it wouldn't be long until he just passed out on the couch, especially if he intended on drinking that beer. The problem was, he wasn't wrong.

Shit had gone on too long.

"You want to know about Sheri?" I put my beer on the coffee table, my voice cold. "Fine, Rick. She hasn't said shit to the papers or to anyone that I've heard of. And that's what I wanted, right? I didn't want it to get out, and I didn't want her to say anything and that's great, right? All it means is that I have to come out and say that my relationship failed. That I got fucking played, *again*. That this girl that I thought I loved and was going to get married to and have a family with and live in this stupid house in our stupid hometown ended up being a complete liar." My face burned and I grabbed the beer, taking a drink. "How in the fuck did I not notice that she was just another gold digger?"

"Because she didn't seem like it," Rick said, sipping his own beer. "I don't know if she ever thought about doing it before you two reconnected, or if she just took advantage of the situation once you had."

I looked down at my beer, shaking my head slowly. "I date women who are famous, and it's like I'm not good enough for them. Not hot enough or talented enough or rich enough or Hollywood enough. I wanna avoid the press and they can't live without it. So whatever, right? Date different people, right? So I date women who aren't, and I'm like an ATM." I laughed, then took another drink. "Maybe I should just accept it. Pick the hottest girl that'll fake it around me and call it a day."

"I don't believe for one second you'd consider getting a trophy wife."

I snorted. "At least I'd be getting laid."

"And there it is." Rick tilted his beer at me. "That's what this is all about, isn't it? You need to get laid."

Despite my annoyance with him, I almost laughed. "Probably wouldn't hurt."

"I'd offer my services if you swung that way."

"I know you would. Still pretty sure I'm straight. Still would friend-zone you."

"I know. Because you love me too much to risk it. But I mean, maybe I can help find you someone to do the... you know. Whatever straight people do when they need to get off."

"Pretty sure it's still called sex."

"Whatever. That. I can find you someone."

I rolled my eyes. "What, you're suddenly some kind of soulmate-finding matchmaker?"

"No, not like that." He twisted his mouth to the side as he tried to find the words. "Look, remember when you played that charity gig last time we were on tour with all the other acts? I overheard some of the other assistants talking about it, and a lot of them just... They go out and find a girl, some superfan who's super hot and wants to sleep with whoever the act is. They... you know. Get her to sign a non-disclosure agreement and bring her backstage and..." Rick looked at me pointedly.

I gaped at him, my mouth hanging open. "I... what? No. That's not... No fucking way."

"You sure? I guess it's pretty common and—"

"I'm not finding some fan of mine who wants to fuck just for the sake of fucking."

He sighed. "Look, I know it's not ideal, but they... like, they consent to it and—"

"No." I took a last swig of beer and put the bottle on the table. "Thanks, but no. I'm calling it a night. You should... you should go get some sleep. You're going to be really hung over tomorrow."

I didn't know if he went to bed right away. Way back when I first started out, when Rick and I would share a hotel or apartment or whatever, I used to be able to hear him puking or snoring, but my house was big enough and soundproofed enough that I couldn't tell anymore. Still, even though my room was silent and dark, I lay awake, staring at the roof as the conversation played over in my mind.

I knew what he was talking about. I even knew other musicians who had done it before or did it regularly. It was one of those things that everyone knew about and took in stride, even though to someone on the outside, it was fucking *weird*. Arguably, it was all ethical, I supposed. The fans got something they wanted, and the musician got something they wanted, and everyone walked away happy. But it still seemed... I don't know. Skeezy. I'd never been able to picture myself doing something like that, maybe because I was almost constantly in a relationship and so had never needed to. Though, now that Rick had planted the thought in my head...

I tried to imagine asking him to find someone for me. What criteria would I even give him? Would I stick to a type, or pick a different kind of girl every night?

"Oh yeah, Rick, find me a curvy one tonight. Make sure she's got a thick ass."

"There's gotta be at least one girl out there with pierced nipples. Maybe get them to flash you first to make sure? Yeah, I know you don't like tits, but just check her nipples first, okay?"

"Hmm, tonight I feel like a blonde. Skinny, but big tits. Make sure she doesn't have an annoying voice."

No, I decided, cringing as I imagined the scenario. It made me sick to even think of trying to order a woman like she was something on a fucking menu. So maybe I'd just ask Rick to find someone. Someone who just seemed... nice. Someone who seemed like she'd actually want to be there.

Then what? He'd send them up to my room. After my shows, I usually showered in my dressing room, then went for drinks with my team. But if I had some girl waiting, I'd go to the hotel right after instead. She'd come into the room. Nervous, probably. They'd have told her what to expect. Asked her for consent, on my behalf. Made her sign to say she'd tell no one about this. She'd be wondering what would happen. Thinking maybe it was a little sketchy. She'd be shy. Worried, maybe.

I'd offer her a drink. Laugh a little, apologize.

"Kind of awkward," I'd say.

She'd chuckle a bit, nod. "Never thought I'd get to meet you, let alone... you know."

I'd laugh. Maybe tell her I'd noticed her in the crowd, thought she was pretty. No, she'd see through that. I wouldn't say anything about why she was picked.

"I'm Theo," I'd say.

She'd tell me her name. I'd ask her to sit on the couch with me. Make small talk. Ask her where she's from, what does she do, did she enjoy the show? Try to make her feel comfortable. Tell her if she changes her mind, that's okay, just tell me and we'd stop, no hard feelings. That I wanted her to enjoy herself and even though I probably totally seemed like *that* guy, I didn't want to be *that* guy.

She'd smile, relax a bit. "It's okay. I'm just so excited."

I'd laugh. "We can keep making small talk, if you want," I'd say. "Or, we could, uhh…"

I'd leave it up to her. Maybe she'd ask for more small talk. Or she'd be funny and say *"Uhh* sounds good…"

She'd put her drink down and take mine from my hand. Lift her hand to my face and pull me towards her. She'd kiss me softly, still a bit nervous, but trying to be confident.

I'd shift so I was closer, put my hand against her neck and kiss her harder. Lift my other hand to her shirt, feel her breast through it. I would keep kissing her as I touch her body through her clothes, run my hand down her arms and to the bottom of her shirt. I'd toy with the hem for a moment, then slide my hand underneath, up her stomach, feel her tremble. Pull away.

"Are you okay?" I'd ask.

She'd nod, smile. "Tickles a bit," she'd say. "Keep going."

I'd smile and kiss her again. Pull her closer to me, resume my exploration. Cup her breast through her bra, feel her nipple harden through the fabric. I'd try to take her shirt off and she'd help, lifting it over her head, blushing as she sat in front of me and I drank in her body with my eyes. I'd tell her to take off the rest of her clothes and sit back, watching her undress. She'd stand in front of me, breathing a little heavily, as I looked her over head to toe, gazing at every smooth curve, hard nipples, glistening pussy. I'd tell her she's gorgeous and she'd giggle. The sight of her blushing would drive me crazy, pink tinges crawling up her chest and collarbone and neck. It'd be too much to handle and I'd stand up and start undressing. She'd watch and it would be my turn to be the nervous one. She'd look at my body and at my cock, hard and ready. I'd wonder what she was thinking. If it was what she'd imagined, because she… she would've imagined this, right? Somehow, this beautiful fucking girl would've pictured herself with me before.

She'd grin at me, taking over. Tell me to sit down, and then she'd kneel in front of me. Her lips would wrap around me and I'd groan, tilt my head back, close my eyes. She'd suck me off, bobbing her head, hands cupping my balls. It would be heaven. Nothing but her mouth around my dick, the slick, wet sound as her head moved back and forth, the muffled gags when my cock hit the back of her throat.

It would take everything in me, but I'd ask her to stop, and she'd look up at me with big eyes as she let my cock slip out of her mouth. She'd tease me with her tongue and I'd be breathing heavily now, and I'd tell her I want to be inside her. I'd get a condom, put it on, and she'd get on top of me. Arms resting on my shoulders, I'd reach down to guide my cock inside her, the tip just teasing her wet entrance, both of us inhaling in anticipation as she started to move down and...

I jumped, gasping as my eyes flew open. For a moment, I was disoriented before realizing I'd fallen asleep thinking about Rick's suggestion. The face of the girl in my dream floated in my mind, as did the flawless tits I'd conjured up, her perfect body naked and hovering over mine. Of course I'd woken up at the best part.

My cock ached, throbbing painfully in my boxers. I couldn't remember the last time I'd been so hard, not that I had much brain power to devote to remembering anything right at that moment. Guided by my cock, I reached down and gripped myself, immediately beginning to stroke hard. The dream was barely fading and I could almost taste the girl's lips. I pictured whoever she was fucking me, imagined what her tits would look like bouncing up and down in my face as she rode me.

It didn't take long, and I stifled a cry as I came. Wave after wave of tension crashed and released and I clenched my jaw, breathing through my nose as cum spilled on my hand and stomach. When I finished, I groaned, resting heavily against my pillow. It had been a very long time since I'd had a dream like that. Carefully, I climbed out of bed to go clean up.

Once I was done and back in bed, I thought about Rick's offer to make that a reality, and immediately felt my face burning.

There was no way I'd ever be able to ask Rick to find me some random fan to have sex with. Hot as the dream had been, I don't think I could handle the humiliation in real life. I rolled over and pressed my face into the pillow, trying not to think about it.

# Chapter Nine

*Aspen*

AGREEING TO DINNER WITH Lisa's family seemed like a great idea when I was in the safety of my office with unwarranted confidence that I could, in fact, handle it. How hard could it be, after all? It was just dinner. I'd had dinner before. And sure, it was with her family, but her husband and kids were just people. I'd been around people before. I'd been around people often, in fact. Theoretically, dinner at Lisa's house was no different than having a plate of nachos at the pub with Darby on one of my stopovers in Montreal.

However, as I followed Lisa to her front door that Friday evening after work, it was very clear that dinner at Lisa's house was nothing like a pub and I wasn't entirely sure why I'd even thought it would be.

We had left my car at the office since Lisa and I lived on opposite sides of Wakeham. The drive over had been fine; it was just me and Lisa and that was manageable. The last couple of days at work had been great and I'd been enjoying getting to know her better. I could even state almost confidently that we were friends. A lot of that was because I'd gone home and, in a moment of boredom, looked up the books she'd suggested.

When I got to work the next day, I immediately went to her desk and put the Post-It note full of recommendations in front of her.

"Lisa?" I said, keeping my voice as steady as I could. "About these..."

She looked up, eyes wide with worry. "Yes?"

"More."

She stared, bewildered. "What?"

I tapped the Post-It note. *"More.* On my desk. By noon." I turned to walk into my office, then stopped. "And don't ever let HR see that list. I very much appreciate your particular brand of depravity, but they might not."

She burst out laughing. "So you liked the books?"

"*More,*" I said again. "Particularly like that one with the pilot and the lawyer. None of the wind-blowing-through-the-hair bullshit, please. I just want the dirty stuff."

I had three Post-It notes worth of recommendations on my desk by noon, with a promise to bring me a stack of paperbacks she'd finished reading if I wanted to go through them and a warning not to think *too* badly of her, which I assured her wasn't possible.

Making friends may not have been my forte, but I figured once Lisa and I knew what we were each getting off to, it counted as being friends. She was also an unreasonably kind person. After our conversation about how out of place I felt, she began making every effort to involve me more in the community. Each time we talked to an employee, Lisa would tell me as much as she knew about them. She'd coach me on how to be a bit more relatable, and even though it was only a few days later, I'd noticed a significant difference. Maybe I was more approachable. More likely, I was less on-guard, and finally just accepting the hand I was dealt for the next year.

However, it had still only been a few days, and picking her brain for new recommendations of things I could get myself off to was a lot different from meeting her family. As we reached the front door, a familiar sense of stoniness began building up brick by brick in response to the nerves fluttering in my stomach.

"I'm home!" Lisa called out as she opened the door and ushered me inside.

Despite spending most of the drive telling me her house was a disaster and not to judge her too harshly, since they were all still getting used to her being a working mom instead of a stay-at-home-mom, there was a distinct lack of chaos. Bright and airy, there were family photos on the walls and books on tables next to armchairs in the nearby living room. Children's toys were in baskets, the occasional straggler sitting on the floor nearby, and a huge shelf full of movies sat next to the TV. A savoury scent of pepper filled the air, something home cooked and comforting in the most unfamiliar way. My mouth watered as Lisa apologized for the mess and I looked at her, raising an eyebrow.

"You must be joking, Lisa," I said.

Her mouth dropped open and I realized how that had sounded.

"Let me try again," I said quickly. "Your house is beautiful. If you think this is a mess, please never come to my house. I'm a single woman in a small apartment and I can't keep things half as tidy as your home is."

That was the right thing to say. Her olive skin turned pink and she smiled, but before she could respond, a tall man with light brown hair and peach-toned skin came through the hallway. He had an oven mitt on one hand, a towel over his shoulder, and a dopey-bright smile on his face as he looked at Lisa.

"Welcome home, babe," he said, and the pink tinge on Lisa's skin darkened even more as he kissed her on the cheek.

"Aspen, this is my husband, James," she said.

I extended my hand. "It's a pleasure, James."

"Nice to finally have a face to the name," he replied, smiling. "Lisa talks about you all the time."

That smile was contagious; I couldn't help but return it as he shook my hand. "She may have mentioned a thing or two about you as well."

He laughed. "Well, that's a relief. Now, in all those things she told me about you, she didn't mention any food preferences, so I hope the basics are okay. Chicken and potatoes, salad, and most importantly, wine."

"That sounds lovely," I said.

Lisa raised her eyebrows at my formalness. I grimaced, shrugging as if to tell her I was trying.

"Now that you mention wine, I, um... brought this," I said, reaching into my work bag and withdrawing one of the bottles of wine Kevin had paid for after my bet with Darby. "To thank you for having me."

"You had *wine* in your purse all day?" Lisa asked, aghast.

"Well—"

"And you didn't tell me? Not even after I had to deal with that idiot Daniel who couldn't figure out how to leave you a voicemail?" She took the bottle from me, smirking. "Probably smart of you. I would've cracked this so fast, I wouldn't have been able to explain to him how voicemails work for the tenth time."

Before I could respond with much more than a laugh, the hurricane began.

"*Mooo-OOO-ooom!*"

Like a battle cry, it echoed through the house, and suddenly three blurs of energy flew into the hallway. Lisa braced herself expertly as two boys and a girl crashed into her legs, flailing arms wrapping around her in the approximation of a hug.

"Okay, okay," she said, trying to cut through their chatter. "Yes, hello, I love you too. I missed you, too. I—oof."

"Mom did you see I cleaned up the *whole* living room by myself except that part where there's still stuff, that was Cole."

"Hey, I helped! Mom, I helped!"

"Mom I didn't help because I got a boo-boo and Daddy gave me a princess bang-daid."

"I see that, Anna. Did you—"

"It wasn't my fault she got a boo-boo, Mom. I didn't have nothing to do with it, right Anna?"

It took some time, but eventually Lisa managed to determine that Cole had stepped on Anna's fingers, Anna had promised not to tell on him if Cole let her watch *Frozen* for the millionth time, and Grayson had cleaned the living room by himself while all of that was going on. It was only once they untangled themselves from Lisa that the kids seemed to notice I was there and, like someone had pressed a mute button, they turned into quiet, shy little angels.

I cleared my throat. "Hello."

I'd been aiming for a pleasant tone, but it came out oddly high pitched, and Lisa raised her eyebrows at me again.

"Kids, please say hi to Ms. Haws, my boss," Lisa said. "Aspen, this is Grayson, Cole, and Anna."

"Hi, Ms. Haws," they replied in unison.

"Um. Hi," I replied. "And it's... you... please call me Aspen, too."

"Aspen?" asked Grayson, the oldest one, who was wearing a neat-and-clean t-shirt and thick glasses. "That's like a tree. Did you know that?"

"That's a stupid name," the middle one, Cole, said boredly as he picked at a hole in his dirt-scuffed jeans.

"Cole!" scolded James.

But something about Grayson's earnest excitement about sharing the fact that my name was a tree paired with Cole's exasperated disinterest made me laugh.

"It is a kind of tree, you're right," I said. "And you want to know something else?" Grayson nodded, eyes wide. "My last name—Haws—comes from a kind of berry. So my whole name is kind of like Tree Fruit."

As much as I'd hated my stupid name growing up, I was thankful for it now. All three kids seemed to think that was the most interesting thing I could have possibly said. Even Anna, who likely didn't understand a single word, expressed her awe.

"Do you think they have haw berries in Arendelle?" Anna twirled, the princess dress she was wearing flaring out wildly. "And they could make cakes with them, and pies, and—"

"Can I call you Mrs. Tree Fruit?" Cole asked loudly.

"Okay, let's get ready for dinner," Lisa said, cutting everyone off. "No, you can't call her Mrs. Tree Fruit. Be nice, that's Mommy's boss."

James managed to wrangle the kids towards the kitchen so that I could finally take my coat off.

"Sorry for the bombardment," Lisa said, putting my coat in the closet. "I know they're a little intense."

"It's fine," I replied. "I apologize for—"

"Uh-uh, nope." She looked at me pointedly. "Stop being so uptight. This is my family, not a business meeting."

"Right," I said. "I'm... I'm trying."

"Would wine help?"

"Lisa," I said, my voice pitching down in a way that made her look just a little nervous. "What do you take me for? Of course wine would help."

She laughed, relieved, and as much as I told myself I really had to stop doing things that made her think I was going to yell at her or something, it was kind of funny.

"I promise you can relax around us. We're all mostly nice people and we're not going to bite," she said as she led me to the kitchen. "Well, except maybe Anna, but we're working on that with her."

As James started dishing out plates for the kids, Lisa poured a generous glass of wine for each of us. Everything looked phenomenal; roasted chicken with crispy skin and fluffy mashed potatoes alongside peas that were swimming in a buttery sauce and a salad that actually looked delicious considering it was a salad.

"It looks amazing," I said suddenly.

James looked up from scooping potatoes onto Anna's plate and smiled again. "Thank you. I hope it tastes amazing."

"It will," I said, not even a hint of doubt in my voice.

Maybe it was the wine, but probably not; the stony nervousness I'd been feeling faded before I'd even taken two sips. As James finished serving the kids and us adults began filling our plates with food, I even started smiling.

The kids regaled me with stories from their day at school and their favourite things. I learned that Grayson was a certified nerd who loved math and astronomy. My guess was that Cole would be the boy some girl's mother warned her about one day, though not because he was actually trouble; he was energetic and curious and free-spirited, which would undoubtedly piss off some poor conservative family who wanted to keep their daughter locked in a tower. Anna was every bit the princess she dressed up as; her brothers doted on her in a way that made my heart ache, for some reason, though I shoved that firmly behind one of those secondary walls I had built up somewhere deep inside. She was a funny kid with big expressions; in particular, she gave a riveting review of her meal that would have given the most curmudgeonly of TV chefs a run for their money.

"...but you shouldn't make it so *mushy*!" she finished, pointing her fork at her father as she scolded him about the 'mushed' potatoes on her plate.

I pressed my lips together, trying my hardest not to laugh, and exchanged a glance with Lisa, who had a similar expression on her face.

"Or," said James thoughtfully. "Or, you could just say 'thank you for making me a nutritious supper, Daddy. I appreciate it very much.'"

"Well, I, for one, think it was the perfect level of mushiness." I put my fork down after finishing my last bite. "Thank you, James, it was delicious."

Anna apparently didn't like that and sat back in her seat, sulking. "Auntie Sheri always used to agree with me."

Cole heaved an exasperated sigh. "I don't want to talk about Auntie Sheri."

"Miss Aspen, you should be our new auntie!" Grayson exclaimed. "You can be Auntie Tree Fruit."

I must have made a face because Lisa hurriedly covered up her chuckle with a cough.

"I don't know about that," I said. "I think your Auntie Sheri is probably doing a good job of it on her own."

"Not really," Anna said. "We lost Auntie Sheri so now we need a new auntie."

My mouth dropped open, likely wide enough for me to stick my foot all the way to the back of my throat and I looked at Lisa, horrified. "I'm so sorry. I didn't know you'd just lost someone."

"Oh, she's not dead," said James casually. "My brother just went through a break-up." He turned to Anna. "When we say 'we lost someone,' it means they've passed away, so we just say that she's not our auntie anymore, okay?"

"Uncle Theo is sad like she died, though," Cole said.

"Do you think he knows she's not dead?" Anna asked.

A practiced look of patience crossed Lisa's face. "Yes, Uncle Theo knows she's not dead."

"Oh, I know!" Grayson's eyes were wide behind his big glasses. "Miss Aspen should marry Uncle Theo. Then she can be our new auntie."

"That's not really how it works," Lisa said.

Grayson looked at his mom in disbelief. "Yes, it is. When Uncle Theo loves someone, that person becomes our Auntie. That's what you said. That's how it works!"

"Well, there's your answer," I said. "Your uncle doesn't love me, so I can't be your auntie."

"He might," Cole said. "He loves lots of women."

James choked back his laugh, pressing a napkin to his throat.

"Is that so?" I asked, amused.

"Uh-huh. What?" he asked, looking at his dad. "What's funny? Uncle Theo loves Mom, right? And Grandma? And he used to love Auntie

Sheri. There's probably more. He'd probably marry Miss Aspen. Like, if you asked nicely."

"Maybe I don't want to get married," I said. "What about that? Besides, I don't even know your uncle Theo. Can't marry someone I don't know."

"That's true," James agreed.

"That's what Elsa says in *Frozen*." Anna made a sweeping gesture with her arm as she started to sing a song from the movie, inevitably knocking a glass of water across Cole's plate.

"Okay, okay!" Lisa shot out of her seat in full Mom mode and began cleaning up the table.

Chaos ensued, so I gathered some of the dishes to help as the kids lost focus on the glass of water and began to focus on dessert. I brought the first stack to the kitchen, following behind Lisa as she went to get more towels for the table, but she didn't notice me until she turned around with a roll of paper towels.

"Oh, you don't have to do that!" Lisa said.

"It's no problem," I said. "You fed me an amazing meal. The least I can do is help clear up a little. Where can I put these?"

"Right here," James said, taking the stack from me. "You're our guest. Thank you, though."

Lisa went back out to the table to finish mopping up the spilled water, leaving me with James in the kitchen.

"At least let me rinse them or something," I said.

"Not a chance, but you could bring the dessert plates out for me, if you don't mind."

"I'd be happy to help."

Smiling, he put the dirty dishes down and opened a cupboard. "I appreciate it. Dinner around here sometimes feels like we're running a full-service restaurant. The joys of parenting, you know?"

"Well, you're doing an awesome job of it. Your kids are wonderful."

"Thanks." James looked proudly towards the dining room. "I can't take much credit. Lisa was home with them until she got hired on with you."

"Well, we consider ourselves very lucky to have her there," I said automatically, then cringed and shook my head. "Sorry. I'm working on not sounding like a corporate robot all the time. That wasn't meant to be meaningless words. I very much appreciate you having me over for dinner. I enjoy working with Lisa and she's been a... a good... friend."

James smiled another one of those dopey-bright smiles that showed just how much he loved his wife, but before he could respond, the doorbell rang.

"Lovely," he said flatly, then smiled again. "Small town life, you know. People stop by without calling."

While James went to the door, I grabbed the dessert plates and brought them to the dining room, where a fresh round of chaos had started at the chime of the doorbell. Lisa was fighting a good battle as she tried to keep the kids in their seats, but Grayson managed to slip out of his chair and darted past his mom to join his dad in the hallway. A beat of silence went by, then:

"*It's Uncle Theo!*" came the exuberant shout.

With the way Cole and Anna responded, it might as well have been Santa fucking Claus himself. Lisa sighed in exasperation as Cole and Anna shrieked, the sound so high-pitched that I was almost certain a neighbour's dog started barking, and bolted to the door.

"Sorry, Lisa!" I heard someone call from the front.

A whirlwind of childish chatter followed. I listened, amused, as the kids recapped the night, including that Lisa's boss lady was in the other room and she was a tree fruit.

"A tree fruit?" he was saying as the kids led him into the dining room. Lisa looked at me, mortified. The newcomer—Uncle Theo, obviously—looked at me from the doorway and grinned.

"I don't know about that, Cole. She kinda looks like a person to me."

I couldn't help bursting into laughing. Lisa shook her head, a smile cracking through her exasperation, and crossed the room to greet Theo with a hug.

"Sorry," he said again. "I didn't know you were eating so late. Or had company."

"It's fine. You're just in time for dessert," Lisa said.

"No, no, I don't want to interrupt. I just wanted to pop in..."

"It's Mom's devil's food cake recipe," James said, coming up behind him. Theo trailed off and James nodded knowingly. "I'll grab a plate for you."

"Theo, this is my boss, Aspen," Lisa said. "She's the director of the office. Aspen, my brother-in-law, Theo."

Theo flashed a smile at me as we shook hands. "Nice to meet you."

And it was nice to meet him, too. Theo was good-looking, in a kind of scruffy, small town way. He shared the same brown hair and light skin as James, but his eyes were a warm, rich shade of brown and his hair was on the shorter side of shaggy. Where James was wearing a button down and nice jeans, Theo was the epitome of casual in jeans and a T-shirt underneath a zip-up hoodie. He was younger than James, it seemed, maybe around my age, though his style made him appear younger still.

And that smile. If James' smile had been contagious, Theo's was devastatingly infectious. It was one of those genuine, warm smiles that lit up a whole room in the most memorable way.

I frowned. Actually, Theo looked kind of familiar. Where had I seen him before?

As he turned to talk to his niece and nephews, I studied him. He didn't work for me, which would have been my first guess. Maybe at the grocery store? Or the gross, shitty bar that one night I checked it out? Maybe that was it.

Yeah, that had to be it. I'd been so focused on not catching some disease that I hadn't been paying a ton of attention to the people there. He must have been at one of the tables or something.

Still... I thought I would have remembered that smile.

Before I could think about it too much, James came out of the kitchen and I fell in love.

Not with him, obviously.

He was holding the most delicious-looking chocolate cake I'd ever seen in my life. It was round, double layered, and coated in thick chocolate icing. Some kind of chocolate sauce or ganache or something was dripping down the sides and chocolate shavings dusted the top, little curls of heaven scattered along the icing.

"Time for dessert!" James said.

My ass was back in my chair so fast that even the kids were laughing at me.

# Chapter Ten

*Theo*

"But Uncle Theo's still here! He'll play with us!"

"Nope, it's bedtime," said James. "You've already stayed up late *and* gotten cake."

Cole looked at me, his eyes pained. "Uncle Theo! Tell Dad we should stay up!"

I shrugged helplessly. "Sorry, guys. You know that what your dad says goes."

Anna started bawling and Cole's desperate gaze turned to Grayson. I saw Lisa wince and glance in Aspen's direction. Aspen barely noticed, as she was still scraping the last bits of chocolate icing off her plate.

"Mommy, please?" begged Grayson on behalf of his siblings. "We want to stay up. Uncle Theo—"

"Tell you what, guys," I said. "If you go to bed nice and quiet right now, I'll ask your mom if it's okay for you to come over tomorrow for a party at my house, okay?"

The three of them glanced at each other warily, communicating in that silent way only siblings seem to be capable of. I knew it well; I'd shared looks like that with their dad my entire life, furtive glances back and forth as we silently discussed our negotiation strategies. I'd offered them a good deal: a party at my house meant no adults—adults being their parents, since Rick and I didn't count—and basically whatever else they wanted. All the pizza they could eat? Done. Or candy for dinner instead? As if I needed to be convinced to have candy for dinner. The only reason those kids weren't wrapped around my little fingers was because I only had two hands and there were three of them, but they knew damn well I'd do anything for them all the same.

"Can we watch movies?" Anna asked, sniffling cautiously.

"All the movies you want," I said.

She glanced at Cole, who looked at Grayson.

"On the big TV?" Grayson asked.

"Well, *duh*," I said, and that made Anna giggle.

"Can we watch *Frozen*?"

"What if I want to watch wrestling instead of a movie?" Cole asked.

"You can each pick something to watch," I said.

"Promise?" he asked.

"If your mom says yes."

Three heads swivelled towards Lisa, who pretended to think about it like she hadn't already secretly celebrated an unexpected day off from her kids, then nodded.

Still, the kids only half-heartedly agreed to it, which was understandable. Future promises weren't as good as immediate rewards. But they'd get over it, especially once they figured out that we were planning to sit around and do nothing exciting, like adults tend to do after dinner. They said goodnight to Aspen, who stiffly but sweetly wished them all pleasant dreams, and I got a big hug from each of them. Once they were done, James herded them up the stairs, giving me a thumbs-up, and Lisa looked relieved as she reached for the bottle of wine to refill Aspen's glass.

Aspen scraped her fork on the plate one last time before putting it down, her shoulders squared and chin up. "Lisa, can your children hear me from down here?"

Lisa's relieved expression faltered. "Uh... no, I don't... think so."

Aspen solemnly looked my sister-in-law dead in the eye. The smile on my face faded as I glanced at Lisa, who looked concerned.

I hadn't expected to meet someone new when I'd impulsively stopped by my brother's place to see what he was up to. I'd expected even less for it to be a pretty woman with wild, dark hair, bright red lipstick, and a quick wit, especially after realizing it was the notorious boss James had mentioned when we'd had dinner at my parents. She hadn't seemed all that bad to me as we all dove into our slices of cake, though in fairness, she hadn't said much and Mom's devil's food cake recipe was known to placate even the surliest of people.

A tense moment passed as she looked sternly at Lisa, dark eyes boring into her with an intensity that nearly made me shiver, even though I wasn't the target of her gaze. She might've been Lisa's boss, but I was going to be hard-pressed to sit there without defending my niece and nephews if she started some shit about it.

"I will never forgive you," she said. "That was the best fucking cake I've ever eaten in my entire life. Your family has ruined chocolate cake for me forever. How *dare* you?"

Lisa cackled, leaning back in her chair. "One of these days, I'll realize you're joking when you do that. Jesus, Aspen. I thought you were going to lose it on me."

Aspen maintained her stoic demeanor. "You think I'm joking? Cake is very serious, Lisa. This is a big deal."

Then, she glanced at me. Those dark eyes had a sparkle in them, something unexpectedly light for someone who seemed so intense. I held her gaze for a moment before raising my eyebrows. A heartbeat passed, then the stony look on her face cracked and she let out a bright laugh that didn't match the stone-cold personality I had expected.

"Well, I'm glad you enjoyed it. You too, Theo?" Lisa asked, standing up to clear the plates.

"Always," I replied. "Need a hand?"

"Absolutely not," she said in a way that was so reminiscent of my mom, I was glad for James' sake that he wasn't in the room. "Don't get up. I'm just putting these in the kitchen and grabbing more wine."

And then it was just me and Aspen.

The room had dwindled from chaos to quiet almost without me noticing. And for someone like me, that was dangerous. Aspen might have been polite, but now that we were alone... I wasn't in the mood for someone to gush about my music or delve into the intricacies of my career.

"So, Theo—"

I blurted the first thing that came to mind. "What do you think of Wakeham?"

She frowned. "What?"

"I... the town," I said. "Lisa said you just moved here? For, uh... work, right?"

She hesitated and then laughed, though the sound was almost nervous. "I don't know how to answer your question."

I raised my eyebrows at her. "Why's that?"

She was silent for a moment. Just as I started to worry that I'd offended her, she looked at me calmly and I realized she'd just been collecting her thoughts.

"I've spent the last five years travelling for work, so not being on the road is weird." She took a sip of wine. "Everything here is strange to me. Maybe it's a nice place, but I haven't got much to compare it to. I haven't spent more than a couple of weeks in one place, so it all seems... overwhelmingly different."

A lot was starting to make sense about her. I nodded sympathetically. "It's hard to travel all the time. Fun, but it's hard."

"You travel a lot, too?" she asked.

"Uh... yeah, a bit."

She waited for me to say more but didn't seem too uncomfortable when I didn't. "Well, from what I can tell, Wakeham is... okay. Better than I thought it would be. It's quiet. The area is pretty. It's just..."

"Boring?" I finished.

She laughed again. "Very. And it's just weird to know that I'm stuck here. Like, I have to watch what I say and do, because I'm not going to be taking off in a few days."

"Small town life," I said. "Everyone knows everyone and everything is open for gossip."

"Well, Aspen coming to town was the news of the century around here," Lisa said, returning to the dining room. "I almost had to do an interview with the paper when people found out I was her assistant."

"I'm surprised no one's tried to betroth you to their son yet," I said.

"Please," Aspen scoffed. "I don't need a betrothal. The big-city business woman comes to a quaint little town to take a job at the local clean energy factory? If those books Lisa loaned me taught me anything, it's that a charming small-town man will hatch a plan to endear himself to me in the hopes I won't shut down his family's struggling coal mine that the factory is about to put out of business, only to fall hopelessly in love with me."

"What books are those?" I asked, amused.

Lisa's face went *red*. "Just books, *Theodore*."

Aspen seemed to realize she'd said something that embarrassed her and tried to laugh it off, an uncomfortable look of uncertainty on her face.

"Well, if that doesn't work out, I don't think I have much to worry about," she said quickly. "I might not have anyone trying to betroth me to their son, but those kids of Lisa's are trying to play matchmaker already, so I'll be a little caught up trying to avoid their cunning plans to set me up."

"I dunno," I said, laughing. "They're pretty clever. You might not have much of a chance. Who're they trying to set you up with?"

I heard Lisa take in a sharp breath, but it didn't register as Aspen smirked at me playfully.

"Well, according to Grayson, his Uncle Theo might marry me if I ask nicely," she said. "Apparently, I've made a good enough impression that they think I'd make a decent aunt."

The weight of tension hit me instantly, a heaviness that sent a cold shock rushing through me from head to toe. Gravity held nausea in the pit of my stomach and clamped down on my lungs as I stared at Aspen blankly, then glanced at Lisa. She was staring at her hands, a grimace on her face and tightness in her shoulders.

To Aspen's credit, her laugh faded instantly. It felt like much longer, but was just a moment that stretched like taffy before she realized something was wrong.

And it was wrong. It was really *fucking* wrong.

"I—"

"What the fuck?" I asked Lisa before Aspen could say anything else.

"Don't swear at my wife."

I didn't know how long James had been standing in the doorway to the dining room, but I looked up at him, my mouth set in a straight line.

"It was just the kids being silly, Theo," Lisa said. "They didn't mean anything."

"I'm sorry," Aspen said. "I didn't—"

"I didn't think I had to remind you guys that this isn't common knowledge," I said, ignoring her.

Awkward silence filled the room and Lisa looked up, her jaw clenched. Aspen looked from her to me, then pushed her chair back from the table.

"Excuse me," she said. "I need to step outside for a moment. I have to... check some emails."

She didn't wait for anyone to respond before turning towards the kitchen. I listened as her footsteps echoed in the kitchen, then the door to the back deck opened. As soon as it closed, I tore my eyes off Lisa and placed my head in my hands on the table.

"The kids mentioned it in passing, just like she said," James said. "It's not a big deal."

"You don't get to decide it's not a big deal. Because it is, okay? It fucking is. Jesus, James. I'm trying to keep this from being a huge issue and you're joking about it?!"

"No one was joking about it," Lisa said.

I shook my head, anger boiling in my stomach. "I thought things were going so well and I might get through this without someone leaking shit to the press. Sheri hasn't even said anything. And now you're telling me your kids are spreading it around town like it's nothing."

"They're just kids, man!" James threw his hands in the air. "They like Aspen and they like you, and in a kid's mind that means you should get married."

"It's not being spread around anywhere," Lisa said. "They made *one* comment and—"

"Yeah, just the one in front of you," I said. "And what are they saying at school? Or at daycare? Didn't you tell them it was private?"

"For your fucking information, yeah, we did," James snapped. "Are you seriously pissed at my fucking *kids* for making a mistake? It's not their fault that you have a job that makes things different for them."

"I'm not pissed at them," I hissed. "What, you want me to apologize for wanting some semblance of privacy in my life? I don't *know* that woman and she's fucking joking about it like it's just common knowledge!"

"So is that what this is really about? You're upset because a woman you don't know made a joke you didn't like?"

"Don't imply I can't take a fucking joke. This wasn't a joke. This is my *life*, James. This shit is a way bigger deal when someone finding out the wrong thing could ruin my fucking career!"

"It's not like this is a common thing!" James was almost growling, his face turning red as glared at me. "You think there are guidelines for explaining to your kids that your rock star brother broke up with his girlfriend? Or why some things aren't okay for them to talk about? It's hard enough when you have that talk *without* taking your goddamn career into consideration."

My face burned. "Well, I'm so sorry that my life is making yours so much more difficult."

"Fuck off, you know I—"

"Enough!" Lisa snapped.

James fell silent immediately. He stared at me, anger still blooming across his face. We held each other's gaze for a moment, seething, before turning towards Lisa. Almost immediately, my anger turned to guilt as I saw tears in her eyes.

"We are sorry, Theo," she said, her voice shaking. "We are doing our best. You know we wouldn't do anything to intentionally cause you problems. But they are just kids. Anna still needs help in the damn bathroom sometimes. They don't understand everything."

"I'm not blaming the kids—"

"I said enough!" I fell silent and she took a shaky breath. "I was going to ask Aspen not to say anything after dinner, when the kids had gone to bed and we could have a private conversation so it wasn't a huge issue like it is now. Not only is she a nice person, but she's new to town. The chances of her saying anything are—" She stopped, shaking her head. "Since that ship has sailed, why don't you go outside and ask her not to say anything, since we aren't doing things how you'd like us to?"

"I never said you weren't doing things right—"

"Theo, stop." Her voice cracked. "That's my fucking boss you just embarrassed me in front of."

The anger that had been boiling in my stomach churned, then twisted, then morphed into shame. I blinked, looking quickly from Lisa to my brother, who had his arms folded and his jaw set.

Of course they were right.

I'd overreacted.

Horribly.

"You're right." I cleared my throat. "Fuck. I didn't mean—"

"It's fine. Just..." Lisa stopped and took a breath, briefly closing her eyes before looking directly at me. "I won't speak for James, but you can make it up to me by going out and apologizing to her yourself. I'm sure she's figured out why you wouldn't want people to know but hearing it from you would mean a lot. To me, at least. She's been nothing but polite to you all night, and it's not like she had any warning that we're related to you."

I paused. "You didn't tell her?"

James rolled his eyes. "We have identities outside you, you know."

"That's not what I meant," I said. "I thought you must have warned her because she didn't say anything. I thought you told her to act like I was... I don't know, normal."

"I've never told her you were *the* Theo Barker," Lisa said. "I told you, she's a decent person. Not everyone is out to get you. I mean, shit, Theo." She looked at me, pain on her face. "She was probably just excited to talk to someone who's been outside of northern Ontario in the past year. Before this, she travelled *constantly*."

I swallowed, staring down at the table. "You're right. I'm sorry. I..." I looked up at my brother, my face red. "Both of you. I'm sorry."

James sighed, his face softening. "Us too, okay? I swear, man, we try to keep your life private. But there's going to be slip ups."

"You're right. I was a dick. And an asshole."

"Well, maybe. You were kind of between a dick and an asshole."

"James—" Lisa started.

"You were more of a taint."

I rolled my eyes. "Can we just agree that I was the whole general crotchal region so I can go apologize to your wife's boss?"

"Only if you specifically tell her you were a taint."

"*James*!" Lisa looked at me pleadingly. "Please don't tell my boss you're a taint. She's cool, but—"

"I'll tell her I was a jerk," I said.

"Well, you can probably tell her you were a dick," she said. "Or an asshole. Just not a taint. That's such an awkward way of phrasing it."

I couldn't quite laugh, but I shook my head as I stood up to go after Aspen.

# Chapter Eleven

*Aspen*

I SHOULD HAVE GONE out the front door.

Maybe if I'd driven myself over to Lisa's instead of getting a ride with her, I would have. I could have gone out the front door, gotten into my car, and driven away, reminding myself why making friends was overrated and resolving to tell Kevin I needed *out* of Wakeham.

But I didn't have my car. Instead, in my hurry to get the fuck away from whatever *that* was, my feet had taken me to the kitchen, where a door led out to the back deck. Perfect, since the goal was to escape. Problematic, since I could still hear muffled anger floating through the walls. The bigger problem, though, was that my jacket was in the front closet and it was colder than I had thought outside.

I shivered, pulling my thin sweater around me before sipping my wine. Thank God I hadn't been in enough of a hurry to forget that, though I'd probably have to finish off the rest of the case Darby had gotten me in order to forget the night itself.

Because seriously. What the *fuck* was I thinking?

I'd embarrassed Lisa. Leave it to me not to realize that she didn't want her brother-in-law to know about the dirty books she read. And then I'd clearly missed some clues on the appropriateness of joking about marrying Theo. Lisa's kids had mentioned *losing* their Aunt Sheri. I mean, I'd thought she was dead, but that wasn't the case. In hindsight, it was obvious it had been a messy breakup—Uncle Theo was sad "like she died," so clearly joking about it was... well, crass, at best.

Cringing, I sipped my wine again. Leave it to me to upset the only friend I'd made in Wakeham.

Then there was Theo.

Theo, Theo, Theo.

What the actual fuck was with him?

He'd seemed nice. Funny. Cute as fuck. A little flirty. A little scruffy. Someone enticing to look at, since he was somewhat off limits given he was my assistant—and my friend's—brother-in-law. But I could look nonetheless, especially given the limited pool of attractive men to look at in Wakeham. And I'd been enjoying talking to him. I very much *hadn't* enjoyed the way he interrupted me as I tried to apologize.

Twice.

Before I had too much time to contemplate, the door to the deck opened and Theo stepped out. Without a word, he sat beside me on the bench, leaning forward to rest his forearms on his knees. I glanced at him sidelong. He was clenching his jaw, his neck tense, and if someone had told me that this man had an infectiously room-brightening smile, I would have called them a moron. There wasn't even a hint of that smile left, and the annoyance I'd had at his interruptions faded. I didn't know the situation—clearly—and it had obviously been upsetting. That didn't excuse him being rude, but at least I could understand it, and I felt bad all over again for creating that situation.

"So, about that—" he finally said.

"Theo, wait," I said, aware of the irony in doing the exact thing I'd just been annoyed about him doing. Worse, the words came out harshly and Theo sat back, grimacing with his eyes cast down, as if I was about to scold him.

Fuck.

"Jesus, I'm bad at this." I put the wine down on the small table on the porch and turned towards him. "Before you say *anything*, I wanted to apologize like I was trying to before. I'm not the greatest at being tactful. I'm used to saying whatever I want with no consequences. And clearly I hit a nerve by joking about things when I should have realized from what the kids said that it wasn't something to joke about. So, I am sorry. It was inappropriate for me to make that comment in the first place."

Theo stared at me, lips parted as he processed what I said. "I... I mean, thank you, but I wasn't expecting that. You don't have anything to apologize for, though."

I could feel myself falling towards the practiced look of composed ease I usually wore to mask my emotions, then pushed myself away from it and frowned with confusion. Theo looked down before continuing.

"Other than my family and a couple of close... um, family-like people... no one else really knows that Sheri and I broke up. I was hoping to keep it that way for a while longer while I sort things out. I know that probably makes me sound like a control freak or something but I just..." He took a deep breath and then let out in a heavy sigh. "... I was hoping for a few more days, at least. But I still let my frustration get the best of me and made a way bigger deal about it than I needed to. I'm sorry I made it awkward."

I didn't know what to say. Was it normal for break-ups to be secretive? I could only think of a few reasons someone would want that, and... well. Theo seemed like a nice guy, but none of the reasons I could think of painted him in a particularly good light.

But I was aware enough about my own flaws to know I could very well be missing something. I may not have known him well, but I knew enough about Lisa to know that if Theo *wasn't* a decent human being, she wouldn't put up with it. Secret breakup or not, the pain in Theo's eyes was real. Whatever *had* happened, he was genuinely fucked up about it, and there was a genuine reason for his worry about it getting out. Maybe it was just a Wakeham thing, where the town was super invested in his and Sheri's relationship for some reason. Some kind of rival clan situation, maybe?

"Anyone I would talk to about literally anything was in that room." I gestured towards the house. "I appreciate your apology, and I accept it, but I wouldn't say anything, Theo."

He looked relieved and a half-smile crept onto his lips. "Thank you. I mean that. Really, thank you so much."

I picked up my wine glass and took another sip, then pressed my lips together. "It's not my place, obviously, but... Look, for my own peace of mind, I have to ask."

He tensed again. "Uh... sure. That's... fair, I guess."

I took a moment to gather my thoughts before I looked up at him. This time, I kept the practiced look of calm composure on my face.

Just in case.

"I understand that whatever happened was... a big deal," I said. "But is it... *normal* to keep breakups a secret in Wakeham? As an outsider, that's concerning to me because I... I mean, I get that it's a small town and everyone gossips like crazy, but..." I trailed off as Theo stared at me, the disbelief on his face growing to a point where I couldn't ignore it. "What?"

He opened his mouth, then closed it and looked down at his hands. After a moment, he looked up again, his lips parting again, then hesitated before laughing uncomfortably. "This is going to sound... I mean, I-I'm aware that it sounds really conceited, but I'm, uh..." He coughed and ran a hand through his scruffy hair. "God, I can't believe I'm saying this. D'you, uh... know? Who I am?"

I stared at him.

Scruffy, light brown hair.

Warm, brown eyes.

A verifiably gorgeous smile.

That nagging sense of familiarity.

Oh, *fuck*. Of course. He was a rival competitor.

No, that wasn't right. I frowned, studying him.

A former employee?

No, Lisa would have said something if her brother-in-law had worked for us before.

But his eyes... they were beautiful. I mean, he was attractive. Very, very attractive.

Oh, *fuck*. Had I slept with him at some point and didn't recognize him? He said he travelled, so maybe I'd seen him somewhere before?

That didn't feel right, though. I may have been something of a hoe, but I *knew* the guys I slept with. I would have remembered Theo.

And none of that made the slightest bit of sense, anyway. Why would he be upset about me knowing about a breakup for any of those reasons?

"Aspen?" Theo asked tentatively.

My mouth was open, but all that came out was a drawn-out "umm."

When he realized I wasn't going to say anything else, he looked incredulous. "I'm... Theo Barker. The musician?"

Oh.

Barker. Lisa's last name was Barker.

Like the musician. Theo Barker. The rock star. Big name, on all the magazines, swooning teenage girls lining the streets hoping for a glimpse of him as he left a hotel. You know, Theo Barker. Theo fucking Barker.

He was *that* Theo.

"You've got to be fucking kidding me," I said.

He looked startled.

"I mean... *shit*," I said hurriedly. "I... okay, I thought you looked *familiar* but I couldn't place you. I thought maybe you worked with me or... oh my God."

I doubted he heard half of what I said as he burst out laughing. "Talk about an ego check."

My face felt like it was on fire. "This is so embarrassing. I just don't follow music all that much. If someone hasn't been in a movie that's played on an airplane in the last five years, I probably won't recognize them. I mean, I've heard your music, of course. Who hasn't?"

He kept laughing and shook his head as I rambled on. Even though I was completely embarrassed, when tears started leaking from his eyes because he was laughing so hard, I couldn't help it. I started giggling—me, *giggling*—and clapped a hand to my mouth.

Of course I knew who Theo Barker was, but it had never even crossed my mind that *this* Theo was *that* Theo.

"I'm sorry," I gasped as we finally started to regain our cool.

"Oh, God, don't be sorry." He wiped a hand under his eyes. "I haven't laughed like that in ages. Talk about the Streisand effect. Christ, I can't breathe."

I knew the feeling.

I cleared my throat and shook my head, drinking my last sip of wine. "I am never going to let Lisa live this down. Never. She could have given me a head's up."

"It's fine. Really, Aspen." Theo wiped his eyes again. "Fuck, that's... I think this might be one of the best things that's ever happened to me."

"Your standards are pretty fucking low, then," I said bluntly, and he lost it again.

"This all makes a lot more sense," I said once we'd calmed down. "I promise, I won't say anything about the breakup, or any of this. That's not my place. I might be a bitch, but I'm not an asshole. I mean, not much of an asshole."

"Blunt, maybe," he said, smiling. "But you're not a bitch, and if anyone was an asshole tonight, it was me."

I tilted my glass at him and shivered again. "Are we good? It's freezing out here and I'm empty."

"We're good," Theo said. "We're really good."

# Chapter Twelve

*Theo*

SHE ENDED UP IN my car at the end of the night.

There were far worse things than having a gorgeous woman in your car. Aspen was a particularly gorgeous woman, so I didn't mind at *all*, especially since the night ended on a far better note than it seemed it would after I'd thrown my tantrum.

Lisa had looked up nervously when Aspen and I returned to the dining room. Aspen, in what seemed to be a trademark for her, had a serious expression on her face. With her chin up and shoulders back, she walked back to her spot at the table, sat down, and looked at Lisa soberly.

"Lisa," she said. "Your brother-in-law is a massive taint."

James spat wine across the table, then choked on whatever was left in his mouth as he howled with laughter. Lisa looked torn between being horrified at her husband and horrified at Aspen saying the word "taint," so simply looked horrified as she turned to me.

"Well, I feel like 'massive' is a bit excessive, but she's not wrong," I said.

Lisa sighed, then looked at Aspen, who couldn't hold on to her sensible demeanour any longer. A sly grin spread across her face before she let out another bright, warm laugh, then tilted her empty wine glass at me.

"Want to fill me up, rock star?"

I was pretty sure she knew exactly how that sounded. So did Lisa, who shook her head.

"Jesus, Aspen." She finished her glass of wine, then held it out as well. "Pour me a little more before I switch to water, Theo. I need it after... *that*."

"S-Sorry," James said, just barely recovering from his laughing fit. "That was—"

"—payback for not giving me a head's up on who Theo was so I didn't embarrass myself," Aspen finished.

"I know," Lisa said, wincing. "I'm sorry. But thank you for not making a big deal about it."

"Yeah, we appreciate you acting like he's a normal human," James added. "I know it's tough when he's such a freak."

"Thanks," I said, rolling my eyes.

"Oh, it wasn't a problem," Aspen said, sipping her wine. "It helped that I didn't recognize him."

I sighed as James looked like it was fucking Christmas morning. "You didn't know who he was? Like he... had to *tell* you?!"

She nodded, and I knew I was never going to hear the end of it.

But it was fun. The entire night was fun. Sure, James toasted Aspen multiple times for "knocking me down a few pegs," but I couldn't remember the last time I had felt so... well, normal. At least, normal around someone who wasn't my immediate family or Rick. But Aspen made it easy to feel comfortable. She was earnest and sincere. I could see how people might take that as abrasive, but it was refreshing to be around someone who was genuinely herself.

A few hours and countless moments of laughter later, Aspen shook her head as James tried to pour more wine into her glass.

"That's it for me," she said.

"Oh, come on," James insisted. "Have one more."

She gave him a *Look*, one eyebrow raised confidently. "That's what you said about the last one."

"Yeah, well, I meant one more *after* that one." He used the bottom of the bottle to nudge her hand. "Come on. One last toast to putting this taint in his place."

"I think he's already been put in his place," she said, glancing at me. "Isn't that why he was being called a taint? Somewhere between a dick and an asshole?"

"I believe that was the reasoning," I said stiffly, but grinned when it made Aspen giggle.

"Besides, it's past my bedtime," Aspen continued. "And that's saying something, seeing as it's Friday night and if I was living my old life, I'd still be out on the town right now."

James blew a raspberry and put the wine bottle down, then finished his glass. "*Fine*, I guess. The kids'll have us up at the ass-crack of dawn, so I guess we should get to bed, too."

Lisa had switched to water earlier in the night, and she stood up as she cleared some of the glasses off the table. "I can drive you home, Aspen."

"Aw, no, stay here," James whined, grabbing at her ass as she moved past him.

She smacked his hand lightly. "My boss is in the room."

"It's fine, she's been saying 'taint' all night," he argued. "And I know you're lending her those books you like, so—"

"James!"

Aspen caught my eye, trying to stifle a laugh. "Well, since I've put Theo in his place, maybe he could return the favour and put me in mine, since I'm assuming you're heading home, too."

I laughed. "Yeah, I can give Aspen a ride."

"Perfect," James said. "Lisa, I can give you a ride, too."

Lisa feigned annoyance as Aspen lost it, throwing her head back as she howled with laughter. "You two are *horrible* influences on each other."

"Absolutely." Aspen stood up, grinning. "Don't say I never did anything for you, James. Theo, let's stop cock-blocking these two and head out."

So, that was how I ended up with a gorgeous woman in my car at the end of the night. We said our goodbyes and thank-yous and goodnights, peppered with those typically-insincere promises that we should make it a regular thing—though I was fairly certain everyone there meant it, especially when Aspen pulled out her phone and emailed her assistant to remind her to book another Friday dinner the following week, causing Lisa to roll her eyes—and I was willing to bet that James had Lisa half-naked in the front hallway by the time Aspen closed her car door.

She told me where she lived, but then fell quiet, the soft music on the radio the only thing breaking the silence. I watched the road, not sure what to say, not sure if the flirty innuendos and risqué quips were appropriate now that it was just the two of us. It was one thing to make those kinds of jokes in the safety of a brightly lit dining room with other people around, but quite another in a car brightened only by a dashboard and streetlights. Aspen clearly trusted me enough to tell me her address so I could drive her home, but she didn't know me well. I didn't want to push things or make her uncomfortable.

"Think they're done fucking yet or did Lisa hold out a little longer?" she suddenly asked.

I let out a startled laugh. "Nah, they were doing it by the time we left the driveway. Guess we'll find out in about nine months if they made it to a condom first or just went for it and hoped for the best."

"No way Lisa would let that happen," she said. "Three's a handful already, no matter how sweet those kids are."

"They are good kids," I agreed. "But uh, yeah. Three is a *lot*. I always thought—"

And then I stopped. From the corner of my eye, I saw her turn towards me. I braced myself for her question—"Thought what?" she'd probably say, and then I'd have to say I'd daydreamed about starting a family with Sheri, who likely would have been more nurturing to a balance on a credit card than to the two kids I'd pictured us having—but she didn't ask.

Like she already knew the answer, and she was kind enough not to push it.

"So what are you up to on your time off?" she asked instead. "What would you call this, like a... a sabbatical?"

"I dunno, a hiatus, maybe." I shrugged as I turned down the street towards Aspen's apartment. "I was working on a new album before I came back to town. I guess I'm still working on new music, but the tone of it's changed a little since things ended."

"Do you mind if I ask what happened?"

I should have minded. But maybe it was the way she asked it. Maybe it was that I was coming down from one of the best nights I'd had in a while. Maybe it was just that I felt like I could trust her and she just... she made me feel normal.

But I didn't mind. "No. It was almost two months ago."

"That's still pretty fresh."

I shrugged as I pulled up to her building and put the car in park. She didn't move to get out of the vehicle, instead watching me with those intense but attentive eyes.

"I knew her when we were kids. She grew up here. We didn't hang out growing up or anything, mostly because I was..." I laughed softly. "Not the coolest guy around. But I ran into her a couple of years ago and we got talking. She was different and kind and down to earth. Before her, I was dating girls who were way out of my league and knew it, so I constantly felt... I dunno. Like, 'less than' enough for them, you know? But with Sheri, I felt comfortable, like she knew where I came from and just kind of got it."

"It sounds nice."

"It was." I smiled, though it probably looked more like a grimace. "Until she let it slip that she was only with me for my bank account."

Aspen winced. "What a bitch."

I half-laughed. "It wasn't unexpected. I had it in my head that people would forget about what a loser I was growing up. But now I'm just a loser with money." I shook my head. "You know how people are. I'm not some rock star heartthrob or whatever but I've got money, so women think they're doing me a favour by throwing me a bone and I'll be so grateful, I'll pay for anything. I've learned my lesson."

"No, you haven't," she said.

"I... what?"

"You haven't learned a lesson because that's a shitty lesson. Not every woman out there just wants the three six-or-mores."

"The... what?"

"The six-or-mores." She held up one finger. "Six figures or more in the bank." A second finger. "Six pack or higher under his shirt." A third finger went up, along with a smirk. "Six inches or more in his pants. The three arbitrary measurements men think all women want and that most of us don't give two shits about."

My face burned. "Sorry. That's not what—"

"I get it, Theo." She smiled and unbuckled her seatbelt. "You're hurting and you're trying to justify how you feel by looking at women as the enemy right now. We've all been there."

She opened the door and got out of the car, then leaned down to peer in at me. I looked over at her. Her hair was pulled back from her face in a bun, but a few loose strands were framing her face. Behind her, a streetlamp splashed warm light, and she seemed to glow as those perfectly painted red lips spread into a sassy, confident smile.

"But you're wrong," she continued. "You *aren't* a loser, and I think you're kind of a heartthrob. Stop lumping women together as a group of people who want to hurt you and I'd maybe even consider you downright sexy."

The burning on my face deepened at her teasing. "I... uh..."

She laughed and straightened up. "Thanks for the ride. See you next time, Theo!"

The car door slammed. I stared after her, watching to make sure she got into her building okay. At least, that's what I told myself. When she got to the door, she turned back and waved. I raised a hand back and nodded before pulling onto the street.

I felt surprisingly good as I drove back home. Despite sounding like a complete taint with what I'd said at the end of the night, she'd been kind. Aspen seemed like the kind of person who had never minced a word in her life, but what good were polite words if they were meaningless? She said what she meant and that was refreshing. And somehow, having known her for barely an evening, she had made me feel like I wasn't just Theo Barker, the musician. That I could be comfortable around her, that I could fuck up and say stupid shit like I had when I dropped her off without needing to worry that it could ruin everything.

That was... something.

Definitely something.

When I got home, Rick was still up. I walked in to see him sprawled on the couch, wearing plaid pajama pants and no shirt with an empty popcorn bowl on the table.

"Not going out to the city tonight?" I asked as I shrugged my jacket off.

He shook his head, still staring at the TV. "Didn't feel like it. And there was a movie on."

I glanced at the TV. "Which musical is this?"

"Not everything I watch is a musical, Theo," he said. "But *The Producers*."

I looked at him suspiciously. "You feeling okay?"

"Uh... yeah. Why?"

"Staying in on a Friday to watch *The Producers*, one of your least-favourite musicals? Doesn't sound like you. Are you finally settling down with a nice guy?"

He snorted. "You'd love that, wouldn't you?"

"Seeing you happy?" I walked over to the couch and flopped on the other end of it with a sigh. "Yeah, man. I would love that."

"Don't worry, I wouldn't dash your hopes like that. I just didn't want another insane cab ride to the city."

"I would've paid for it."

"Good to know, but not what I meant." He yawned, stretching widely. "There's only like one driver who'll make the trek out to the middle of buttfuck nowhere—a.k.a. here—and I wouldn't want him to get the wrong idea after last weekend."

I frowned. "What happened last weekend?"

"Hooked up with him." He shrugged. "Didn't want him to think it was going to be a regular thing."

"What—here? I didn't even hear you. When did he leave?"

"Why would I have brought him here? He had a perfectly good backseat in his cab." Rick yawned. "How's your brother? I didn't think you were staying late."

"Ended up catching them at the tail end of dinner. They invited me to stay for dessert."

"And you didn't bring me any?"

"Nope. Wasn't any left."

It was Rick's turn to look at me suspiciously.

"What?" I asked.

"You seem awfully happy," he said. "Were you really at James and Lisa's?"

"I was at James and Lisa's."

"Were you?"

"I was," I insisted.

"And?"

"And what?"

He folded his arms. "Theo."

"Rick."

"*Theodore*."

"*Richard*."

"What else happened?"

I rolled my eyes. "Nothing *happened*. I went to my brother's. Lisa's boss was there for dinner. She seemed nice. James made cake, so I stayed for dessert then stuck around and we all chatted for a while. Then James and Lisa wanted to fuck, so I gave Aspen a ride home."

Rick sat up straight. "And was that it?"

"Just a ride home, Rick. Didn't get out of the car."

"I mean, neither did the cab driver, technically. Just kind of leaned the seat back and—"

"Nothing happened. Trust me, she's out of my league."

"You know damn well that's not true. No one is out of your league, okay?" He twisted his mouth to the side, tapping his fingers on his thigh. "Look, I'm the first one to say that you need to get laid, but—"

"I just said she was nice. I'm not hopping into anything here."

"And she didn't hop *onto* anything, either?"

"Nobody hopped into or onto anyone else. I gave her a ride home. That was it."

"Look, the offer is still there for me to find you that womanly babe you can just—"

"I'm not fucking some fan just to get laid," I snapped. "And you *just* said I shouldn't hop into anything."

"A one-night stand is different," he said. "But you shouldn't have a one-night stand with Lisa's boss. That's shitty."

I groaned in frustration. "Jesus, Rick. Nothing *happened* and nothing is *going* to happen. It was just nice to talk to someone who treated me like a normal person."

"Oh, I don't treat you like a normal person?"

"You know what I mean." I stretched and yawned. "She didn't recognize me at all until I opened my fat mouth and said something."

He tried to hold back a smirk. "That must have been quite the blow."

"Nope. It was awesome."

"And you swear you didn't—"

"If I have to say one more time that I—" Rick threw one of the cushions at me and I barely caught it before it hit me in the face. "—I didn't and I'm not going to."

"Look, I want you to get over things and move on from Sheri," he said. "I do. But you tend to see a pretty face and fall in love with it before anyone can tell you to keep your feet on the ground."

"Thanks for the vote of confidence."

"You have a history of letting your emotions take over. Even you have to admit that. Which brings me to my second point: you can't fuck Lisa's boss, even just as a one-night stand. You can't do that to family."

"Man, I wasn't joking. Aspen is gorgeous, honest, and sensible. She wouldn't touch me with a ten-foot pole." Standing up, I threw the cushion back at Rick. "I'm going to bed."

Despite his lack of confidence, I was still smiling as I got ready for bed. I hoped Lisa was serious about doing another dinner next week. Rick was right: Aspen was off-limits. I wouldn't do that to Lisa, obviously, but I wouldn't want to do that to Aspen, either. Wakeham was pretty safe—there weren't a ton of photographers dogging my every move or anything—but even a single hook-up had the potential of dragging someone into the mess and noise that was my life. I wouldn't want her to deal with that.

Still, I couldn't help wanting to be around her, and what was the harm in seeing a pretty girl who made me feel good about myself once in a while?

# Chapter Thirteen

*Aspen*

FOR WHAT IT WAS worth, I started that day smiling.

Smiling. *Me.*

And it wasn't even the first time it had happened.

At first, it was just Fridays. Fridays were Dinner-At-Lisa's-Day. I had been invited for Friday dinner every single week since that first one, and I'd actually attended them.

Me. Attending a thing. *Regularly.*

Sometime after the second Dinner-At-Lisa's-Day, I started my Saturday smiling. Weekends were boring; some weekends, I drove into Timmins, which was the closest "city" to the middle of buttfuck nowhere, but that had gotten old fast. Sure, there were some bars there, and some shopping, but there were only so many things to do by yourself in a "city" of forty-some-thousand people.

But after Dinner-At-Lisa's became a regular thing, my trips into Timmins became less frequent. I started smiling on Saturdays, even if I was just staying in and reading whatever depraved novel Lisa had suggested for me that week.

Maybe those fucking novels were part of the problem.

Because the thing was, Fridays weren't just Dinner-At-Lisa's-Day. Fridays were also Hang-Out-With-Theo-Day. And that, paired with the dirty shit small town working moms like Lisa got off on—and trust me, I wasn't judging her at *all*, because *damn* were those books something—had me pining for the days when I could just walk into a bar, point at a man like Suave Jerome, and insist he take me home for some B grade sex that featured something other than a purring piece of silicone.

Things were purely platonic between me and Theo. He had continued coming to Dinner-At-Lisa's, just like I had, and he had continued to drive me home after. And each time he had, we stayed outside my apartment building talking just a little longer than the week before, until I was ending my Fridays with a smile that lasted until Saturday morning.

We seemed so very, very different. Theo was a family-comes-first kind of guy who regaled me with stories of growing up in Wakeham and the kind of shit he and James got into. I was a "hey, look over there" kind of person when it came to talking about my family. When he was travelling or touring, he drove his team crazy by requesting to eat at, in their words, "the most generic, boring, basic-bitch restaurants in every city" instead of trying all the different cuisines he could, like I did. I loved trying new things and discovering new restaurants; Theo was at his happiest anywhere he could get a basic burger, no onions, with fries and gravy on the side.

But the similarities were there, too. We were also both dedicated to our respective careers. We both worked hard and held ourselves to high standards. We had the same sense of humour and we both got competitive, which led James and Lisa to insist the two of us team up whenever we played card games after dinner on Fridays.

"Okay, but we're going to kick your ass, you know," Theo had said the first time she'd told us we were on the same side.

"I'd rather risk that than losing my dining room table when one of you decides to flip it," she'd replied.

"Lisa, we're not animals," I said. "I might launch myself across it to throttle him if he cheats at crib one more time, but I wouldn't flip the table."

"Because she doesn't have the upper body strength," he added.

It took everything in me not to cackle with laughter. "You know damn well I could flip this table twice as fast as you—"

"No flipping tables!" James cut in. "You're on the *same team*!"

I had kept my word about Theo's breakup. In fact, I hadn't mentioned even meeting Theo to anyone, including Darby. Why would I? If he had been anyone else in the world, it wouldn't have even been a concern. He wasn't someone I was sleeping with, nor was he someone I was going to sleep with, so telling Darby about him would have been the same as informing her I'd met and enjoyed spending time with Lisa's husband, another man I wasn't and would never sleep with. Pointless.

Yes, he was attractive. That was a simple fact. And he was my age—less important, but still something relatable. He was funny, almost surprisingly so, and far more laid-back than I'd expected for a literal rock star. I had thought if there was any one career that attracted people who found the love of their life every time they looked in the mirror, it was rock stars. But that simply wasn't the case with him. When he relaxed, it was almost impossible to picture him the way the magazines did. The confident man who graced front pages and tabloids was so different from the humanized version that graced Lisa's dinner table, they could have been completely separate people.

As I got to know him better, I saw hints of Rock Star Theo in Normal Theo, usually when he wasn't paying attention to himself and let those moments of confidence creep through. The Theo I knew was insecure; for someone who spent so much of his life under a spotlight, he had some big hang-ups about himself. The problem was that made him especially relatable in a way I wasn't entirely comfortable with.

I considered him off-limits. He was my assistant's brother-in-law. He was a close family member to one of the few friends I'd made in my adult life. But that didn't mean I couldn't enjoy his presence, of course. And, frankly, bereft of any and all sexual encounters as I was, I would seriously reconsider that "off-limit" status if he ever made a move or any sort of indication he was interested in me.

The smiling-more thing was helping with my concentrated effort to be a better version of myself in Wakeham. I'd made friends—three friends, actually, if friends-by-association counted, which meant I could count James and Theo as well as Lisa. And work, while boring and mindless and exhaustingly numbing, wasn't as terrible as it could have been. Lisa being there made it fun, and I'd started having lunch with some of the managers and getting to know them as well. Basically, Dinner-At-Lisa's-Day was helping me make the best of being stuck in that place for the year. And aside from causing me to reach a little more frequently for my vibrator, there was nothing remotely unsavoury going on with Theo.

To reiterate: we weren't fucking.

We had never broached the subject.

Aside from car rides between his brother's house and my place, we were never even alone together. He was just a person who made me smile.

That was the smile I started the day with when I walked into the office that Friday morning and passed a couple of employees in the foyer.

I nodded at them less stiffly than I used to. "Good morning."

Both muttered something of a greeting in return and averted their eyes.

Big Scary Aspen would have liked that—the whole eye-averting thing. That was a hallmark of doing pre-audits: my job was to whip people into shape, which meant I sometimes had to rely on fear. Fear was good; audits were scary and there was a lot riding on them.

But Director Aspen didn't like that. Director Aspen was trying to be approachable and relatable so that she could function in this godforsaken town for the rest of the year, and employees averting their eyes was something of a red flag.

Confused and more than a little concerned, I made my way to my office. The receptionist busied herself at the printer when I walked by. The managers I usually ate lunch with responded with tense smiles when I said hello. A young woman I didn't know well but who I thought might be an admin with the operations department dove into a nearby supply closet when she caught sight of me. By the time I reached my office, the smile I'd started the day with had been replaced by the beginnings of a cautious wall.

Lisa was at her desk just outside my office door and I rapped my knuckles on it as I walked by. "Good morning."

Terror exuded from her. She made a face that must have intended to be a smile but came out as a grimace. "M-Morning, Aspen."

That was the last straw. "Okay, what the *actual* fuck?"

Lisa jumped, her eyes wide, and I sighed.

"My office. *Now*." I walked to the door and threw it open, holding it as I motioned for Lisa to follow me. She did with the enthusiasm of a child resigned to attending a Love of Broccoli convention and I closed the door once she was in there.

"What the fuck is going on?" I asked bluntly. "Did someone die? Is it a national day of mourning that I forgot about? Is this sick Wakeham tradition meant to confuse the shit out of me?"

Lisa grimaced. "So you didn't see it then."

The shakiness of her voice did nothing for my stress levels. "See *what*? Did someone actually die? Is the company going under? What happened?"

"No, no. Not that." She pulled out her phone and fiddled with it, then looked up at me. "Just so you know, Aspen, I know it's not true. The... the first part of it. The rest... I mean, if you... like, it's fine if you two *are—*"

I snatched the phone out of her hands. She might have said more about it, but if she did, I didn't hear it. My bewildered annoyance faded and was replaced with a bubbling sensation of anger, though not on my behalf.

On Theo's behalf.

It was a great picture. Grainy, but identifiable. We were seated in his car. The photographer had zoomed in, but I could tell we were parked outside my building. The splatters of rain on the windshield told me the picture was from the previous week. Theo was smiling that infectious smile of his, looking happy and relaxed and very much like the Dinner-At-Lisa's version of himself that I knew.

And me? Damn.

I looked disgustingly phenomenal. My head was turned to the side and my eyes were half-closed because I was looking down. There was a girlishly delighted look on my face, an expression caught in laughter.

I looked happy. I mean, obviously, on account of the smile. But I also looked... softer, somehow. Sweeter. Maybe even younger. Had that picture been on the cover of one of those romance novels Lisa kept lending me, I would have pushed it back at her with an eye roll and a reminder that I wanted nasty, carnal debauchery, not whimsically wholesome daydreams.

Luckily, the idea of me as the demure and charming lead of a love story was not extended to the article beneath the photo.

## HOMETOWN SWEETHEART CAN'T STOP THEO BARKER FROM CHEATING: MEET THE WICKED WITCH IN THEO & SHERI'S FAIRYTALE ROMANCE

*He might be known for his love songs, but Theo Barker sure seems to have trouble limiting himself to one woman. After Barker was spotted spending his Friday night with a woman who was decidedly* not *his long-time girlfriend Sheri Wilson, an anonymous source has confirmed the rumours that the fairytale romance is over for these two childhood sweethearts... all on account of one anonymous wicked witch.*

*We should have known a guy who writes all those love songs can't help himself from falling for every pretty face that comes along.*

*Sources state that Ms. Wilson is devastated by the split. The pair grew up together in Wakeham and it seemed like the real deal, with many touting their love story as the stuff of fairy tales. But unfortunately for Ms. Wilson, it seems like someone has cast a spell on Barker to make him tire of his princess. After an evening out, Barker spent around 45 minutes cozied up in his car on a rainy Friday night with this mystery woman and we can only speculate on what happened after that.*

**UPDATE 8:07 AM EST**: *Two independent sources have come forward claiming that the homewrecker pictured here is Aspen Haws, a businesswoman living in Barker's hometown of Wakeham, Ontario. Unconfirmed is if Ms. Wilson knows Haws, though in a small town like Wakeham, it seems only natural that there would be some*

*history between these two women vying for the attention of
one rock star.*

*A source who asked we only identify him by his first initial,
J, indicated that was unlikely to fly with Haws.*

*"She's dead set on what she wants. She'll take whatever she
likes and disregard other people's feelings. I had a fling with
her once and she loved to emasculate me. She would even
give me grades after sex." J declined to share what grade she
had assigned to him.*

*Another source says she worked with Haws before she was
made director.*

*"She told me if I wasn't willing to work a bunch of extra
overtime, I should just quit my job, then blackmailed me
and threatened to tell everyone a secret I didn't even know
she knew. I'm surprised someone like Theo Barker would
even give her the time of day. She's not even that pretty."*

The article went on to speculate about other affairs Theo may or may
not have had, but had little else to say about me. Slowly, I held out Lisa's
phone, trying to process everything I'd just read line by line. I could feel
her eyes on me, warily watching as she took her phone from my hands.

"Aspen?" she said.

I finally looked at her. "They got all that from a picture of Theo
dropping me off at home?"

Lisa nodded nervously. "The... um, sources who talked about you—J
and the... whoever the other one was—were added to the article after it
broke. It was released last night, I guess. I only saw it this morning after
Br—I mean, someone. Someone in another department had seen it and
brought it to my attention."

I pressed my lips together, nodding slowly. "Traded his princess for a
witch, huh?"

"If they think that's true, they've never actually met Sheri."

I looked at her and she looked back at me. After a moment, a repressed
squeak bubbled out of my throat. In trying to stifle it, I snorted, and
suddenly both Lisa and I were doubled over in hysterics to the point that

I had to brace myself on my desk. For a few minutes, every time I glanced at her, we broke down again.

"Okay, so I'm super interested in those sources," Lisa finally managed to say, flapping her hands in front of her face as she sat in her usual spot in front of my desk. "Do you think you know who they are?"

"Oh, I know for sure." I walked to my side of the desk, collapsing into my chair. "J—the one with the grades—is Jerome. I slept with him literally once, just before moving here."

"And... the grading thing..."

I rolled my eyes. "It was a joke. Sort of."

"Sort of?"

"Well, I thought it was funny. Maybe he would have, too, if he'd been more focused on making me come. I don't even know what he's complaining about. I gave him a B." Lisa stared at me and I shifted uncomfortably. "What?"

"You gave him a B even though he didn't make you come?" she asked.

"Oh, he did. It just took some prompting. He was very surprised I didn't allow him to just flop over and fall asleep."

"Right. That's... I guess pretty much the definition of B grade sex."

"Yeah, but I'm dropping that to a C after this bullshit."

That started us on another round of hysterical giggles.

"Okay, and the other one?

I rolled my eyes again. "Oh, God. She was... Marissa, I think? No, no. Marina. She was the office manager at the location I audited just before Kevin 'promoted' me. Sleeping with the owner's son and dumber than the rock on her finger."

"What was the—"

"She'd been fucking around for so long that her paperwork was nearly three years behind," I said. "So basically, she was salaried, not doing her job, and then offended when I said she'd have to do her job."

"But you didn't actually blackmail her, right?"

"Of course not. And everyone knew her 'secret' because that's what happens when you have no self-awareness." I snorted and shook my head. "Neither of them knew me very well, obviously, if they thought shit like that would embarrass me. Their arguments were literally 'I was bad at sex and she called me out on it' and 'She told me to do my job.'"

"So you're not upset?" Lisa asked.

"Upset? No. They didn't even give their names. Who gives a fuck what they have to say about me?" I shrugged my coat off and put my purse in my desk drawer. "Annoyed, on the other hand... a little. I can't say I've ever dealt with something like this before. Have you heard from Theo?"

She shook her head. "I asked James to call him, but so far, nothing."

"But he's got... you know. People to deal with this, right?"

"Oh, for sure. A whole team of people."

"Well, keep trying him for me." I turned to log onto my computer. "I could use a hand figuring out what to do and I want to know what his people are planning on saying. I'm going to have to talk to head office about this."

"On it." She stood to head back to her desk but paused. "Look, it's... I just have to ask."

I looked up at her. "Ask what?"

She shifted uncomfortably. "Are you and Theo...?"

I raised my eyebrows. Lisa had gotten pretty good at figuring out when I was being jokingly serious, but it must have been obvious that I was absolutely not joking right then because she started speed talking.

"I know you weren't involved with the breakup, obviously," she said. "I mean, *obviously*. That was before you'd even met him. And—"

"Lisa."

"—those reporters will say anything that sounds good for a story. It's just that the two of you get along so well and it wouldn't be—"

"Lisa."

"—a stretch to think that you're both a little lonely or—"

"*Lisa!*" I said firmly. "We're not. Don't get me wrong, he's great, but—"

Whatever I'd been expecting her reaction to be, it wasn't for her to look triumphant and slap her hand on the top of the chair near my door. "I knew it!"

"Knew... what?"

"James said you two were for sure sleeping together. I said you would have told me first." She grinned at me. "If he doesn't believe me, will you tell him?"

"I... I guess so? Why doesn't he just ask Theo?"

"That's what I said, but you know how James is."

I didn't, really, but didn't bother telling her that. She turned to leave, but stopped one last time.

"Aspen, for what it's worth... if you *wanted* to—"

"You're my friend, Lisa. Don't make this weird."

"It wouldn't be weird. You're an adult, he's an adult—"

"We're not sleeping together."

"I know you're not right *now*—"

"Logistically, it wouldn't make any sense." I turned towards my computer again. "One, I don't do relationships. Two, I'm not even going to be in Wakeham after next year. And three, he's too sweet. I wouldn't be able to give him an honest grade if he sucked and I will *not* tarnish the acclaimed reputation of my grading system."

"I'm pretty sure he could handle your grading system," she said. "He's used to being critiqued on stuff. Comes with the rock star territory."

"Pretty sure that regardless, the romantic rock star who's looking for his fairytale princess isn't the right fit for the big city hoe who doesn't do commitment."

"Well, you never know." She shrugged. "Maybe Theo could do with a little casual hook up now and then."

"Are you trying to pimp your brother-in-law on me?"

"No, ma'am. Just know two people who would be good together when I see them." She left the room before I could give her shit for calling me ma'am and I sighed, turning back to my computer.

The good news was that my so-called scandal wasn't the end of my career. Darby said as much when she called a short while later. She didn't say much more than that, even though I knew she was *itching* to find out what the whole story was; she simply didn't have time between requests for comments and more information about me from the media, who had discovered where I worked. Instead, she passed my call over to Kevin, who was more concerned about what the "anonymous" source in the article had claimed.

"I didn't blackmail her, Kevin," I said, rolling my eyes. "I overheard her say something in the office that *everyone* overheard."

"That's good to know, but I'm not pleased about this 'work a ton of overtime or quit' statement," he said. "I don't want our company to be known for that."

"And on top of it being an 'anonymous' source with no verification, you're not interested in the context?" I asked.

"And the context is...?"

"It was the Lac La Biche location."

Kevin waited. "And...?"

"And the office manager sucks at her job."

"So you did tell her to work overtime or quit?"

"I gave her my professional opinion, which was to let her *father-in-law* hire someone qualified for the role, and that expecting overtime of salaried employees isn't illegal."

"So... you told her to quit. Or work overtime."

I didn't respond.

"Aspen."

"Kevin."

"That isn't the kind of thing we want our directors to be saying."

"Hmm," I said. "Good point. Maybe I should go back to doing pre-audits, like I was when I made that statement before you forced me to take a director position I didn't want."

Before he could respond, my phone buzzed and I glanced down to see a message from Darby.

*board member standing nearby he's pretending to give you shit just go with it*

I sighed heavily. "Jesus, Kevin. Fine. I apologize for doing my former job to the best of my ability and will endeavor to do better."

There was relief in his voice. "I appreciate that, Aspen. Now, can I assume that you have contact with Mr. Barker?"

"I'm not fucking him. Not that it's any of your business, but it's not true."

"For HR purposes, I'm stating very clearly that was not what I was going to say. But I imagine he'll be making a statement of some sort about the situation and, given what was said by one of our employees, perhaps a request could be made for him to clarify that aspect of the article was also untrue."

I sighed. "I mean, I can ask, but—"

"Perfect, please do."

I glared hard enough that I was sure Kevin could hear it through the phone. "I will *try*. You can thank me for my diligence and dedication to this company by having Darby charge another case of wine to your credit card, since I've finished the first one.

"I will let Darby know."

I spent a bit longer chatting with Kevin, who made a big show of doing something meaningless and ineffective to address the situation, which was to do a company-wide reminder about our policy for talking to the media. Luckily for Marina, there was no way to prove it was her, though I was fairly sure Kevin had an off-the-record conversation with George after I got off the phone with him.

It was likely that conversation that was behind my inability to get anything done for the rest of the day, since *someone* leaked my company email address on a Theo Barker fan site shortly after.

And the front desk phone number.

And my private office phone number.

Within an hour, we were getting so many calls that I told Lisa and the receptionist to let them all go to voicemail. The emails were pouring in so quickly that I couldn't even filter through to find work-related messages. Finally, I closed it down in frustration and spent the rest of the morning bugging Lisa about getting in touch with Theo.

"I swear, I'm trying," she said after I'd asked her the fourth time.

"Does he know we're getting phone calls? And emails?" I paced in front of her desk, agitated.

"I mentioned it when I texted him. James has been calling him too. No answer. I don't know if he's just busy with his team or what."

"When is James done with work? Can he go over and talk to him?" I continued pacing back and forth.

"Not for a while."

I checked my email again, then paced my office, then went back to Lisa's desk. "How about now?"

"Still nothing."

"Okay, get your coat. Let's go."

She frowned. "Where?"

"You know where he lives. Let's go over."

"Aspen, no. He's probably stressed. Just give it a little longer."

"I can't! This is unreasonable. I can't get any work done, and I don't want to put up an auto-response or something until I hear from him." I marched into my office and grabbed my purse and coat. "Come on, I'll drive."

She looked at me pleadingly. "Give it another half hour. This is the exact thing he was dreading when they broke up."

"Yes, but this affects me, too. And maybe I can help." I shook my keys at Lisa. "Let's go."

"Just give him some more time, obviously something's..."

We were interrupted by Lisa's phone vibrating on her desk. She snatched it up. "It's Theo."

I threw my purse and keys on her desk, grabbing the phone out of her hand.

"'I released a statement,'" I read.

"And?" Lisa said.

"That's it." I passed the phone back to her.

Lisa was already on her computer, bringing up Theo's website. She turned the monitor towards me and I leaned over her desk.

*Regarding the recent unauthorized article about my relationships with Sheri Wilson and Aspen Haws, I'd like to set the record straight and address the disgustingly sensationalized rumours.*

*Yes, Sheri and I have broken up.*

*We have been separated for a couple of months now. I am currently spending time with family, working on music, and working through the emotions that accompany the end of any romantic relationship. This was not due to an affair of any kind by either party. Both Sheri and I appreciate your respect for our privacy during this difficult time.*

*Aspen Haws is a family friend who I met after Sheri and I broke up. The photo in the article shows two people sitting in a vehicle talking. It was taken without permission from*

*either of us as I dropped her off after dinner with my brother*
*and his family. We are not in a relationship.*
*To my fans, as always, thank you for your support.*
*Theo*

I straightened up. "He didn't write that."

"Of course not. His publicity manager or someone would have." She closed the page. "But at least it's something."

"Sure, it's something." My heart was racing. "Too bad that 'something' didn't include some kind of request to stop harassing me at my workplace or any sort of indication that I'm not some homewrecking witch or, God forbid, denying that I tell employees to quit or work overtime since now I'm getting heat from head office and—" I stopped, taking a cooling, calming breath. "Could he not have talked to me before releasing the statement? Wouldn't that have been the decent thing?"

Lisa's phone was to her ear. She listened, then looked up at me before hanging up. "Still no answer."

I picked up my keys and jangled them at Lisa. Exasperated, she grabbed her purse.

# Chapter Fourteen

*Theo*

THERE WAS HALF A beer on the table.

I wanted to drink the beer on the table.

All I had to do was reach forward and grab it, but my arms didn't want to move.

"I just want to know who took the goddamn picture."

Rick paced the living room furiously, grumbling aloud for the billionth time. My phone punctuated the rant as it vibrated against the table. I had long since begun ignoring it in favour of staring at the wall, though now the half-empty beer beside the phone had my full attention.

"I know," I responded for the billionth time.

Rick stopped his pacing and looked at me. "You need to get some sleep."

That might have been the millionth time he'd said that one. "I know."

"Man, I'm serious. You haven't slept since this was released." He crossed his arms, frowning at me. "It's a shitty situation, but you still have to take care of yourself."

"I know."

Rick threw his hands up. "Will you say something—*anything*—else?"

"Nope."

I knew I was pissing Rick off. I knew I was acting immature. I knew the sleep deprivation wasn't helping, and the sense of dread and embarrassment would likely fade if I just had a fucking nap. All I had to do was stand up and go to my room, but my body didn't want to move.

Each time I tried to leave, my brain threw memories of Sheri at me. Sheri meeting my family. Watching Sheri play with my niece and nephews, my heart swelling as I imagined having kids of our own one day. Sheri telling me she loved me. Those moments with her, kissing her, touching her, making love to her like she was The One. Sheri sitting on the deck we'd once tried to make love on, laughing at me, mocking those moments with her friends. Revealing every moment with her had been a lie bought and paid for with my bank account.

When my mind wasn't forcing me to relive those moments, it was coming up with scenario after scenario of what would happen now that I'd been labelled a cheater.

Because it didn't matter what was true. It didn't matter that I'd never so much as thought about cheating on *anyone* I'd been with, just like it didn't matter that whoever had taken that photo knew damn well I hadn't gotten out of the car. It didn't matter that Aspen and Sheri had never knowingly been in the same town at the same time. Some clever fucking pseudo-journalist put the words on paper and that was enough to make people believe it.

Those things would follow me. People would wonder, no matter how much I denied it, if I was telling the truth. And I couldn't think of much that was as insulting as being labelled a cheater. There was a ball of disgust in the pit of my stomach.

I should have released a statement about Sheri sooner.

I'd known that all along. I'd been putting it off, ignoring the whole situation, focusing on the things that made me happy. In doing that and trying to keep everything private, I'd inevitably made it all worse for everyone.

Well, everyone that mattered. Sheri was coming out perfectly fine in the whole thing, just like I'd expected. Because even though she was a gold digger, I was too proud to let people find out I'd been played by her. But I'd made it worse for myself. For my team, who was now in high-gear trying to get everything dealt with. For my family, who'd end up being peppered with intrusive questions from people in town who "just wanted to know the real story." And for Aspen.

Especially for Aspen.

The ball of disgust in my stomach tightened. A witch, they'd called her. A homewrecker, for no reason other than her proximity to me. They'd made her out to be this monster of a person when that wasn't the case at all.

I mean, shit. My friendship with Aspen was probably the main thing helping me move past the bullshit experience that was my relationship with Sheri. It wasn't fair to put that kind of pressure on any sort of friendship, but I couldn't help it. Everything about Aspen was a bright spot in my life. Her humour, her brand of blunt honesty, her desire to be a better person—all of it was refreshingly positive and made me want to be a better person, too.

It didn't hurt that she was hot as fuck, of course.

Rick had warned me not to let my emotions get the best of me when it came to Aspen, and I wasn't. I wasn't at all. I just couldn't help wanting to be around her and, for what it was worth, she seemed to enjoy being around me, too.

She made me feel like I was just another guy. Like it didn't matter that I had a bank account or an unusual career. With Aspen, I was just... normal.

Unfortunately, she was now caught up in the very not-normal parts of my life. It had only taken a matter of weeks before she was exposed to how harshly the world treated the people around me. But maybe... maybe she'd understand. Maybe she would still want to be friends.

Unlikely, but maybe.

"You have to know that this will pass," Rick was saying as my attention slowly faded back in.

"I know," I said.

"This site is nothing but a rumour mill. They're only making up stories about an affair because it brings in the views. Anybody who thinks you cheated on Sheri is an idiot. Your fans—the people who matter because they're the ones who pay your bills—won't believe you cheated. Not for a second."

"I know."

"Theo, for the love of *God*, stop saying—"

Before he could finish, the doorbell rang, and *that* was not a sound I wanted to hear. It was alarming enough that I tore my eyes off the half-empty beer on the coffee table and looked towards the entrance at the same time Rick did.

"Who in the fuck..." He inhaled, then let out a calming breath. "I'm going to see who it is, but I swear to God, if it's reporters I'm going to punch someone."

He stormed across the room and into the hallway. I listened as he unbolted the door and flung it open.

"What do you—oh. Shit, I mean... Look, it's not a good time, Theo doesn't want to see anyone."

"I literally do not give a fuck what he wants."

It was her.

I looked back at the beer bottle as her voice floated through the house, punctuated by a surprised cry from Rick.

"Sorry, Rick," I heard Lisa say. "She's kind of upset. Sorry!"

Well, that answered the question of if she would want to stay friends. A big, fat, completely expected "no."

I felt her storm into the living room. From the corner of my eye, I saw her stop, eyes tracing the room as I slouched on the sofa, hoping to blend into the cushions. When she didn't say anything, I absurdly wondered if I'd *actually* hidden myself among the couch cushions. But when I forced myself to look up, her eyes were on me. Her face was unreadable: not blank, but not an expression I could name with my currently limited vocabulary.

The silence was broken by my phone vibrating again. Aspen glanced down at the table, and my gaze followed hers to the buzzing rectangle a few feet away next to the half-full beer bottle. It felt like ages that we stared at my stupid phone, but I could see from where I sat that it was a text, so really it was only the second it took for it to vibrate twice before Aspen spoke.

"So, why did you not respond to Lisa, since you've clearly been getting her messages?"

Time was definitely acting strange. Rick and Lisa stumbled into the room just behind her, clearly having rushed to follow her, but I could have sworn it had just been Aspen and I for a few minutes. I blinked, staring at the phone a moment longer and forcing myself to fight against my exhaustion before I responded.

"Want a drink or something?" I asked.

Aspen looked furious. Apparently, that was the wrong thing to say. I looked back at the beer bottle, which was also apparently the wrong thing to do.

"It's barely noon, Theo," she said, storming further into the room so she could stand in front of me. "And it's a workday—not that I'm getting anything done today—so no, I don't want a drink. Why didn't you answer your phone?"

"Do you often just storm into people's houses and start berating them?" Rick asked.

"Who are you, again?" she asked.

"I'm Rick," he said in a crisp voice. "Theo's assistant."

"Right." She looked back at the phone on the table. "So you're the one who should've been answering the phone?"

"Leave him alone," I muttered. "He's my best friend. I can answer my own phone."

Her eyes were back on me. "So why didn't you?"

"I've been dealing with some shit. Minor scandal. You know. Just some personal stuff."

"Oh yes, *so* personal." She waved a hand dismissively. "Obviously it doesn't affect anyone else. It's not like I'm getting more emails than usual telling me what a whore I am. I doubt anyone leaked my contact information—it's normal to not be able to work because your inbox is flooded with hate mail, right? And I'm *totally* used to the CEO of my company wanting to know about my sex life or lack thereof so he can figure out what he's supposed to do, since our damn head office is getting phone calls about this. It's nothing, right?"

I just stared at the phone on the table.

"You don't think maybe you could have touched base with me about this? Let me know you were putting out a statement? Or like, maybe your people could have called my people? I don't have as many people as you do but I'm sure Rick could have called Lisa, just as a little head's up?!"

My eyes flicked to the half-bottle of beer.

"Hello? Earth to Theo? I'm talking to you!" Aspen waved her hand sarcastically at me until I looked up at her. "Oh, there he is! Hi, yeah, the minor scandal about your personal stuff affects me too, did you know that?"

"Aspen, maybe tone it down just a little..." Lisa said from behind her.

"Are you kidding?" Aspen asked. "Does *everyone* baby him like this? He's an adult, Lisa. He can respond himself."

"It's not babying," Rick said. "You just have no idea how—"

"You're right I have no idea," she said. "I have no *fucking* idea how to handle this because I've never had a goddamn tabloid article written about me. So maybe, Theo, you could do the decent thing and *talk to me* instead of sulking like a fucking *child*."

Everything felt very hot all of a sudden. Feverish, almost. Anger and shame bubbled up in my chest from that spot in my stomach that had been full of disgust.

I didn't remember choosing to stand up, but it surprised me less than it did Aspen. She recoiled so suddenly that she stumbled into Rick, who was behind her.

"You're right," I said. "Sorry that my entire life falling apart is such a *fucking* inconvenience for you."

The half-beer was in my hand. I didn't remember grabbing it. Turning, I left the living room to... something. To leave. To go... outside. I was too warm. Outside was a good idea. Pushing the back door open, I heard Lisa's voice pitch up shrilly just before the door slammed behind me.

The air was crisp and bit at my flushed skin as I collapsed into one of the porch chairs and finally took a swig of the beer I'd been staring at.

Bleugh. Warm.

But I took another swig, choking it down as I blinked back tears, then leaned back in the chair and closed my eyes.

# Chapter Fifteen

## Aspen

I WOULDN'T HAVE DESCRIBED Rick as intimidating because of his height.

Was he tall? Yes. Broad shouldered? Yes. Did he have a Viking-esque stature with skin that seemed surprisingly tan for a red-haired white man? Yes. And was all of that—well, except his hair and skin—stopping me from physically being able to walk past him? Absolutely.

But that wasn't why he was intimidating.

He was intimidating because of the anger in his eyes, an almost maternal sort of protectiveness in them as he folded his arms and blocked my path through the living room.

"Nope," he said, stepping from side to side each time I tried to get around him. "No way. Uh-uh. You have done more than enough damage."

"Oh, I'm just getting started." I whirled around, intending to go back to the front hallway and find another path through the house, but Lisa touched my arm and I stopped.

Not because of her touch. It was nothing more than a light brushing of her fingers against my bicep, but I froze all the same as I saw tears in her eyes.

"Please," she said.

"Lisa, I—"

"Rick is right." Her voice shook. "Look, I know you didn't... I mean, I probably wouldn't—" She stopped, then shook her head. "Please don't fire me, but if I'd known this is what you were going to do, I wouldn't have agreed to come over here."

I gaped at her. "Do what? Get angry? Lisa, I've been telling you all morning how upset I am!"

"Yes, but I didn't think you'd..."

"What?"

But she couldn't bring herself to finish the sentence.

"You didn't need to yell at him like that," Rick said.

"Like what? Like I was upset? Because I'm upset, Rick. I know it's the first time we've met so you may not have noticed, but yeah, surprise, I'm pissed off."

"And you claim *he's* the one acting like a child," he muttered.

"Excuse me?"

He glared at me. "You come in here, stamping your feet like a toddler and all 'poor me, did you even think about me in all of this' when you haven't given a single thought to how any of this is going to affect him."

My mouth dropped open. "So it's okay for him to not care about how it'll affect me because I didn't *think of him* hard enough?"

"I didn't say that."

"You kind of did," Lisa said.

"Whose side are you on?" Rick asked.

"Neither. You're both being horrible." She folded her arms, looking at Rick. "Theo could have *absolutely* answered his phone or his texts. This *isn't* just about him and not even talking to Aspen when he knew damn well what was being said about her makes him kind of a taint."

Rick looked taken aback. "A... taint?"

Lisa ignored him, turning to me with her eyes still watering. "And you? You got me to bring you to my brother-in-law's house and walked in yelling. You didn't even give him a chance to respond and—"

"I absolutely did," I said coldly. "I asked him a question and—"

"And he offered you a drink, which set you off. It's not like he completely refused to answer until you started mocking him."

"I was not *mocking*—"

"You walked in and the first thing you said was that you literally did not give a fuck what he wanted," Rick said. "He doesn't respond well to aggressiveness."

"Doesn't respond well... are you serious?" I was incredulous. "He's a grown-ass man! You're talking about him like he's a child, or a particularly sensitive dog! So fine, I'm sorry I didn't act overly mature myself, but that doesn't excuse him doing the same thing. He might be some big-shot musician but anyone else in the world would get the same reaction from me."

Rick looked at Lisa, who said nothing, then back at me. I held my ground, my chin tilted up as I glared at him.

"If you want to treat him like a spoiled princess and tip-toe around the absolute immaturity he's displaying, then fine," I said. "But I refuse to."

"You know what?" Rick stepped out of the way. "Fine."

I looked at him warily.

"Seriously, fine. Go. You're not wrong." When I still hesitated, he rolled his eyes, then moved to the nearby armchair and gestured towards the rest of the house. "Theo's been my best friend since we were kids. Am I overprotective? Yeah, I fucking am. He deals with a lot of shit that other people don't ever have to deal with. Like his relationship being dragged through the media when he's still not over it and being made out to be the bad guy when he was the one who got hurt."

He slumped into the chair with a tired sigh.

"But yeah, I could've probably handled this better. He hasn't slept since it came out. He's upset and being dramatic and I'm letting him instead of trying to get him to do the right thing. I probably should have taken the beer away, too." He sighed again. "You wanna go yell at him, go yell at him. Maybe he'll say more than two words to you."

I didn't move. Beside me, Lisa fidgeted, then folded her arms.

"I'm not apologizing," she said, her voice shaking. "I know you're my boss and if that's a problem then... then I guess it's a problem. But Theo is family. I don't think you should have yelled at him, even though... I mean, yeah, I'm a little overprotective of him, too."

Lisa was a badass. She didn't seem to realize it, but I admired her.

"I won't hold that against you," I said. "You're right. I made you take me here and then lost my shit. I'm sorry I was being kind of a taint."

"What is with you people and taints?" Rick asked, bewildered.

I ignored him as Lisa smiled and I knew at the very least, I hadn't lost her friendship.

"Thank you," she said. "And thank you for not firing me."

"Thanks for not quitting." I took a deep breath and exhaled loudly, looking in the direction Theo had stormed off in. "Damn both of you. I was ready to go out there and keep yelling. Now I have to go be an adult and have a level-headed conversation. Thanks a fucking lot."

Rick chuckled as I left the room, which I considered a good sign.

Theo was sitting outside on his deck, back to the window. He tensed when I opened the door, but said nothing as I closed it behind me. His eyes were shut and it wasn't until I sat in the chair across from him, a small table between us, that he opened them.

I was used to seeing him smile, so this version of Theo—the overtired, stressed, vulnerable Theo—was new to me. Rick had clearly been telling the truth about his lack of sleep; the circles under his eyes were dark and swollen and his skin was chalky, more of a grey-white than the usual light peach tone. Even his hair—shaggy, as usual, but dirty and flattened against his head—seemed dull. And while he always dressed casually, it wasn't usually quite so casual as a pair of baggy pajama pants and a faded hoodie that enveloped him like a security blanket. He watched me with guarded eyes, his jaw tight and his fist clenched around the beer bottle he was holding.

"You look like hell," I finally said, breaking the silence.

His eyebrow twitched and a ghost of the smile I knew crossed his face. "Thanks. I wasn't sure."

I grimaced. "Sorry. That was... you know what I meant."

Theo nodded and motioned with his free hand, then sipped his beer. I took it to mean he wasn't offended.

"I'm pissed off," I said. "Well, I was pissed off. I couldn't get a hold of you and I just... I was worried about you. And it was easier to be pissed off than worried."

"I'm fine."

"You're not."

"I am."

"Bullshit. Don't lie to me." I crossed my arms and Theo looked away. "People who are fine don't lose a full night's sleep and then ignore their phones while people who care about them are calling."

"What do you want me to say?" he asked tiredly.

"I want you to tell me what's going through your head."

"What does it matter?"

I twisted my mouth, trying to stay patient. "I might not be pissed off anymore, but that doesn't mean I understand why you didn't answer your phone. And since it's not entirely about you..."

"I'm fine."

I glared at him. "That two-word answer shit might fly with Rick, but I will lose it if you try it on me."

Shock crossed his face. "What do you—"

"Your best friend—who is very confused about why Lisa and I kept talking about taints, by the way—is far more willing to put up with your shit than I am. I want you to talk to me and I'm not leaving until you do."

"Okay. Fine. I'm fucking upset." He played with the bottle in his hands, but didn't drink from it. "It wasn't enough to just have my entire personal life posted online. They dragged you into it. They made me look like a dirtbag. I'm pissed at myself for not addressing it before this happened. I'm pissed at whoever took that goddamn picture. And you're pissed at me and that... sucks."

Finally, we were getting somewhere.

"I'm pissed at the situation," I said. "I'm annoyed that I'm being bothered at work. Mostly, Theo, I wish you would have just talked to me before making your statement so I could have some say in it. The stuff they said—"

"It wasn't true." He took a swig from the bottle he was holding. "People are going to think I'm a cheater forever now because of one stupid story, but they couldn't just leave it at that. They had to go and make you out to be this awful person when you're not. You're—" He cut himself off, looking down. "You're not a witch."

"That you know of."

He frowned. "What?"

"Maybe I've taken up witchcraft in my spare time. You know. Spells and... and broomsticks."

He smiled a little more. "Any chance you can cast me a spell to figure out how to deal with this?"

"No, but that's only because I already know how you can deal with it."

He raised his eyebrows. "Yeah?"

I nodded. "There are three options. You've already said your bit. Happened months ago, no one cheated on anyone, leave me alone now please. So option one, you leave it at that. Some people won't believe it, but next week someone else will do some other thing and people will forget about you. Option two, you tell everyone what really happened. It means everyone finds out more of your private information, you defame your ex, and people will think it's petty. And of course, some people won't believe it. Option three..." I thought for a moment. "Murder."

He snorted back a laugh, sounding a bit more like himself.

"I couldn't think of a third option," I admitted. "But it's either tell everyone what happened, or just get on with your life."

"But it's not just my life it could affect," he said. "We're from the same place. Her family still lives here. It's a small town. I mean, people have had generational feuds over way smaller shit than this. If I don't say anything, she could tell people—"

"But she won't."

He fell silent, his eyebrows furrowed.

"Look, you're a man."

His mouth twitched, amused. "Thanks for noticing."

I didn't laugh. "It means that in a situation like this, you're going to come out on top, regardless of which of you was in the wrong. Even if you *didn't* have a video of her admitting she was using you, you'd be able to bounce back from it in a way that she wouldn't because you're a guy. No one likes to talk about it, but it's true. She knows that."

"How would you know?"

"Because she didn't go to the press and make up rumours about you."

"She threatened to."

I raised my eyebrows. "Really?"

He shrugged. "Sort of. When... right after we broke up. She implied she was going to tell everyone Rick and I were fucking again."

"When did you and Rick fuck before?"

He laughed. "We haven't. I meant she was going to start the rumours up again. Rick's open about being gay and I'm open about not giving two fucks about it. There have been more than a few stories about how we're secret lovers, which is bullshit because neither of us would keep that a secret. It's just that I'm—according to him, unfortunately—straight." He sighed, the smile fading. "It has nothing to do with that, though. Sheri knows it would upset me to be called a cheater. That's what it was about."

"Right," I said. "And did she start those rumours up? Did she tell anyone you were a cheater?"

He stared at the beer bottle. "I don't think so. Not that I've heard."

"I've known you for a while now, Theo. And Lisa for even longer. Maybe I don't know everything, but I think if her family was on the cusp of an intergenerational feud with your family because Sheri made up a lie about you being a cheater, someone would have mentioned it. On the off chance she decides to lie about why things ended, you can easily prove it's a lie. She's more likely to eventually come back and try to rekindle whatever you two had."

He snorted. "Yeah, right."

"Trust me. One day when you're not expecting it, she's going to sidle up beside you and tell you how good you're looking and how wrong she was, and isn't there *anything* she can do to get you back?"

"You think so, eh?"

"Despite the fact that you currently look like you might be sticky if I touched you, yes."

He chuckled. "And what would I do in this hypothetical scenario? Take her back?"

"You better fucking not." I looked at him pointedly. "You could take the justified route of telling her that's she full of shit and to go fuck herself, or the slightly classier route of accepting her apology but telling her it's not going to happen, or the incredibly petty route of grabbing the nearest person and—"

"Pretending to date them?" he finished, eyebrows raised.

"Oh, no," I said. "You would pretend they're your sugar baby and tell her that after you broke up, you realized you were into the whole findom thing and thank her for clueing you into it. But I swear, I will personally track you down and yell at you if you believe her bullshit and take her back."

"Findom?" he repeated.

"Financial domination," I said. "Some people get off on that."

"Financial—what?"

"It's a fetish."

"How do you—" He stopped and shook his head. "Never mind. Like I'd do that after doing everything I can to keep my personal life out of the spotlight, I'd just hand the press a fucking bombshell like that."

I shrugged. "It's not any of your business what other people think of you. Everyone who gives a shit about you knows the truth behind all of this, so who cares what these other fuckers think? You're just giving them more power by letting it upset you."

He didn't respond right away, instead picking at the label on the beer bottle as he considered what I said. I studied him as he did, unsure of what it said about me that I still found him attractive, even though he looked like he'd been lost in the woods for a week and survived by stumbling across an abandoned frat house. I knew he was a good person. He was kind. And he deserved better than this kind of shit happening to him.

I didn't say it, but I also thought he owed it to himself to figure that out.

"You know, when you say it like that, it seems like common sense." His voice was soft, though the vulnerability and sadness still came through. "Why can't I think of it that way without someone telling me to?"

"It's hard when you're in the middle of it." Part of me wanted to reach out and take his hand, but I didn't. "It sucks, but it happens. You can't control what other people do, only how you react to it."

He nodded, smiling down at the beer bottle. "I wish I had your voice in my head."

"I can yell louder next time, if that'll help."

He chuckled, which made me smile. "I hope there isn't a next time. And I'm sorry. You have every right to be pissed. I should've at least talked to you before... I push people away when I'm upset, and I need to stop doing that."

"Apology accepted. I'm sorry for losing my shit at you. I should have at least tried to let you speak."

"It's okay." He took the last sip of beer from the bottle and put it on the table, then leaned back and closed his eyes again. "Honestly, I probably wasn't going to say anything useful."

"I still could have handled it better."

He yawned. "It's just bullshit that you got dragged into this mess. I try to keep people in my life out of the spotlight."

"It is what it is. An annoyance, at most. If that's the cost of friendship with you, I'm okay with it."

"If I'd known that, I would've actually asked you to come back to my place."

The words were drowsy and half-mumbled, so it took a moment for me to register what he'd said. His eyes were still closed, so he didn't see my mouth drop open as I stared at him.

"Did you just... did I hear that right?" I asked.

A beat passed before Theo opened his eyes. He sat up, his face flushing completely red. "I didn't say that out loud. I-I didn't—fuck. I did not mean to say that out loud."

I was speechless, which was not a common experience for me. That must have been obvious, since it only made Theo squirm more, panic flashing across his face.

"I'm so sorry... Shit, I thought I was thinking, not... words."

I burst out laughing. I couldn't help it. The look on his face as he tried to form a coherent sentence was more than I could handle.

"It's okay," I tried to say.

He didn't seem to hear me. "I know I don't have a shot with you. Not that I should want one. You're Lisa's boss and I'm an idiot. You're gorgeous and funny and you treat me like a normal person and I'm a mess. But that's not... I mean, like, of course anyone would want to bring you home... Sorry, that's crude, I mean... you're just beautiful and I can't..." He stopped, burying his face into his hands with his elbows propped up on his knees. "How deep is the hole I'm digging myself into here?"

He sounded like he was about to cry. I had a hand over my mouth, forcing myself to stop laughing. "Theo, it's okay."

"It's not. I'm so fucking sorry."

"Please don't be."

I stifled a last chuckle and stood, walking over to him. He didn't look up, so I put a hand on his shoulder and leaned down, slowly pressing my lips on that shaggy, scruffy hair of his, lingering just long enough for him to realize what was happening. As I pulled away, he sat up, his eyes wide.

"It's all okay," I repeated. "Let's talk when you've had some sleep."

I knew his eyes were on me as I went back into the house. A small smile escaped, and both Lisa and Rick looked alarmed and confused when I re-entered the living room.

"He's fine," I said.

"He's fine?" repeated Rick. "Really?"

"Yep," I said, heading towards the front door. "Bye, Rick. It was a pleasure to meet you."

"No, it wasn't. It absolutely wasn't. It might be next time, but this was awful."

"Fair." I picked up my purse and dug my keys out and looked at Lisa. "Let's head back to the office."

# Chapter Sixteen

*Theo*

I WENT STRAIGHT TO my bedroom after Aspen left, laid down on the bed, and didn't move again until three in the morning when my internal clock was like "Why the fuck have we been asleep for over twelve hours?" and jolted me awake.

Lying in bed, I groggily reached for my phone, where there were a handful of missed calls and texts, including two from Lisa:

*No pressure, but we're still doing Friday dinner if you want to join us. Aspen will be coming. I imagine you're probably exhausted, but wanted you to know the invitation is there.*

And then, a few hours after that:

*Assuming you're asleep, as you should be, and that you're not coming—we'll save you a piece of cake if you want to stop by and see the kids tomorrow. Aspen says hello.*

I smiled, then laughed when I saw the follow-up message from James:

*You know, super inconsiderate of you to make Lisa drive her boss home after Friday dinner. That's my 'drunkenly feeling up my wife' time. Cock-blocking's not cool, bro. Hope you're okay. Love ya.*

Yawning, I replied, knowing he wouldn't see it until he woke up:

*Sorry. If you don't mind losing the 'drunkenly' part, I can bring a game for the kids and distract them when I pick up my cake. I'm okay, you too, see ya later.*

Then, I closed my eyes and tried to trick my body into thinking it hadn't had enough sleep. It was a hard battle, especially as I fought with the pangs in my stomach, partially from hunger after missing two or three meals.

Mostly, though, they came from what I'd said to Aspen.

At first I tried to convince myself I'd imagined the whole thing, which I knew I hadn't. I might have been tired enough to mix up thinking and speaking, but I knew damn well the laughter I'd heard as I rambled about what I'd said was real. I knew the sparkle in her eyes had been real.

And I knew—I fucking *knew*—the feel of those beautiful red lips against my hair had been real.

She'd kissed me. Not the way I wanted her to kiss me, but she'd fucking kissed me. And her mouth was a hell of a motivator. She'd said we'd talk about it after I had some sleep, which is why I'd immediately gone and passed out. Because unlike all the stammering and backtracking and blathering I'd done right after I'd let it slip that I would've asked her to fuck me if I'd known all this would happen anyway, now I wanted to talk about it.

It made it a lot easier knowing that there was a pretty good chance she wanted it, too.

Right? I mean, she had to. Probably.

No, she totally did.

Maybe.

She'd kissed me. I wanted to see her. To talk about it. To figure out if... well. I shouldn't have even been considering it. She was Lisa's boss. But maybe... maybe there was something there. And maybe that would make it okay.

I wouldn't know until I talked about it with Aspen. And now that wasn't going to happen for another week, since I'd missed Friday dinner.

It was a blessing, in some ways, that it forced me to wait to talk to her. It gave me time to think things through, to mull it over in my mind, to go back and forth as I tried to figure out if jumping into something new with someone was a good idea. Logically, I knew it was a terrible idea, especially when that someone was my sister-in-law's boss and I was still fucked up from my relationship with Sheri.

But was I? Was I really still fucked up from that?

It had been some time. I was doing better. A big part of that was because of my friendship with Aspen. Week after week, I saw her, talked to her, got to be myself around her. She didn't judge and she didn't treat me differently than anyone else. Simply being around her was freeing.

And no one said it had to be something serious. She had talked numerous times about how she wasn't staying in Wakeham permanently, about how she was going to go back to her old job once her year was up. I didn't want a one-night stand, but that didn't mean I couldn't do casual.

I could totally do casual.

Probably.

I spent the next few days dealing with the fallout from the article, working on new music, and trying to figure out if it was too bold for me to try getting Rick out of the house in case Aspen wanted to come over after Friday dinner. I decided it was, since I hadn't even talked to her yet, and if by some chance everything worked out, there was always her place.

And that was if she was even interested. There was always the chance I'd misinterpreted the whole situation and was about to be bitterly disappointed. But I was excited, even as the week dragged on and on, that I'd get to see Aspen on Friday.

Then James went and fucked it up.

"Theo, man, I need a favour," he said when I answered the phone Thursday afternoon.

"Okay, but if it involves hiding a body, I'm going to have to get Rick in on this," I said. "There's no way you can dig a six-foot hole by yourself and I'm not getting my fingerprints on a shovel."

"Ha fucking ha. Can you pick up the kids from school tomorrow and watch them until Lisa's done work?"

"Uh... yeah, I guess. They're done at what, three? Three-thirty?"

"Noon. It's a half-day tomorrow."

"Okay... and you're not working half a day like you usually do?"

"Nope, I'm currently shoving my suit into a carry-on so I can go down to Toronto and try to convince our biggest client not to drop us. My boss is flipping out. I'll be back Saturday, hopefully, and if it wasn't for the fact that the kids have a half-day, Lisa could just leave work early, but she can't take the whole afternoon off and—"

"Man, it's fine, don't... don't worry about it. I can pick the kids up."

He let out a relieved breath. "You're a lifesaver. Lisa's bummed we have to cancel dinner but I'll bake you a whole fucking cake for yourself when I'm back."

Shit.

I didn't know if I could make it another week wondering where things stood with Aspen. I'd barely made it to that point; another eight days would be impossible. But the heavy disappointment faded when I realized I had the perfect reason to see Aspen—and sooner than I would have if dinner *wasn't* cancelled.

And that was how I ended up trying to corral three very excited children into an office building at lunchtime on Friday.

After pulling up to the building and parking, I turned around in my seat and looked at my niece and nephews. "We're going to surprise your mom. But we have to be very quiet, since this is where she works."

"I'm good at sneaking," Anna said solemnly.

"No, you aren't," Cole replied.

"Yes, I am," she insisted.

"I'm better at sneaking," Grayson said. "That's why I'm being a ninja for Halloween."

"Yeah, well, I'm the *best* at sneaking," Cole said.

"No, I am," Anna said, pouting. "I wanna be a ninja for Halloween."

"You're already being a princess for Halloween!"

"Princesses can be ninjas too, *Cole*."

"No they can't, princesses are—"

"—totally able to be ninjas, but they have to practice," I interrupted, then grinned at the three of them. "Luckily for you, I'm a professional ninja."

"I thought you were a musician," Grayson said.

"Musicians *have* to be ninjas." I looked at them conspiratorially. "I can show you, but we all have to be very sneaky and quiet."

They all nodded.

"Okay. Here's the plan."

The kids promised to be quiet and listened eagerly as I explained how we would sneak through the building to their mom's office. Then together, we all crept across the parking lot and into the building.

When we got into the lobby, the receptionist was staring at her phone. I glanced at her, then crouched down to whisper loudly to the kids.

"Okay, now we have to get past security." I looked back at the receptionist. "Let me do the talking."

The kids covered their mouths as they tried not to make a noise, eyes shining as I approached the front desk and leaned on it.

"I'm here to see Lisa Barker."

"Are you?" asked the receptionist.

"Yep."

She glanced at me, then at her computer. "She doesn't have any appointments this afternoon."

"I didn't think we needed an appointment to see their mom."

"Hmm. What did you say your name was?"

"Theo."

"Theo," she repeated, then *finally* looked up at me. Her eyes went round immediately. "Oh! You... you're Theo Barker."

I smiled in what I hoped was a charming fashion. "Yes, I'm her brother-in-law. These are her kids. We wanted to surprise her."

Wide-eyed, she handed me four visitor passes and gave me directions to Lisa's desk. The kids hissed in excitement when I handed them each a badge and told them to pretend that we totally belonged here.

It took a little longer than I'd expected, on account of all the sneaking and stopping at every hallway intersection to take a careful look around the corners to make sure we weren't "caught." But eventually we reached the hallway at the top of the stairs that the receptionist said led to Lisa's desk—and, by association, Aspen's office. I could hear Lisa's voice floating down the hallway and tilted my head towards the open door at the end.

"She's in there," I breathed.

Anna, Cole, and Grayson all seemed to tremble with anticipation, scurrying towards the office. Once we were close, I directed them each to look around the door frame into the office, moving slowly as they poked their heads in. I couldn't help sneaking a look in myself once the kids were in place. Lisa's back was to the door, her hands resting on the top of a chair as she chatted idly with Aspen, who was leaning against her desk.

Cole couldn't hold in the excitement anymore. He let out a high-pitched giggle, followed by Anna and Grayson both shushing him with zero self-awareness of how loud they also were, the way only kids seem to be. Aspen glanced up and caught sight of us, a secretive smile spreading across her face.

"Lisa, your next appointment seems to have arrived."

"Appointment?" Lisa looked over her shoulder and a bright look crossed her face. "Oh! Hi!"

Giggling, the kids rushed into Aspen's office, and the whirlwind started.

"Hi Mom! Were you surprised?" Grayson said.

"Did we sneak up on you good?" Cole added.

"Very surprised! You did an excellent job sneaking," Lisa said, laughing.

Anna threw her arms around her mom's legs. "Mommy, it was Uncle Theo's idea!"

"You don't say." Lisa looked up at me, grinning. "Thanks, Theo. This is so thoughtful."

I shrugged, trying to keep myself from looking at Aspen, even though I could feel her eyes on me. "Wasn't a problem. I figured they might like to see where you work."

I hung back in the doorway as the kids explored Aspen's office, which seemed to take forever even though it was just a standard office. There was a bookshelf and a filing cabinet along one side, her desk with a computer in the middle, and some generic paintings on the wall, yet somehow, the kids found it fascinating. Anna in particular loved the colourful stack of Post-It notes Aspen had in her desk drawer.

"Well, if you think that's cool, you should see the supply closet," Aspen said. "There's even more Post-Its in there."

Anna's eyes went wide. "There's *more*?"

Aspen nodded, then glanced at me, laughter hidden in her eyes. "There is. And you know, there might even be some pink ones in there that your mom could give you as a souvenir if you want a tour of the whole office."

I tried not to grin as Lisa herded the kids towards the door to go on a tour of the office. Neither Aspen nor I spoke until their excited voices faded as they ran down the hallway and it was just me left standing in the open doorway of her office. Finally, I let myself look at her.

She was as gorgeous as ever. Her hair was in its customary style, pulled back off her face, but a few curls had escaped, framing her cheeks. She was wearing one of those jacket and skirt outfits that made her look so intimidating, but so, so good, and had removed the blazer so she was left in a solid button-up shirt. It was tucked into the skirt, accentuating the curves of her body and making me picture how good the entire outfit would look on my bedroom floor.

"Thought I'd hear from you sooner," she said, her voice teasing and low.

I half-shrugged, leaning against the door frame. "Well, I don't have your number. And I couldn't think of a good reason to stalk you at work."

"I'm glad you found one."

Smiling, she motioned me into the room. I looked over my shoulder at the deserted hallway, then stepped forward. She waited, then raised an eyebrow with another little laugh playing on her lips. "You should probably close the door."

I swallowed hard, then reached for the knob and let it swing closed behind me before looking at her.

"How are you doing, Theo?" she asked.

A thousand times that week, I'd agonized over what I was going to say to Aspen. I'd played it over and over in my mind, planning out what suave but sincere thing I'd say. I wanted her to know that I liked her and respected her and would absolutely drop it if she didn't want to go down that road, but also that I wanted her. Just straight-up wanted her, so badly, and that I couldn't stop thinking of her lips and that was after she had just kissed my *hair*.

And of course, I couldn't remember a single syllable of any of that.

"I meant what I said," I finally said. "About... about what I'd have asked. I wanted to be honest. I'm sorry if that makes it weird."

"Why would that make it weird?"

I sighed. "Because of this. Who you are to me and to my family." I shook my head, laughing softly. "And because you're this total badass who sort of scares the shit out of me. I look at you and I feel like you're so far out of my league because you're just so different from anyone I know. And even if I did have a shot with you, I'm not ready to jump into anything else, which isn't fair to you either. But I can't help being attracted to you."

As soon as I finished speaking, I regretted it. So much for being suave. I couldn't even look at her. For a moment, the only noise in the room was the sound of Aspen drumming her nails lightly on her desk.

"I can't help you with a lot of that," she said. "If I scare the shit out of you, that's a you problem. And yes, I know me being Lisa's boss makes things... complicated. But I also know how Lisa would potentially feel about it."

That was news to me. I looked up, surprised, and a small smile spread across Aspen's face.

"She brought it up, not me," she said. "But as for feeling like you don't have a shot... you know I'm only in town for a little while. This isn't a permanent thing."

"I know."

"So jumping into anything serious isn't realistic for me, either. The only thing I can really jump into is someone's bed."

It was my turn to be quiet for a moment. My heart started beating faster, hoping I was interpreting her right.

"So do you mean maybe you'd be willing to jump into bed with me?" I glanced up quickly at Aspen, willing my cheeks not to burn and give me away.

She grinned, a sultry kind of smile. "Why, Theo... Are you propositioning me?"

Just then, with the worst possible timing in the universe, we heard the kids' voices hollering back up the hallway. Clearing my throat, I stepped away from the door just in time for it to swing open. Grayson, Cole, and Anna bounded into the room, followed by Lisa, who gave me a meaningful look as she walked past me.

"Did you have fun?" Aspen asked them. "Did your mom show you everything?"

"Everything they're allowed to see," Lisa answered. "But I ran into Debbie and she has some stuff she needs taken care of right away."

"That's our cue, guys." My voice came out hoarse. "Say thanks to Aspen and bye to your mom."

As they each hugged Lisa, Aspen came around her desk towards the door. Barely even glancing at me, she pressed something into my hand. I didn't look at it, just slid it into the pocket of my jeans as she said her goodbyes to the kids.

I waited until we were partway down the hall before looking at it. Making sure Grayson and Cole were still excitedly jumping from tile to tile in some made-up game and Anna was thumbing through her new pads of Post-It notes, I withdrew the item and glanced down.

A glossy white business card with the company logo on the top and a full-colour portrait of Aspen on the left side. It wasn't quite the Aspen I knew; her face was serious and the sparkle of laughter in her eyes wasn't there. But it was her, and she was as alluring as she always was. Her company phone number and email address were on the front, but more important was the back of the card.

*CALL!!!* was scrawled in spiky blue ink, followed by what I assumed was her cell number.

Grinning, I slipped the card back in my pocket.

# Chapter Seventeen

*Aspen*

"YOU ARE THE WORLD'S worst friend."

"I find that hard to believe."

"You—oh my God, Aspen, you are the *worst*! I can't believe you kept this from me!"

I flopped backwards on my bed as Darby freaked out. I could picture her on the other end with her blonde-highlighted hair knotted on the top of her head and a mud mask plastered to her face. It was Get Sexy Friday, she'd said, which was Darby speak for "I couldn't find anyone to go out with me tonight and I didn't have a date so I'm pulling out all the stops to find some hot piece of ass when I go out tomorrow."

"—absolutely unacceptable that you didn't even *call* me this entire week—"

"I was busy," I said. "Working? You know? That job that I have?"

"Don't give me that shit. There was a weekend in there. And you could have called me after work. It's been a *week*, Aspen."

"Maybe I didn't want to."

She let out a high-pitched noise of offense. "Why would you not *want* to talk to me?"

I sighed, closing my eyes. "Maybe because I knew you'd freak out like this."

"Oh, you think this is freaking out? Wait until I remember to start giving you shit for not telling me *before* all this went down that you'd met *Theo Barker*!"

"There was nothing to say until that article got written."

"Nothing to say? Jesus, Aspen. The fact that you made a friend is noteworthy in itself."

"Bitch."

"Not sorry. On top of that, you met a friggin' celebrity—in the middle of buttfuck nowhere!—and he started driving you home from dinner at his brother's house because you just happened to befriend them too, and you think that's nothing? You've made like, three friends!"

"Jesus, with friends like you, no wonder I've been looking for new ones," I muttered, picking at my blanket. "I have some friends, you know."

"Not in Wakeham, you don't. Unless you're not telling me more. Who else have you met? Does the Queen have a cottage nearby? Perhaps you and the Pope are in the same book club?"

I glanced at my bedside table, where I'd reluctantly put down the novel I'd been reading when Darby called. I'd been in the middle of a particularly riveting gang bang between the main character and her reverse harem and had just been about to grab my vibrator when my phone rang.

"I don't think the Pope and I read the same books."

"Not the point."

"I know, I'm just saying. I'm pretty sure he'd send me straight to Hell. Like, he wouldn't even wait for me to be smited or whatever. Just whap me upside the head with a Bible and let the devil take me."

That got her cackling. "If anyone could get the Pope to commit murder, it's you."

"Thank you for your confidence in me."

"Anytime. But I still can't believe you didn't tell me about Theo Barker."

"I told you I was having dinner with Lisa and her family. Theo's career doesn't define him as a person, you know. If it was anyone else, it would be non-news."

"He's not just anyone else, though. And, umm, excuse me, but you just said that you were flirting with him today and gave him your number."

"Well, yeah, but I told you about that. Like, just now." I grinned as Darby let out a groan of frustration.

"I can't believe this," she repeated for the millionth time. "And I also can't believe you're actually hitting on him. He's your assistant's brother-in-law. Don't you have a 'don't shit where you sleep' policy with guys you're fucking?"

"Yeah, but that policy was put into place when I didn't live in a town that had approximately twelve men. I haven't got laid for months, Darb. I'm wearing my vibrator out."

"That basically makes you a nun, doesn't it? Maybe you and the Pope would get along after all."

"Basically," I agreed. "But anyway, I don't think he'll call."

"The Pope?"

"What?"

"You don't think the Pope will call?"

"Correct, I very much doubt His Holiness the Grand Priest of Jesusness will call me. I also doubt Theo will call."

She snorted. "Why wouldn't Theo call you? You said he seemed into it."

I twisted my mouth to the side. "Well, maybe he will. But I don't know if…"

"Girl, let me be clear with you right now." She paused and I heard her shift in the background. "Are you listening?"

"I'm listening."

"Okay. I'm going to say this very slowly so you—"

"Just fucking say it, Darby."

"If you don't fuck him, please give him my number. I'll be on the next flight out there, panties down and legs spread."

I burst out laughing. "I think that's the problem, Darb. Theo's kind of a romantic type. I'm kind of a hoe."

"Is he an actual romantic type, or does he just write songs that say he is?"

"He's an actual romantic type." I grinned in spite of myself. "He's a nice guy, actually. A little dramatic sometimes, but nice. And he's only dramatic because everyone around him babies him. Not that he needs it, because he's unexpectedly smart for a rock star. And he's hilarious. Just, all around not what I would expect from someone who does what he does, you know?"

"Uh-oh. Did you hear that?"

"Hear what?"

I could picture the shit-eating grin on her face. "Sounds like someone's catching feels."

I almost gagged. "Don't say catching feels. You sound like you're trying to be hip with the kids these days and it's not a good look."

"I don't hear you denying it."

"Is sexually deprived a feel? If so, then yes, I've caught that feel."

She cackled again. "I think you like him, Aspen. Like, like-like him. I think you want him to be your *boyfr*—"

"Enough."

I wasn't laughing. Darby cut herself off immediately and changed the direction of the conversation without missing a beat. No apology, no acknowledgement, no mushy "Oh, I'm so sorry, I didn't mean to offend you" bullshit: she just changed topics and kept going.

The fact that she knew to do that was part of the reason we were such good friends.

"You could always hire an escort," she said. "I'm sure someone out there provides those services."

"Yeah, but he probably doubles as the local butcher or something. That news would spread around town instantly."

"Well, I'm all out of ideas. Better order a new vibrator before that one bites the dust, since it'll be at least a fortnight before the delivery carriage makes it all the way out there. More if the horse dies on the way."

"Ha fucking ha. Wanna put the case of wine Kevin owes me on the carriage while you're at it? Actually, maybe I'll expense the vibrator, too. It's you and Kevin who stuck me out here. If I can write off mileage on my car, I should be able to write it off on my vibrator."

Darby's laughter was so loud, I had to pull the phone away from my ear.

"Ah, fuck," she said suddenly, still giggling. "Kevin's on the other line, I gotta go."

"What?" I asked, bewildered. "It's Friday night."

"Yeah. He's probably having issues checking into the hotel. Did I tell you he's off to a conference this weekend? *Without* me? I'm never going to find a rich husband this way. I'll call you later."

She hung up before I could respond. The unexpected loss of her laughter made my bedroom feel jarringly quiet. Annoyed, I tossed my phone beside me and stared up at the ceiling, frowning.

I thought Theo would call me after work. Maybe he wasn't as into me as I thought he was. I mean, yes, I had only given him my phone number earlier that day, but I knew he didn't have plans that night, seeing as the plans we usually had *together* were cancelled. My hope had been that he wouldn't be able to wait and we could have made new plans.

I'd changed into comfy yoga pants and a tank top while I waited, then curled up with the newest novel I'd gotten. I figured reading my book counted as multitasking: it gave me something to do, obviously, but it was also basically foreplay.

But it was dark now, and late enough that the sleepy little town was tucked in for the night. Darby had called and Theo hadn't, and my panties were still aggravatingly wet from the scene I'd been reading before I answered my phone. Resigning myself to give up on Theo completely, I reached towards the nightstand and fumbled around for my trusty little vibrator, which I'd plugged in to charge just before Darby called.

Unfortunately, I hadn't bothered plugging the other end of it into the actual wall, so it was still dead.

An almost-anguished cry left my lips as I realized that. Fucking vibrators. It used to just be that people could buy batteries in bulk and change them out whenever needed. And then we all decided that was *so* bad for the environment—which it totally was—and developed vibrators that were way better than they used to be. They were quieter, more powerful, with countless different options and settings and modes. And sure, there were some magical ones that didn't require batteries *or* recharging because they just plugged right into the wall. But I didn't have a magic wand, or a way to make one appear.

I flopped back onto my back, shifting uncomfortably as that unrequited spot in my lower stomach begged for release. I could wait for the vibrator to finish charging, but ugh. That would take time, and I wasn't exactly known for my patience when it came to sex.

"Guess I'm doing this the old-fashioned way," I muttered out loud.

Not that there was anything wrong with that. The vibrator was just more efficient and more intense and I could make myself come multiple times way faster. But beggars couldn't be choosers, so I wriggled out of my yoga pants and slid my hand into my panties.

I closed my eyes and sighed as my fingers made contact with my clit, soothing that needy ache in my stomach just enough to make me relax. I rubbed gently, then circled my fingertips around my clit before trailing them down to the pooling wetness in my slit. Teasing my entrance for just a moment, I let my fingers collect the juices there before moving back to my clit and running my now-slick fingertips across it.

Despite my impatience, I let myself develop a slow, tantalizing rhythm. A few caresses of my clit before trailing my fingers down to my slit again and again. When I couldn't take it anymore, I slipped the tip of one finger in my entrance, satisfying my desire to have something—anything, really, at this point—inside my pussy, before starting the process again.

Closing my eyes, I pictured Theo and the warmth of his rich, brown eyes. It was stupid how attractive he was. His wardrobe consisted of jeans and hoodies, his hair was a mess half the time, and he had a goofy smile that lit up a room like nothing else could. He shouldn't have *been* so attractive, but he was. I wanted to feel his hands—large, I'd noticed, and strong, and slightly calloused on the fingertips—tracing down my body. I wanted to feel him inside of me, because of course I did. And I wanted to know what his cock looked like, what it tasted like, what it would be like to have it buried deep.

My other hand wandered up to my breast and under my bra. Biting my lip, I matched the same slow rhythm on my nipple, teasing myself as my hands worked in unison on those sensitive spots. The arousal that had been pooling deep in my stomach started to change. It built and surged, preparing to boil over, but I resisted speeding up my motions and focused solely on the journey towards that release.

Thoughts of Theo's lips floated through my mind. Not kissing them—I didn't like kissing—but what that mouth could do between my legs. And what he could do with his tongue, which I could almost feel tracing between my folds and teasing my entrance and—

My bed decided to interrupt me by vibrating.

The distraction was so sudden and intense that I jumped, eyes flying open as I was startled away from my task. Then, realizing what it was, I scrunched my face, closing my eyes again and debating whether to let it go to voicemail before groaning and answering the phone.

"Seriously, Darby? I'm trying to get off here. If you interrupt my solo session one more time, I'm legitimately going to tell Kevin you approved of me expensing like twelve dildos to his card."

The response that came back was not one I expected. Instead of Darby's raucous laughter, I heard the banging of a phone being fumbled and almost dropped.

"I... uh... it's not... I'm not Darby..." he stuttered once he regained control of the phone.

I bolted straight up. "Oh, fuck. Theo?"

He chuckled nervously. "I can call back if you're, uh, busy."

"No, I'm... well, yes." I pressed my lips together, trying not to laugh. "God, what must you think of me?"

"A lot of things," he said. "All good. I mean, some bad, but the kind of bad I'd like to encourage."

I almost pulled my phone away from my ear to double check I was *actually* talking to Theo. That was unbelievably smooth for him. "Was that a pickup line?"

Another nervous chuckle confirmed I was definitely talking to Theo. "Did it work?"

Licking my lips, I traced a finger along the waistband of my panties, making myself shiver as my fingertips dragged across my flushed and sensitive skin. "I don't know. Were you calling because you wanted to join me?"

"Well, I was calling because I wanted to see if you'd like to come by my place for a drink tomorrow night." He hesitated. I licked my lips, hoping he'd continue. When he spoke again, his voice was hoarser than usual. "But that was just a front, really, because... because, yeah, I wish I could be there."

"Hmm." I shifted on the bed, moving up to lean back against the headboard. "I mean, you could have been, if you'd called a little earlier, maybe."

He groaned softly. "I know. I wanted to."

"Why didn't you?"

"I was with Lisa and the kids. Then Rick was hanging around and..."

He trailed off, but I understood all the same. "Are you alone right now?"

"Yeah."

"Good." I spread my legs, knees up, but didn't move my hand yet. "I am, too. I'm in my room, on my bed."

Theo made a soft noise. "What are you wearing?"

"A tank top. Bra. Panties."

"That's it?"

"Mm-hmm. I told you, I was in the middle of something."

There was silence. Even though I was alone, I tried to hide my smile. I could almost see his face, beet-red as he tried to cover his eagerness. The chances of him ever having done anything like this before seemed slim. Theo was a "sweet nothings" kind of guy. I imagined most of his sexual encounters featured deep looks into his lover's eyes and maybe candles or something. So this? This had to be new to him.

Which made it all the more fun.

"I don't know what to say," he admitted. "Shit. Sorry."

I laughed. "Say whatever you want. Ask me something else."

"Ask you..." He hesitated again. "What colour?"

"What colour are my panties?"

"Um. Yeah."

"Black. Cotton. The boyshort kind."

"Sorry. Was that a stupid question?"

"Depends. Did it do anything for you?"

He exhaled. "Yeah. I'm picturing you."

"Mmm. And was there anything else you wanted to ask me, something maybe you wanted to ask the first time instead of the colour of my panties?"

"Yeah." His voice was quiet, almost timid.

"You should ask me that, then." I tried to sound soft, inviting, less demanding than my usual self, but still self-assured.

A beat went by, tense and enticing, a moment that hung on the edge as I waited for him to gather the courage and take things further.

"When I called..." he finally said. "What were you..." He cleared his throat. "Where were your hands?"

I couldn't help grinning and resisted congratulating Theo on getting the words out. "I was touching myself. I had one hand in my panties, and the other under my bra."

"Yeah?"

"Yeah."

His voice was low and feverish. "What were you thinking about?"

It would have been easy to make something up. "One of my books," I could have said. "Porn." "Fond memories of anonymous B grade sex in Montreal." Something that wouldn't have made Darby accuse me of catching feels even though I was only thinking about Theo in an entirely physical sense.

But I wasn't in the habit of lying to Theo.

"You."

There was no mistaking the low, groaning sound that came from his mouth. "What about me?"

"I was wishing you had called. Wondering how good you are with your mouth." I left it at that.

"How were you touching yourself?"

Something in my stomach fluttered. Theo seemed to be getting into it. He was stammering less, asking more honest questions. I moved my hand between my legs, grinding my palm down over top of my panties.

"What do you mean?" I asked.

"Soft or hard? With, like a... a toy or something, or...?"

"Mmm. Soft. Kind of rhythmically. It was difficult because I just wanted to get off but I know it's better when I take my time." I pushed my fingers a little more firmly on top of my thoroughly soaked panties. "No toy. Battery's dead. So just fingers."

"And now?"

"I have my hand between my legs. Not in my panties yet. They're soaked, though, so I might have to take them off soon." Almost immediately, I heard a quiet, metallic noise, and I bit back a laugh. "And what about you, Theo? Where are your hands?"

"I just unbuckled my belt," he answered, confirming my suspicions in a surprisingly bold way. "I've been thinking about you too."

"What have you been thinking about?"

"Kissing you." His voice grew stronger with each thing he listed. "How much I'd like to sleep with you. What your tits look like. What your pussy tastes like. I'd eat you out for days if you'd let me."

Oh, *fuck*, Theo.

I licked my lips, a shiver running through me. "Keep talking. I'm taking my panties off."

"Right... right now?"

"Yes, right now. I'm going to slide them down my thighs and kick them off so I can touch my pussy more easily."

Theo groaned. "I imagined that. Undressing you, I mean. And what you'd look like. I want to touch every part of you."

He paused briefly, and I was almost certain he'd gripped his cock. Whatever he'd done, he made a strangled but satisfied noise before he spoke again.

"In your office earlier, you were... when you leaned back on your desk, your shirt kind of... opened."

"It did?" I asked, shocked.

"Just a little. The space by the buttons, it was pulled back a bit. Not enough to see anything, but I could imagine and... I could just see the outline of your bra against your shirt. Fuck, Aspen, I barely saw anything and I wanted to lock your door and fuck you right there."

"Jesus, Theo," I gasped. His sudden confidence had me dripping, and my nipples were growing painfully hard.

He cleared his throat, his voice bolder than it had been. "What are you doing right now?"

"Touching my pussy. I have one finger inside and I'm grinding against my thumb. I'm so, so wet right now." I moved my other hand up to my breasts, cradling the phone between my shoulder and chin. "I just started touching my tits. I like having my nipples sucked, but since it's just me, I'll just have to do with pinching."

"G-Good to know. I'll have to... I mean, I... I want to see your tits so bad."

The longing in his voice was almost painful and I pictured him with his cock in his hand. The image sent another wave of delight through me and I bit my lip.

"And you? Are you stroking your cock for me yet?"

"Oh, fuck yeah." He breathed heavily. "I wish you were here. I wish you were jacking me off while I fingered you."

I took the finger out of my pussy and started rubbing my clit harder. "I would want to suck you off first, though. Find out what you taste like."

"Fuck, Aspen." His breathing got just the slightest bit faster.

"Mmm, that, too. But first I'd like to have you in my mouth. I'd love to make you lose control and..." I couldn't help fingering myself harder. "Theo, I was half done when you first called. It's not going to take me long to get there."

His voice was hungry, eager as he groaned again. "Tell me. Tell me what you're doing to yourself."

"I'm rubbing my clit." I closed my eyes, focusing on the sensations running through my body. "I'm picturing having your face buried in my pussy. I can't... it just..." I moaned suddenly, almost losing the ability to speak. "I want to see your face when you come and feel your cock so deep inside me..."

"Keep going." I could hear the rustling in the background as he stroked himself.

"I'm so..." I panted. "I need to come, Theo..."

"Do it," he demanded. "Let me hear you."

I'd never, ever expected to hear his voice sound like that, and *fuck* did it work for me. Suddenly I was crashing over the edge, bucking my hips against my hand. My body tensed and relaxed, wracked with pleasure as I cried out, pushing against my fingers again and again as I tried to draw out my orgasm. At some point in that mindless ecstasy, my phone fell from my shoulder, though I didn't realize it until the stars faded from my eyes and all that was left was a pounding heart and limbs like jelly. Breathing hard, I picked the phone up, my hands shaking.

"I dropped you," I whispered. "Sorry."

He didn't hear me.

"Fuck, I'm..." He grunted, short and intense, and his breathing became erratic.

"Yes, Theo..." I urged into the phone.

"Fuck. *Fuck*!"

I grinned, listening to Theo as he came. He was quiet, restrained, but intense. I tried to picture him, to imagine what his face would look like as his cum coated his hand and stomach, but I knew whatever I pictured would pale in comparison to the real thing.

And fuck, did I ever want to see the real thing.

"Still there?" I asked once it sounded like he was finished.

"Yeah." Theo sighed deeply, his breathing returning to normal. "I... wow."

"You're alright?"

"Oh, fuck yes."

I laughed. "Good."

"Are you?"

"I am."

He made a soft noise. "Good. That's... that's good. Fuck. Sorry. I haven't done anything like this before."

"If this was half as good as actually fucking you, I can't wait."

"So, come by for a drink tomorrow night?"

*Fuck* yes.

"I'll be there." I grinned, leaning back against my headboard again. "Good night, Theo."

# Chapter Eighteen

*Theo*

I WAS CONFIDENT ABOUT two things in my life.

The first was that I was a good fucking musician. I had no problem saying that. Getting to where I was took a little confidence, a little luck, and a whole lot of working my ass off. My passion for music had defined my life: I might have been Thtupid Theo with the Lithp growing up, but *no one* would have said that lisping little fucker couldn't play the guitar. I'd fought through years of speech therapy to get rid of it because I wasn't going to let the way my mouth moved stop me from succeeding.

And I mean *fought*. It took years; I was a teenager before any of the therapy stuck, but it didn't matter as far as the teasing went. People never forget flaws like that, and in a small town like Wakeham, there would always be people who remembered me as Thtupid Theo no matter how many hit songs I wrote or concerts I played.

But I wrote those songs and played those shows all the same. I knew how to make music. I knew I was *good* at making music. Music was something I understood, a force I could conjure up from nothing and shape into something beautiful. I knew I could walk onto a stage and stand under the lights, hold my guitar, and make people *feel* what I felt.

The second thing I was confident about was my family.

There had been no point in my life where I questioned that my family loved me or that I loved them. I suppose a third thing I could be confident in was that most people would eventually try to fuck me over or get something out of me, at least since my career had taken off and I'd learned quickly what trusting implicitly would get me. But that had never been the case when it came to my family. There was no question that they would always be there, that they believed in me, and that I

140

would be there for them, too. I might have been bullied growing up, but I had a good life at home and that was more than a lot of people could say, so I was grateful for it.

There were my parents, of course, and maybe I was biased, but I thought they were the best parents in the world. My mom, protective and nurturing. My dad, emotional but pragmatic. Both working together to bring up two boys who ended up doing pretty well for themselves.

Although, James did have one up on me when it came to the whole marriage-and-kids thing, but his family was still my family. Lisa, who was the sister I'd never had. She was a voice of reason and sensibility, the person I knew I could always trust to be down to earth. And the kids: enigmas made up of energy and excitement who looked up to *me*, of all people.

Sure, James and I had gotten on each other's nerves so many times growing up that it was surprising either of us had nerves left, but he was my brother. He was one of the two people in the world I knew I could count on for anything, anytime, no questions asked.

The other was Rick, who was as much a brother to me as James was. Maybe we weren't blood-related and we didn't look or act anything alike, but other than that, we could have been twins.

Except that we didn't have the same birthday.

But we'd been raised together. We'd been friends since we were in diapers, before we even understood what the concept of a friend truly was. As much as I got bullied as a kid, I knew it would have been ten times worse if it wasn't for Rick. He'd always been taller than me, though he'd been gangly until puberty kicked in. But that, paired with the fact that people just generally *liked* Rick, was enough to keep at least some of the bullying at bay.

At least, it did until he came out when we were in high school.

He'd never come out to me, specifically. I'd just known. Rick liked boys, and I liked girls, and it didn't matter to us but it might to other people. And a lot of the people close to him had suspected, I'm sure, especially as we got into our teens and he kept ignoring all the girls who were swooning over him as he grew into his gangliness.

His mom had *known*, though, which was good because she was prepared to take on the world when it turned against Rick. I think he'd expected that would happen, though he'd held out hope that maybe it wouldn't. But small towns aren't always known for their openness, so one day he was the guy almost everyone was friendly with, and the next he was more of an outcast than I was.

He'd gotten through it, though, and when things took off for my career a few years later, it hadn't even been a question in my mind that I wanted Rick there with me. He called himself my assistant, but he was far more. He was my wrangler, my go-between, my sanity, and my connection to the ground when I was at risk of letting myself float away.

There was no one in the world who knew me as well as Rick did, and that meant getting him out of my fucking house without suspecting anything so I could have Aspen over for a drink was next to impossible.

"Going to the club tonight?" I asked as we ate breakfast that morning.

He shook his head and swallowed a piece of bacon. "Still haven't found another cab driver."

"Did you actually talk to the guy?"

"I mean, briefly, but if you must know, my mouth was kinda full for most of—"

"I meant about if *he* was looking for anything serious. You guys hooked up in the back of a cab. Maybe he wants something casual, too."

Rick shook his head. "Nah, he seemed like the clingy type."

"How would you know if you never talked to him?"

"You can just tell with some people," he said, yawning and pouring more coffee into his mug. "Some people just aren't built to do the casual hookup thing. Like you."

I raised my eyebrows. "'Scuse me?"

He blinked at me. "What?"

"I could totally do a casual hookup."

It was a while before Rick's laughter faded. When it did, I looked at him, unimpressed. "Done?"

"Oh, come on, Theo," he said, still half-chuckling. "*You* are not capable of a casual hookup. How many times have I suggested you have a one-night stand or just get laid, and you always—"

"Just because I want to know someone at least a little before I have sex with them doesn't mean I'm not capable of keeping things casual,"

I grumbled. "I just wouldn't want it to be *totally* anonymous. That can still be casual."

Rick started laughing again. He finished the last bite of bacon and picked up his plate, clapping me on the shoulder as he brought it to the sink. "Sure, man. Whatever you say."

So trying to plant that idea didn't work.

"Hey, you talked to your parents lately?" I asked a while later.

"A few days ago," Rick replied. "Why?"

I shrugged. "Just wondering. I noticed you hadn't gone over for dinner or anything in a while."

"Jesus, Theo," he groaned. "Have you been taking guilt trip lessons from my mom?"

"It was just a question."

He studied me for a minute, then frowned. "Or was it?"

"Uh, yeah."

"What's going on?" he demanded.

"Nothing's going—"

"You're trying to get me to go out."

"I was just *asking*, Rick."

"You're hiding something."

"I'm not—"

"Tell me." He folded his arms. "Tell me now."

Silently, we stared at each other, holding each other's gaze until I sighed. "I'm not hiding anything."

"You're so full of shit," he said. "Are you trying to get me out of the house? Or did my mom put you up to this?"

Rick might've known me well enough to suspect something was up, but it went both ways. I knew him well enough to get into his head, too.

I raised my hands in surrender. "Neither. Forget I said anything."

"*Theo*—"

"You said you wanted to come back to Wakeham to see your family. I was just curious if something was up. Don't worry about it."

A few hours later, I was in the studio messing around with a song when Rick walked in.

"Your guilt trip worked," he said. "I'm going to my parents for dinner and a movie. Mom's decided she wants to torture me with *Fiddler on the Roof* for the thirty thousandth time. Wanna come?"

"Not to say you didn't do a good job selling it, but no."

"Not even a little bit? I was even going to let you DD so I could get through the movie by chugging a bottle of wine."

"Why don't you just stay over?" I asked.

He folded his arms. "You *are* trying to get me out of the house. What's—"

"Oh my God." I tilted my head back exasperatedly. "It was a suggestion. That way you could still drink your bottle of wine and I wouldn't have to sit through *Fiddler* to drive you home. We both win."

He eyed me suspiciously, but eventually agreed that I was brilliant.

I hated to hide things from Rick, but this... I had to. He'd made his feelings about me hooking up with Aspen clear and his complete lack of faith that I could keep things casual didn't exactly help. There was no way he'd approve of what I was doing, and maybe I should have considered that a red flag. After all, he was my best friend. If he didn't think it was a good idea, maybe it wasn't.

Then again, he was avoiding his only method of safe transportation into Timmins after not thinking through a casual backseat hookup, so it wasn't like Rick was the king of good ideas, either.

Mostly, I just needed to keep this for myself.

Just for now.

I texted Aspen to let her know what time she could stop by, a couple of hours after Rick had left so there was no chance of them running into each other. It also gave me enough time to shower and try to find something to wear that didn't scream out how hard I was trying while still looking... well. A little more presentable than the last time she had been at my house.

Not that the bar was high for that, since I'd been in the baggiest pajama pants I owned and a hoodie that looked like I'd had it since high school, mainly because I'd had it since high school. Still, I wanted to look decent. She was hot as fuck and I still wasn't entirely convinced this whole thing was really happening, but I wanted it to.

When I heard a car door close at exactly eight o'clock, it took everything in me to resist running to the front like I was a golden retriever who couldn't contain his excitement. Instead, I hung out just around the corner, waiting impatiently for her to come to the door.

Despite listening for it, the sound of her firm, authoritative knock made me jump. I ran a hand through my hair, then went to the door and opened it.

"About time," Aspen said, even though it had only been a matter of seconds since she knocked before I opened the door. "I wasn't expecting it to be so cold tonight." Her lips curled up into a smile as she shivered. "Let me in?"

I stepped to the side, trying not to grin like an idiot. "Of course."

She stepped in and I let the door swing closed behind her. "Thanks. I don't know why I thought it would be warmer. I guess winter starts earlier up here."

"It does," I agreed. "Can I, uh... take your coat?"

A playful smirk crossed her lips. "I didn't expect such personable service."

I couldn't help chuckling as she let me help her with her jacket, which was probably good because it covered the moment I saw what she was wearing.

It wasn't anything outrageous. Just unexpected. The Aspen underneath the coat wasn't one I'd seen before. Lisa had started picking Aspen up at home on Friday mornings so they could go straight from the office to dinner at Lisa's, which meant I'd always seen her in her work attire. For Aspen, that was skirts with stockings or tailored slacks, paired with silky blouses that skimmed along her curves and well-cut blazers. She usually had her hair pulled back from her face, though there was no way to completely tame the wild curls on her head.

Even though I'd pictured Aspen at what was probably her most casual—black panties, a tight tank top, and her hand between her legs with her phone tucked against her shoulder as she masturbated to the thought of me, which, like... *fuck* was that a good picture—I'd never seen her dressed like she was that night.

Everything about her exuded sexiness in the most effortless way. She still wore her signature red lipstick, but I'd never seen her hair down. I'd never realized how long it was or how much I'd want to feel it wound through my fingers. She wore jeans that framed an ass somehow even better than the one I'd been fantasizing about and I couldn't help but wonder what it would be like to peel them down her thighs as she lay on her back on my bed. And her sweater, hugged her curves and teasing just the slightest bit of cleavage...

"Something wrong?" Aspen asked.

We hadn't moved from the entrance way, and I was still holding her coat.

"Nope." I hurried to hang the coat up, then motioned to the living room. "Come on in. Can I get you a drink? I've got water, beer, uh... orange juice. Or something warm, maybe? Coffee or hot chocolate?"

That bewitching smirk played across her lips again. "Hot chocolate, you say?"

I made a cup for each of us as she settled in the living room, then joined her once it was ready. As I set the cups on the table, I couldn't help letting my eyes trail down her body and back up again, taking in the way her curls grazed the line of her neck as it fell against her shoulder. When I glanced at her face, she was watching me, a laugh sparkling in her eyes.

Normally, I would have been embarrassed to be caught gaping at a woman like that, but I didn't feel like I had to be that way around Aspen. Instead, I just chuckled as I sat beside her. "You look amazing."

"Thank you," she replied. "You're looking great yourself."

I glanced down at my clothes, not sure how jeans and a t-shirt compared in the slightest to what she was wearing, but glad she thought so all the same. "Thanks."

"Anytime."

Things were quiet as we each took a sip of hot chocolate. I swallowed, suddenly at a loss for words, and shifted in place.

"How's your, uh... weekend been? So far?" I asked, like a total fucking dork.

Aspen looked at me, then put her mug of hot chocolate down on the coffee table. "Let's not beat around the bush, Theo. Not that your hot chocolate isn't delicious, because it is, but we know why I'm here. So let's talk about that instead."

Holy fuck.

I'd suspected it already, but Aspen's directness was waking something up. Well, it was waking multiple things up, my cock being one of them, but she was also waking up something that I hadn't known was there with the way she spoke. The matter-of-fact way she said things. The confident way she simply knew what she wanted and wasn't afraid to say it. There were no games to play with her, no complicated social structure to navigate as we tried to figure out how interested the other person was.

She wanted to fuck. I wanted to fuck. So we were gonna talk about how to make that happen.

"Gladly," I said, my voice already hoarse.

"You already know what the situation is, but is there anything we should talk about before we... explore things?"

I nodded. "Can I ask a couple of questions?"

"Yes, please." She licked her lips and looked down at my lap, which was so fucking hot I almost forgot what I wanted to ask. "Things work best if we get as much talking out of the way before we start."

"Makes sense," I said. "Okay, so the... uh." I stopped, thinking for a moment. "Shit, I hope this doesn't make you mad or anything, but you know the guy in the article? The one you graded?"

She looked amused. "Yes, I did know him. Why?"

"I just wanted to know what happened. I mean, specifically, how does one obtain a... good grade?"

She burst out laughing. "Don't tell me you're hyper-fixated on grades, too."

I couldn't help but join in her laughter. "Not really, but it doesn't hurt to know what I can do to get to the top of the class."

She licked her lips again. "Well, it'll please you to know that Jerome—that was his name—had a B but was demoted to a C after the article was put out."

"Fair. What'd he do to earn a B in the first place?"

"I'm not going to lie to you, he was an okay fuck," she said, then shrugged. "But *only* okay. There was potential, but he didn't seem to fully know what he was doing and didn't reciprocate the way I'd hoped. And I can work with potential, most of the time, but when he blew his load and thought that was it—like he was just off the hook and it was too bad, so sad that I didn't come—that was a major strike."

I was incredulous. "And he still got a *B*?"

"I'm not totally unfair. He ended up getting me off, but only after I practically ripped his arm off and made him finger me. So, desired result, but needed a little *too* much guidance."

"I can't believe there's still guys out there who think it's not a priority to help their partner finish."

She smirked. "Already swinging for extra credit?"

I shrugged. "A guy's gotta try."

"A guy's willingness to make an effort always makes a difference."

"Good." I glanced at my hands, serious again. "Okay, second thing. Again, if... I don't want to piss you off. If I'm asking something—"

"You seem very concerned about upsetting me," she said. "Unless you ask me to do something illegal, I'm pretty open-minded."

"It's not that. I mean, people aren't supposed to ask about previous hookups or anything, right?"

"Sure, but I think that's a stupid rule." She shrugged. "I don't care all that much about where your dick's been before, unless it's been somewhere that's going to affect me."

"Fair. And, uh, it... hasn't. After Sheri, I... you know. Got checked. Just in case." I cleared my throat. "This one is a bit more selfish. I mean, I'm not... it's just, I wanted to know if..."

She waited as I trailed off, then smiled. "Come on, spit it out."

I sighed. "Look, I know we said it's casual, and I can do that. But I want to make sure we can... you know. Keep this just between us. You saw the kind of shit people say and that was just because I *know* you. I don't want you to get dragged into anything else."

"Is that the only reason you don't want people to know?"

I shook my head, not quite able to meet her eye. "Honestly, I don't want to deal with questions or lectures or anything. You saw how Rick can be. He's overprotective. And my parents mean well, but they'll read into any little sign that I might be seeing someone. Plus, the less people who know, the less chance it gets out to the media." I stared down at the mug in my hand. "I get it. It sounds shitty of me to even ask, but—"

My words were cut off as her hand covered mine and an electric thrill rushed through my skin. "Theo, let me be clear that I'm saying this from the very bottom of my cold, cynical heart."

I looked up at her, and she gazed back with an earnest expression.

"I can't express to you how perfect that sounds in every single fucking way."

"Oh, good," I said, laughing.

She grinned. "I don't need people getting their noses in my business. We can keep this between us. No problem."

"You're a dream come true," I said. "Anything you want to talk about before we, uh... How'd you put it? Explore things?"

"Yes." She put the hot chocolate she'd grabbed down on the table again and started counting things off on her fingers. "Number one, you're not finished until I am, but you seem to understand that already so I doubt it's a problem. Two, I don't like kissing. Three, no excessive hair pulling. Especially if I'm going down on you. Firmly grabbing is okay, yanking it isn't."

Before I knew what was happening, she reached for me with both hands. It was all I could do to stare into her eyes as she placed one on either side of my head, grasping a handful of my hair in each hand and tugging gently.

"Like this," she said.

A shiver ran through me. Her face was not far from mine, so close I could feel the warmth of her breath against my face. My cock throbbed, fully hard now and begging me to do *something*, but I couldn't even bring myself to speak. Instead, I nodded, my heart racing as she let go of my hair and continued.

"Spanking is okay, but hands only. Biting is okay, but be warned that I'll bite you back. Same place, same strength, so be careful with your teeth if you want me to be careful with mine."

"You know what you like." I cleared my throat. "I like that."

"Good."

"Is anything off-limits?"

She shrugged. "I'm open to almost anything. Just ask first. Or give me a head's up. Like, if you suddenly decide you're totally into coming on my face? Cool, just let me know so I can close my eyes. Want to try anal?"

I'd made the mistake of sipping my hot chocolate and nearly spat it out, but she didn't seem to notice as she continued.

"I'm game, but I need some notice to make things work. That is, if you want to fuck me in the ass. If you want to be on the receiving end, it'll take a little longer since I don't imagine there are many discreet places to buy a strap-on in this town."

"Good to know," I managed to say. "I, uh, don't... haven't considered that before but if I change my mind, I'll let you know. The strap-on part, I mean."

Her bottom lip curled between her teeth as she looked at me.

"Here's the thing you need to understand, Theo," she said, her voice husky and seductive. "I want this because I really like sex, so if there's stuff you want to try or specifically like, I'm probably open to it. Mainly, I like being fucked. I like to tease men, and make them want me, and make them come."

My throat was incredibly dry. I drank more hot chocolate, trying to steady my heartbeat so my voice didn't shake when I responded. "I like those things, too."

She reached for her mug. "Good. I think we can make this work."

"One last thing," I asked. She looked at me expectantly as she sipped her hot chocolate. "You said you don't like kissing."

Of course, the one thing I hadn't been worried would upset her caused her to stiffen in her seat.

"Yes. That's correct."

"I just wanted to know why."

She sighed, looking away as the smile faded off her face. "I just find it weird. It doesn't do anything for me."

"Is it off the table completely, or—" I cut myself off as she looked at me, one eyebrow raised. "I like kissing. A lot. I'd... I'd say it's the thing I like most about sex. If it's a hard line, then I get that, totally, but just... if it's..."

"It's not... no. It's not completely off the table." She tilted her mug, swirling her hot chocolate as she contemplated what I said. "For one-night stands, it would be. But this is... I mean, it's still casual, but you and I are friends and—"

"I don't want you to do something you're uncomfortable with," I said. "I don't want to be that guy, Aspen. I'd just like to understand, I guess."

There was something unreadable on her face as she looked up. Her eyes met mine and she studied me for a moment before nodding.

"I haven't had great experiences with kissing," she said. "I know I don't have to, and I appreciate you saying that, but I'd be open to it if it's something you enjoy."

Part of me felt undeserving of that, but Aspen didn't say shit she didn't mean, so I nodded slowly. "Okay. I mean, it's a big responsibility, but I'd be happy to show you how awesome kissing can be."

She bit back a smile. "Okay. I'll give you one chance."

"Come on. One chance? That's hardly anything. I need at least five, to show you all the different... you know. Facets of kissing or whatever."

She twisted her mouth to the side. "Three. Final offer."

I raised an eyebrow at her. "Three kisses, or three sessions of kissing?"

She rolled her eyes, but grinned. "Okay, three kisses, where each 'kiss' is defined as the moment you put your lips on mine, to the moment you pull away."

"Okay, so we're defining 'kiss' as an instance that could potentially contain multiple occurrences of lips meeting?"

"Sure, Theo," she said, laughing.

"Then it's a deal. I'll agree to three."

She playfully stuck her hand forward to shake on it. I glanced down, then back up at her eyes. Holding her gaze, I put my mug on the coffee table before enveloping her hand in mine and squeezing it gently.

"Can I cash in on one of those kissing sessions right now, or is there more I should know first?"

Her eyes flicked down to my lips as she licked hers, almost subconsciously. "We can definitely start cashing in now."

Fuck yes.

I kept hold of her hand, using it to guide her towards me. She shifted, the warmth of her thigh pressing against mine as we grew closer and closer still. I leaned in, slowly, carefully, and once our faces were almost touching, I stopped. Her eyebrow twitched up questioningly and I slowly brought the hand I was holding up to the side of my neck.

"When you pulled my hair earlier, I almost lost it," I said quietly. "We can probably add that to things I'd like you to do to me again."

Her face was so close to mine that I almost felt the motion of her lips as they curled into a sultry smile. "Noted."

Fingertips trailed up my neck to just behind my ear, weaving the strands between them. The sensation of her fingers running through my hair made me shiver, and I exhaled softly before bringing my hand behind her neck, closing my eyes as I finally captured her mouth with mine.

It was heaven.

Her lips were soft and warm and tasted somehow even sweeter than the hot chocolate on them. I tried to hold back my eagerness, forcing myself to be patient and careful and attentive to any sign she might want to change her mind about kissing, but she kissed me back without hesitation. Without pulling back too much, I pressed my lips to hers again, and again, and then nipped her bottom lip to see if she'd keep her word on returning the favour, which she did. I almost groaned into her mouth as her teeth sank into my lip before she sucked on the spot that she bit down on.

Shifting closer, I ran my tongue along her bottom lip. Her grip on my hair tightened and my cock strained painfully against my jeans as she parted her lips, the taste of chocolate still on her tongue as it met mine. I moved my hand to her waist, unable to stop myself from pulling her closer, and that's when I heard the front door open.

"Theo?"

Aspen released my hair and pulled away just as Rick called out.

"You've got to be kidding me," I said.

"Whose car is in the driveway?" he shouted, his voice coming closer as he left the entryway.

Luckily, Aspen could think faster than I could. She wiped her thumb across my mouth as her face morphed to a practiced look of professional blankness, then moved back on the couch so she was a respectable distance away before grabbing her hot chocolate.

"It's mine, Rick," she called out, her voice steady and calm.

Rick was in the living room a moment later, his eyebrows so high on his forehead that they looked painted on. "Aspen. What a surprise."

"Hey," I said, trying not to sound as aggravated as I felt. "You're back early."

"Mm-hmm. Too early?" he asked, his voice falsely light.

"Not at all. Otherwise you would have missed Aspen."

"Well, maybe if you'd told me you were having someone over tonight, I wouldn't have risked it."

"He would have had to have known I was stopping by," Aspen said pleasantly, then finished the last sip of her hot chocolate. "I decided to get in on the old Wakeham tradition of dropping by unannounced so I could see how Theo was doing. But I'll get out of your hair, Theo. Thanks for the hot chocolate and the chat."

"Any time," I said. "Thanks for stopping by."

"It was nice to see you too, Rick," she said. "Far more of a pleasure than last time."

"Glad to hear it," he said.

I stayed on the couch as she saw herself out, willing Rick to leave the room so I could stand up without my erection being so obvious. He waited until the front door closed before turning to me, arms folded.

"A hot chocolate and a chat, hey?"

"Yeah."

"Really?"

I tried to look confused. "What?"

"Oh, come *on*, Theo. I'm not buying it."

"Sounds like a you problem." I sipped my hot chocolate. "Aspen and I are friends, you know. And I haven't seen her in a while, so considering everything that happened... I'm allowed to have other friends, Rick."

"Don't play that game. You know my concerns have nothing to do with her being your friend."

"You don't need to be concerned."

Rick picked up her empty mug from the table and went towards the kitchen. "Sleeping with your sister-in-law's boss is a bad idea."

"Thank you for your input." I hurriedly adjusted my cock, relieving the straining against my jeans. "I thought you were staying at your parents'. Did you even have enough time to watch *Fiddler*?"

"No. I got a call from the label."

I frowned as he re-entered the room. "What?"

"The label. They want you to come in for some meetings next week."

"I... what? Why are they calling you on a Saturday night?"

"Probably because you've been 'on hiatus' for months now and they're getting worried." He flopped onto the couch. "And because I was texting them."

I stared at him. "And why were you texting them?"

He sighed. "Because my dad is still having issues with his back and is refusing to acknowledge that he's in pain, and Mom's pretending everything's fine because if she doesn't, he gets sulky. But he was obviously not going to be capable of sitting through a three-hour movie and needed to take his meds and go to bed, so I messaged Alice to see if I could fake a work emergency—"

"Why didn't you text me?"

"Because it's far more convincing for you to have no idea about any work emergencies," he said without missing a beat. "And Alice actually did have some stuff she wanted dealt with, so I told my parents that I had to get home because the label wanted us back in Montreal for a few days and we have to leave tomorrow."

"I... are you serious?"

He gave me a pointed look. "I know you're still on a break but we can't ignore them forever."

"Yeah, but... what if I had stuff I wanted to do tomorrow?"

"Like Aspen?"

I glared at him. "Nothing *happened*, Rick."

"Sure. So you have nothing to do tomorrow? We can go to Montreal and get a few meetings out of the way this week? Then they won't need to see you until after Christmas at the earliest, I'd think."

Maybe it was because my blood was all still concentrated in my dick, but I couldn't think of a reason to say it wouldn't work, so that was that.

I moped about it when I ended up in my room a short while later. Cock-blocked by Rick *and* now it was going to be a few days before I even had a chance to see Aspen again? After kissing her and touching her and getting so, so close to being able to fuck her?

It fucking sucked.

But I had more pressing matters to deal with. I was still half-hard and my cock was *aching* for me to do something. Groaning, I grabbed my phone and figured I'd find a video or something to jack off to, only to see a message from Aspen from a while earlier.

*Sorry our night got interrupted.*

I smiled in spite of myself. She must have texted me as soon as she got home.

*Me too. It's my fault. I insisted on keeping it from Rick. No one to blame but myself for losing out.*

I didn't think she would respond right away, but before I could even open my browser, my phone vibrated again.

*Shit happens. I liked where it was going though.*

I raised my eyebrows. *So the kiss wasn't too bad?*

*It wasn't terrible. That's the highest compliment I can currently give. So take it as a good thing.*

I couldn't help but grin. *I'll wear it as a badge of honour.*

She sent back an emoji blowing a kiss and I bit my lip. Sure, I could pull up some porn to jack off to, but maybe...

Maybe I needed to take a page out of Aspen's book and just say what I was thinking.

*I wish I'd gotten to fuck you,* I typed. *You looked so good tonight. I can't stop thinking about your ass in those jeans.*

I sent it before I could stop myself, then waited. When a few minutes went by and she didn't respond right away like she had with her other messages, I cringed, my face burning as I clicked out of my messages app and pulled up my browser.

But I hadn't given her enough credit.

My phone vibrated and her name was on the notification that dropped down, but there was no message. I should've realized what that meant, but I wasn't thinking, so I nearly exploded when the message opened and I was face-to-photo with a perfectly round ass clad in black boy short panties.

Holy *fuck.*

My mouth was half open as I stared. Her ass was... Phenomenal didn't even begin to cover it. Her panties looked like they were painted on, clinging to every curve and dipping into her crack so that her ass cheeks peeked out on each side. Her hand was resting on one hip, fingers tucked into the waistband teasingly, like she was about to peel them down her hips.

My phone vibrated again. *Which view is better, this or the jeans?*

*I can't even tell you how hard I am right now,* I replied.

*I can imagine. Wish I could help.*

God, so did I. But she couldn't, so I brought the picture of her perfect ass back up and unbuckled my belt, pulling my jeans down just enough that I could shove one hand in my boxers and grab my cock. It was so sensitive that I winced as I started stroking, barely letting myself blink as I stared at Aspen's ass.

Another message came through seconds later. *You're jacking off now, aren't you?*

*Can't help it,* I managed to type with one hand.

*Show me.*

I shouldn't have. A picture like that could easily come back to haunt me. But somehow, Aspen had become one of the people who I trusted. I couldn't explain why, nor did it matter as I pulled my boxers the rest of the way down and let my cock spring free. I wrapped my hand around it again, my face burning as I snapped a quick photo.

The message sent and nerves thrummed through my body, which only seemed to fuel my need to jerk off. I moved my hand faster, pre-cum leaking from my tip and coating my shaft with each stroke as I waited for her response.

It didn't take long.

*MMMMMMMMM* was the first message.

*I love your cock,* was sent right after that.

*I want that inside me. SO much.*

*Seriously, your cock is so gorgeous that I'm pretty sure I would love having you come in my mouth.*

I groaned, the sound embarrassingly loud. Each message sent a sharp wave of pleasure and pressure through me and I moved my hand faster, incapable of responding.

She seemed to not only understand that but encouraged it. Right after planting the image of her lips wrapped around my cock as I came in her mouth, my phone vibrated again and another picture came through. In this one, she was standing completely naked in front of a mirror, one hand occupied with her phone and the other between her legs, spreading her pussy lips so I could see the glistening wetness between her legs.

I barely had time to appreciate the perfect, hard nipples on top of her perfect, firm breasts or the perfect placement of her finger overtop of her clit. The familiar pressure built and built until it was more than I could take and I came, muffling my cry as I shot ropes of cum across my stomach and hand. Waves of release crashed over me as I stroked every last drop out, gasping breathlessly as the image of Aspen's perfect—fucking *perfect*—body was seared into my mind.

*Fuck,* I managed to text back. My hand was covered in jizz, but I couldn't bring myself to move quite yet.

*That's what I thought,* came the response, followed by a winking face. *My vibrator battery is all charged up, so I'm gonna stare at this picture of your cock and finish up. Good night, Theo.*

I almost laughed.

Fuck, this girl was amazing.

# Chapter Nineteen

*Aspen*

Kissing Theo was a problem.

It was a *big* problem.

Not because he'd pressured me to do it. I refused to fault him for daring to ask for clarification and trying to understand what the boundary was rather than just silently accepting what I'd said. And I hadn't been lying when I said I was okay with doing it if it was something he enjoyed. Theo was trustworthy, and even though we didn't get a chance to explore things the way I wanted to, I was confident he would respect any boundary I put in place. In fact, he almost had; despite me saying I was okay with kissing him, he'd made a point of saying he didn't want me to do something I was uncomfortable with.

That, more than anything, had cemented my decision to let him kiss me. He didn't want me to do it for just him; he didn't want to pressure me; he didn't want me to feel obligated or like I owed him anything. He didn't act judgmental or press for more information about what I knew was a somewhat unusual boundary. He just enjoyed kissing.

The surprising thing was that I'd enjoyed kissing him, too.

That wasn't a problem, either. It had been unexpected, that enjoyment, but it wasn't a problem. I had my reasons for not liking kissing, but kissing Theo was... different. Maybe it had been the dizzying sweetness and heat from the hot chocolate that had lingered on his lips. Chocolate did make everything better, after all. Or maybe it was that pause, the extension of anticipation as he admitted he'd loved the way I pulled his hair.

Whatever it was, it didn't matter. The problem wasn't the fact that Theo had kissed me *or* that I'd enjoyed it.

It was that kissing him was so good, I couldn't stop thinking about what his mouth would feel like everywhere else on my body. I couldn't stop wondering what that tongue would feel like tracing my pussy lips or if he'd suck on my clit the same way he'd sucked on my bottom lip. If he'd graze his teeth along my nipple the same way he'd gently nibbled at my lips.

Kissing Theo had turned into an oral fixation, and the big problem—the biggest *fucking* problem—was that he gave me that fixation and then left town for the rest of the week.

I'd been in Wakeham for months at that point. Despite the goddamn romance novels and the complete lack of sexual contact with anyone, I'd been managing pretty well. And then Theo came along, pressed his lips to mine *once*, and I turned into a mess of unrequited horniness and moody desperation.

Sure, the texting afterwards had been nice. The slightly blurry picture of Theo's cock was... well. Strictly from a technical standpoint, it wasn't anywhere near as hot as the ones I'd sent him. That wasn't to say he didn't have an absolutely gorgeous cock. Because he did. There were dicks, and then there was Theo's dick. Theo's dick was like how someone would describe the ideal dick. It wasn't excessively huge, though he was fairly blessed, and it was just... perfect. The shape, the colour, the glisten of pre-cum just beginning to drip from his enticingly swollen tip...

He just had a really fucking nice dick.

The only reason it wasn't as hot as I'd hoped was because of the quality. The blurriness, the angle, all of it was just a little off. But it was serviceable, and I mentally gave him extra points for trying after he admitted the next day that it was the first dick pic he'd ever sent. Knowing that it was his first one increased the hotness factor, too, as did the simple fact that he trusted me enough to send it. Embarrassingly, it wasn't until then that I considered just how big a thing it was for Theo to send those pictures to me. He was famous; a dick pic could have serious repercussions for him. And he got even more bonus points for improvement when he sent me another dick pic two days later—by my request, of course. Theo was a gentleman who didn't send unsolicited dick pics because of course he was.

That picture—and the next one—had been a problem, too. Mainly because they were reminders of what I wanted and couldn't have, since I was in Wakeham and Theo had taken the pictures at his place in Montreal.

The first one wasn't a true dick pic, since said dick was hidden beneath the fabric of Theo's boxers, but it was enticingly erotic all the same. He'd taken it in his living room while watching a movie with Rick, who had excused himself to the bathroom just long enough for Theo to snap the photo and send it to me. We'd been texting all day, but I still hadn't expected it when I'd teased him about needing another photo from him for my gallery.

*Like an art exhibit?* he'd asked. *I dunno if I want my dick on display in a gallery.*

*My collection of privates is a private collection, thank you very much,* I replied. *For my own personal viewing pleasure.*

*Oh, well in that case...*

The message had come through first and I frowned, trying to figure out what he meant. Then, a few seconds later, a picture of an unzipped pair of jeans, his hand pushing the waistband down just enough that I could see a spattering of hair above the bulge in his boxers. I licked my lips, delightfully surprised.

*I think I have a new main attraction,* I wrote. *How can I ever repay you for this generous donation to my gallery?*

*Maybe you could help me start a gallery of my own.*

"Be careful what you wish for," I said out loud, laughing to myself as I wiggled out of my yoga pants.

*This one's called Response to Dick Pic #2,* I sent a short while later, along with a photo. *Fingers on pussy, created as a gift for Mr. Barker, date unknown.*

*Jesus Christ, Aspen.*

I smirked. *Not your style? I can take a different one.*

*I might explode. Literally. There's 30 minutes left in this movie and the risk of me ruining these pants is insanely high right now.*

*So... don't take another one?*

*Not what I said.*

He didn't give himself enough credit. He didn't explode until later that night, after the movie was over and I'd added a few more photos to his exhibition. That was when I got Dick Pic #3, which had been a massive problem because I'd just finished cleaning my vibrator when he sent it. But the sight of his hand wrapped around his still-hard cock, coated with cum that dripped from his fingers down his shaft, was enough to get me going all over again.

The dirty messages and pictures were torture, but what was worse were the messages that came between those.

*Do you finish work at the same time every day?* he messaged me on Monday afternoon while I sat on a conference call, trying with everything in me to not interrupt Daniel as he droned on about the pre-audit process my facility was about to go through as if I hadn't spent five years doing his job better than he did.

*Usually, yes,* I replied. *Why?*

*I'm done my meetings and Rick's not home.*

I licked my lips. *Mmm. Sorry, can't sneak away. I'm on a call and you're in another province.*

*Shit, sorry. Didn't mean to bother you while you're busy. Text you later?*

*Oh, God, no. Please keep texting me now.* I sent the message without even considering what I'd just said. *It's probably the only thing stopping me from losing it on this fucking idiot.*

He sent back a laughing emoji. *What fucking idiot?*

*Daniel. One of the other pre-auditors. Not only is he explaining a pre-audit to me like I'm five years old, he's wrong about the things he's explaining.*

*Hmm. Would a new addition to your gallery help distract you?*

"Aspen?"

I jumped as Daniel said my name. "What?"

He sighed condescendingly. "Are you even listening to me?"

"I—"

"Because this is very important information about your pre-audit. If you don't have the—"

"Don't interrupt me," I said flatly. "And no, Daniel. I'm not listening to you. If I was, I'd be fucked when it came to getting ready for my audit."

I could almost hear him gaping through the phone. "Excuse me?"

"If I were to take your advice, I would fail the audit," I said slowly and clearly. "Do you understand?"

"Aspen," Kevin said warningly.

I sighed. "Right. Please continue, Daniel."

Rolling my eyes, I glanced back down at my phone.

*Too far? Sorry. I won't send you pics if you don't want them, promise.*

*No, not too far at all,* I replied quickly. *Idiot called me to attention in the meeting. My boss was reminding me I'm supposed to be on this call to "help" train Daniel how to be better at the job he's fucking paid to do.*

*Ugh. Frustrating. Isn't he the one who's been doing it almost as long as you have but has done half the number you've done?*

*Yep.* I couldn't stop myself from smiling. *Bonus points for remembering that.*

*Of course. You've called him an idiot so many times, I feel like I almost know him.*

I didn't end up with a dick pic from him during that exchange. Instead, I ended up stifling my laugh so poorly that Kevin eventually reprimanded me, assuming I was laughing at Daniel.

"I would have had to be paying attention to be laughing at Daniel," I told him, but that apparently didn't make it any better.

There were more dirty texts and at least one orgasm apiece that night after I got home from work, but when I was bored during a mandatory social media training the next morning, I texted him again.

*What are you up to?*

I received a photo in response: Theo sitting in a boardroom somewhere, surreptitiously taking a selfie. The hood of his hoodie was pulled up, covering his shaggy brown hair, and he had his chin resting on his hand, just barely concealing the unimpressed look on his face.

*Listening to someone who doesn't know shit about music tell me how to write a hit single.*

*Hmm. Sounds like a real Daniel.*

*She is. We should take care to make sure these two never meet. The world wouldn't be able to handle it if they reproduced together.*

Thankfully, my training was a webinar with my mic muted because I burst out laughing.

And that was why those messages were torture. Because for as many pictures as I sent Theo of my tits, I also found myself itching to message him about the hilarious HR-inappropriate thing I'd overheard one of my employees say in the break room. For as many messages I got from Theo telling me to come for him, he'd send me memes or gifs that made me grin stupidly at my phone.

We were friends. Before we'd ever approached the idea of sleeping together, we'd been friends. I saw him on a weekly basis, which was unheard of for me; other than Lisa, I didn't see my friends that regularly. So all those extra messages did was get me even more excited about the whole thing. A guy I got along with, who could match my humour and enjoyed my directness, that also only wanted a casual thing and was showing a lot of promise to be an exceptionally good fuck?

It was a dream come true.

But *waiting* for certain aspects of that dream to come true, specifically the ones that involved having Theo's cock inside me rather than just on my phone? That took patience, and I was not known for my patience.

That was why, when my phone went off with a new message from Theo during my usual Thursday morning management meeting, it took everything in me not to tell Debbie to shut up about deliverables so I could celebrate. Instead, I listened to the rest of whatever it was she was saying, then called the meeting and walked back to my office. Lisa was thankfully on the phone, so all I had to do was nudge my door closed with my hip before doing a dorky celebratory dance.

*Just got home,* said the message. *Already checked with James, he says dinner's on tomorrow night. Need a ride?*

*Yes,* I replied after I finished dancing with joy and collapsed into my desk chair. *But if you could drive me home first, that would be great.*

*Dinner, then home, then ride. Got it.*

*I'll move my car so you can park in the back.*

*Oh, I'll be staying for a while?* A winking emoji accompanied the message and I smirked.

*You better be.*

*Hope you don't have plans Saturday. Once I'm done with you, you won't be walking straight.*

I couldn't stop myself from grinning at my phone. I'd liked Theo before, but this confident, bold side of Theo I'd gotten to know over text was even better.

*Big promises. I'm holding you up to that.*

"Ooo, who're you texting that's making you smile so much?"

I jumped as Lisa entered my office, holding a stack of papers. Apparently, I hadn't closed the door all the way.

"No one," I said, locking the screen of my phone.

"Yeah, right," Lisa snorted. "Come on Aspen."

"I was looking at memes."

She burst out laughing. "No you weren't. That was not a 'laughing-at-memes' smile. That was a 'someone-made-me-smile' smile."

"You're right." I tucked my phone into my desk drawer as Lisa raised her eyebrows. "Whoever made that meme made me smile."

She rolled her eyes and I laughed.

"Fine then," she said. "Keep secrets from your most trusted assistant."

"Thank you, I will."

She put the stack of papers on my desk. "Well, whoever it is, tell them good job. Also, Kevin called while you were in the meeting and wants you to call him back right away."

I frowned. "Kevin called? Not Darby?"

She shook her head. "Trust me, I almost had a heart attack when he said who it was."

"Why?"

"What if I'd done something wrong?"

I grabbed the stack of papers, rifling through them. "What would you have done wrong?"

"I don't know. Maybe I answered the phone wrong. Like, I always say 'Thank you for calling Aspen Haws's office, this is Lisa, how can I help you?' But what if I'm supposed to say, like, 'It's a green energy-alicious day here in Aspen's office, you've got your friend Lisa on the line, how can I—'"

"I would fire you personally if you answered the phone like that."

She laughed. "Let me know if you need anything."

"Just get the door behind you, please."

Nodding, she left and closed my office door as I picked up my desk phone to call Kevin. Not that I was worried, but it was unusual for the CEO to call me directly. That's what he had Darby for—that, and answering his calls, of course.

"Kevin Wu's office," she said after picking up on the second ring.

"It's me, Darb."

"Aspen!" she said, delighted. "Just the person Kevin wanted to talk to."

"So I've heard." There was a long pause and I tapped my nails on my desk. "Uh... are you going to transfer me to him?"

"You didn't ask me to."

I sighed. "Can I assume it wasn't that important on account of all the fucking around you're doing?"

"Oh, not at all. It was super important," she said. "But he just went into another meeting, so that means I get to tell you the good news about all the fucking around you'll be doing!"

"What?"

"That's right, Ms. Haws, you can thank me personally for getting you a break from the ho-hum drudgery of Wakeham, Ontario! Pack your bags because you've won—" A muffled drumroll sounded as she slapped her palms on her desk "—a week-long stay in Montreal because Kevin wants you in head office next week!"

"Seriously?" I asked, sitting up with excitement.

"Mm-hmm." She sounded positively giddy.

"A whole week? What does he need me for that's going to take a whole week?"

"No need to panic. He wants a progress report on Wakeham and to get you in on some meetings, plus—and I know, you're going to hate this, but just remember the bright side of not being in Wakeham for a week—he needs you to do some training with Daniel."

I groaned. "Daniel is an *idiot*, Darby. I'm going to tell him that to his face. You know that, right?"

"That's what I told Kevin, but he insisted."

I sighed. "Fine. As long as—"

"But *wait*!" she said. "There's more!"

I smiled, shaking my head. "What else?"

"Because I am *such* an awesome friend, guess who booked your ticket for tomorrow morning and your *return* ticket for next Sunday so we can go fuck around at the bar *two whole weekends in a row*?! I'll give you a hint, it was me, but also I had to justify the extra expense by telling Kevin you'd attend a dinner with some big clients on Saturday night so he can show you off. He won't stop calling you a superstar. Literally. Be prepared for him to parade you around and brag like he physically gave birth to you. But *after* that, we can go out on Saturday, too."

Tomorrow morning.

My smile was gone, replaced by a half-open mouth as I stared at the wall ahead of me, trying to figure out why the fuck I felt so disappointed.

I mean, yes, obviously I'd been looking forward to fucking Theo. But a week and a half in civilization? A week and a half where the world didn't shut down at nine and I could order food from a restaurant that wasn't pizza or frozen deep-fried appetizers? Think of all the sushi, I told myself. I could have Indian food. Poutine from that place I liked downtown. Korean barbecue. Pizza, but from the Italian bistro I liked rather than a chain restaurant.

I would have a whole week and a half in a place where I had a company-expensed hotel room that, knowing Darby, was near at least four different bars I could scope out for random one-night hookups. Where I could find a different guy to fuck each and every night, giving my vibrator a much-needed vacation and my pussy a much-needed workout.

Except I didn't want to fuck a different guy each and every night.

I wanted to fuck Theo.

After all the work I'd put into it, after all the texts and pictures and anticipation, I wanted that prize. Not this one that Darby was giving me.

"Aspen?" she asked when I didn't say anything.

"Yeah," I said, shaking off the sudden letdown. "Sorry, I was... That's great, Darb. That sounds awesome."

"I have to say, I am absolutely shocked," she said, her voice full of concern. "I thought you'd be ecstatic. This is kind of meh."

"I am," I said. "I just... There was a thing I wanted to do tomorrow and I was... thinking about how to reschedule it. It's fine."

"Damn right it's fine," she said. "Okay, so here's the plan. We do dinner when you get into town, then a mini Get-Sexy-Friday, and then the bar. I figure that'll get you someone to fuck as efficiently as possible, which I'm assuming is your number one priority."

"You know me," I said.

Darby went silent again. "Okay, what the fuck?"

"What?"

"What's going on with you?"

"Nothing."

"You aren't even remotely excited about Get-Sexy-Friday and going to the bar, are you?"

"I am, Darby," I said exasperatedly. "It's just that picking up random guys hasn't been on my priority list, given that there are no random guys in Wakeham, so I'm a bit rusty."

"Bullshit. What's really happening?"

"Nothing is happening."

"You're a liar. Who—" She gasped suddenly. "No way. Are you?"

"Am I *what*?" I asked. "And whatever it is, no, I'm not."

"Aspen!" Her voice was giddily high. "You're fucking Theo!

"Darby!" I hissed, my face going red. "If that were the case, I'd be asking you to lower your goddamn voice because I wouldn't want it spread around everywhere!"

"Oh, don't worry," she said flippantly. "No one's here. They're all in that meeting. So tell me *everything*."

"There's nothing to tell you because I'm *not* doing... that."

I could almost hear her roll her eyes. "Please. When did it start? How is he? Is he as big as I'm imagining he is? I want all the details."

"There are no details!" I snapped. "Nothing's happened."

She fell silent, then made a low noise of understanding. "You have a dick appointment with him sometime soon and this interferes, doesn't it?"

"I can't really talk right now."

She hooted like a fucking owl on a bender. "That's totally it, isn't it?"

"I'm not confirming anything."

"Oh, I'm so sorry," she said, and she genuinely did sound apologetic. "Really, I am. If I could change the flights, I would, but I don't think Kevin will sign off on a change fee for a dick appointment."

"Work comes before I do," I muttered.

"What?"

"I said work comes first." I sighed. "Look, I have to get some stuff done so things are ready for me to be gone for a week. We'll catch up tomorrow night, okay?"

"I want details. *All* of the details."

There was no point in denying it. "I will give you *some* of the generalized information and you'll like it."

After we hung up, I put my elbows on my desk and rested my head in my hands.

All I wanted was to fuck Theo. Was that so much to ask? Was it really so much to ask that roommates stay out when they were supposed to be out? Or that business trips be scheduled around my sex life? Was this the universe somehow telling me I shouldn't have sex with Theo? If I believed in that kind of bullshit, maybe.

But I was stubborn and I wasn't about to let some kind of karmic message tell me who I could and couldn't have sex with.

"Lisa?" I called, not moving my head from my hands.

"What's up, boss?" she asked cheerily, though her tone changed when she walked into my office. "Oh, no. What's wrong?"

"Nothing's wrong." I sat up and forced a smile. "Kevin wants me to go up to head office for a week and they booked me a flight for tomorrow. I guess I'm missing Friday dinner again. But I need you to clear my schedule for next week. I'll have my laptop and phone, so I can still work if you need me for anything. Just no meetings."

"Don't worry about dinner. We'll manage to get there one of these days." She smiled. " And don't worry about anything here. I'll take care of the schedule."

"Thanks." I opened my desk drawer and grabbed my phone and purse. "I'm going to take a half day so I can pack. You're in charge. Don't burn the place down."

"No promises, but I'll try."

I smiled and set up my autoresponder and out-of-office voicemail, then grabbed my coat and slung my purse over my shoulder. As casually as I could, I walked down the hallway. The moment I was sure I was out of Lisa's hearing range, I called Theo.

"Hey," he answered, sounding surprised. "What's up?"

"I need you at my place in twenty minutes."

"Uh... what?"

"I have to go out of town tomorrow and I won't be back until next Monday." I passed by one of the managers and smiled at them before continuing. "I can't do two more weeks of this. Be at my place in twenty minutes."

I gave him the code to the main door so he could let himself in, then hung up.

# Chapter Twenty

*Theo*

EIGHTEEN MINUTES LATER, MY hand was poised to knock on Aspen's apartment door.

I'd dropped everything when she called, including my phone when I saw her name flashing on the screen. Rick had gone out for the afternoon and I was in the studio, fucking around with the song I'd been working on. The moment my phone went off, my mouth went dry and my heart started to race.

There was no way to describe the messages I'd been exchanging with Aspen. They were the best part of my day, and the worst. They sucked because they made me miss her in a way I shouldn't have missed her, especially since we hadn't *done* anything together. And they were amazing because... well. I could easily have said because she was hot as fuck and I kept getting glimpses of her tits or her ass or her pussy, but it was more than that.

It was the laughter. The inside jokes we'd developed. The silly things she'd text me and the updates about her day. Messages that were more than just two people wanting to fuck.

So when she called to tell me to be at her house because she couldn't wait any longer to see me and would be leaving town, I... well.

I needed to see her.

Before I could actually knock, the door swung open. Aspen caught my hand and tugged me inside, pressing against me to close the door behind us.

I'd seen her looking business-like and put together. I'd seen her looking casually sexy. And they might've just been pictures, but I'd also seen her half-dressed or naked from more angles than I could count.

This version of Aspen was a mix of the three. She'd already let her hair out of its bun, but unlike that night at my place, it wasn't neatly styled. Instead, it flowed wildly around her face and neck, giving her an untethered and carefree look. Based on the fitted grey skirt, I assumed she'd been wearing a blazer and probably also a blouse, but she'd shed them and was just wearing a thin strapped camisole that teased the hint of her bra beneath it. She'd taken her shoes off, leaving her legs and feet clad only in stockings.

Of all the ways I'd seen her, dressed or otherwise, this had to be my favourite. This had me wanting to turn her around, bend her over, and start *fucking* her with her skirt around her waist, her panties pulled down just enough to give me access to her pussy.

But there were other things I wanted first.

"I can't take another week of waiting and flirting and staring at pictures of your cock," she said. Her hand was still on my arm as she looked up at me. "I need it. You. Now."

My throat went dry and all I could do was nod. The corners of her mouth flicked up and she let go of my arm, taking it as permission to continue. Her hands twisted around to her back and I heard her unzip the skirt.

"Wait." I reached out and grabbed her arm. "Just wait a second."

"Wait?" she repeated, her eyes wide. "I haven't waited enough?"

I half-laughed, pulling her a bit closer to me. She held my gaze as I brushed a piece of hair off her face, then let my fingers trail down her cheek.

"You don't have to leave until tomorrow," I said. "That means I've got time to do this right."

Her tongue poked out of her mouth, wetting her lips as she looked up at me, though she didn't say anything. I kept moving my hand, tracing a pattern down her neck and across her shoulder before walking my fingertips down her arm. Once I reached her wrist, I slipped my hand between us so I could put it on her hip and guide her closer to me. Only then did she put her hands on my arms, pulling me in even more. My cock twitched as I moved my hand from her hips to her ass, finally letting my pelvis press against her.

"What does 'doing it right' mean?" she asked.

"I have been picturing this moment all week," I said, my voice low and strained. "I've been looking at your pictures again and again, reading your messages about all the things you're doing to yourself, and dreaming about doing all those things to you. And I only get three chances to prove to you why kissing is amazing—"

"I believe you're down to two."

I shook my head, grinning triumphantly. "Nice try, but I've been thinking about this. We defined kissing as from when our lips touch to when I pulled away. Since *you* pulled away, I don't think that kiss should count."

"Is that so?"

"Mm-hmm, and I'll also have you know that half the people I met with this week gave PowerPoint presentations and I think I have a good understanding of the platform now, so if needed, I can give you a twenty-minute presentation about why I'm right."

"You realize that's twenty minutes that could be spent fucking me instead of giving me a presentation?"

"Trust me, kissing you even once is well worth those twenty minutes."

She pressed her lips together, laughter behind her eyes. "Fine. I'm not wasting any more time fighting you about this. You're back up to three."

I squeezed her ass gently. "Perfect. So I have three kisses and all night to fuck you right. I hope you know I plan on getting an A+ for this."

She threw her head back and laughed again. "Theo, I'm so fucking horny that it would take a severe misstep to earn anything below an A. Like surprise anal or spitting on me or something."

Her laugh had barely faded when I leaned down, my lips trailing along her cheek towards her mouth.

"I absolutely insist on earning my grade," I whispered against her mouth, and then kissed her.

The grip on my arms tightened before she kissed me back. Then, she surprised me. Her hands moved from my biceps to my chest, then up to my shoulders and to the back of my head. She wove my hair through her fingers and let me feel the small smile on her lips before she tightened her grip.

I still wasn't entirely sure why I liked that so much, but I did. Enough that my cock went from half-hard to full in a matter of seconds as she pressed her face closer to mine.

She melted against me, just a bit, as I slipped my tongue into her mouth. I trailed it along her teeth before tasting her lips, then kissing her again before grazing my teeth against her bottom lip. There was a sudden sensation of coolness from her drawing in a sharp breath as I sucked on her bottom lip. She mirrored the action and I groaned softly as her teeth sank into my lip, but as soon as she let go, I pulled back. Her eyes opened, looking questioningly at me.

"Show me your bedroom?" I asked.

Taking my hand, she led me urgently through the apartment to the room. The shades were drawn and her bed was neatly made. I tried not to laugh when I spotted her nightstand, where she'd made sure we had everything we would need. A box of condoms sat prominently in the middle, along with some tissues, lube, and a couple of bottles of water.

"Here it is," she said, then folded her arms as I looked around. "How long are you going to make me wait, Theo?"

I turned back to her, grinning. "I'll make you wait just as long as you need to."

"Hmm. Someone seems to be forgetting who was just amiable enough to oblige his negotiations for additional kissing sessions." She took a step towards me, her hips swaying enticingly. "It sure would be a shame if I changed my mind about that."

"It sure would," I agreed, then took her back into my arms. "Luckily, you won't have to. Two kisses left, for those keeping score."

She laughed and I moved my mouth to her neck, kissing and licking her skin. Her laughter changed to a small noise of delight as I nipped her neck, then pressed a kiss against her throat. I ran my hands down her back to the waistband of her skirt, where the zipper was not quite halfway undone. Pulling it the rest of the way, I guided the skirt down her hips and let it drop unceremoniously to the floor. Then, while moving my mouth's attention from her neck to her collarbone, I lifted the camisole over her head and let that drop beside the skirt.

Despite her threat to renegotiate how many kisses we had left, I had to make her wait again, though this time it was because I couldn't help it.

After all, I'd seen pictures of her in various stages of undress, but never in person. Never where I could reach out and run my hands along her smooth skin or cup her ass or push my face against her breasts.

I needed to *see* her.

And it was worth it. The view was astounding. Aspen's bra was plain, just an everyday kind of bra, but the way she stood made it seem like it was the kind of thing that would walk down a runway. Cotton panties hugged her hips, curving forward to make a triangle that pointed to the delicious center between her legs. Her stockings ended at her thighs and were the only one of her underthings that were embellished: tiny bows adorned the bands at the top, a distinctly feminine touch that fit her look so, so well.

I indulged in the sight of her, drinking her in until she folded her arms and raised her eyebrows at me. I licked my lips and swallowed, shaking my head slowly.

"Where to start?" I murmured.

She opened her mouth to respond, not realizing it was very much a rhetorical question. I interrupted whatever she was about to say by placing a kiss between her breasts and making her words turn to a soft, giggling sigh. Kissing along the cups of her bra, I nuzzled against her, then glanced up before falling to my knees in front of her. I kissed her stomach, tracing my tongue around her belly button and feeling the way she shivered beneath my touch before moving my mouth towards the waistband of her panties.

I stopped there, pressing my lips to the fabric of her panties as I ran my hands up her legs from ankle to thigh. Unhurriedly, I peeled one stocking off, then kissed the spot the band had rested on her thigh while I repeated the action on her other leg.

Once her stockings were off, my hands moved to her hips. I squeezed gently before guiding her towards my face. As I pressed my lips to the cotton triangle covering her mound, her breath quickened, a soft noise reaching my ears and making me fight back a smile. I could smell her arousal through the fabric and placed another kiss lower, and lower again, and again until I felt the wetness I knew was waiting for me. Holding firmly on her hips, I buried my face against her slit, nuzzling her pussy, inhaling all I could.

"*Fuck*," she said, her voice throaty.

Moments later, her hands were pressed to my head, fingers winding through my hair again. My cock twitched as her fingernails raked against my scalp and I groaned, then hooked my fingers into the waistband of her panties. A soft noise of approval urged me on, and I moved my face away from her just enough to reveal her pussy. The moment her panties were out of the way, I leaned in, bringing my lips so close that I could almost taste her.

Not quite, but almost.

I kissed the top of her mound instead, pulling her panties the rest of the way down lazily. She made another noise, then a frustrated one of longing as I kissed just above her clit.

"Something wrong?" I asked, my voice muffled by her pussy.

"Stop. Teasing. Me." Each word came through clenched teeth. "Goddamnit, Theo. *Please*."

I grinned, then used one hand to spread her pussy lips so I could immediately start licking her clit. Despite her pleading, she seemed surprised that I went straight for it and gasped, then let out a satisfied sigh as I sucked on her clit. She pressed my head hard against her and I slipped my other hand around her hips and grabbed that perfect ass, steadying her as she pushed her pussy against my face.

There was nothing like listening to a woman moan, of course, and the noises Aspen made were enough to make my cock throb needily, but her hands spoke more about what she needed from my mouth than anything. She guided me with her fingers, encouraging me as she loosened or tightened her grip. I alternated licking and sucking, twirling my tongue around the swollen nub, and experimented with slipping a finger inside the dripping entrance just below. Given the response—gasping, and a hard grinding of her pussy against my face as her fists tightened in my hair—I assumed it was positive and eased my finger in and out as I used my mouth to worship her clit.

Since she seemed to like that so much, I decided to experiment a little more. She'd indicated more than once that she was open to having her ass played with, so I slowly let the fingers of my other hand explore her crack, lower and lower until I could feel her tight hole beneath the tip of my finger. Glancing up, my eyes met hers, and I raised my eyebrows to ask if I should continue.

"Yes," she breathed. "God, yes."

Trying not to grin so I could keep my full attention on her clit, I collected some of the wetness from her pussy before moving my finger back to her asshole. Still staring into her eyes, I pressed it forward, carefully pushing it past the tight ring of muscle. Her breathing came faster, her breasts shifting as she watched me, and I barely had the tip of my finger inside her ass when her knees buckled and she tugged on my hair *hard*. Grinning, I took my mouth off her pussy.

"I was just getting started, and you can't stand?" I asked innocently.

"Jesus, Theo," she said. "You're like a completely different person right now."

A surge of insecurity washed over me. "Is that bad?"

She shook her head. "I like this. I like both sides of you."

The insecurity faded and my stomach fluttered as I looked at her. I couldn't bring myself to say it, not right then, but I fucking liked her too.

A lot.

Instead, I stood and motioned for her to go to the bed. "Get on your hands and knees."

She looked amused. "And if I don't want to?"

I looked at her as solemnly as I could. "I've been dreaming about this since the first photo you sent me of your ass. I think you're going to want to."

She smirked but took the position I requested on the bed. I couldn't help but stare at her perfect, round ass in the air, her legs spread just enough to see her dripping pussy.

Fuck, she was gorgeous.

She was slightly twisted, trying to look over her shoulder as I stepped forward. In hindsight, I think she expected me to grab a condom and unbuckle my belt so I could fuck the hell out of her. And I wanted to; my boxers had to be a mess from all the pre-cum leaking into them and my cock was throbbing hard, but I was having way too much fun indulging in Aspen's body.

Instead, I placed a hand on each of her cheeks and spread them, admiring her perfect ass before dipping my head down and licking her soaked pussy a few times. She moaned softly, then gasped as I moved my mouth up to her ass.

"Oh my G—*oh.*"

Her legs trembled. Whether it was from the two fingers I pushed inside her pussy or the fact that I started licking her asshole at the same time, I didn't know, but it didn't matter. Her reaction was more than I could have hoped for as the stunned *"oh"* turned to a wailing cry, followed by a steady stream of words:

"Oh fuck. Oh, Jesus, oh fuck, oh *fuck, Theo!*"

I ate her ass enthusiastically, fingering her pussy all the while. Her face was pushed against the bed and she was grinding back against me, her perfect ass in my face as I fingered her and licked her. Sooner than I had anticipated, her stream of words changed and I felt her pussy clenching around my fingers.

"Fuck. *Fuck*, Theo, I'm... oh *fuck* I'm gonna—"

Her pussy tightened impossibly around my fingers as she screeched. I kept licking, enjoying every second of her orgasm until she began to come down from it. Her hips fell forward and I grabbed them, guiding her onto her stomach as she gasped for breath. Grinning, I planted a kiss on her ass cheek and nipped it playfully before standing up.

"I'm going to wash up quick," I said.

A quiet groan was her only response.

I still had plenty of places I wanted to lick and suck and finger, and I didn't want to cause any kind of discomfort for Aspen. Sometimes sex has parts that are decidedly unsexy, but every second of eating out her beautiful ass was worth it. When I returned, she had rolled onto her back and removed her bra.

"Okay, you did good," she said, still semi-breathless.

"I'm not done with you yet."

"I know. It's my turn to be in charge." She sat up and motioned towards me. "Clothes. Take them off. Now."

"Yes, ma'am," I murmured.

I stripped quickly, leaving my clothes on the floor, then stood at the foot of her bed to wait for my next instruction. Her eyes travelled up and down my body, then she slowly shook her head.

"Damn, Theo," she said. "You need to get better with that camera. Those pictures don't do any of this justice."

I blushed but smiled.

She twisted her legs under her to kneel and patted the bed beside her. "Come sit here."

I crawled onto the bed next to her. "Can I kiss you again first?"

We were both kneeling, and she glanced up at me. Instead of responding, she put a finger under my chin and drew my face to hers. I closed my eyes as she took control, pressing her lips against mine, exploring my mouth with her tongue. She balanced her other hand on my thigh, tantalizingly close to my cock. As I reached up to cup her face to deepen the kiss, she let go of my chin and pulled back.

"That counts as one," she whispered.

I could only nod as she gripped my hand that was in mid-air and brought it to her breast. A groan escaped my lips as I finally got to cup her beautiful tits. I kneaded her gently, feeling her hard nipple against the palm of my hand, watching the way her breast overflowed my grip. As I fondled her, she moved her hand off my thigh and reached for my cock. I shuddered as she wrapped her fingers around me, her motion slow and deliberate, letting me feel each finger gripping me.

"Finally," she said. "I've been waiting for this."

She started stroking me lightly, just enough to provide the slightest bit of relief to my swollen cock. I kept playing with her tits, but as she increased her speed and intensity, my hands seemed to stop working. I felt my eyes close as I relaxed into the pure bliss of her touch, only opening them again when I felt her pulling away from me a bit.

"Lie down," she commanded, releasing her grip on my cock.

I did as she said, leaning back against her pillows. She crawled forward, positioning herself between my legs, and regained her hold on me. Leaning forward, she took the tip in her mouth in one quick movement.

"Fuck," I gasped.

I felt the vibration as she giggled. She sucked the tip of my cock, twirling her tongue around it, licking the pre-cum off me and exploring the ridges as her hand increased speed. I looked down at her, watching the movement of her head as she sucked me off. She began taking more in her mouth, little by little, going deeper each time she bobbed her head. Finally, my entire cock was in her mouth, and I could feel myself pressing against the back of her throat.

I couldn't help groaning. I couldn't help winding my fingers in her hair. I couldn't help thrusting forward just the smallest bit. She made a soft gagging noise and readjusted, then began to deep throat me. With each movement, I hit the back of her throat, and that, along with the wet sounds she made as she sucked, was more than I could handle.

"Aspen," I breathed. "Aspen, stop."

She looked up at me, eyes wide as she released my cock from her mouth with a soft pop. "What's wrong?"

"Not wrong," I panted. "Too good. I'm not done with you yet. As much as I want to come in your mouth, I need to fuck you."

Aspen's face wasn't always easy to read, but in that moment, I felt like I surprised her.

"You're damn right," she said. "I believe there was talk of making sure I couldn't walk straight the next day?"

I reached for her, guiding her onto my lap so I could take a few minutes to cool down. She placed a leg on either side of me and I wrapped my arms around her waist, holding her body against me. I don't think I was the one who initiated that kiss, but it didn't matter. She had her arms on my shoulders, wrapped around my neck, and for a moment, we just kissed, breathing in one another, touching each other. Her hands moved up and down my arms, and I explored her hips and back, spending more time grabbing that amazing ass of hers. Soon, she started grinding against me, and I could feel the wetness of her pussy against my stomach. Reaching down, I slid a hand between our bodies and pushed it between her legs.

She pulled back from the kiss and tilted her head back. I took in the sight before me: her elongated neck, her hair tossed over one shoulder, the heaving of her chest as she panted. Dipping my head, I took her breast in my mouth, sucking on her nipple and running my tongue back and forth over it.

"Oh yes," she moaned. "Yes, just like that."

Her hip gyrations increased in speed as she ground her clit against my fingers, using my hand to get herself off. I obliged, taking every moment of pleasure I could out of sucking those gorgeous breasts. Before long, she came again, not quite so hard as the first time but enough that she dug her fingernails into my shoulder. As she came down, I took my hand back and pulled my mouth away from her breasts, then kissed her.

"That's four," she mumbled against my mouth, but even as I pulled back, she kissed me harder. "Not that anyone's counting."

I smiled against her mouth, then groaned as she nipped my lip again.

We kept kissing until she'd caught her breath and was squirming delightfully against me, my cock nestled against her ass. Between kisses, I asked her how she liked to be fucked.

"Any way. Just pick quickly."

I knew exactly how I wanted her. Wrapping an arm around her waist, I steadied her, then rolled so we switched positions. She squealed with delight, laughing madly as she ended up on her back.

"Where did you learn to do *that*?" she giggled.

My face burned, but I laughed. "I'll tell you after I fuck you."

Aspen watched as I reached for the condoms on her nightstand. Her hand was between her legs, touching herself as I unrolled one before moving between her legs.

"You just want me like this?" she asked.

"I want to watch you," I said, gripping my cock in one hand and positioning it at her entrance. "Is that okay?"

"God, yes."

I didn't say anything more, just pushed forward and entered her waiting pussy. We groaned in unison as I slowly pushed forward, feeling her tight walls around me. I stopped halfway in and pulled back before pushing forward again, this time as deep as I could go. My hips met hers, skin pressed against skin, and a contented noise left my lips as the long wait to bury myself inside her was finally over.

Her head was tilted back and eyes were closed. Carefully, I touched her face.

"You okay?" I asked.

"Almost," she breathed back. "I need you to start fucking me now."

And I was more than happy to oblige.

There was no way to describe sex with Aspen except fucking amazing. The sounds she made, the feel of her around me, the look in her eyes as she urged me on—it was all fucking *amazing*. She wrapped her legs around my waist, urging me deeper, forcing me to submit to my need to fuck her harder.

When she came again, she gripped the sheets of her bed, fists full of fabric as her back arched and pussy clenched around my cock. She cried out, spasming beneath me, and I couldn't hold back. I pounded her hard, giving into the instinctual need to just *fuck* her until I came, just on the tail end of her orgasm. My body tensed and my mind went blank, relief and release washing over me again and again as I finished.

Panting, I looked down at Aspen. Her eyes were closed and small shivers ran through her body.

"You okay?" I asked.

She opened her eyes and looked up at me, her face full of relief and satisfaction and...

And something else.

Something good.

"Theo," she whispered, and I fucking *fell* for her breathless little smile.

# Chapter Twenty-One

## *Aspen*

WHO IN THE FUCK did Theo Barker think he was?

I mean, shit.

*Shit.*

My nerves were confused. Little twitches ran from the tips of my toes to my pussy, along my arms and down my hips and through my arms. I felt like the end of a cut wire, my body buzzing, small zaps of electric thrills jolting through my limbs.

I loved sex.

I had a lot of sex.

I owned my hoe-esque image. I wore it like a badge of pride. The Toronto Maple Leafs would win the Stanley Cup on an ice rink in hell before I felt an iota of shame for indulging in the pleasure my body was capable of.

I liked fucking and being fucked. I knew what I liked, what I didn't like, which positions would make my body shake and my toes curl. I had fucked in bedrooms, hotel rooms, the occasional bathroom—so long as it was reasonably clean—the backseat of cars, beaches, workplaces—never my own, mostly because I'd never had a permanent desk—and one time, had given a covert hand job and in return received the most furiously furtive fingering of my *life* in a semi-private-but-still-riskily-visible cabana at the water park at West Edmonton Mall. I'd had a lot of different partners. And a lot of those partners had tried a lot of different things.

And none of them—not a single fucking one of those people—made me react the way he did.

Who the fuck even *was* Theo Barker?

The audacity. The sheer fucking *audacity* to make me come like that. After all that time thinking he was some insecure cinnamon roll of a man. How dare he take my breath away like that? The very nerve of him, to make my mind go blank and my vision cloudy when I was supposed to be sharp and aware and in control. And then to lie there, those warm brown eyes studying me, a half-smile on lips swollen from kissing every inch of me and then some? Like he didn't even *realize* how he'd shaken me?

The more that I thought about it, the more it made sense. Theo was unreasonably selfless; he didn't give himself enough credit for that, likely because he didn't even notice it. I mean, the first night we'd met, he offered to drive me home. Me, a woman he didn't really know and who had opened a wound she didn't know he had.

He put other people's needs ahead of his own, which was a strange quality for someone who was a literal rock star, but it was what set him apart. Theo was genuine. He was real. And that was likely a big part of his success. He wasn't just about the fame or the fortune; somehow, he'd maintained that firm sense of self through a journey that usually stripped that away from people. He was different and open and relatable. It was why people liked him.

It was part of why I liked him, certainly. Though, a big part of me liked him because his mouth was fucking delightful and he knew how to use his dick *damn* well. But even so, that stemmed from his selflessness. His pleasure had been dependent on mine, his focus on it almost obsessive until he finally gave in. Like the request for me to stop sucking his cock, even though he'd already given me one amazing orgasm.

No, that wasn't enough for Theo. He'd needed to give me two more after that before he took his turn.

And then there was the kissing.

Fuck, the kissing.

I'd thought I would never enjoy kissing again. In fact, I'd been *determined* to never enjoy kissing again. But Theo... It was *aggravating* how good kissing him felt. How his lips dissolved any tension or worries I had. How he was passionate, deliberate in his movements, his mouth intoxicating no matter where on my body he placed it.

The *audacity*.

I loved that he had it.

And I hated—fucking *hated*—that I felt that way.

I was drawn out of my thoughts by the bed shifting beneath me as Theo recovered enough to move. Turning my head, I watched idly as he cleaned himself up, grabbing a few tissues off the nightstand. There was a light sheen to his skin, just a hint of sweat, and his already scruffy hair was sticking out in a wildly charming way.

Fuck.

He got up to discard the condom, then looked at my nightstand with the fake casualness of someone who was trying to cover the fact that he didn't know what to say. I suppose I could have been nice and said something first, but watching a delightfully naked Theo wrestle with his awkwardness was more fun.

"Good book?" he asked, picking up the novel that was on the bedside table.

"Not terrible," I replied. "I prefer the ones where they don't take three pages to describe the love interest's monster cock. It just sounds painful."

He looked up, eyes wide.

"Actually, I finished with it yesterday," I continued. "Would you mind bringing it back to Lisa tomorrow night? You can tell her that she's crazy and the scene with the two firefighters was nowhere near as hot as the pilot and the lawyer one. I just don't see how fucking on a Ferris wheel is a turn on."

He seemed to realize I was joking and smiled as I patted the bed beside me.

"You don't think she'd wonder why I ended up with her romance novel?" he asked.

I shrugged. "Tell her you ran into me at the grocery store or something."

He made a non-committal noise as he leaned against the pillow resting on my headboard.

"So where'd you learn the porn-star flip move?"

He groaned. "Damn. I'd hoped you would forget."

"Not a chance. That was one of those things I'm committing to memory for those lonely nights with my vibrator."

He chuckled and ran a hand through his hair. "Well, if that's the case, you definitely don't want to know."

"Refusing to tell me is just making me want to know more."

"You sure?" he asked. "Once I tell you, you can't un-learn it."

I grinned up at him. *"Tell* me."

Resigned, he sighed. "Okay, so you know, like... wrestling?"

"Yes."

"That."

I rolled my eyes. "That *what*?"

"I learned it from wrestling."

"... and?"

His face was turning red. "And what?"

"Come on, Theo." I propped myself up on my elbow. "You can't honestly be embarrassed about wrestling when you were growing up. Were you on, like, a wrestling team or something?"

He opened his mouth but didn't speak. After a moment, he grimaced. "No, but that's one hundred percent what I should have said. I meant like, watching wrestling. Like—"

"Like WWE?" I asked incredulously.

His face was *so* red. "Mm-hmm."

"Well that's still... impressive," I said, trying not to giggle. "I mean, you learned it just from watching TV and—"

"Oh, no. Nope." He shook his head slowly. "I should let you think that, but I've admitted this much already, so nope. James and Rick and I all used to watch wrestling together and James, being older, convinced me and Rick that it was how you could escape from a bear if you ever got attacked and that they used to teach kids how to do it in school. Kinda like how they teach you stop-drop-and-roll. But he said they'd had to stop because it was *so* effective that the bears kept getting hurt and they didn't want them to become endangered so now people just had to let the bears attack them."

I stared at him. He couldn't quite bring himself to look at me.

"And I mean, we believed him, but Rick and I were like... well, endangered or not, we don't want to get eaten by a bear." He sighed heavily. "So, we decided we'd watch that wrestling match over and over and learn how to do it. And, uh, a move like that... you gotta... you know. Practice it."

I pressed my lips together, trying not to laugh. "Of course."

Theo looked up sheepishly. "Anyway, Rick was sure I couldn't manage it since he was so much taller than me, but I fucking nailed it, so he was kinda embarrassed when it was his turn. So he... well. When Stella—Rick's mom—walked into his room to see him sitting on top of me after hearing a huge bang, she was like... maybe sixty percent sure I had a concussion and probably about ninety-eight percent sure we were lying when we said we were practicing to fight bears. I think for a while she thought Rick and I were like... you know, trying to hook up or something, but—"

"Wait, hook up?" I asked. "How old were you?"

He cringed *hard*. "Uh... fourteen."

I tried very, very hard not to laugh. I really did. But picturing a fourteen-year-old Theo dazed on the ground after being convinced that this was how a person fought bears—at *fourteen*—was more than I could handle. My face hurt from laughing so hard and I tried to gasp an apology for laughing at him.

Theo, luckily, was chuckling along with me. His face was still red, but he seemed to understand that my laughter wasn't *at* him. At least, not maliciously. I suppose it made sense; in order to trust me enough to tell me the story in the first place, he would have had to be very comfortable with our friendship. And I knew he was. He'd sent me dick pics, after all. But it was still a relief to know he wasn't taking my uncontrollable giggles as an insult.

"I know," he said as I caught my breath. "Just when you thought the lisping loser kid couldn't get *any* cooler..."

"I mean, yes and no." I wiped a hand across my cheek. "You learning how to do it from entertainment wrestling so you'd be able to fight a bear may not be the *sexiest* backstory, but using it? Definitely sexy."

He chuckled and ran a hand through his hair. "I guess that makes it worth it."

"Absolutely."

"Alright. Enough about my WWE obsession. I have a real question now." He looked at me expectantly and I raised my eyebrows. "What's my final grade?"

I burst out laughing, shaking my head. "Really?"

"How else will I know if I'm a certified freak in the sheets?"

"Hmm," I said, tapping a finger against my lip. "Well, even after considering docking points for that absolutely *awful* joke—"

A bright smile spread across his face as he laughed.

"—I have to admit your performance was... exceptional." I licked my lips as I looked up at him. "It was an A+ for sure. Congratulations, certified freak."

He let out a victory cry and pumped a fist in the air and I grinned at his show of celebration.

"Wow, what an honour," he said, his voice taking on a low, rumbling sound that made more of those little electrical thrills buzz through my body. "I'd like to thank the Academy and everyone who made this possible, even though it's kind of weird to be thanking my brother and Rick for their role in it." He smirked as I lost it again. "And I promise I won't let it go to my head too much."

I shrugged. "Or do. I mean, you probably deserve to let it go to your head at least a little. I don't think..."

"What?"

"I don't think I've ever come like that before. I didn't even... I liked kissing you, even."

I don't know why I admitted it. Almost as soon as the words came out of my mouth, I felt my skin crawl and my face turn red.

"You're not just saying that?" Theo asked, almost innocently.

"You know I don't say shit I don't mean."

"Yeah, but..." He trailed off.

I frowned. "But what?"

He shook his head, then looked back up at me with a shy sort of smile on his face. "Just glad you enjoyed. I mean like, I obviously enjoyed it, but I didn't want to disappoint you after how awesome this whole..." He motioned between the two of us. "...you know, *thing* has been."

"Why would you think I'd be disappointed?"

He shrugged. "It seems to be a common thread with some of my exes."

"You don't seem like the type to take criticism from people who don't know their head from their ass."

He laughed, shocked.

"I'm serious." I sat up slightly. "Your last girlfriend was with you for your money. I don't know about your other exes, but you can't take their complaints at their words when they weren't with you for the right reasons." I hesitated, then bit my lip before I continued. "You don't think highly of yourself, but you should, Theo."

He looked up at me. "You think so?"

"Considering how many times I just came, yes."

He chuckled, glancing back down. "Good point, I guess. I don't think I've ever been with someone who likes sex as much as you do."

"When you're with someone who wants the same things you do, it's not hard to do well," I said. "Look, I'm the *least* qualified person to say this, but even I know that if you're killing yourself trying to make something work, it's not worth it."

He nodded, pulling his lower lip between his teeth thoughtfully. "That's a good point. It should be... easy. Natural."

"Exactly," I said, stretching as I leaned back against my pillow. "Someone you can just be yourself around and have fun with."

"Right," he said softly. "That's... I've been missing that."

I smiled at him. "She's out there."

A heavy beat went by before he looked at me.

"What?" he said.

"The right person," I said. "She's out there. You just haven't met her yet."

"I... haven't."

"You will." I stretched again. "You're going to find the perfect girl and treat her just like you treated me and she'll never want to leave. Just be patient. There's some amazing woman out there who wants to be with you."

When he didn't respond, I glanced over to see him staring at me, an unreadable expression on his face. A strange sensation prickled up my spine, something that had nothing to do with the way my nerves were still sparking inside of me.

Fuck.

"So this—" he started.

"I mean, you obviously know I'm not that girl." I laughed, trying to break the tension. "I mean, you're hot and all, but there's no way I could be with you."

His throat flexed as he swallowed. "Yeah, no. You're... right."

*Fuck.*

"Not because of *you*. Because... because that's what we agreed to, Theo," I said. "We went into this knowing it couldn't be anything serious."

"Right, yeah." He nodded slowly. "So this was just, what, like a precursor to finding some guy to fuck on your business trip, then?"

Those words did something to me. I didn't know why. There was no reason for me to feel that surge of guilt or the coil of shame in my stomach. Theo and I were friends; nothing more. *Nothing* more. There was absolutely no *fucking* reason for the instinct to apologize and claim I'd misspoke to flare up inside me.

Emotionally, I recoiled as if I'd been stung. Physically, I stayed still as that default look of total composure built itself up on my face.

"Excuse me?" I asked.

"Since whatever this is isn't serious? That's what you mean, right? You want to fuck other people."

"We're not—"

"Just say it, Aspen." He sat back, looking at me with angry hurt in his eyes. "It's just sex, right? Nothing more than that. Any other guy could be sitting here with you right now and you would've had the same experience we just had, right? So why wouldn't you find someone else to fuck while you're out of town?"

Burning anger crawled up my chest and neck as my heart began to race. "Not that it's *any* of your fucking business, since you don't get to tell me what I can and can't do—"

"That's not what I was—"

"Don't interrupt me," I snapped. "It's none of your business, but no, okay? I wasn't planning on fucking anyone on my trip, even though I haven't gotten laid in months. Even though this—" I motioned between us "—was all we ever agreed on, turns out I kind of like you. That's why I wanted *you* to come over before I left."

"Okay, so you're enjoying whatever *this*—" He mirrored my motion almost sarcastically "—is, and you *kind of* like me, but not enough that you couldn't stop yourself from saying that you didn't want to be with me. As we're lying in bed. After having sex. Like that's what anyone ever wants to hear, even if you said it was just a casual thing."

I took a deep breath, willing myself to calm down as that practiced look of professional poise stayed on my face.

"Okay, that is... not what I meant, but I can see how it may have sounded like that," I said carefully. "I apologize. That wasn't my intention. But the fact remains that you also knew this was a casual thing."

"You said that this was awesome," he said. "That you never came like that before. That you liked kiss—"

"It was just sex," I interrupted, my face burning again.

"You sure? Because I didn't think it was just sex."

My wall broke.

Not the emotional wall. Not the one that would make me reveal my deepest, darkest secrets to Theo and fall into his arms, sobbing like some kind of fucking stereotype. No, it was my professional wall, the composed one, that came down like a tragic, massive explosion caused by a wrecking ball that was intended for an abandoned building and smashed into a children's hospital instead. Whatever self-control I had vanished, scattering as fear and anger and panic burst in my chest.

"You were mistaken!" I snapped. "You were *very* mistaken. This was only ever about sex."

"But—"

"But nothing!" My voice was shrill. "There is no 'but' here, Theo. It was about sex."

"To you."

"You *agreed* it was—"

"Things changed!" he said. "The fucking—Jesus, Aspen, we've been texting and sending shit to each other and just, this whole time, we've been—"

"We've been nothing!" I was moving back on the bed, subconsciously separating myself from him. "We've been friends and we've fucked. That's *it*."

"So us being friends didn't make it different?" he asked pointedly. "It's been like this with all those other guys you've fucked?"

I stared at him, my mouth half-open. "Are you calling me a slut?"

"No, I—"

"Just fucking say it, if you are."

His face flushed. "I'm *not*. I'm just not understanding how you can say something like this—" Another one of those gestures between us "—is just fucking. Like us being friends doesn't stop this from being on the same level as a one-night stand?"

"That's—no, it's not the same, you're right, but it's... Just because we're friends doesn't—" I stopped, trying to collect my thoughts. "I'm not just going to suddenly decide I'm madly in love with you because you're good in bed, Theo."

"You're right. It's fine." He sat up and turned away from me. "Don't worry about it. I'm not good enough for you and you got what you needed out of this. I'm used to people using me, Aspen. You know that."

"*Using* you?"

He laughed, not the warm, bright laugh I was used to but something cold. Something almost demeaning. "It had nothing to do with me, right? It's all about you getting some dick and it doesn't matter whose it is. I ended up being that dick because there no other guys for you to fuck in this town. It had nothing to do with us being friends, did it?"

The words stung.

It had never been about a relationship. He knew that. I knew that. We'd fucking discussed it. But he was right: we were also friends. It wasn't *just* sex. I felt comfortable and safe enough to relax around him—or I had, anyway, before he opened his fucking mouth and ruined it. I didn't want it to have to be one or the other: either me using him for sex, or a full relationship.

And I'd been under the impression that he was okay with that, given that's what we *agreed* to.

Relationships terrified me. I had my reasons and I had no desire to share those reasons with Theo, not at that moment. And I shouldn't have *had* to share those reasons. Not after we'd communicated about it. I didn't know when or why he'd decided he wanted something more than what we'd talked about.

But I wasn't about to fucking put up with it.

Getting out of bed, I stormed across the room to my dresser and wrenched the top drawer open. "You need to leave."

"What?"

I took an oversized T-shirt out of the drawer. "Leave. Now."

His disbelief was palpable. "You're kicking me out?"

"Yes."

I tugged my T-shirt over my head, then spotted his hoodie on the floor. Picking it up, I tossed it at him. He caught it, his mouth half-open as he sat at the edge of my bed. Angrily, I turned back to my dresser and dug out a pair of panties.

"This was a lot of fun," I said as I put them on. "I don't know about you, but I had a great time, mostly. Your tongue? Excellent. Your dick? Even better. But you?" I walked over to his jeans and kicked them in his general direction. "You're trying to make this something it's not. Something we never agreed to. And I do not have the time to deal with your dramatics."

"Dramatic? I'm not—"

"Are you for real?" I asked. "Jesus, Theo. At least own it. Like I get it, you're insecure about a lot, but oh my God. You think people are always using you when you're the one changing the parameters of the situation without saying anything and then getting all mopey about it. That's fucking *dramatic*."

"You don't even know what kind of stuff I put up with."

"How often have you been used for sex?"

He looked taken aback. "I—"

"Never? Once? Enough times that you're used to people using you for it? Or are you just claiming I'm doing that so you can find something to be upset about because you're pissed I don't want a relationship?"

"I fucking *told* you about Sheri and—"

"Yeah, and I'm sorry your ex was shitty, but for fuck's sake, Theo!" I snapped. "You know what? You're a good guy. You're fucking hot, even though you don't think so for some reason. You're great in bed. Like, this slut gave you an A+ and—"

"Don't say you're a slut," he said heatedly. "I *didn't* say that."

"Yeah, well, I did." I slammed my dresser drawer shut. "If you think it's something I should be ashamed about, that's your fucking problem. And you know what else your fucking problem is? Somehow you still have it in your head that you're a pre-pubescent loser with a lisp that people couldn't possibly want to be around other than because—what? Because you have money?"

His face went red. "It's not like it's that unheard of. I mean, it literally just happened to me."

"And you think I'm that kind of person?"

"No, I—"

My hands were shaking so much I balled them into fists. "Are you sure? Because you apparently think I'm using you for... what? For sex? Like we agreed to? Because I don't need your fucking money. I don't need your career or your connections or any of that shit. I don't *need* you to be my friend. I *wanted* that, but this—" I cut myself off, shaking my head. "So you got bullied growing up. So people were mean to you. Get over it, Theo. You're a fucking adult now, a goddamn successful one at that, so fix your shit and get the *fuck* over it."

I stormed across the room towards my bathroom, stopping suddenly to turn and look at him. He was still sitting on the bed, looking shocked, holding the hoodie I'd thrown at him.

"Until you start thinking better of yourself, people are always going to take advantage of you because that's what you'll expect of everyone. You didn't even give me a chance. We have sex one time—one time!—and somehow, in your mind, me sticking to the parameters *we agreed on* is me *using* you for sex. Like I can't possibly also like you as a person if I'm not willing to instantly fall in love with you. If you think that's being taken advantage of, no wonder you're so fucking *miserable*."

I slammed the bathroom door behind me. My hands shook as I reached for the sink, turning the water on full-blast and shoving them beneath the ice-cold stream. The shock of cold was meant to calm me, to jolt me out of that heightened state of anger and frustration and pain, but I was so wound up that it didn't. Heart racing, I cupped my hands, filling them with water and splashing it onto my face.

That didn't help either. Now I was just wet, and not in the fun, sexy way. Seething, I grabbed a towel and mopped the water off my face, opening my mouth and screaming silently into the cloth. I shoved the fabric against my lips hard, but even harder against my eyes as they threatened to water.

I did not cry.

I would *not* let myself cry.

Once I was certain my eyes would stay dry, I carefully pulled the towel away from my face and turned the tap off. On the other side of the door, I heard Theo moving around my room. My heart still racing and hands still shaking, I sat on the edge of my bathtub and glared at the door as shadows played behind it, light flashing and fading from the crack beneath the door as he dressed, communicating his actions in a nonsensical version of Morse code. Staring, I watched as the shadows crossed in front of the door, pausing as if in contemplation.

I knew he was on the other side. Why, I didn't know.

I didn't want an apology.

I didn't want to talk to him.

I didn't want to see him ever again.

The moment stretched on and I stared hard at the blockage of light that represented Theo's feet, refusing to even blink as I wished for him to leave.

As if he heard my thoughts, he walked away. It was only when I heard the door of my apartment close that I let out an angry cry and kicked the side of the tub.

# Chapter Twenty-Two

*Theo*

CHOOSING WHERE TO SIT at a bar was a problem.

I wanted to sit on one of the stools at the far end of the bar. It was a clear signal I was here alone and, more importantly, that I had no desire to change that. But sitting at the bar meant that every single person would walk past me to get a drink. Even though I had traded my contacts for thick-rimmed glasses—Rick had been nagging me to get laser eye surgery for years but I just couldn't stomach the thought of lasers cutting up my eyes—and covered my hair with a Vancouver Canucks hat—worn in the hopes that people wouldn't look closely at the face beneath the cap because they were too busy being disgusted that someone would wear a Canucks hat in northern Ontario—it was too likely I'd be recognized.

Instead, I tucked myself into a booth, the high-back bench enough to shield me from most angles. The problem was that a mostly empty booth invited people to approach and try to sit with me, which I was *not* in the mood for. My solution for that was to open the book Aspen had asked me to return to Lisa and that I'd impulsively grabbed as I was leaving the house and prop it in front of me as if I was reading.

The problem with *that* was Aspen hadn't been lying about the content. I'd hurriedly flipped past what, at a glance, seemed to be a gang bang in the back of a firetruck to something slightly more innocuous. Thankful that the cover didn't scream "dirty romance novel" like some of the books I knew she and Lisa read, I let my eyes glaze over as I pretended to be engrossed in the story.

I don't know why I'd grabbed the book as I was leaving. I shouldn't have, but I wasn't thinking. It had been sitting on the table in my front entranceway, discarded there after I returned from Aspen's on Thursday.

I'd skipped out on Friday night dinner because that would have required leaving my studio, where I'd spent pretty much all my time since our blowup. Rick rarely bothered me there, but when he realized I'd missed every meal on Friday and then didn't go to James and Lisa's for dinner, he'd barged in on Saturday morning.

"What's going on?"

"Nothing," I muttered. "Working."

"Theo—"

"Get out, Rick."

"You need to eat."

"Get *out*, Rick."

He'd left reluctantly but returned Saturday afternoon, only to wrinkle his nose and leave again. A few minutes later, he returned with a candle.

"How can you sit in here? It's starting to stink," he said as he lit it.

"Get out and you won't have to smell anything."

"Theo—"

But I'd started strumming my guitar, drowning out whatever it was he was trying to say.

On Sunday morning, he brought in a coffee that I didn't touch and a plate of food. I ate half a slice of toast and ignored the rest of it.

"Tell me what's going on," he demanded when he returned to a plate of cold and congealed scrambled eggs sitting next to three empty beer bottles.

"Nothing. I'm working."

He tried again that afternoon. "Theo, you're worrying me."

"Stop worrying. Everything's fine."

"What the *fuck*?" he asked Monday morning when he came in.

I startled, lifting my head off the desk I'd apparently passed out on. "What?"

Rick's mouth was open as he glanced around the studio. "Theo, this is—"

"Fuck off," I muttered blearily.

"How fucking much did you *drink* last night?" He picked up a not-quite-empty bottle of vodka that was missing its cap. "Is this the one we just bought?"

"No," I said.

"You drank almost the whole goddamn bottle in one night, Theo. What the fuck is going on?"

"I didn't drink the whole bottle."

He clenched his jaw, then tucked the vodka in the crook of his elbow and silently picked up the empty beer bottles from around the room.

"Leave them," I muttered. "I'll get them later."

He didn't respond, just continued collecting the bottles.

"Just fucking *leave* them, Rick!"

He sighed. "You're not leaving me much of a choice here."

I didn't know what he meant until a little while later, when my phone went off with a call from James. Annoyed, I clenched my jaw and ignored it. But an hour after that, when it rang and I saw my mom's name flash on the screen, I'd had enough.

After calling her back—I wasn't a *complete* taint, after all—and assuring her nothing was wrong, I was just "in the zone" or some bullshit like that, I finally left the studio. I took a nap and then had a shower. When I got out a while later, Rick started hounding me immediately.

At least, until I walked through the living room.

"You've got to be *fucking* kidding me."

Rick almost pitched himself through the front window as he stumbled towards it to verify that his eyes were not, in fact, fucking with him and that there was, in fact, a cab in the driveway of my house.

"I cannot *believe* he fucking came here," he said, lunging across the room to the front door. "It was *one* blowjob and now he's stalking me at home because—"

"He's not here for you," I said.

He stopped, frowning as he turned to see me grabbing my jacket off the hook. "What?"

"I called it. I'm going out."

"What? In a cab?" He looked towards the door. "In *that* cab?"

"Yep."

"Where?"

"Figured I'd check out one of the bars in Timmins."

He stared at me, then sighed heavily.

"For fuck's sake," he grumbled, reaching for his jacket.

"You're not coming."

Again, the stare of disbelief. "Who are you going with?"

I shrugged my coat on. "No one."

"What the fuck, Theo? You can't go out alone. And I would've driven you or—"

"I just need to get out. Don't worry about—"

"I'm going to fucking worry about it," he snapped. "That's my job, and this isn't like you."

"Well, consider it a night off for you," I said, shoving my shoes on.

"Man, you can't—okay, what the *fuck* is this about? Does it have to do with Sheri?"

"Nope."

"Aspen?"

I rolled my eyes. "Why would this have to do with Aspen?"

"Because you've been locked in your fucking studio since Thursday night and aren't telling me what the *hell* is going on with you! Do you know how much you've fucking drank?"

I couldn't bring myself to look at him. "Look, I just need... I need some time to myself. Away."

"Theo, *talk to me*. Whatever's going on, you can't just—"

"Would you stop mothering me for a bit and just chill?" I grabbed my keys and shoved them in my pocket. "It's Monday. I'm going to a bar in Timmins. It'll be dead and nothing's going to happen. No one's even going to notice me."

He was aggravated enough that he did the only thing he could think of to stop me from opening the door, which was to grab me by the arm. I stiffened, looking over my shoulder at him. "Let go."

"No, I—"

"Take your hands off me or I'll fire you."

He called my bluff and didn't move. Unfortunately for him, I wasn't bluffing. I stared directly into his eyes, my face cold.

"I swear to God, Rick."

"Theo—"

"You called my brother. You called my *mom*. I'm leaving because I'm fucking pissed at you. Let go. *Now*."

He hesitated, then slowly took his hand off my arm. I glanced at the spot he'd grabbed, almost stunned that he'd *actually* listened to me and so uncertain that I froze. That was when I spotted the book on the front table and, to cover my awkwardness, grabbed it. Before he could open his mouth again, I was out the door.

Hiring that specific driver made me kind of a taint. I knew that. But I needed to do it. I'd hoped it would be enough to stop Rick from demanding to come with me, but he was stubborn. Still, he wasn't stubborn enough to follow me out of the house, especially since it would require him to sit in proximity to one of his many casual hookups for over an hour in each direction. Little did Rick know that the cab driver didn't want to see him, either, and for the same reason: he wasn't looking for some nice guy to settle down with. He'd almost refused to let me hire him, but when I told the cab company I'd pay double in each direction and triple if they'd send that specific driver, he'd decided the risk of driving around a guy he'd casually exchanged blowjobs with in the back of his car was worth it.

The bar he brought me to wasn't the one Rick usually went to, mostly because I wanted to be alone and that bar was more for people looking to get laid. Instead, I got him to drop me off at a sports bar that was half a health violation away from being a dive. It wasn't as bad as the nasty-ass pub in Wakeham, but that was because there was more than one bar in Timmins, so they had to have some standards to keep up with the competition. They specialized in having cheap beer on tap and deep-frying the shit out of anything that came out of the kitchen, so at least the chances of getting food poisoning were pretty slim.

It was busier than I'd expected, which was good. I blended into the crowd, practically invisible amongst the guys scouting for the hottest woman they could find on a Monday night and the women weighing their options from a limited pool of suitors. After ordering a pint of their finest beer, which was the same as their shittiest beer, and whatever the fuck a "sampler plate" was, I opened Aspen's book and let my mind wander.

Which was a bad idea.

Thinking of her hurt. Picturing her lying beside me, beautiful words spilling from her lips as my heart started racing, as I started to think that holy *shit*, she'd felt it too, she'd felt her world shake and the sky tumble around her, enclosing us in a little bubble that was just for us. That everything felt as right for her as it did for me when I slid inside her, a sensation of breathless satisfaction that I'd never truly felt before taking over my mind.

It hurt, because even without picturing what happened next, I knew what was coming.

Angrily, I flipped the page. *Get over it*, she'd said. Like she understood what it was like to have people hurt you again and *again* and fucking *again*. Like anyone could just get over spending their life feeling like they'd never be good enough, no matter how fucking hard they worked. Because sure, I was doing good for myself. I was a fucking success.

But all that had done for me was make finding love even harder.

I flipped another page, trying not to remember the look on Aspen's face when she admitted she liked kissing me, then trying to ignore the guilt as I remembered what her face looked like when she asked if I was calling her a slut.

I wasn't. I fucking *wasn't* calling her that.

Another page. Another moment trying to shut down my mind. The look on her face when I'd accused her of using me. Another page. Then another.

I don't know when I started actually reading the pages I flipped, but it was only when there was a particularly in-depth description of a woman getting Eiffel-Towered that I realized I was. And honestly, that was okay, because while I was focusing on trying to figure out how that worked in the confines of a seat on a Ferris wheel, I stopped thinking about Aspen. When the waiter came by a while later with my plate of grease wrapped around various types of battered food-like items, I thanked her and asked for extra napkins, then kept the book in one hand while I ate with the other.

The book did a damn fine job of distracting me, which was good, except that meant I didn't notice it had failed at its main purpose of stopping people from approaching me until it was too late.

Though, in fairness, I couldn't entirely blame the book.

"Have you read the first one in the series?" asked a familiar voice.

I looked up, annoyed, and my breath fled my body.

It wasn't the book's fault that she recognized me. It was my fault that she knew every inch of me intimately and had seen me in this exact outfit countless times. And it wasn't the book's fault that she was there that night; that was just fucking fate, I suppose. Nor was it the book's fault that she made the choice to walk up to me, her eyes full of nerves and her hair brushing against her shoulder.

"No," I finally said. "It's a series?"

She smiled. "A trilogy, I think. The first one's about a bunch of paramedics and the last one is about police officers."

I'd forgotten how beautiful her smile was.

"I didn't know you liked romance," she continued. "Though I guess it makes sense. But we could've shared books, you know. I have about a million of them."

"What are you doing here, Sheri?" I managed to ask.

The woman who had almost been my fiancée, who I'd almost asked to marry me before finding out she was with me for my bank account, smiled again, though it was much sadder that time.

"I could ask you the same," Sheri replied. "A bar in Timmins, by yourself, reading a smutty book? Where's Rick?"

I couldn't think of a lie. "At home. And I... I didn't know it was smutty."

She nodded, then glanced behind her. Without asking, she slid into the booth. The bench wrapped around the table and it wasn't until she was sitting beside me that my brain processed what the *hell* was happening.

"What about your new girl?" she asked. "The one from the picture?"

I didn't say anything. Sheri pressed her lips together.

"You were telling the truth, then? She's just a friend?"

"I... it's none of your..." I shook my head slowly. "What are you *doing* here?"

"Well, after we broke up, I moved in with Betty. She lives here. And Angela came up to visit, so we thought we'd go out and—"

"I mean *here*," I said. "What are you doing *here*, in my booth, talking to me?"

The harshness of my voice seemed to stun her, but she nodded gracefully.

"I deserve your anger," she said. "I know that. I... I just wanted to apologize."

I stared at her.

"For everything." She folded her hands in her lap. I followed her gaze as she looked down at them, noting the chipped red polish on her nails. "I'm sorry. For what I said and what I did. I wish I could take it all back because I…"

Her voice caught and my heart started beating just a little faster.

"Because what?" I asked.

She looked up, her eyes wide and earnest. "Because I miss you."

I almost rolled my eyes. "You miss my bank account, you mean."

"No." Her voice was so soft, I found myself leaning in to listen. "If I…" She stopped and took a breath as if to steady herself. "If I tell you the truth, will you try to believe me? Even if… if part of it hurts?"

Hurt was becoming my default state, so I just nodded.

"You asked me when… when we were breaking up," she started, then cleared her throat. "You asked me if I ever loved you or if it was always just about the money."

"I remember," I said coldly. "And I remember you couldn't answer, which said enough."

"I did."

"Uh, no, you didn't say a single—"

"No, I did love you." She looked down at her hands again. "I can't… I *won't* lie to you. It started because of the money. You were right about that. But I fell in love with you, Theo. I *loved* you. I still—" She stopped herself, her lip trembling. "I was embarrassed about it. I said horrible things to my friends because I didn't want to admit it to myself. I know that makes me awful and that I don't deserve your forgiveness for it. But I wanted you to know that I did, okay? It stopped being just about the money."

After all this time, she'd finally given me an answer.

"When?" I asked.

She looked up at me. "When did I know I loved you?"

"Yes."

"The first time we were at the cottage," she said without a moment's hesitation. "When we were on the patio and you… you had this whole fantasy in your head about hooking up out there, but when you realized I was getting eaten alive by the bugs and wasn't having fun, you stopped and brought me back inside. You gave up that entire experience for me and I..."

She trailed off, smiling sadly again.

"Your ass was covered in mosquito bites," I said.

That made her laugh. Fuck, I'd forgotten how beautiful her laugh was.

"And you put that lotion on all of them for me," she said.

I nodded slowly, smiling in spite of myself. Sheri lifted a hand off her lap, letting it hover for a moment before placing it over mine.

"Theo, if I could do anything in the world to get you back, I would," she said. "I know I don't deserve that, but if you... if you *ever* want to... to try again..."

Fuck.

"Sheri, I—"

"You are the one who got away," she said, captivating me with wide, intense eyes. "I realized it too late. And I won't beg you to take me back because I know, okay? I know begging you for forgiveness will make it look like I just want something. But just... just *if*. I'd sign any prenup you wanted. I'd do *anything* you wanted. I—"

Her voice caught again and her forehead wrinkled into a pained, pleading expression.

"I still love you," she finished, her voice barely above a whisper. "I never stopped loving you."

My mind was swirling with thoughts and memories. Bits and pieces of those thoughts flashed and flickered as they surfaced and sank. Rick offering to find me a one-night stand from my fans. Rick insisting I wasn't the kind of person who would have a trophy wife and insisting I wasn't the kind of person who could do "casual" relationships. Sheri at the cottage, wine glass in hand and head thrown back with laughter. Aspen sitting with me on my deck, telling me I better fucking not take Sheri back if she ever did something like this. But what did Aspen know? She'd been so certain about what she thought I should do, yet didn't have any sort of feelings for me. What gave her the right to tell me what to do?

More thoughts came. My dad's hands tightening on his lawn chair when he found out what Sheri did. The kids telling me they missed Auntie Sheri. So many nights alone, by myself, wondering if I'd ever find the person out there for me. Aspen telling me to leave her apartment, throwing my clothes at me before slamming her bathroom door. The guilt of what I'd said to her, the shame, the burning and roiling in my stomach as I threw away whatever little chance I'd had with her, and for what?

For *what*?

And then, in front of me, Sheri. Sheri with tears in her eyes as she looked up at me. Sheri sitting there with a vulnerable openness I'd never seen from her before. Sheri being *honest* with me, for once, and telling me the bad along with the good.

"Theo?" she breathed.

"Yes?" I replied quietly.

"Kiss me?" She bit her lip. "Just one last time? Let me show you I love you, even if you don't want me anymore. Let me show you I'm sorry."

She was a good actress, I knew that. And sure, she could have been acting right then, pretending she'd changed, saying whatever it took to convince me she really, truly loved me. But the way her eyes flashed, the shimmer behind them and the pain on her face...

Maybe she would be enough.

Maybe she was what I was meant for. I thought I'd found someone different, someone who made me feel like no one else had before—and considering I just about put a ring on the woman sitting in front of me, that was saying something. But there was hurt there too. Worse, in a way, because I'd hoped... I'd hoped.

I'd just fucking hoped.

Maybe I could be happy with Sheri. No one knew why we'd broken up. Well, except for all the people in my life who mattered. But publicly, no one knew what she'd said or done. People went back to their exes all the time. We could just say we realized we were better together. That we had gone through a rough patch. That we'd gotten over it.

Her pull was irresistible. I leaned in, entranced as her face grew closer and closer. Inch by inch, moment by moment, she drew herself to me. My hand raised of its own accord, reaching for her face, my fingers dragging along the smooth skin of her cheek. Just as she closed her eyes so I could capture her lips, I stopped, so close that my breath brushed against her as I spoke.

"Sheri," I whispered. "I forgive you."

Her eyes opened again, hopeful and bright. "Theo, I—"

"But you're so full of shit." I dropped my hand away from her face. "Fuck off."

# Chapter Twenty-Three

## *Aspen*

THE HOTEL DARBY BOOKED for me was full of wrestlers.

Fucking *wrestlers*. WWE superstars at some convention or event or something that was taking place at a conference center nearby. Guys who were a little too swole, a little too loud, and a little too unreal before turning off their acting abilities and deflating to regular human men.

The muscles stayed, though. The over-the-top bravado may have faded, but there was no question that those boys were *ripped*.

Somehow, that made their presumed ability to flip me over and toss me around like a rag doll less impressive than when Theo had done it. Theo was the kind of "in-shape" that a guy who had an active job would be. He spent a lot of time jumping around on stages and was constantly on the go, but he didn't spend a lot of time in the gym or anything. I knew he had a treadmill at his place, and he'd said that when he was on tour for his shows, his team made sure there was a private gym either in the hotel or nearby. I also knew he hated jogging outside, but he did enjoy hiking. And I knew that his chest wasn't overly muscled, and he didn't have a six-pack, but that absolutely did not stop him from being able to command my every movement when we were in bed together and—

"Again, Aspen?"

I jumped back into the present as Darby startled me. That she could startle me was startling enough on its own, which was clear from the expression of disbelief on her face.

"What?" I asked.

"You're thinking about him again."

I glanced at the off-duty wrestler sitting across the hotel bar, the Edmonton Oilers cap on his head and rimmed glasses doing nothing to conceal the fact that he looked like he was about to burst out of his dress shirt. Those buttons had to be on salary because they were definitely putting in overtime as they tried to hide the fact he was *someone* so he could eat his very boring looking salad in peace.

"Him?" I said, tilting my head towards the wrestler. "Yeah, of course I am. I was wondering if he'd be strong enough to fuck me against a shower wall or—"

"You're thinking about Theo." Darby folded her arms and leaned back in her chair. "Again."

I looked at her, my mouth in a straight line. "Why the fuck would I be thinking about Theo? There's nothing to think about."

"Right." She sipped her martini. "Not a thing."

"Darby, I told you. It was just sex. Good sex, yes, but I was right and we're too different, so it's not happening again." I sipped my wine. "Life goes on."

"You're so full of shit. You haven't stopped thinking about him since you got here."

I looked at her, unimpressed. "Taking out all the times *you've* brought him up, I have thought about Theo exactly twice since I've been here." I lifted a finger. "Once when I realized you booked me in a hotel full of wrestlers and I thought 'you know who would be fangirling like crazy right now? Theo.' Just like anyone would think when someone they knew was into wrestling." I raised a second finger. "Then when, at your insistence, I told you I fucked him—"

"Yeah, and you promised me *all* the dirty details—"

"I promised you nothing and you *still* got to hear about how he stuck his tongue in my ass, so count your fucking blessings." I shook my two fingers at her. "He's no different from any other guy. I fucked him. I left him. I've thought about him twice since then."

She reached forward and flicked one of my still-tucked fingers before prying it away from my hand. "And then a third time when he sent you that text and you *still* won't tell me what the hell it said. Also—" She tried prying more of my fingers open. "—since you haven't *stopped* thinking about him since, you can go ahead and put the rest of these up."

"Darb, stop it—Stop it!" I wrestled my hand away from her. "You are being obnoxious."

"Admit it, then." She picked up her martini glass and gave me a *Look*. "We've been friends for years. I know you well enough to know this wasn't just sex and something else happened. You've been moping around Montreal for four days now. You haven't even *tried* to hook up with anyone. That's alarming because you're a *giant* hoe."

"Excuse me?" I glared at her. "How dare you? This hoe does not *mope*."

She sipped her martini. "This hoe is barely even a hoe anymore."

"You and Kevin can be blamed for that. I'm not the one who sent me to buttfuck nowhere. Actually—" I picked up my wine glass and looked at it thoughtfully "—it's not really buttfuck nowhere. There has been a severe *lack* of buttfucking in Wakeham, so I guess that means it just fucking sucks."

I sipped my wine as Darby laughed in spite of herself.

"Look, Aspen—"

"I am looking." I nodded towards the wrestler again. "At him. Wanna take bets on how long before those buttons pop? I bet if I went up there and 'accidentally' dropped a napkin, I could make him turn his head so fast the button on his neck would bounce off my ass before I could stand up. We could put another case of wine on it."

"You know I don't believe you, right?" she said. "If you have feelings for Theo, you can just *tell* me."

"Does annoyance count as a feeling? Because that's about the only feeling I currently have that has anything to do with Theo, and it's mostly your fault." I sipped my wine, putting on a carefully selected and well-practiced expression of stoic ambivalence. "But since you're insisting, do you want to know what I *have* been thinking about?"

"No, I want to continue this aggravating guessing game for the rest of the week." She picked up one of the roasted chickpeas we'd ordered to snack on and threw it at my face. I caught it mid-air and popped it into my mouth. "Yes, of *course* I want to know."

"I'm thinking about quitting."

She spilled her martini. "*What*?!"

Patiently, I handed her my cloth napkin and waved the waiter over. While Darby mopped up her wasted drink, I ordered us another round.

"You can't be serious," she said when she'd finished cleaning up her martini. "Aspen, you *can't* quit. Who will I complain about Daniel with? And... *why* are you even thinking about this?"

I hadn't actually been thinking about it. It was an impulse as I wracked my brain for anything that might make her stop talking about Theo fucking Barker. But now that I'd said it out loud, it made sense.

"I'm bored," I said, swirling the last sip of wine in my glass. "I don't like Wakeham. Being back in Montreal has reminded me of that." I gestured around the bar. "I haven't been here in so long and I feel so out of place that the thought of picking someone up so I can get laid is exhausting, not exciting. And even if I found someone to fuck, I'd still have to leave at the end of the week knowing it might be months before I get laid again, and somehow that makes it even harder."

She didn't look convinced. "And this has nothing to do with Theo, who you *just* fucked?"

"Sure, it has to do with Theo. Sex with him made me realize how much it's going to suck to not get laid for a while. I told you." The waiter came back and I paused as she placed our drinks on the table. "Theo's a romantic. I'm a hoe."

I stopped for a moment, sipping my wine.

"Now, this week..." I waved my hand again. "I'm training Daniel how to do a job he's not suited for and that I can do better. It's exhausting, and it's just reminding me I gave up something I enjoyed doing to go to the middle of nowhere, where I'm not even getting a good buttfucking. I already asked for my job back and Kevin said no, so I don't see another option."

Darby pressed her lips together. "This isn't you. What did Theo do to you?"

Anger flared up so suddenly that it almost smashed my wall. "I swear to God, if you say his name one more—"

"He either did something that got you all messed up or fucked you so good that you've lost all common sense," she interrupted. "It's gotta be one or the other. Or..." She tapped her chin. "Does Wakeham have a large alien presence?"

That caught me off guard. "What?"

"Aliens." She sipped her martini. "I guess a pod person or something could have replaced you, because the Aspen I know isn't such a fucking moron."

I stared at her. "That was almost offensive."

"Sorry."

"Don't be. I'm proud of you."

She rolled her eyes. "Look, you have an end in sight, okay? You agreed with Kevin that you'd stay for a year and you could go back to doing pre-audits at the end of it *and* keep the raise he gave you. So sure, quit, but you know as well as I do it would be stupid to do it. Not to mention the company pays for your apartment, and your car, and if you quit while you live there, you'd have to pay to move back yourself."

I pretended like I'd thought of all those things and shrugged. "Like I said. I've been thinking about it. I haven't decided yet."

"And you're sure this sudden thought of quitting your job has nothing to do with whatever did or didn't happen with Theo that's got you so hung up, you haven't even considered fucking someone else while you're in Montreal because you've thought about him eight thousand times since you've been here?"

Closing my eyes briefly, I took a steadying breath as I reminded myself that Darby was my friend and that the police probably wouldn't believe me if I said I'd body slammed her in an attempt to impress the wrestling stars at the hotel.

I hadn't thought of Theo eight thousand times since I'd arrived in Montreal. It wasn't a lie when I said I'd thought of him twice since the previous Thursday. It couldn't *count* as multiple thoughts if I never stopped thinking of him in the first place, and it was only twice instead of once because Daniel had said something so fucking *idiotic* when I saw him that morning, my mind went blank to protect itself from his Monday morning stupidity.

It was so stupid that I'd reached for my phone so I could immediately tell Theo about it, stopping only when I opened my messages and saw the one I'd received the previous day.

*Can we talk?*

That was it. *Can we talk?* Just underneath the exchange we'd been having before I called him to come over to my place on Thursday afternoon.

*Can we talk?*

I hadn't responded.

And I wasn't going to.

I didn't want to talk to him. I didn't want to admit that at the corporate dinner Kevin had forced me to attend on Saturday night, there was a mouth-watering piece of chocolate cake that made me think of him. Or that I'd smiled a bit when I saw the table of desserts laid out because it made me think of his sweet tooth. That I'd heard one of his songs on the radio and felt a shivering thrill at the sound of his voice, or that the hotel had a daily special on his favourite type of beer as part of their happy hour. Or that I'd thought about him while lying alone in the king size bed of that generic hotel room, my mind wandering as I wondered what he was doing.

"Let me say one thing," Darby said. I opened my eyes and looked at her. "One thing about Theo, and then I'll drop it."

"You can't just drop it completely, given all the *other* things you've said about Theo?"

She shook her head. "Just listen. One thing. Regardless of whatever happened, you should at least try to repair your friendship with him. I'm the first to admit that Theo is fine as *hell* in that kind of approachable, unintimidating sort of way, not to mention a literal rock star and probably not doing too badly in the finance department, so I don't understand why you wouldn't consider at least trying to date him."

My temper flared again. "Because I'm not—"

"Just *listen*," she repeated, waving a hand at me. "You have your hang-ups about relationships, I know. But you told me you enjoyed hanging out with him even before you two hooked up, and given that you've made what, three friends in your adult life? You should probably try to hang on to that."

"You think I haven't considered that?" I asked.

"Yes, I do." She looked at me pointedly.

"And why do you assume this whole thing didn't work out because of me?" I asked. "How do you know he didn't do something? Maybe he's an asshole, Darby. Did you ever think of that?"

"I sure did." She took a patient sip of her martini. "And maybe he was an asshole. But if you felt like it was entirely his fault, you wouldn't be hiding it from me."

"Enough."

She fell silent as I stared at my glass.

She had me there.

Because I didn't feel like it was entirely his fault. It was *mostly* his fault because he'd decided sometime between us agreeing to a no-strings-attached hookup and the hookup itself that he wanted something more. And he was the one who'd been an absolute taint while we were in bed, saying things that were as hurtful as they were almost true.

Things I didn't want to think about.

He was the one who thought I was using him. He was the one who assumed that because I didn't want to make things more than they were that I didn't care about him. *He* was the one who thought it didn't matter who I was fucking, as long as I was fucking someone, and couldn't quite believe me when I said it wasn't true. That was *his* fucking issue.

My anger at Theo was still there. The problem was, it wasn't the only feeling that was still there.

That feeling meant I didn't know if I could go back to being his friend. It meant I had to face things I didn't want to face and admit things I didn't want to admit. Thinking about Theo in the context of things *not* just being about sex was terrifying. Discovering I missed texting him, and not just because I liked the pictures he used to send me of his dick, was horrifying. How he'd made me feel that in the span of a few kisses and some fucking good fucking was beyond me. My mind had been mush when he finally came, floating in a haze that was beyond anything I'd experienced.

Although...

I glanced down at my wine glass, my mind swirling. Darby had said she thought Theo either did something that got me all messed up—which he had—*or* that he'd fucked the common sense out of me, which he also had.

So maybe being hung up on him was part of that. Maybe it hadn't been that good. Maybe it was like being ravenously hungry and someone finally comes along and gives you a bologna sandwich, and when you take that first bite it's like it's the most delicious, decadent meal you've ever eaten. But it's just a bologna sandwich, and after you've eaten a few other meals, you realize that the sandwich itself wasn't all that good.

You were just really fucking hungry.

"I need to get laid," I said.

Darby's eyes almost touched her hairline. "What?"

Lifting the glass to my lips, I swallowed the last of my wine in one large gulp. "Laid. I'm gonna find someone to fuck."

"Are you?" she asked, uncertain.

"Mm-hmm." I put the glass back down, then undid the top button of my blouse and patted my curls down, hoping they weren't too frizzy. "So how about that bet? If Mr. Wrestlemania's button bounces off my ass, we charge another case of wine to Kevin's card."

She looked at me, then at the wrestler sitting across the bar. After a moment, she shrugged and sipped her martini.

"Go for it."

# Chapter Twenty-Four

*Theo*

THE HIGHWAY BETWEEN TIMMINS and Wakeham made for a beautiful drive.

Maybe I was biased because I knew home was on the other side of that almost rigid line of road. Certainly, some people didn't see the beauty driving kilometer after kilometer of highway that stretched through trees and fields. But in the spring and summer, the world around the road was green and lush, and in the fall, that same world was ablaze in reds and oranges and greens.

At least, that's what it looked like under daylight. At night, it was just dark.

But driving at night during the winter was a different experience. Winter brought a stark contrast: a world coated in shimmering white, trees capped with mounds of snow that glimmered reflections of moonlight and starlight and headlights.

About halfway between Timmins and Wakeham, located somewhere near the middle of nowhere, there was a decent sized lake. A few minutes off the main road was a parking lot surrounded by trees, far enough off the beaten path that, although everyone *knew* about it, no one paid much attention to what happened there. During summer days, people would treat it like a hidden swimming hole, dipping their toes in the water and exploring the surrounding woods. At night, local kids sometimes went there and started bonfires, huddling around them with plastic mickeys stolen from their parents' liquor cabinets. But that was in the summer and sometimes in the fall. In the winter, no one wanted to shiver in the darkness around the frozen lake.

That's not to say it wasn't busy in the winter. It was, maybe even more so than during the warmer months. There were more than a few couples in Wakeham who had arrived there as a couple but departed with a surprise third party brewing in someone's uterus. And I didn't have a single doubt in my mind that was where Rick's cab driver had taken him to fool around on their way back from the bar. It was understandable. A place like that screamed romance in a small town, back roads kind of way: shielded from the world by tall pines, overlooking a quiet lake, the starry sky unmarred by the light pollution you would see in urban centers.

So of course, that romantic spot tucked away off the highway was where my best friend pulled over during the awkward trek back to Wakeham after I'd hurriedly left Sheri scream-sobbing in the sports bar.

I was able to ignore her dramatics just long enough to chug the rest of my beer and pop a last piece of greasy batter into my mouth before going up to the bar to pay. Just as heads started to turn and the first hint of a whisper started— *"Hey wait, isn't that Theo Barker? Holy shit, I think that's... quick, get a picture of him!"*—I slipped out, grabbing my phone and figuring I'd walk down the street to the next bar while I waited for the cab.

Except I didn't need to, since my car was parked directly in front of the entrance with a shivering Rick leaning against the hood, his cheeks red and arms folded across his chest as he tugged his winter coat around him.

"What are you doing here?" I asked.

"Wasting my paycheck bribing cab drivers to tell me where the fuck you are," he grumbled. "Are you done or are you barhopping?"

"None of your—"

"I told them I'd double whatever you offered them if they agreed *not* to pick you up," he said. "So your options are to get a ride home with me or walk. If you're not done drinking at shitty bars yet, that's fine. I'll follow you and just freeze half to death out here while I wait."

I meant to argue with him more, but the door of the bar I'd just left flew open.

"There he is," said a snide voice that I immediately identified as belonging to Betty Schultz. "Thtupid fucking Theo Barker. What the *hell* is wrong with you?"

"Yeah, no, I'm done," I said.

Despite looking both affronted and alarmed, there wasn't even a second of hesitation before Rick rounded the car to the driver's side. I didn't pause either, though Betty was quick enough to shriek a horrendously loud "How *dare* you?!" before I got the door closed. As I tugged my seatbelt on, Rick started the car, and seconds later he was pulling out of the parking lot and onto the main road. He buckled his own seatbelt as he drove, then mashed the buttons on the dashboard until the heater was running full blast.

Then, aside from the whoosh of hot air as it rushed to fill the car, there was silence.

"Okay, I know you don't want to talk to me about anything and I'm still fucking pissed at you, but I have to ask," Rick finally said. "What was Betty doing there?"

"Hanging out with Sheri."

He whirled towards me. "You saw Sheri?!"

I nodded.

"Theo, what the—"

"Not on purpose. Give me some fucking credit, Rick."

"You deserve absolutely no credit, but that's an issue for another time." He looked back at the road. "Are you okay?"

"Mm-hmm."

"Did she..."

"Did she what?"

He made a scoffing sound. "I don't know, talk to you?"

"Mm-hmm."

"And?"

"She apologized and said she still loved me."

Rick clenched his jaw. "Okay."

I waited a moment, staring out the window. "Then she tried to kiss me."

"Mm-hmm." The sound came out high-pitched. "And?"

"I forgave her."

The strangled noise he made was probably audible to every dog within a five-kilometer radius. "And then...?"

"I told her she was full of shit and to fuck off."

A beat passed. I glanced at Rick out of the corner of my eye as he processed what I said, then jumped when he slapped his hand on the steering wheel and let out a loud hoot. "*Fuck* yeah, you did!"

I smirked just as both of us remembered we were still mad at each other. My smile faded and I turned, staring out the window as snow-capped trees flew by.

"So are we gonna talk about this or—"

"No," I said.

Rick sighed. "Man, you can't keep—"

In a show of astonishing maturity, I reached forward and turned the radio up loud enough to drown out both his voice and the sound of the heater running full blast. He glared at me, his lips pressed into a straight line. A moment later, he turned the volume down to a reasonable level, but took the hint and stopped talking.

I rested my elbow against the door, propping my head up as I stared out at the world flying by us. Trees and fields and starlight, snow and asphalt and endless sky, the occasional car passing us in the other direction the only reminder we weren't in a world that was completely abandoned. My mind wandered aimlessly, which meant I started thinking about Aspen again. My hand twitched, almost itching to text her and tell her what had just happened; that she'd been right, that Sheri had tried to get me back. That I'd done what Aspen had believed I could, even when I hadn't. She would've laughed, I thought, her eyes crinkled shut and her hair bouncing as she tossed her head back and *howled* at the thought of Sheri with her face almost up against mine, only to be told to fuck off.

That was exactly her humour. She would've loved it.

The familiar clicking of a signal light being turned on pulled me out of my thoughts. I frowned, disoriented by the world fading back into something I didn't expect. We weren't anywhere near Wakeham; nondescript trees surrounded us, and it was only when I saw the almost-hidden sign at the intersection that I realized Rick was heading to the romantic picnic area by the lake.

"What are you doing?" I asked, glancing at him.

He didn't say anything and I sighed.

"Can we please just go home?"

He didn't so much as glance at me.

"I'm still straight, man," I said glumly as he turned into the parking lot a few minutes later.

"Fortunately," Rick said, finally breaking his silence. "Since you're also not my type, so no one's really missing out here."

I snorted at the jab. He was still pissed, obviously, but not enough that he wouldn't insult me, which was a good sign. Silently, I waited as he parked the car. He left it running and looked out at the frozen lake, collecting his thoughts before turning to me.

"You're a gigantic fucking baby," he said.

Ouch.

"Tell me how you really feel," I muttered.

"Okay." He held up his hand and counted off on his fingers. "One, I've never been this fucking angry with you before. Two, part of that's my fault, since—"

"Since you called my *mom* and told on me?"

"No, since I enabled you to act like a gigantic fucking baby." He held up a third finger. "Three, I'm not sorry for calling your mom or calling the cab company *or* pushing you to talk about this because you are worrying the hell out of me. I'm your assistant second, your friend first, and you know what? If you're going to fire me, fine. If you *really* think you're going to find someone else who's going to put up with this dramatic bullshit and who also knows how you take everything from your coffee to your eggs to your women while simultaneously being the absolute fucking delight I am, go ahead. You're scaring me. You're fucking *terrifying* me. I will absolutely get James and your mom and everyone involved in this, even if it means you throw away an entire lifetime of friendship."

My mouth fell open, but Rick just held up another finger.

"Four, I'm really fucking proud of you." His voice cracked slightly. "I'm *so* proud of you for responding to Sheri the way you did."

I nodded gruffly, trying to ignore the pricking sensation of tears building up in my eyes. "Thanks."

Rick cleared his throat. "Five—" He held up his last finger. "We're going to talk about Aspen."

"There's nothing to—"

"I went into your studio."

My head snapped up. "What?"

He stared hard at me. "I went into your studio. Partly because it smelled like someone died in there and desperately needed to be aired out, but mostly because you're spiralling and refusing to tell me what's happening."

"You are an unrelentingly petulant pain in the ass, you know that?"

"Look at you with those ten-dollar words," he said. "And I prefer to think of myself as insistent and tenacious."

"Either way, you were out of line and you fucking *know* it." I glared at him. "And there's nothing happening with Aspen so there's nothing to—"

He interrupted me by opening the middle console and withdrawing a stack of semi-wrinkled papers covered in chicken scratch writing.

"You had like six *albums* worth of music in there and you were using it as a coaster for your empty beer bottles," he said, shuffling the papers.

"Yeah, 'cause it's all garbage," I muttered.

He took out one of the papers and held it up to his eyes, squinting. "In this one, you tried to rhyme 'Aspen' with 'grasping,' 'happen,' and 'slapping' before scribbling everything out and writing—"

I snatched the paper from his hands, my face burning. "It's nothing."

"Why don't we talk and I'll be the judge of that?"

I opened my mouth to protest again, then shut it as I stared down at the paper in my hands. I couldn't see it, not when I was in a small space lit primarily by the light from the dashboard and stars billions of miles away, but I knew what was there. I remembered scribbling out the bullshit lyrics I'd tried to come up with and scrawling three words across the bottom of the page over and over again.

*Get over it.*

*Get OVER it.*

*Get over it.*

"I slept with her," I forced myself to say.

"No, really?" Rick replied flatly.

I stared down at the paper. "It was supposed to be casual."

He sighed. "You can't do casual."

"Yeah, well, I know that *now*," I grumbled, my face still burning.

"You knew that before, but you've always been an unrelentingly petulant little crybaby." Rick opened the center console again. I raised my eyebrows as he withdrew two tall cans: one beer and one energy drink. He handed me the beer, put the energy drink in the cup holder, then dug back into the console and pulled out an open bag of chips sealed with a kitchen clip.

"Did you pack an entire picnic in there?" I asked dryly.

He glanced up, half a smirk on his face. "I figured the story would take a while, or I'd have to stage some kind of sit-in. Either way, I knew I'd need something to stay awake, and you'd need snacks. You get grouchy when you're hungry."

In spite of myself, I laughed.

"So," he said, opening the bag of chips and offering it to me. "Start from the beginning. Wait, don't start from the beginning. Start from when I walked in on you two at your place and then backtrack. *Please* tell me you didn't fuck on the couch where I watch my musicals."

I took a last glance at the piece of paper in my hand before putting it on the dashboard. Cracking the beer open, I took a deep breath, and then I told him everything.

How I accidentally forgot how thoughts worked and blurted out my desire to fuck her when I looked like a shabby mess.

How she brushed it off, then kissed me.

How I'd looked forward to seeing her again, only to be thwarted by James, so took the kids to her office so I could talk to her.

The phone call. The dirty pictures, which made Rick wince as I hurried to assure him she wasn't the kind of person who would share those, and that no one would be able to tell it was me, anyway. The fact that we didn't fuck on the couch where he watched his musicals.

And then the texts. The jokes. The way I felt like she just fucking *got* me. The frantic phone call from her on Thursday afternoon that made me drop everything and hurry across Wakeham to her place so I could *finally* be with her.

"... and it was good," I said, reaching for more chips only to realize I'd polished off the bag. "And then she started talking about how she didn't want a relationship and I told her it was kind of offensive to bring that up while we were literally still lying in bed."

"Mm-hmm." Rick took a sip of his energy drink. "And?"

"And what?"

"That's not it."

I fidgeted with the kitchen clip that had been around the chip bag. "She didn't want me."

"Right. And?"

"And nothing."

"Theodore."

I bristled. "We talked about how happy we were and how good things were. I thought she was saying one thing, then she turned around and shot that down. I was upset and told her I felt used. Then she got mad and kicked me out."

"And?"

"And that's it."

Rick raised his eyebrows. "I find it hard to believe that was it."

"That's the gist of it."

The energy drink made a crinkling noise as he casually squeezed the can. "You said you felt used?"

I fidgeted with the clip again.

"Or did you put it on her and say she used you?" he pressed.

"That," I muttered.

"Mm-hmm." He sipped his drink again. "So you fucked up."

"I thought she wanted to give us a chance."

"So you changed your mind about the parameters you'd agreed on and got pissed when she didn't. You fucked up."

"I was being honest with how I was feeling. Based on the things she *was* saying."

"And instead of asking her about it, you got upset when she couldn't read your mind. You fucked up."

"Fine!" I threw my hands up, unable to bring myself to look at Rick. "You're right. I fucked up. I fucked up *bad*. I really liked her, I got defensive when she didn't want to make things more than what we'd talked about, and I said—fuck, I said horrible shit to her, Rick. I told her she was using me, that all she wanted was someone to fuck, and that it didn't matter to her that we were friends. I said shit that made her think I was calling her a—" My voice broke and I leaned forward, putting my elbows on my knees and resting my head in my hands. "I wasn't. I didn't call her that. But it sounded like that and I know, okay? I fucked up, and I hurt her, and I feel like garbage about it. I *know* it's my fault."

The muscles in my throat tightened and I swallowed, trying to hold back the stinging tears in my eyes. A moment passed, then Rick's hand was on my shoulder, a weight that provided comfort I definitely didn't feel like I deserved.

"I came back home to get away from all the bullshit and drama," I mumbled into my hands. "Everyone else was the problem, in my head. Everyone was out to get me. But it's always been me, hasn't it? I'm the one looking for ways that people are trying to fuck me over, even when they're not. I'm the problem."

"That's good."

I turned my head slightly. "What?"

"It's good." He patted my back. "Figuring that out shows you're not completely hopeless."

"Thanks for the vote of confidence."

"You're welcome. It means you know there's something wrong and we can work on fixing it."

I half-laughed. "How? How the fuck do I stop feeling like this? 'Cause I can't take it, Rick." I shook my head, my voice desperate. "I shouldn't have anything to complain about, but I can't get *past* this."

"I don't have an answer for you," he said. "You're in a unique situation. But it doesn't matter who you are, some asshole out there is always going to try taking advantage of you. The key is knowing that not everyone's an asshole."

Rick's voice was calming, and finally admitting that the problems in my life were my own fault had lifted a weight off my chest. I sat up a bit and his hand dropped away, returning a moment later with a napkin he'd dug out of the center console. I took it gratefully, wiping my face.

"Look, you have people who love you, no matter what," Rick continued. "Lisa and James are always there for you and they've never asked for anything in return. Kids aren't cheap and they've got three of them, but they've never asked you for anything except to stop spoiling the shit out of them. Your parents, same thing. They give and give and then when you try to give back, they're surprised. Not because you don't usually try to give back, but because of who they are. And like, not to brag or anything, but you've got an awesome best friend who is ruggedly good looking and willing to look out for you to the point of literally driving you away because he knows what's best for you."

I chuckled softly.

"You've got more friends than just me, but it gets complicated. Aspen was like that. Someone new, someone you didn't know, someone who wanted nothing extra from you. But you're so used to that not being the case that it's hard to get past that, and that's kinda understandable, man. It's easy to be suspicious of people. A lot harder to trust them, especially when you have a life like yours. Finding that balance isn't easy, and it's gonna take work on your part."

"Think I've maybe started learning that lesson." I closed my eyes, almost grimacing as I thought of Aspen and the look on her face when I'd said what I said. "I lost a good thing over this. Maybe it never would've been anything more, but she was my friend and I was a total asshole to her."

"I dunno if you were a total asshole," Rick said. "I mean, I'm sure you had some good points."

"I was still a dick."

"Hmm. Maybe something between a dick and an asshole." He stopped suddenly and gasped. *"Taint!"*

I stared at him. "Uh... yeah."

He shook his head. "That explains so much. Anyway, why don't you just text Aspen?"

"I tried texting her yesterday," I said. "She left me on read. Should I... text her again?"

He shook his head. "If she saw it, she saw it. You did what you could. Now it's time to move on."

"Yeah? I shouldn't break into her studio and rifle through her papers, then bribe a cab company to tell me where she is so I can follow her there?"

"Just because I can pull that off without looking like a stalker doesn't mean you can." Rick folded his arms across his chest. "I need you to promise me something."

"I won't press charges, stalker. Don't worry."

"I'm being serious. I need you to... to work on this." He gestured vaguely at me. "Look, you know I've talked with other assistants and stuff before. Never about anything specific, but there are... you know."

I must have looked confused because he sighed.

"There are some psychologists and stuff who work specifically with people who are famous or powerful or whatever. I know there's a couple in Montreal and Toronto. And LA, of course. Probably New York, but I'd have to check."

"You think I need therapy," I said.

Rick shifted uncomfortably. "I know no one wants to hear that. I can only do so much and it's killing me to see you like this. And frankly, you're kind of a taint to me sometimes too. This just isn't healthy, man. I'm sorry, but—"

"Can you make me an appointment?"

He looked shocked. "What?"

"At one of the psychologists. Whichever seems like it might be the best fit. Probably one of the ones in Montreal." I picked up the crumpled piece of paper. "It's time for me to get over this."

"I... okay," he said, sounding hopeful. "When do you want to go?"

"Soon as possible. I think I wanna go back to real life." I folded the sheet of paper, then grabbed the romance novel I'd been reading and tucked it between the pages so I wouldn't lose it. "Record a new album. I've got enough music. Then go on tour maybe."

"Oh thank you dear, sweet Jesus," Rick breathed. He yanked his seatbelt back on and put the car in reverse. "I'll email the label when we get home."

I smiled. "Tired of Wakeham?"

"*So* tired. Let's get back to civilization."

# Chapter Twenty-Five

## *Aspen*

To MY CREDIT, IT was months before anyone noticed that Theo and I weren't friends anymore.

I say "my credit" because Theo skipped town, so it wasn't like he had to pretend like nothing changed. Which was probably a good thing. The man's acting was about as good as his ability to keep a casual thing casual—that is, he couldn't do it worth shit—so it was better that I took care of things myself. It was better that I be the one to sit in Lisa's dining room and listen to her and James laugh about how Theo had finally had enough of Wakeham, just like he always did, and pleaded with them to let the kids skip school so he could spend the day with them before he left.

I smiled and laughed along, wishing that they would change the subject. Then, when James left to get the kids ready for bed and Lisa turned to me with a saucy look on her face as she asked if I'd "met anyone" while I was on my business trip, I started wishing I'd stayed in Montreal.

Not because I'd met anyone there. Mainly so I didn't have to deal with all of *this*.

I told Darby I didn't fuck the wrestler because he wasn't swole enough, since his buttons didn't even strain when I walked up to the bar and "accidentally" dropped my napkin. Maybe it sounded vain, but I knew I had a great ass. Great enough that Theo had taken one look at it and shoved it in his face with the same enthusiasm he had when he devoured the devil's food cake James made every Friday. There was no denying I had an amazing ass, so that wrestler's buttons should have *absolutely* flown across the bar when he saw it.

Darby said it was because I bent down in front of him so it wasn't like he had to turn his head or anything. I pretended that was unintentional.

It wasn't just the wrestler, either. I didn't fuck anyone while I was in Montreal. That's not to say I didn't think about it, because I did. And it's not to say I didn't try to pick anyone up, because I also did that. But each time I started talking to someone, something was off.

One guy's smile did nothing for me.

Another's hair wasn't long enough to wind my fingers through.

A third didn't laugh at my jokes and a fourth didn't turn red or stammer charmingly when I told him he had the kind of gorgeous fingers I'd love to come all over.

And yes, I realized how that sounded. I wasn't so obtuse as to claim that I wasn't comparing them to Theo. I was *absolutely* holding those men to the standard that Theo had set for me, at least on a physical level. Logically, it made sense. Why *wouldn't* I want to experience that level of pleasure again? Theo was fucking phenomenal at fucking. Just because I missed his dick didn't mean I missed *him*. Frankly, the fact that he'd raised my standards for sex so high only to reveal that he was a pouty drama queen was just another reason for me not to like him. How was I supposed to go back to the kind of men I'd been with before when I'd experienced *Theo*, for fuck's sake?

It weighed on me heavily enough that by Thursday, I wondered if I was wrong.

Me.

Wrong.

I didn't do relationships, but maybe Theo and I could work something out. What that would be, I didn't know. I couldn't give him romance or sweet nothings, just like he couldn't give me casual. But as I sat in yet another meeting staring at Daniel as he failed to string together two coherent thoughts again, I thought... maybe.

Maybe it would be worth at least talking about.

And maybe if I was one of those people who believed in fate or any of that karmic universe crap, I would've thought Darby rushing up to me after that meeting to let me know she'd had to change my flight was a sign. A sign of what, I didn't know. I might've thought it was a sign that I was making the right choice, that bringing things up with Theo was what I was supposed to do. After all, why else would some bullshit cosmic force cause the airline to overbook the Sunday flight and contact Darby to tell her she'd have to switch me to the Friday morning flight instead? Why else would I conveniently end up back in Wakeham just in time to make it to Dinner-At-Lisa's if not to see Theo so we could figure things out between us? And why else would I decide not to fucking text him first in case he decided not to go to Lisa's when he found out I'd be there, if it wasn't meant to be a sign that I was doing the right thing?

As it turned out, if it was a sign, it was just a sign showing that fate and karma and the universe in general were fucking bullshit.

"Welcome back!" Lisa said cheerfully as she let me inside. "Hope you're hungry."

"Starving," I said, kicking my heels off. "I haven't eaten anything but a pack of airplane cookies since lunch."

"Perfect!" James called from the kitchen. "It's just about ready. And there'll be extra dessert, too."

"Now you're speaking my language," I said, laughing as I followed Lisa to the dining room.

Figuring it out took me longer than I'd like to admit. The table was empty when I walked in, but I thought maybe he was just running late. But Lisa began helping the kids into their seats and James brought the food to the table and as I settled in my usual spot, I realized there was one place setting less than usual.

"No Theo tonight?" I asked as casually as I could.

"No," Grayson said glumly. "He left to go back to work again."

"Oh," I said. "Just like that?"

"Yeah, but that's Theo," James said with a laugh as he put a bowl of potatoes on the table. "He gets restless."

"That was sudden," I said. "I thought he lived here."

He shook his head. "He's slightly obsessed with real estate, so he has houses all over. He hires Rick's dad to watch the place for him when he's not in Wakeham, which is most of the time."

"He told me to say goodbye for him," Lisa said to me. "I told him he should apologize."

My mouth went dry. "For what?"

She laughed and picked up the wine bottle, reaching across the table to pour me a glass. "For costing you your DD. Now *I* have to drive you home after Friday dinner."

"Should've apologized to me," James grumbled, and I forced a laugh as Lisa shushed him with a red face.

So that was it. The flight change was just a flight change. The feelings I'd had were just because Theo was good at fucking. There was no karmic message, no fateful meeting, no deeper meaning to what had happened between us. There was just me, my renewed commitment to avoid commitment, and my vibrator.

Well, vibrators. I was starting to get quite the collection.

See, this was why both vibrators and one-night stands were superior. Just sex, no friendships broken up, no dealing with stupid feelings, no getting involved in strange dynamics with famous musicians. No confronting uncomfortable truths about myself for no reason when the person responsible for that left town without so much as a word. No staring at a three-word text message wondering if I should text back, only to stop myself because what fucking good would it do?

He wasn't *there* anymore.

So that was it, whatever *it* was. It was over, and I was over it, and it was time to move on. Weeks and months passed. Christmas came and went. It was Lisa's parents' year to have her and James and the kids visit, so I did what I did every Christmas: cooked chicken wings and drank wine by myself while watching true crime documentaries. Winter passed with snow, and more snow, and work passed with meetings, and more meetings. Lisa and I exchanged novels, Darby kept me up to date on what life was like in civilization, and I existed.

I simply existed.

When Lisa walked into my office one morning a few months later, winter hadn't quite started giving way to spring. It was close, though, and close enough that I was almost ready to shift my countdown to the end of my contract from months to weeks. I mean, there were still months left, but somehow framing them as "weeks" seemed easier.

"Thanks," I muttered, distracted by a report on my screen as she placed a folder on my desk. Out of the corner of my eye, I could see her hovering by my desk. "What's up, Lisa?"

She pressed her lips together, then sighed. "Can we talk? Friend to friend?"

I turned away from my computer, concerned. "Of course. We're officially on a coffee break. Grab the door?"

Nodding, she closed my office door, then sat in the armchair on the other side of my desk. She didn't look up, instead staring at her hands in her lap as she chewed on her lip.

"Is this work or personal?" I asked. "Not that it matters. It's just so I know what level of worried I should be right now."

She half-laughed. "It's sort of personal, I guess."

"Sort of?"

"It's... I need to..." She stopped, then took a deep breath and let it out. "Okay, it's personal, but please don't get mad. Please?"

"I won't promise you that," I said. "You know I won't make promises I can't keep. But I'll try to, I don't know, keep an open mind."

She nodded, her neck flexing as she swallowed again. "I know. And I kind of expect... you know. That you will. But..."

I waited as she trailed off, then took a calming breath of my own. "Please just tell me what's going on. I don't enjoy guessing games."

"Okay." She took another breath, then looked up and met my gaze directly. "Alright. Friend to friend. Did something happen between you and Theo?"

I was usually quite good at anticipating things, but that? I wasn't expecting that. A muscle in my neck twitched as my default expression of calm, bland professionalism manifested itself on my face. I felt each brick of the wall go up, shooting up from the ground of my emotional boundaries.

"I haven't seen Theo in months," I said, my voice measured. "He left town. When I was on that business trip. Remember?"

"I know," Lisa said. "But, as my friend, would you please be honest with me?"

"I am being honest."

"Would you be for-real honest with me and answer the question you know I'm asking? Did you and Theo have something going on that I don't know about?"

I wasn't a liar. I wouldn't flat out deny it. But even as I opened my mouth, nothing came out. I didn't know how to answer that question. The answer was yes, of course, but it was more than yes. And more importantly, the answer had already ruined one of my precious few friendships: the one between me and Theo. It had the power to ruin my friendship with the person sitting in front of me, too.

And somehow, I'd become the kind of person who cared about that, enough that the idea of losing my friendship with Lisa made my stomach curl. Enough that I felt my eyes start to burn, even though I was *not* the kind of person who cried. Enough that despite being the kind of person who had no shame in who I slept with or how many of them there were, despite being someone who unapologetically did and said what she wanted, I couldn't even bring myself to respond.

Which, apparently, was enough of a response.

"What happened between you and him?" Lisa asked.

It took looking away from her for me to find my voice. "Why do you need to know?"

Her voice was gentle. "I'm not sure if you remember James mentioning it, but Theo's been working on a new album. The first single is about to go out and I think he's releasing the entire album next month, but he... he always sends a copy to James before it gets released." She paused. "I think the single is about you, Aspen."

Maybe it was the way she said it. The softness of her tone, the delicate way she phrased things. Maybe it was the knowledge that whatever this song was, it was so obviously about me that she'd figured it out, which meant it almost certainly wasn't complimentary. Or maybe it was just the feeling that I was about to lose my friend.

Whatever it was, the lump in my throat grew and the stinging in my eyes grew strong enough that I had to put my elbows on my desk and rest my head in my hands so Lisa couldn't see that I was almost crying. "Please don't hate me."

"Why would I hate you?" she asked. "You and Theo had so much chemistry, the *kids* could see it. James and I were betting on whether you'd hooked up. Clearly something... happened. But I know you're both good people and that whatever it was, neither of you were trying to hurt the other."

I swallowed hard and nodded. "I slept with him. Not like... not before that article was written. I didn't know him or Sheri then, and I had nothing to do with that."

"I know you didn't," she said, but I barely heard her.

"When the article came out, he... he admitted he was attracted to me and I was attracted to him and I just... I gave him my number, that day he was here with the kids. We just started talking and texting and—" I shook my head, squeezing my eyes closed as an odd sort of pain started in my chest. "He was so much fun. Like he was... we were friends. And I *told* him that it would never be serious because I wasn't staying in Wakeham and I don't do relationships and he fucking *agreed* to that, okay? It was all fine and good and really, *really* hot and—" I stopped myself again, choking on a laugh. "I mean, you don't want the details, seeing as he's your brother-in-law."

"It's not like you're talking about my mother or something. I'm aware Theo is a grown man who has sex. I have three children with his brother, Aspen."

I couldn't help but laugh a bit. "I know, I just... I've never been with someone like him before. It's never been like *that* before."

I had to stop. My voice was shaking, my throat so tight that I was sure it was going to cut off my breathing. Lisa waited a moment, then pulled her chair closer to my desk.

"What happened?" she asked. "If it was so good, why did—"

"He accused me of using him for his dick."

Even with my head down, I saw her wince.

"We... hooked up," I said bluntly. "That Thursday, right before I went to Montreal? That's why I left early. And it was..." I sat back a bit, semi-confident that I could control myself. "It was just really great. But I... I told you, we said it couldn't be serious, and it was supposed to just be casual, but I was..." Sighing, I looked up at the roof. "I said some things that made it sound like it wasn't just casual. Then, when he started thinking I might want something more than what we agreed to, I shot that down. He turned into this stupid, whiny drama queen and I got mad and... we both said things that weren't cool. But when I was in Montreal I just..."

"Just what?" she asked when I didn't finish.

"I missed him," I said miserably. "I liked him. A lot. I wanted to at least be friends. I thought, you know, I'd come back and we could talk it out. Solve something. That maybe he was..."

I couldn't bring myself to say it out loud.

"You didn't try texting him?" she asked.

I shook my head. "He texted me once. I wasn't ready to talk. So I didn't respond. I just came back here, and he was gone. So I told myself that was it and I had to get over it."

"It's funny you should say that, actually," she said, pulling her phone out.

"Why?"

She tapped the screen a few times. "You can't tell *anyone* I showed you this, okay? It's a huge breach of confidentiality, and Theo's legal team scares me."

"He wouldn't do anything to you. You're family."

She smiled, then put her phone on the desk and pushed it towards me. "Just don't say anything. Just listen."

"This is the single?"

"Mm-hmm."

I picked up the phone and glanced at the song waiting to be played. Then, despite everything, I started to laugh.

# Chapter Twenty-Six

*Theo*

"Welcome back! You're listening to the Raj and Jill Show on The Buzz FM and oh, man, do we have a surprise for you today. Spoiler alert, if you're watching our livestream online, you already know the surprise."

I grinned at the webcam and waved as Raj looked across the desk at me.

"But if you're doing something boring like driving or working, you don't know," Raj continued. "Because that's how radio works."

"No, really?" his co-host, Jill, said.

I couldn't help it; I laughed.

"Shh, man!" Raj scolded. "There you go, ruining the surprise."

"Is it a surprise?" I asked. "I mean, before the break, you said—"

"Details, details." He slapped his hand on the table lightly. "Alright, listeners, if you haven't already figured it out by the sound of those distinctive tones, we've got a good friend of mine here in the studio with us. Now, he's a little unknown, so you'll have to bear with me as I introduce him. The first time I met this guy, he was puking backstage at the—"

I burst out laughing again. "Oh, come on."

"Ah-ah-ah, let me tell the story." Raj wagged his finger at me. "I was hosting and DJing between sets at a live music venue downtown more than a few years ago now. It was just about the end of the night and I'm getting ready to introduce the next act when someone starts *frantically* waving at me from backstage. And I'm trying to figure out what they're saying, right? Because they're mouthing something at me that I can't hear, and I eventually figure they're saying 'Stall! He's not ready yet! Stall!' So I do my thing, I stall, and stall, and *stall*, and this guy's still not ready, so I throw on some generic beats and go to figure out what's happening."

I tried not to laugh as my face turned red.

"I walk back there and what do I see?" Raj gestured at me. "This up-and-coming act, some guy I've never heard of before, just *dragging* himself towards the stage as three different people try to tell him he can't go on. He's white as a ghost, sweat on his forehead, one of the stagehands is holding a garbage can next to him. Like, dude is *sick*-sick."

"It was just a little food poisoning," I said.

"Just a—" Raj heaved a huge sigh. "Whatever. I tell the guy, 'Look, man, you can't go on, that garbage can is half-full, you're not gonna make it through your set without puking and I don't want puke on my stage, I gotta be up there all night.' And buddy looks at me, white as white can be, and opens his mouth..."

"Oh God, Raj, where is this going?" Jill asked as I cringed.

"Nah, nah, it's fine," he said. "Dude opens his mouth and goes, 'Just watch me.' Then *snatches* the garbage can from the stagehand, hurls into it again, and—"

"This is *disgusting*!" Jill said.

"—*hands it to me*," Raj continued. "Then grabs his guitar and marches himself out onto that stage, no intro, nothing. The generic music is still playing, I'm holding a garbage can full of puke, and I rush out there to turn the music off so he can start his damn set." He laughed and tapped his hand on the desk again. "I swear to you all, I was clutching that gross garbage can the whole time he was out there, eyes glued to him so at the first sign of upchuck, I could pounce and get the can under his mouth, but wouldn't you know he managed to do a twenty-minute set without puking."

"Unfortunately, it was a twenty-five minute set," I said.

"Oh, *no*!" Jill cried as Raj cackled.

"Uh-huh. So as he finishes, he lurches offstage and I grab my puke bucket and go after him, getting it under his face just after he puked all over his shoes," Raj finished. "And that, my dear friends and listeners, is how I met the one and only Theo freakin' Barker, who's here in the studio with us today."

Jill grinned and clapped rapidly. "I'm so excited to meet you! Raj said he knew you, but I thought he was lying.

"I never lie," Raj said. "But since you didn't believe me, Jill, you can have the honour of—" He stopped and dug beneath his desk, then withdrew a small silver garbage can that had my name on it in giant black letters "—holding this upchuck receptacle for Theo. *Just* in case."

I laughed as Jill made a face. "Thanks, man. You're always so thoughtful."

"It's the least I can do, considering what you're here for." Raj looked at me, genuine gratitude in his eyes. "For anyone who isn't aware, we're about to be the first radio station in the entire *world* to play Theo's latest single. That's gonna happen in just a few minutes here, so you've got some time to grab your friends and family and huddle around the old radio set while he's blabbering on about whatever he's been up to recently before we get to the good part."

I grinned again. This was one of the best things about having my career take off. I could debut my music the standard way, but I was popular enough that I could insist that it be done on shows like Raj's. It didn't matter where my music was released: within hours, it would be everywhere. But this let me help boost smaller shows and stations with hosts like Raj, who asked me fun and insightful questions rather than the standard stuff from the typical press cycle. Not to mention that he was one of my biggest supporters from back when I had no choice but to drag my ass onstage with food poisoning.

He asked the standard questions to start: what I'd been up to, when my album was coming out, how many marshmallows I could fit in my mouth and still sing the lyrics to my last number one song. You know, the usual stuff people chatted about while counting down to the pre-determined yet meaningless time we'd picked to officially release my single. Then, when we got the signal from Rick, who was standing outside the studio window, Raj sat back in his chair and interlaced his fingers.

"Okay, everyone," he said. "You're just a few minutes away from being among the first to hear the new single from Theo's latest album. I think it's a good time for us to learn a little more about the song. Now, I gotta say, one perk of having Theo as a friend is that I got a sneak preview of this album and man, it has some of the best music we've seen from you. Seeing as all your music is awesome, that's saying something. I know it's still a few days before the full thing drops, but I'm excited for the world to hear it. So what do you say? Wanna tell us a bit about your latest jam?"

"Absolutely." I sat up a bit, clearing my throat. "So, uh, this is probably the most personal song I've ever written. I think it's going to give people a bit more insight into who I am, like, as a person. When I wrote it, I never intended for it to be released. It was, uh..."

I took a breath. Raj and Jill both knew what I was going to say. I'd told them what I wanted to talk about on the show since it went a little beyond what I'd usually say on a show like this, but they'd both been on board. Everyone had been. There were countless people who had my back, but now that I was faced with actually saying the words, my heart was racing and my mouth felt dry. I glanced at the window, where Rick smiled encouragingly, then cleared the tightness from my throat again.

"It was something my therapist suggested I write," I said, my voice far steadier than I felt. "Music is how I process a lot of my, uh, feelings and emotions and stuff. That's probably obvious."

"It makes sense," Jill said. "So it was like, a therapeutic exercise sort of thing?"

I nodded. "Yeah. I've been seeing a therapist for a while now for help with some... some personal stuff. I was having trouble letting go of some stuff that had happened in the past, to the point that it was affecting my relationships with people."

"Like romantic relationships?" Raj asked.

I shook my head. "No, this was after my last breakup. It was friendships, family, everything. It took me destroying a really good friendship to realize how much I needed to, uh..." I laughed softly. "To get over it."

"That explains a lot," Jill said.

"It was good advice, on her part," I said, laughing. "The friend, I mean. The person who... who inspired this."

"There are some interesting lyrics here," Raj said, looking at the page of notes he had in front of him. "You say at one point *And I'm gonna say thank you, gotta thank you, you couldn't have chosen better.* What does that mean?"

"Basically, it's like, 'thank you for breaking my heart,'" I said. "And that I mean it sincerely. That she chose the right thing, which was ditching my sorry ass—oh, fuck—I mean—crap."

Raj cackled. "Don't worry, we're on a slight delay so we can have a producer on bleep duty. I know how you are."

I shrugged, my face turning red as I smiled. "You know me. Well, anyway, that was the... the gist of it. She was right to end things with me because she deserved way better than how I was acting."

"You've said she was a friend a couple of times," Jill said. "But the lyrics and the way you're talking about her now... Clearly, this wasn't about Sheri, the woman you were seeing from Wakeham."

"Correct," I said stiffly, even though I'd agreed that Jill could ask me that question.

"Whoever it was, it sounds like you may have had some feelings for her. Do you think there's any chance you could get back together?"

"We weren't in a relationship in the first place," I said. "It's... it's a little more complicated than that. But regardless, that wasn't the point of all this. I started seeing a therapist because I needed to get my shi—stuff. Get my *stuff* sorted out and do some work on me. And that's where a lot of this album comes from. Most of it's not as personal as this song, but overall, it's a pretty strong representation of my life over the past year and the growth I think I've gone through in the past few months. This song kind of represents a breakthrough in that."

"Well, man, I think it's an awesome song," Raj said. "And I think our listeners are gonna riot if they don't get to hear it soon. So, what do you think? Should we play it for them?"

I grinned and nodded. "Let's do it, Raj."

"Excellent!" He leaned towards his mic as Jill clapped her hands again. "Alright, everyone, listen up. You're about to hear the world premier of the newest Theo Barker song right here on the Raj and Jill Show on The Buzz FM. This is a seriously awesome jam, so turn the radio up, settle in, and enjoy Theo's latest single. This is *Get Over It*."

# Chapter Twenty-Seven

*Aspen*

THE SONG WAS EVERYWHERE.

Regardless of Theo's feelings about his childhood in Wakeham, the town stood behind him. Even though his family still lived here, I doubted he knew about the absolute celebration of his talents that occurred whenever he released new music or won an award. He'd been so worried when the article about me and him had been released, so worried what people would think and how they'd treat his family, but I don't think Theo ever considered the other edge of the sword that is living in a small town.

Because they were proud of him, those people. Oh, sure, they'd never say it to his face, because you simply didn't *do* things like that in small towns like Wakeham. They'd never actually *tell* Theo that whenever he released a new album, the grocery store played it on repeat for days at a time. Or that when a new single came out, you wouldn't be able to walk down Main Street without hearing it blaring from the rolled down windows of a beat-up old pickup that looked like it should be blasting Garth or Johnny, not the sort of heartfelt pop-rock that Theo was known for.

But they did, and when that single just so happened to be about you, it made living on Main Street a fucking nightmare.

Not because it was a terrible song. That would have been better, actually. If the song sucked, I wouldn't have wanted to listen to it all the fucking time. But it was catchy and sincere and *good*. No, it was a nightmare because even days after I'd first heard it, days after it had been released worldwide, it kept forcing me to confront things I didn't want to confront. To feel things I *didn't* want to feel. It reduced me to sitting at home after Lisa apologetically cancelled our usual Friday night dinner because Anna's birthday was the next day. She and James were frantically trying to prepare to have an army of family members, friends, and sugar-hyped five-year-olds overtake their house while I lay on my bed in leggings and an old T-shirt, counting each time I heard *the song* blasting from the street below my window.

> *Gonna kiss me once and kiss me twice*
> *Kiss me 'till you can't count no more*
> *Gonna take my heart and hold it tight*
> *Then tell me to get the fuck outta your door*

"Three," I muttered to myself as the opening verse rose and faded beneath the dulcet tones of a jacked-up truck racing down the street. The latest novel Lisa had lent me was beside me, abandoned in favour of toying with my phone as I processed my thoughts in a strange cyclical ritual.

Screen on. Messages open.

*Can we talk?*

Stare, stare, stare.

Power button. Black screen.

Stare, stare, stare.

Screen on.

As if burning out my phone battery by reading those same three words over and over would somehow magically solve everything. As if I'd come up with some new solution just from looking at a message I was too afraid to respond to.

Me. *Afraid.*

Fuck.

> *You weren't the one who made me hurt*
> *But you got caught up all the same*
> *Thought you were the one who broke my heart*
> *But baby, I'm the one to blame*

"Four," I said, then nearly slapped myself across the face as something wet pooled in the corner of my eyes.

Not. Fucking. Again.

Growing up, I was a weepy kid. I was that kindergarten kid who teared up at lunch if she opened her snack bag and her mom had packed the wrong flavour of yogurt. When paired with my tendency to be an absolute perfectionist, it led to a lot of tears over things that didn't warrant tears. In first grade, I once cried after stepping on a bumblebee, then cried even more because I'd been mistaken and it was just a scrap of black and yellow pipe cleaner. The mistake was ten times worse somehow. A year later, I cried when I fell off the swings. Not because I was hurt, but because I was trying to jump further than all the other kids had and miscalculated the point at which I should have jumped, so ended up having the worst distance of the entire second grade class. And a year after that, I was so distraught over only getting nine out of twenty questions right on my multiplication tables test that the teacher had to call my mom, who had to leave work to come pick me up.

My mom was a good mom. She was. There was no one in the world I loved the way I loved my mom, and I never doubted for a moment that she loved me fiercely. But moms make mistakes sometimes. Moms are human. They say things or do things that stick with their children for years and years, often in ways they weren't intended to.

She'd taken me to Dairy Queen that day. I remembered that clearly, because we never went to Dairy Queen unless it was report card day. As a kid, I'd thought it was because ice cream was something that had to be earned with good grades, but once I was older, I realized it was because we couldn't afford stuff like that except on special occasions. And that day was a special occasion, since it was one of the few times my mom got mad at me.

"Tell me something," my mom said after she parked, but before we got out of the car. "Was it worth it?"

"What?" I asked, confused.

"The crying." She turned to me, frustration on her face. "Sometimes we make mistakes. You made eleven of them on that test. That just means you have to work harder next time. Was it worth getting *so* upset that I had to leave work to come get you?"

I didn't answer because I didn't know how. The answer, to me, was yes. Yes, it was worth being that upset. But that clearly wasn't the answer my mom wanted.

"When was the last time you cried?" she pressed when I didn't respond.

I thought for a moment. "Yesterday when Mr. Lebraun said I couldn't play with their kitty anymore 'cause it ran away."

"Mm-hmm," she said. "And was this worse than that?"

I twisted my mouth to the side, weighing the two scenarios.

"No," I said.

"Do you think it was worth me leaving work early?" she asked. "You know Mommy doesn't get paid if she's not there, right?"

I didn't.

"Aspen, next time you want to cry over something, I want you to think *really* hard about if it's worth being upset over," she said. "Think of the last time you cried, and if it's not worse than that, then maybe it's not worth crying at all."

I nodded and we got out of the car. She held my hand as we entered the Dairy Queen and let me pick anything I wanted off the menu, which was unusual—normally, she had a coupon.

But it was a special occasion.

If my mom knew how much that conversation would mold me, I don't know that she would have said any of it. I don't think she meant for me to take away what I did, which was that I should only cry if I was experiencing something worse than I'd ever experienced before. But that was what my little brain decided she meant, and even though she'd brought me to Dairy Queen to show me that it was okay to make mistakes sometimes, the little perfectionist in me associated mastering the ability to not cry over things to earning ice cream like I did when my report cards were good.

There was logic in there somewhere. Not necessarily sound logic, but logic all the same. And it worked out. I stopped letting things upset me so much. Why would I bother crying over a breakup when Nick Ivy, my eighth-grade boyfriend, took me to a school dance only to spend the whole time grind-dancing with a ninth grader named Sara Pensylton?

Why would I cry when someone called me a home wrecking witch? I'd been called far worse before.

Why would I cry over *anything* when I'd already had my whole life crumble around me? When the dream I'd had since I was a child who realized how fucking *poor* we were evaporated like mist?

But that song.

That fucking song and what it meant.

> *I gotta say thank you,*
> *Baby, thank you*
> *Fuck, I miss you, but I get it*
> *Didn't get over it*
> *So now I gotta get over you*

Thank God Lisa had thrown her legal obligations of confidentiality to the wind in order to show me Theo's single when it was just me and her sitting in my office. At least that way, when I burst into tears, she was the only witness. Before the final repeat of the chorus, I'd broken down, which seemed to alarm Lisa to no end. She'd fretted for a moment before grabbing the tissues on my desk and emptying nearly half the box as I sobbed into my hands.

"Oh my God, what happened?" she kept asking as she shoved handful after handful of Kleenex at me. "What did he *do*? Aspen? You need to tell me what *happened*."

I kept shaking my head, trying to answer and failing, before I calmed enough to ward her off by grabbing the box of tissues away from her.

"It just wasn't what I expected," I said thickly, then blew my nose hard enough that it could have been mistaken for a convoy of semis honking a mile away. "He... he took the blame for everything."

"He needed to, from the sound of it."

I nodded, then shook my head. "It's complicated. Some of it is my fault. Some of it isn't. We might not have meant for things to... you know. Be more than sex. But I... ugh." I blew my nose again, though it was slightly less thunderous. "I miss him. He was a good friend."

She awkwardly clumped the tissues I hadn't grabbed in her hand. "Why would it have been such a bad thing for it to be more than just sex?"

"It was. I just said we were friends."

"You know what I mean."

I threw the Kleenex in the garbage and grabbed another one. "I don't do relationships."

"So I've heard."

She waited, apparently expecting me to say something, then sighed when I didn't.

"Will you at least tell me why, Aspen?" she asked. "Just between us. I'm not saying you have to consider it with Theo but I just..." She leaned back in her chair, then sighed. "Okay, don't be mad or anything, but I just think you two would be so fucking *good* together and I want to understand why you don't think so."

"It's not Theo," I said stiffly. "I just don't like relationships. I don't like who *I* am when I'm in a relationship."

She frowned. "What do you mean?"

I fidgeted with the Kleenex in my hand. "I was in a relationship with someone for a long time. It didn't end well, and I realized I was completely different when I was with him. Not just a different person, but a... I was like an object. I don't like feeling like someone owns me and I don't want to go through that again."

"That's... that's not what relationships are about," she said, almost incredulous. "You don't belong to anyone. You're supposed to be a team."

I didn't reply.

"Theo... you know Theo wouldn't... like *ever*. Aspen, you know he wouldn't be like that. James would kick his ass. *I* would kick his ass. His *parents*—"

My jaw was tense. "That's not the point."

"Having one bad relationship isn't—"

"It wasn't just *bad*, Lisa," I snapped. "Okay? I don't *do* relationships."

My tone was harsh enough that she recoiled in her chair, her eyes wide. Maybe it was that I was particularly emotional that day, but I felt an immediate surge of guilt that almost made my eyes water again.

"Sorry," I said quickly, my face burning. "Sorry, I just... I just can't. I can't."

"It's okay," she said. "I'm sorry. I was clearly over the line."

"It's... complicated." I forced myself to laugh, hoping it would make the wetness in my eyes go away. "I guess I should take Theo's advice and get over it."

"From the sounds of the song, that was your advice to him," she said.

"Well... yes."

She pressed her lips together, looking at me thoughtfully. "He told James that he started seeing a therapist."

"Okay."

"Because of all this." She motioned at her phone sitting on my desk. "He didn't say specifically it was because of your advice but it's not that hard to make the connection. He really does want to 'get over it,' Aspen. James said it's been a long time since him sounded so *grounded*. Theo said he feels like he's sabotaging himself and—"

"Should you be telling me all this?" I asked. "If it's something he told James?"

"That's the thing," she said. "He *wants* to talk about it. He told James when he releases the single in a few days, he's planning on making that part of the discussion around the song and how he owed it to himself to 'get over it' so he could be happy." She looked at me pointedly. "I've known you for months now. You're this tough, uncrackable, intimidating person who says what she thinks and doesn't apologize for it. You're also super kind-hearted and sweet. But I've never seen you look this vulnerable."

"You mean crying like a pathetic baby?" I muttered flatly.

"No, I mean you're showing that you're an actual human being and that this whole situation has clearly caused some emotional turmoil. That's not a bad thing, and it doesn't mean you're pathetic. I'm not saying you need to see a therapist or something, but I think you deserve to be happy just as much as Theo does. And if that means figuring out why you keep denying that you want a relationship when you obviously want to be with Theo in *some* capacity, I think you owe it to yourself to do that."

*Get over it, you said*
*And baby, you were right*
*Just wish I figured that out*
*Before it cost me you*
*'Cause you, baby*
*You didn't deserve what I did to you, baby*

"Five," I whispered as yet another repeat of *Get Over It* floated up from the street below, cutting through the memory of my conversation with Lisa a few days earlier. Given the revving sound that accompanied it, I thought it might be the jacked-up truck that had gone by earlier, and I wondered vaguely when people in Wakeham started spending their Friday nights driving up and down Main Street blasting the same Theo Barker song on repeat.

Biting my lip, I stared up at the ceiling and repeated my cyclical ritual. Screen on.

*Can we talk?*

Power button. Black screen.

Screen on.

The music faded as the truck took off down Main Street again, replaced by the sound of Lisa's voice in my mind.

"Just try talking to him," she had said before leaving my office. "Just call. Or text."

"What, so I can make him feel better about everything?" I asked cynically.

The patient look on her face was more than I deserved. "Talk to him for *your* sake, Aspen. Not his."

Screen on.

*Can we talk?*

Black screen.

Lisa had made a lot of valid points. I couldn't deny that and still consider myself a logical person. And I knew there were some logical fallacies behind my actions. But that didn't make it any easier.

What if Theo didn't want to talk to me?

What if he was *actually* over it and by reaching out, I set him back from that progress?

What if he blocked me? Or told me I was shit and that he was glad we'd... Broken up wasn't the right phrase, but that was as close as I could get.

Screen on.

*Can we talk?*

I stared at the words, chewing on my lip. What if I was going through all of this—actually considering making myself *vulnerable* to him—and he hurt me?

"But what if he doesn't?" I asked out loud.

*Gonna tell me I'm just not your type*
*'Cause your type just don't exist*
*Gonna break my heart and not think twice*
*Tell me to just get over it*

"Six," I said, aggravated as someone drove by listening to the song fucking *again*.

And that's when I got mad.

Because really.

Fucking *really*?

There I was, sitting at home by myself on a Friday night, moping around indecisively and pussyfooting around the entire thing instead of just fucking *dealing* with it, while the rest of the world moved on. There was some dude out there in his goddamn truck, driving around and listening to the same song repeatedly, doing more with his Friday night than I was. Doing more with his *life* than I was as I sat around braless, wearing a T-shirt that had holes in the armpit. Sure, he might be driving around in circles, but I was literally just opening and closing the same fucking text message on my phone like I, Aspen fucking Haws, was the kind of person who did that sort of shit.

No.

So what if Theo didn't respond? So what if he blocked me or laughed at me or hurt me? So fucking *what*?

I sat up, glaring at my phone as I clicked the keyboard and started typing.

*I know it's been months but I wanted to say I'm not happy with how things ended and I freaked out because...*

No, that wouldn't do. I deleted it.

*When you said you wanted a relationship I was scared.*

Nope. Delete.

*I like the new song. I'm glad you see it from my point of view.*

Ugh. That was terrible. Delete.

I went through line after line, trying to phrase things the way I wanted to. Finally, I found the perfect solution. Something that showed I was, at the very least, open to talking to him, and that I wanted to know if he was, too. Something eloquent, but sincere. Something friendly and casual, but with the appropriate amount of solemnity given the fact that we hadn't talked in months.

*Hey. Can we talk sometime?*

I re-read those five words about eighty times before hitting send, then immediately threw my phone to the other side of my bed and flopped onto my back, my heart racing.

There. I'd done it. And if he decided he didn't want to text me back, he could go to hell.

I was so convinced that he wouldn't text me back that when my phone buzzed barely a minute later, I jumped so severely that my bed shook and my heart ended up in the base of my throat. Almost instantly, my palms started sweating. As I snatched my phone up from the other side of the bed, I told myself it was probably Darby. Because reasons. Because it couldn't fucking *possibly* be—

*Yes. I'd absolutely love that. Are you busy? Like, right now?*

Fuck.

Oh, *fuck.*

My hands started shaking and it took three tries before I got the message written with no typos.

*Nope. Just at home. Friday dinner was cancelled. Call me when you're free?*

And then I waited.

A minute went by, then two, then five. I glared at my phone, annoyed with Theo as much as I was annoyed with myself. I shouldn't have left an open-ended time. I should have told him specifically when to call me. Or at least, I should have asked when he would. Though, he'd said "right now," so it wasn't unreasonable for me to expect—

I shut that shit down as quick as I could, shaking my head as I scolded myself. This was *not* who I was. He would call when he was free.

Still, I kept my phone nearby as I got out of bed and walked to the kitchen, grabbing a glass from the cupboard. I was thirstier than I realized, apparently, which I figured out when I opened the refrigerator to fill my water glass from the jug I kept in there, only to down nearly half the glass before I even shut the door. Once I had to stop for air, I closed the fridge. I'd just brought the glass back to my lips to take a more conservative sip when three loud knocks at my door made me jump and slosh almost the rest of the glass down my shirt, gasping as the cold water soaked my skin.

Cursing, I glanced at the clock over the stove and wondered who the fuck was knocking at this hour. Then, I immediately cringed. Shaking my head at the thought that it was just after nine p.m. and I was having "at this hour?!" thoughts, I strode to the door, still annoyed as I flung it open to see Theo.

Theo.

My mouth was open, but I was speechless. He looked great. Like, *really* great. His eyes were brighter, somehow. His hair was still shaggy, but it had been cut recently. As always, he was dressed casually, wearing a coat that was far too light for the weather over a grey hoodie. And even though there was a nervous expression on his face, the way his shoulders were squared and his head was held up gave off an air of confidence I hadn't seen from him before. Even at a glance, he seemed more self-assured.

A lot of feelings came tumbling back, very suddenly and very intensely. How attracted I'd been to him. How attracted I still *was*. How hurt I'd been. How amazing things had been.

How much I missed him.

"Hey," he said, breaking the silence.

"Hey," I replied, still staring. It took another moment of gaping before my brain caught up and I burst out laughing. "I mean, *hey*! Oh my God."

He grinned, then joined in my laughter with a pleasantly surprised one of his own as I reached forward to hug him.

"I had no idea you were in town," I said.

His arms wrapped around me, firm and warm and comforting. "It's Anna's birthday this weekend, so I decided I'd drop in to surprise her."

Of course he had.

"When did you get in?" I asked.

"About twenty minutes ago," he replied. "I dropped Rick off at his parents' and then came here."

He was still holding me. I could feel the heat of his body paired with the coolness of the fabric surrounding it, still chilled from him being outside. The hug was going on far longer than it should have but I just...

I didn't want to let go.

"Why is your shirt wet?" he suddenly asked.

"I... spilled some water," I said, forcing myself to step away.

His arms let go almost hesitantly and when I glanced up, there was something vulnerable and sincere on his face. I swallowed hard, then stepped to the side.

"Come in. We should talk."

# Chapter Twenty-Eight

*Theo*

SHOWING UP AT ASPEN'S door unannounced could have gone one of two ways, so it was a major relief when it went the way that resulted in her laughing and throwing her arms around me.

I hadn't expected to run into her while I was in Wakeham. I knew she was still there, obviously, and I'd worried a bit that she might be at Anna's birthday party. Part of me hoped she would so I could just *see* her, but the part of me that was starting to sound suspiciously like my therapist insisted—rightly so—that would be unfair to Aspen. As far as I knew, she still didn't want to talk to me, so I'd wanted to avoid texting her if I could help it. Instead, I tried to bring it up casually when I was on the phone with James to figure out the details.

"Rick and I might be able to make it in Friday afternoon," I had said. "Are you still doing Friday night dinners?"

"Yeah, but not this week," James said. "We need the time to get ready. Besides, I thought you wanted to surprise Lisa and the kids at the party."

"Right, yeah," I said. "But I figured if you *were...*"

"Nah, Lisa's already told Aspen it's off. Poor Lisa." He laughed and I could almost picture him shaking his head. "She was so worried about whether she should invite Aspen to Anna's party and as soon as she brought it up, Aspen asked how big a gift she had to get in order to avoid showing up for the party."

"Oh yeah?" I asked, chuckling. "What'd Lisa say?"

"Same thing she says to you, which is always that the kids don't need anything and to stop spoiling them, and that it was fine for her to skip the party without getting a gift for Anna."

"Mm-hmm. So what's she getting Anna?"

"She suggested a Barbie Dream House while Lisa was in the bathroom and I told her that even I wouldn't be able to justify something that expensive, so I talked her down to this Barbie convertible sports car thing Anna's been talking about. She wants it so she can race the boys' Tonka trucks."

That conversation answered two of my questions: I needed Rick to go out and buy a Barbie Dream House for Anna, which he was ecstatic about, and I wasn't at risk of seeing Aspen unexpectedly while I was in Wakeham. Which was one of those good things that really sucked, but that was just the way things were.

Just like my therapist said: I felt sad about it, I accepted it, I got over it. Time to move on.

And I had. I'd spent most of Friday doing interviews and other press stuff for the new album, then caught an evening flight to Timmins with Rick. Rick's dad had been having some health issues and since we wouldn't be in Wakeham very long, he'd decided he was going to stay with them for the few days we were back. I'd felt the slightest pang of sadness as we drove down Main Street and passed Aspen's apartment, then was forced to stop thinking about her when some jacked-up truck nearly ran me off the road as he sped down the street.

"Wanna come in and say hi?" Rick asked when we got to his parents' place.

"Sure, why—"

And then my phone, which had still been connected to the dash of the rental car, had gone off.

*New message from: Aspen H.*

"What the *actual* fuck, Theo?!" Rick growled. "Again?!"

But it only took him half a second to realize I was just as surprised as he was. I stared at the notification on the dashboard, my lips parted.

"Do you think Lisa told her?" he asked.

"Lisa doesn't know I'm here," I said.

"James?"

I shook my head, reaching for my phone sitting on the center console.

"Oh, hell no," Rick said, and mashed the touchscreen on the dash. "I wanna know what it says."

"What if it's something—"

"Sexy? She's pissed at you, man. She's not sending you sexy pics. And the car doesn't *read* pictures."

"Message from: Aspen H.," said the cool metallic voice of the automated assistant. "Message: *'Hey. Can we talk sometime?'* Would you like to reply?"

"No," I said.

"Okay," the metallic voice said.

Rick looked from me to the screen. "What? What do you mean, no?"

"I mean no, I would not like to reply while you're sitting there listening to me," I said, grabbing my phone and typing out a response. "Can I take a raincheck on seeing your parents? Maybe Sunday? Or before we leave on Monday?"

Gently, he plucked my phone from my hand. "Man, wait one sec. Think this through."

"I have. I want to talk to her. Give me my phone."

"I know, but—"

"I want to apologize." I grabbed my phone away from him. "I want to tell her I'm sorry. If that's all that happens, that's all that happens."

"Over the phone, right?" he asked.

"What?"

He looked at me, unimpressed. "You're not going to just go over there and hope for the best, are you?"

"Of course not. I'm going to text her back, then go to my place and call her."

I doubt either of us believed me, but Rick at least pretended to and unloaded his bag from the car while I texted Aspen. Then, before he'd even shut his parents' front door, I was pulling out of the driveway and beelining back to her place.

I hadn't been lying when I said if all that happened was that I got to apologize, I'd be fine with it. If her message had literally said *Hey, I want you to apologize to me and then never speak to me again*, I would've fucking done it. But for some reason, after the moment it took for her to reconcile her shock when she opened her door to see me standing there, she smiled, then laughed, then hugged me.

She hugged me.

For a few moments, she was in my arms, pressed so close against me it was almost like nothing ever happened. Until, of course, I had to make things weird by wondering aloud why her shirt was so wet I could feel it through my hoodie.

Her face was the slightest hint of pink when she let go of me and stepped back, gesturing me inside. She led me to the couch in her living room, making awkward small talk and offering me a drink. I watched as surreptitiously as I could as she bustled around her apartment, almost hating how good she looked. Almost hating how, even in simple black leggings and a, for some reason, damp orange T-shirt that had holes in it, she took my breath away. Her hair was twisted into a blossom of tangled curls sitting haphazardly on the top of her head and her face was clean and fresh, her skin smooth and glowing.

Fuck, she was beautiful.

I'd missed those eyes. Those lips, not wearing their usual shade of red, but as enticing as ever. The sound of her voice. Even through the small talk and general uncertainty, I could feel the spark we'd had. The chemistry that had surged between us returned with an ease that was impossible to ignore. As she settled beside me on the couch, fingers wrapped around a bottle of beer, all I wanted to do was take back everything that had happened. I just wanted to plead with her to forget what I'd said the last time I was here and just kiss me, just give me one more chance, just let me hold her again.

But that wasn't why I was here.

"So," she said softly.

"So," I agreed.

Then silence.

"I don't know where to start," she said.

That made two of us. I nodded, looking down at the beer she'd brought me, then took a deep breath.

Alright, I thought. Start simple.

"I dunno if you've heard, but I have an album coming out," I said. "I, um, just released a single. And I wanted to tell you it's about you. Or, well... us. What happened with us. I hope you're not... I dunno. Offended or upset. I feel like I should've let you listen to it first or something."

The corners of her eyes crinkled as she smiled down at her beer. "Don't tell your legal team, but I heard it a few days before you released it."

I raised my eyebrows. "Oh?"

She looked up, her eyes sparkling. "Lisa figured out that it was about... us. Or what happened with us. But she's terrified of your legal team."

I chuckled. "I wouldn't call a lawyer on Lisa."

"That's what I said," she replied.

Silence fell again. I picked at the label on my beer. "What, uh, did you think of it? The song, I mean."

She sipped her beer thoughtfully. "It's good. Catchy. I'd say it's a solid B+, as far as songs go."

"Damn," I said. "There goes my GPA."

More laughter. The tension between us was dipping dangerously low, dissolving and fading as we fell back into the ease of our friendship. Things might have changed—hell, *we* might have changed—but that spark was still there, and it was catching.

"I'm a hypocrite," she said suddenly, looking up at me. "That whole song is about you taking responsibility for what happened and it makes it sound like I was the one who, I don't know, inspired you to 'get over it' and treat yourself better. But I can't even do the same thing myself. I don't deserve the amount of credit you're giving me."

I frowned. "What are you talking about? You absolutely do."

She looked up. Her eyes seemed bright, but after a moment, I realized it was because they were wet.

"I told you to get over it and fix your shit, but I haven't gotten over any of *my* stuff, and that absolutely had a part in how things ended for us." She drew in a breath, as if to steel her resolve, then slowly let it out. "You deserve an explanation."

"You deserve an apology first," I said.

"But—"

"Aspen, whatever happened, however you feel about your role in it, it's mostly my fault." I paused, looking at her and hoping she could see that I meant it, wholly and completely. "I don't know why you don't want a relationship. I don't understand it. But that doesn't *matter*. I made things about me when it wasn't about me, and I took it personally when it wasn't meant to be personal. I put pressure on you to take things further than we agreed on and when you weren't interested, I got upset. I projected my issues onto you and the shit I said... I don't know how you didn't just punch me in the face or something. *None* of that was fair to you. So, I'm sorry. I really, really am."

She nodded, glancing down. "Okay. Thank you."

I licked my lips, then took a steeling breath of my own. "And I disagree with you."

"About what?"

"The amount of credit you deserve." My hands threatened to shake, but I swallowed hard and kept them steady. "That whole thing was the kick in the ass I needed to get my shit together. If it wasn't for you, I'd still be miserable. I dunno how much you, uh..." I trailed off, then winced. "This is gonna sound kind of conceited."

"You don't have to ask me if I know who you are again, Theo. I know now."

I couldn't hold back a laugh and she grinned.

"Well, it's kinda along those lines," I said. "I dunno if you've been like, following my... interviews and stuff—"

"I may or may not have listened to your interview with Raj and Jill a time or eighty," she said. "Did you really puke on your shoes backstage?"

"Uh-huh," I said, laughing in spite of myself. "Okay, well, then you know, I guess. That I've been seeing someone for help and that I've..." I stopped and shook my head. "Look, whether or not you want the credit, I wouldn't have gotten to where I am if this hadn't happened. I'm still pissed with myself but regardless, it's because of you that I'm better than I was. I'm just sorry it cost me your friendship to get here, and I'm sorry I hurt you."

I wasn't looking at her, so when she reached out and touched my hand, it was a surprise. Half in shock, I stared at the soft hand covering mine, almost scared to even breathe, just in case she pulled away.

"Thank you," she said. "And I'm sorry, too. I freaked out and I'm going to tell you why, even if it doesn't excuse things. I just hope it helps make sense of them." She paused again, then almost subconsciously tapped her fingertips against the back of mine. "I haven't told many people this before."

Heart racing, I risked turning my wrist so my palm was facing up. When she didn't take her hand back, I wrapped my fingers around hers. "I'm listening."

She looked at our hands, then took another breath and started speaking. Her voice was soft but direct, and to anyone else, it might have sounded like it was void of emotion.

But I could hear it, hidden behind that matter-of-fact tone.

I could hear *her*.

"My dad died," she said. "When I was a little kid."

"I'm sorry," I said.

She nodded once, briskly. "I hardly knew him. I wish I did, but I barely remember him, and the stuff I do remember might just be me filling in memories from stories I've heard from other people. I wasn't even old enough for my parents to have even tried having another kid, even though I knew my mom had always wanted a huge family. But after he died, she didn't date much, at least that I knew about. She always said she was too busy with work but I think she just..."

"She missed your dad?" I finished when she trailed off.

"I think so," she said. "So it was just me and her, growing up. And she was just that total badass single mom who was a superhero, you know? Everything I am, I owe to her. And it wasn't until I was a little older that I realized just how much she was giving up for me. Like, she worked all the time. She made sure I never even *knew* how close we were to not being able to pay bills or have groceries or..." She stopped and sighed. "I had this dream once I found out how much she'd given up. I was gonna go to college and get a degree so I could get a good job. Then I was gonna find the love of my life and marry him and buy a big house. And we were gonna have a bunch of kids and my mom was gonna come live with us so she could be around her grandkids and she could stop working and just *relax* finally. It might not be the kids she'd wanted to have herself, but it was what I could do."

"That sounds beautiful," I said.

"It was all I wanted." She smiled down at our hands again. "So I finished high school. Got into college. Worked my ass off and graduated. That was step one, right? Found my reasonably good job. Step two, done." She stopped, and I felt her hand tremble just the slightest bit. "Then I met Wyatt."

"The love of your life?"

She snorted. "Mom never liked him. I thought she just hadn't given him enough of a chance. I was still living at home with her when I met him. But we'd been together for almost a year and I was sure I loved him and that he was The One, you know? I thought maybe if I moved in with him, it would give a bit of separation and she'd see he was a good guy. And she *had* to like him because if my dream was going to come true, she'd have to live with him someday, so I was going to do what it took to make that happen. So I moved out." She sighed again. "She thought I was settling and I thought she was being unreasonable. She thought I couldn't see who he truly was and I thought she was being overprotective."

"That must have been frustrating."

She nodded. "I was still sure it was going to work out. Wyatt had a good job. He was fun. He knew what he wanted out of life, just like I did. I was so fucking *sure* my mom just needed to see that and that when she did, we'd be this big happy family and she would come live with us in the house we were gonna buy one day. I was so *certain* that it would work out. Then she died."

It took me a second to process the words. Her tone hadn't changed in the slightest; she could have been talking about the weather or traffic or the score of a hockey game she didn't care too much about. I didn't know *how* she could say something like that with a voice that was so steady, so direct, so easy and blunt and plain.

But when I looked at her, I understood.

This was who Aspen was. She wasn't some emotionless robot; she felt pain and sorrow and hurt just as strongly as anyone, but her approach to handling those things was different. It had to be, when she'd experienced so much of those things so early in her life.

And I knew there had to be more, simply by the look in her eyes. The slight wetness. The vulnerability. The dread that I felt, knowing her mother's death wasn't the end of the story she was telling me.

"I'm sorry," I said, squeezing her hand. "What happened?"

"A brain aneurysm," she said. "One of those 'out of nowhere' things. They told me that even if I'd still lived with her—she was at home when it happened, in the kitchen cooking dinner for herself—it wouldn't have mattered. She died that fast. But I still..."

She looked away. Her eyes glistened again, but she didn't blink. Instead, she stared hard at the wall, her throat flexing as she swallowed before she looked back at me.

"I ended up in this complete haze where I wasn't really present at all. It was a shock. I was lost and confused and everything I'd wanted didn't seem to matter. The big house, the success, the kids... what did it matter if my mom wasn't there? And Wyatt, he just kind of... swooped in." The look on her face darkened. "In my mind, he was helping me. He was supporting me. He made sure I was eating and drinking water and being taken care of. When people pressed for me to move on, he told them they were being insensitive. That I wasn't ready to 'get over it.'"

My stomach clenched as I realized where the story was headed.

"It was slow, at first. Little things. I shouldn't go out with my friends because they didn't understand. There was some sort of indiscretion that made them unsuitable to spend time with because they would just hurt me. Then it was what I should wear. He wanted me to be comfortable, so why was I wearing heels? I should wear flats. Why was I wearing skirt suits and stockings when I could wear flowy dresses that didn't restrict my legs? Why did I need to wear red lipstick? Who was I trying to impress?"

She laughed, then shook her head. "Then my career. Why would I apply for a promotion at work? He was the man of the house. I didn't need to worry about those things. He would take care of me. Why would I want a job where I had to travel? Was I trying to get away from him? Was I hiding something?"

"Aspen," I breathed. I had no idea what else to say.

"I didn't notice any of it," she said. "And he'd do this thing. He'd... he'd order me to do something. Like, let's say he wanted dinner. I'd make dinner because of course I would. Because of course I was a good little lady who spent all her time in the kitchen after I spent all day fucking *working*. And he'd sit on the couch, and he'd tell me to bring it to him. I'd go put it down, but before I was allowed to leave, I'd have to kiss him. And if it was the wrong thing? He'd berate me or make fun of me or yell at me. Then, when he was done, he'd grab my wrist, and I wasn't allowed to walk away until I kissed him.

"It became his way of claiming me. If we were in public, no matter where we were, he would force me to kiss him, like he was showing the world how much control he had over me. And I fucking *hated* it, Theo." There was anger in her eyes as she looked up at me. "His mouth was always *wet*. I felt like I was drowning, like I would pull away and my face would be shiny because he'd slobbered all over me. He treated me like one of those bratty kids at lunch, you know? 'I licked it, so it's mine.' And I just... I let him do it."

"That explains the dislike of kissing," I said. "I'm sorry I made you—"

"No." She squeezed my hand so hard it almost hurt. "You did not *make* me do anything. No one *makes* me do anything anymore."

I nodded, gently squeezing her hand back. "Okay. Alright."

"I despised it," she said. "And when I realized that, when I realized how much I hated kissing him and that I was *still* doing it, I started to figure out that he was manipulating me. I started realizing it wasn't right. That it wasn't normal. That he—"

Her voice broke and she shook her head, her face darkening even more.

"It was right around then that I came home one day and caught him balls deep in some girl, right on our bed." I winced, but she didn't notice. "She was humiliated. The poor thing. He hadn't told her about me so she was completely shaken up. So she left while I just... sobbed."

She laughed suddenly. "So then Wyatt, the sick son of a bitch, starts telling me how it's my fault and I should be the one embarrassed because he felt the need to cheat and if I was doing 'my job' he wouldn't have needed to cheat. And that was just... it. The haze was gone, and I realized I was standing in my bedroom with the man my mom had seen *long* before I did. That she'd been right, and I was wrong, and I could have avoided so *much* if I'd just..."

"It wasn't your fault," I said, mostly because I had no idea what else I *could* say.

She squeezed my hand. "I know that now. And I realized it then. It was like I woke up. I told Wyatt we were done and I started packing my things.

"Then, as I'm packing—just basic shit, clothes and whatever—he's screaming about how I owe him everything, and he's taken care of me, and I'm not allowed to take certain things because they're his. That he'd done *so* much for me after my mom died and was I really that ungrateful? And I had enough and screamed back at him that he was a piece of shit and no one would ever love him. And Wyatt was, of course, not used to anyone—but specifically, me—standing up to him. So he came across the room and pushed me into the wall hard enough that the one picture I had hanging of me and my mom fell off and smashed on the floor and my head left a hole in the drywall."

Again, the matter-of-fact tone. Again, I gaped at her, my heart fucking *breaking* as I realized what she'd said.

"He *what*?" I choked.

"Pushed me into the wall hard enough to leave a hole," she repeated. "The picture was okay. Just a little scratched."

I'd never wanted so badly to hurt someone I'd never met. "He fucking hit you."

Startlingly, she smiled. "I didn't respond in the best way."

"How?"

She blinked up at me. "I kicked him in the nuts. Hard. Hard enough that he just like... crumpled. And I'm not going to lie. I relished every second of it. I told him if he ever came near me again I'd..." She coughed and her cheeks went pink. "I'm not proud, really, of what I said. But he was on the ground, so I just kind of stepped over him, picked up my stuff, and walked out of the room. And I never heard from him again after that."

"I'm glad," I said softly.

She smiled. "I hate that this sounds like some woeful sob story. I hate that I lived it. I hate *him*. But I was done, Theo. I walked out of that room telling myself I'd never be in a situation like that again. That I wouldn't let my mom down like that ever again. That relationships... They're all just power dynamics. I never wanted to feel indebted to someone or like I belonged to them. I was so *wrong* about Wyatt. I'd thought he was so amazing and that he was the man I'd have all those kids with, that we'd have this beautiful family and live happily ever after. And he took advantage of that."

She sighed heavily, looking up at her ceiling. "I didn't have many friends left, since Wyatt had isolated me from all of them. Mom had a place in Toronto that I technically inherited, but I'd been renting it out so I could keep living with him. But Darby and I were friends and she let me stay with her for a while. She told me Kevin still hadn't hired someone for that promotion Wyatt hadn't wanted me to apply for, so I applied and got it. And then I just kind of buried myself in work until my boss made me come here for a break because he figured I'd burn out.

"And then I met you. And I liked you. And then you accused me of taking advantage of you and I thought I was going to hurt you like Wyatt hurt me because I didn't know how to... to *be* with someone and I couldn't..."

It explained so much.

This Aspen, the Aspen trying so hard not to cry, the one reliving her pain, the one sitting in front of me with anger and shame and so many other warranted and unwarranted feelings... this explained the Aspen I knew, the stubborn, independent, blunt woman who knew what she wanted. The woman who was unapologetically herself, who was self-assured, who did and took what she wanted because she'd been denied that right at one point and she refused—fucking *refused*—to be in that position again. The one who was so guarded, so careful, so terrified of being manipulated again.

"You aren't capable of hurting someone like that," I said firmly. "I'm sorry if I *ever* made you think you could, but I know, okay? I know you aren't that kind of person, Aspen."

"I don't know about that. I mean, I canned him pretty good. He went down. *Hard*." She shook her head. "I shouldn't have... I regret getting physical. I should have tried to be better than him. But I was scared and he was... I didn't know what he would do."

"You protected yourself," I said simply. "And it seems fairly cause-and-effect to me. 'Don't hit Aspen and she won't kick you in the nuts.'"

She smiled, looking down at her lap. "Well, that's it. That's my tragic backstory."

I wanted nothing more than to pull her into my arms and hug her, kissing her hair and her neck as I told her it was going to be okay. But

I couldn't. I knew damn well I couldn't. I was lucky she was still even touching me. So even though I wanted to hold her close and give the comfort I thought she deserved, I simply squeezed her hand again.

"I'm sorry. For all of this."

"Why? You weren't the one who hit me."

"I'm sorry you lived it. That you had this asshole in your life and that he didn't see you for the person you are. That your parents... that you went through that." I thought about my parents and wasn't shocked to feel tears prick in the corners of my eyes. "Thanks for trusting me enough to share this. I just... fuck. I don't even know what to say."

She nodded once, a tiny jerk of a movement. "It happened, and I survived. It's not the sole thing that defines me, but you deserve to know what was holding me back from... from making 'us' a thing. Because even after all that, I wanted..."

I stared at her after she trailed off. She wasn't looking at me and my heart started to race, so hard that I was almost certain she'd feel it through my fingers as I held her hand.

"Wanted what?" I asked.

She didn't answer. When I couldn't take it anymore, I swallowed hard and took a breath.

"Was there a chance, Aspen? For us, I mean?"

# Chapter Twenty-Nine

*Aspen*

How was I supposed to answer that?

Yes?

No.

*Yes.*

But no. No.

I stared down at our hands, trying to think before I spoke. Trying, for fucking once, to compose a sentence that was honest but not hurtful. That made sense. That explained the most contradictory of answers in a way that didn't cause any more pain than I'd already caused.

Not just for Theo, but for me.

"I would have kept insisting we were just friends," I said. "And I would have believed it. Then I probably would have woken up one day and realized we weren't just friends. And I might have been okay with it, even. But when I had to face that before I... before I got to that point..."

"There was a chance it would be more until I pushed for it to be more, instead of letting it get there on its own," he said softly.

"I guess," I said. "But you didn't know. And I was too fucking afraid to even consider it."

"Doesn't matter." His fingers tightened around mine again. "I shouldn't have pushed. I'm sorry. I'm sorry I did that to you."

His hand was so warm. The calluses on his fingertips were rubbing along the side of my palm, their roughness soothing and comforting in a way that didn't quite make sense.

None of it made sense.

I mean, it all made sense. Obviously. Logically, I understood what was happening. But the part of me that was scared, the vulnerable version of myself that hid behind all those walls—she didn't want it to make sense as much as she *did* want it to make sense.

"I've missed you," I said.

"I miss you, too." He hesitated for a moment. "I liked what we had. Even if it was never meant to be more than that, I dunno if I'll ever get over the fact that I made a mess of things. I miss it. A lot."

Every bit of me felt raw. My heart, my soul, even my body. I felt like I was vibrating and the only reason I knew I wasn't was because I was still looking at our hands. His thumb moved across my knuckle and I swallowed, tearing my eyes away and looking across the room. Side by side, we sat in silence, contemplating, facing forward on the couch.

It didn't make sense.

I was expecting some kind of reaction. People always had *opinions* with stories like mine. What I should have done instead, or what I shouldn't have done. Pity. Sympathy. With some women, the thinly veiled relief that it hadn't happened to them. With some men, the sudden desire to go into alpha mode and puff out their chests as they planned a crusade on my behalf. There was always someone who felt like I needed to be saved, like I was some poor, broken little thing that was nothing more than that experience. Like it defined me, shaped me, and was all I was: a victim, or a survivor, or anything besides a human that still fucking *existed* outside of it.

But Theo hadn't run away when I'd told him what happened to me. He hadn't judged me. He hadn't made me feel helpless. There was no moment of him declaring he would hunt down my shithead ex and kick his ass, even though realistically, he probably had the resources to do so. Like, he might not do the actual hunting or ass-kicking, but had he been a different type of person, he could've easily sent Rick to intimidate the hell out of Wyatt.

He didn't do that, though.

He just listened.

Maybe that was where the sparks between us had started. Theo wanted to be treated like a normal person. Whether that was when he was a child being bullied for a speech impediment or as an adult, wanting to be loved for something other than his money or fame, he just wanted to be treated *normally*. Logically, part of his attraction to me likely stemmed from the fact that I treated him as I'd treat anyone.

And in this moment, with my hand in his as he sat beside me on my couch, he was giving me the same thing.

I wanted to be treated as more than what had happened to me. And I'd been so afraid that I wouldn't, and that I'd end up in the same situation all over again, that I'd insisted I didn't want relationships with people. I was certain that no one would ever see past what Wyatt had done to me. That they would either run the other direction or take advantage of me.

Yet, there he was, with the fucking *audacity* to prove me wrong.

"Theo?" I said suddenly, staring straight ahead at the wall.

"Yeah?"

"I don't know how to be in a healthy relationship," I said. "I've never had that experience. There is a very good chance that I'm absolute shit at it. I don't know if I'm what you need and I can't promise I'll even be able to figure out what that is. But I'd... I'd like to spend more time with you. And maybe see where things go. If you'd be willing to."

My mouth was dry and my stomach felt like it was imploding in on itself. I couldn't so much as glance in his direction. I couldn't even *blink*. I would have probably felt less exposed if I'd stripped naked and marched down the stairs, then jumped in the back of the pickup truck that was revving up and down Main Street and started dancing to Theo's song. My palms were sweating and I was certain Theo could feel it, though he still didn't let go of my hand.

"Aspen?" he said.

His eyes were on me. I could tell. Still, I was frozen, staring straight ahead with my lips pressed together, a chill snaking down my arms and legs.

He said my name again, then let go of my hand. The couch shifted as he moved and half a heartbeat later, he was in front of me, crouched on the floor and looking up with those big, warm brown eyes. I closed my eyes briefly, then reopened them and forced myself to look into his.

"I will not treat you like he did," he said, each word said in a ringing, clear voice. "I promise you, I won't. I won't cheat. I won't try to control you. I won't stop you from living your life. We can take it slow. We can be friends who just see what happens."

"I'm only here for a few more months," I whispered. "I can go back to doing pre-audits at the end of my contract."

He shrugged, a lopsided smile spreading across his face. "If you want to go back to your old job, we'll make things work. I mean, I travel a lot, too. I'll have another tour coming up soon."

My jaw trembled.

"If you are ever uncertain, or scared, or worried, all you have to do is tell me," he continued. "We'll step back. If you don't want me, we can end things. We can stay friends. Or we can work it out. Look at things together. Whatever you want, I'll respect it."

I studied him for a moment. "And what if you can't? What if you start feeling like I don't think you're good enough or that I'm using you again?"

The words were harsh. I knew that. But I was honestly asking. I needed to know. It wasn't meant to be a test or anything, but when Theo paused thoughtfully and considered it, he passed.

"I can't promise you I won't," he said. "Like, I think there's always gonna be some self-doubt. I'm trying to get past that, but even my therapist said it's not something that will probably ever really 'go away.'" He shrugged. "What I can do is say I'm working to make sure it doesn't control my life. I'm trying to look at things positively. Like, when I look at you, I'm not gonna think 'this girl is too good for me' anymore, even if I feel like it's a little true. I'm gonna think 'I'm so fucking lucky that this amazing girl likes me.'"

I snorted, but couldn't keep myself from smiling. "You're so sappy."

"Is that a problem?

I shook my head. "One of us has to be."

His teeth raked across his lower lip as he looked up hopefully. "Us?"

"Us," I repeated. "If you want."

"I mean, yeah, Aspen," he said. "As long as it's—"

I assumed he was going to finish that with "—what you want," but the words got lost as I slid forward on the couch and put my hands on either side of his face, tilting it up so I could kiss him.

It caught him off-guard, but he recovered quickly. One hand found my knee as he straightened up a bit, the other making its way to the back of my neck as he pulled himself closer. He was smiling: I could feel it as he kissed me back, his lips eager and soft. Eyes closed, I relaxed into him, enjoying the way my body began to sing, exultant in the moment and demanding more of him already. Still cupping his cheek with one hand, I let the other trail down his neck to the front of his hoodie and grabbed a handful of the fabric, tugging him gently towards me.

He pulled back as I did, glancing down at my hand. "Should we, uh, slow down?"

His eyes betrayed him as much as the breathlessness of his voice did. I knew he would respect whatever answer I gave him, but the one he was hoping for was written all over his face.

Biting my lip, I tugged on his hoodie again. "I thought you were aiming for straight As, Theo. Don't you want a chance to get your GPA back up?"

A shock of laughter fell from my mouth as he practically launched himself off the floor and onto the couch, guiding me to lay on my back. I obliged, looking up at him as he nudged my knees apart and moved between them, hovering over top of me. Wordlessly, he kissed me again, his lips searing hot against mine. The weight of his body was comforting and I could feel him responding to me already, his cock growing beneath his jeans and pressed between my legs. A shiver ran through me as my own arousal started to dampen my panties and I shifted just slightly, just enough that his bulge gave me a delightful taste of friction.

With one hand, he held himself up while the other began to move down my body. His tongue worked against mine as he touched me through my clothing and he groaned softly when my lack of bra meant he could feel my nipple harden through the thin fabric. His thumb flicked back and forth across it, making me squirm again before he cupped my breast and traced his fingers along my cleavage.

"Your shirt is still wet," he murmured against my mouth.

"You know you don't need an excuse to take it off, right?"

He smirked, then sat back just enough to help me wriggle out of my T-shirt. Once it was off and unceremoniously discarded on the floor of my living room, he stopped and looked down at me.

"Something wrong?" I asked.

He shook his head. "You're just so beautiful."

Before I could make a wildly snarky but clever remark about his hopeless romanticism, he dipped his face down and took one of my nipples in his mouth. Whatever I was going to say evaporated as a bolt of arousal shot through me and I moaned, shocked, as he began to worship my tits. His tongue traced patterns around my nipples, circling and flicking in an intricate dance that I couldn't keep track of. Fingers groped and prodded, trailing along my breasts and ribs and stomach as he explored and indulged in my skin. Each movement seemed to make his cock harder, and harder, and before long he was grinding it against my pussy subconsciously as he worshipped my breasts.

One of my hands found its way to the back of Theo's head. I worked his hair between my fingers, intending mainly to urge him on as he worshiped my breasts, but delighted when he shivered and moaned against me. Scratching his head lightly, I made a soft noise as he groaned again and sucked on my nipple harder. He pushed his hips forward and I responded, grinding up against him and revelling in the roughness of his jeans and hardness of his erection through my leggings.

With something like reluctance, he moved his mouth away from my nipple, kissing the top of my breast before moving back to my lips.

"I feel like you're trying to tell me something with all this grinding," he said against my mouth.

"Are you not getting the message?" I responded.

"Hmm." He thrust forward and I let out a gasp before shifting my hips so I could rub myself against him. "It *kinda* feels like you want me to fuck you, but I might be translating wrong, because it also kinda feels like you want me to eat your pussy until you're screaming."

Thankfully, he captured my lips immediately, giving me enough time to recover from those enticing words and come up with a response.

"I want both," I whispered.

"Mmm." He nipped my lip. "What a coincidence. So do I."

Then his mouth was gone from mine and he was kneeling between my legs. Before I could sit up, his hands were on the waistband of my leggings and he pulled them down, along with my panties. As soon as I kicked them off, his head was between my legs. He slipped a hand beneath me, cupping my ass as he licked up and down my pussy lips, teasing along my entrance and just barely letting his tongue graze my clit. Biting my lip, I stifled a moan and pushed up against his face.

He smiled, which I felt, then carefully guided each of my legs over his shoulder so my thighs were pressed against his ears. Even with him so close and held so tight against me, he continued to tease, licking and kissing everywhere except where I wanted his tongue and making me absolutely *ache* for him.

Squeezing my thighs around his head, I groaned. "Please, Theo."

"Patience," is what I think he muttered, but it was so muffled against me that I wasn't sure. Whatever he said, it was spoken right against my slit, and he snaked his tongue out and just grazed my clit to punctuate whatever point he was making. I gasped, gripping the couch cushion as I looked down.

He looked so fucking good with his head between my legs. His eyes were closed, blissfully indulgent in his task until he must have felt me watching him and looked up. Eyes sparkling, he dragged his tongue along my pussy lips one last time before finally, *finally* taking my clit into his mouth and sucking gently.

My eyes squeezed shut as I cried out, my legs trembling around his head. Luckily, he seemed to be done with his teasing and set to work, licking and sucking my clit eagerly before bringing his hand up to my pussy and slipping one, then two, fingers inside of me. He kept a steady rhythm with both his mouth and fingers, bringing me closer and closer to the edge until I was there, right fucking *there*. I grabbed at his head, whispering and gasping and urging him to not stop, to *please* not stop.

And he didn't. Instead, he flicked his tongue against my clit, then curled his fingers so he was hitting my G-spot *perfectly*.

The noise I made wasn't quite a scream or a moan or anything even remotely human-sounding. I came with a crashing force, my body seizing as I clenched my thighs around Theo's head like a vice. He kept licking, kept sucking, kept absorbing every moment of my orgasm and extending it by maintaining his attention to my pussy until I couldn't take another moment of it and had to tell him to stop.

He grinned, kissing my stomach and belly button as he sat up. Before he could stand, I pulled him towards me and pressed my lips to his, tasting myself on his mouth. He smiled and kissed me back, brushing the hair off my face as I caught my breath.

As soon as I could, I sat up, pushing on his chest. He parted from me, a surprised look on his face as I wriggled out from beneath him and stood. He started to say something, but I leaned down and kissed him again before tugging him to his feet and unbuckling his belt.

"Need a hand?" he asked as I fumbled with the buckle.

"Naked. *Now*," I demanded, abandoning his belt and moving to pull his hoodie over his head.

He laughed and unbuckled his belt, then patiently pulled his hoodie off while I pushed his jeans and boxers down. I didn't care how eager or needy or desperate I seemed; I'd just had a taste of sex with Theo and I wanted the rest of it.

*Now.*

"Sit down," I said when he was naked. "I need to get a condom."

It took seconds for me to cross my apartment and get the box of condoms from my nightstand before making my way back to the living room. Theo had sat obediently, his lovely cock in his hand and stroking slowly as he watched me. I took a condom from the box and handed it to him, watching impatiently as he put it on. As soon as he was done, I straddled his lap and positioned my entrance over his cock.

"Aspen," he whispered, his warm brown eyes wide and awed as he looked up at me.

I didn't respond, at least not with words. What I needed to tell him took more than words. It took his mouth against mine, a breathless kiss that he returned eagerly before moving his hands to my hips. Mouths still pressed together, I lowered myself onto his cock, both of us making noises of relief as he entered me. Inch by inch, I took him inside of me, only stilling when he was buried in my pussy. I paused, simply enjoying the feel of him, the way his cock pressed against the walls of my pussy, stretching me, fitting so perfectly in my body. Then, when I couldn't take it any longer, I began to move, slowly rocking back and forth and letting him slide almost completely out before taking him again and again.

He gasped and groaned, and his hands guided my hips in their movements. His head dipped, and suddenly he had my breast in his mouth, sucking my nipple as I rode his cock. I cried out as he sucked, flicking his tongue across my nipple, my pace increasing both out of necessity and from his hands grabbing my hips and guiding me faster and faster. His fingertips dug into the side of my ass, almost painfully, but it felt so good I couldn't ask him to stop.

I could feel my orgasm building again, and I steadied my pace, not ready to stop, wanting to feel more and more of him inside of me. Theo's mouth never left my breast, even though I could hear and feel him groaning against me. His other hand moved suddenly and I tensed, expecting him to spank me, but instead it just slid onto my ass, and closer and closer to my asshole, until his fingertips were pushing to be let in.

"Yes," I urged, and he thrust his finger forward, pushing it inside me.

I moaned, my hips bucking wildly. I could hardly take all the stimulation: the tongue flicking my nipple, the cock fucking me, the finger inside my ass. Whimpering, I clutched at his shoulders, trying to tell him I was close, that I was going to come, that I—

I don't know if I managed to say it before my orgasm ripped through me, from my toes to my neck. White light flashed in my eyes as I shattered, pleasure overwhelming every sense I had at once. It wasn't until it began to fade that I realized Theo was holding me in place, his arms wrapped around me as he held on for dear life. He'd taken his finger out of my ass at some point, but my breasts were practically smothering him as he thrust up into my pussy and I realized he wasn't done. I leaned back, letting him breathe, then began riding his cock as hard as I could.

"I need you to come for me," I whispered.

"Not gonna take long," he grunted.

And maybe that was true, but I liked to think it was the way I kissed him just then that sent him over the edge. He moaned against my mouth, a sound I just fucking *loved*, his fingertips digging into me again as that long, drawn-out sound accompanied his orgasm. I kept moving my hips, riding him slowly and gently until I was sure every last drop of cum was out of him and he was leaning heavily against the back of the couch, his head tilted back and his throat bared to me.

I kissed his neck softly, then rested against him as he held me, my eyes closed as I listened to his heart and felt his skin pressed to mine. Silence filled my apartment as we caught our breaths, a moment of quiet that said more than any words could.

"Where's that coming from?" Theo asked suddenly, his voice almost groggy.

"What?" I asked.

"The music."

I listened, then started laughing. "Seven."

"What?"

"That's the seventh time I've heard this tonight. There's some guy driving up and down the road listening to it on repeat. I think he's probably working through some shit right now."

Theo laughed. "Shit. So you're probably already sick of it."

> *Know it's too late to get you back*
> *But gonna be the man that you deserved*
> *Gonna get over it and fix my shit*
> *'Cause baby, lesson learned*

"A little," I teased, kissing the side of his neck. "But I'll get over it."

He groaned, and I started laughing, and I was still laughing when he found my lips and kissed me again.

# Epilogue

"So, THIS IS IT. What's the decision?"

Kevin is looking at me, and I smile: calm, confident.

"Both," I say.

"Both," Kevin repeats.

He's wearing a confused look, and I'm sure Darby would be too, had I not already told her what I was planning.

"Both." I open the file folder in front of me and withdraw the proposal report Lisa helped me make before the meeting. "Wakeham is a money maker no matter who's in there. You know that. I know that. Everyone knows that. Even Daniel could run the place, and he's an idiot. I can run it better, and we all know that, too. But I miss traveling. I liked doing pre-audits."

I slide the report to him.

"You can have me in Wakeham half the time and doing pre-audits half the time. I've done the math. It's not only possible, it's more efficient."

Kevin looks through the proposal, his expression difficult to read. I catch Darby's eye and she shoots me an encouraging half-smile. The board room is quiet, the only sound the shuffling of the paper as Kevin turns the pages.

"Why?" he says. "You're right, of course. If anyone can do it, I know it's you. But why in the hell would you *want* to do that?"

I shrug. "It turns out I like Wakeham."

Darby snorts and I shoot her a dirty look.

"I like the people in Wakeham. But I'm not a small-town girl. I miss my old job, too, even though I do enjoy directing the facility."

"And how much is this going to cost me?" Kevin asks.

"The deal was that at the end of the year, I keep the raise, or it increased to fifteen percent if I stayed." I pull out a copy of my contract, and a final page of the proposal. "Now, since we're exploring a third option that we didn't consider when I signed this, obviously that needs to be taken into consideration, but I think you'll find I'm asking for a fair deal."

I pass him the page and he reads it, then re-reads it, then looks up at me before reading it a third time.

"Are you fucking crazy?" he asks.

"No, his name is Theo," Darby says.

Kevin and I both ignore her as I shake my head. "I just want a better work-life balance."

He regards me carefully. "So aside from wanting to book the next two months off and use up some of your already-banked time, you want nothing except more time off and the salary you already have." He taps his fingers on the table. "I'm getting the deal of the century here. What's the catch?"

I shake my head. "No catch. This is what I want."

"I thought you wanted to travel."

"Yes, sometimes. But it's not like Theo's tour schedule aligns with the pre-audit schedule and you were right: it's a fast way to burn out. This way, I have a life outside of work, and you get to keep me around longer because I won't get sick like Dean Bradford did."

Kevin still doesn't agree to it right away, but I don't expect him to. I leave the meeting with a smile anyway. As I walk down to my car, I call Theo.

My heart aches a little as the phone rings. I haven't seen him in ages. But I will, soon, almost as soon as Kevin approves my brilliant plan. The Asian leg of his tour is about to wrap up, and then it's onto Europe, where we'll be together for two months.

Part of me is scared. Two months is a long time, and Theo and I haven't had more than few days together here and there since we agreed that *we* were a thing. That same part of me questions whether I'm doing the right thing, whether being with Theo is worth all this trouble. That part of me is small, but present; I don't think it will ever go away completely.

A bigger part of me knows that Theo is absolutely worth it. That even if I can't completely quiet my fears, I can get past them.

"How's Singapore?" I ask as he picks up.

"Lovely. Can't buy gum here, did you know that?"

"I've heard that before, yeah."

"How'd the meeting go?"

"Great. I'm hoping he'll have an answer for me soon. I think he's trying to figure out if it's a scam. He did ask if I was crazy."

"You are a little crazy."

I smile as I get into the car. "You are, too. Have a great show tonight. I miss you."

"I miss you, too. Talk later."

We'll do more than talk later. There will be pictures. He's wondered more than once when I'll get tired of seeing his cock, and I've told him more than once that I'll get tired of seeing his cock when he gets tired of seeing my ass.

He'll then concede that I'm right, and we'll each end up with a new addition to our respective collections.

I miss him.

I can't wait to see him.

My name is Aspen Haws, and that was how I, of all people, fell in love. And if you didn't like it, well... I guess you're just going to have to get over it.

# What's Next for Theo + Aspen?

*The story continues...*
Get your free copy of the exclusive follow up novella *More Than Words*
by visiting ***bit.ly/ct_words***
Then, read on for Rick's story in ***The Devil Made Me***

# Acknowledgments

**My books would not be possible without some very special people:**

My proof-readers, editors, and beta readers are extraordinary people who I am incredibly grateful to. Special thank you to Jason Caldwell, Nora Fares, John, and Chasten.

To Paul M, Kevin Matheny, centralsquareguy, KW, AG, PM, N, ED, KJ, MidNyt, RP, Caleb Waters, and all my incredible supporters on Patreon and in my Cheryl's Terrors group - thank you. Your enthusiasm, support, and belief in me means more than I can ever say.

I am lucky enough to be surrounded by friends and family who have read, supported, and encouraged my writing. To all of you, thank you, and I stand by what I said: you're the one who has to look me in the eye if you read something you didn't want to think about me writing! But also, thank you for not making it weird. I am so grateful for the special people in my life.

And finally, to the man I love more every single day: I love you. You're my everything. Thank you for standing with me, encouraging me to follow my dreams, and being my happily ever after.

# About The Author

Cheryl Terra writes romantic and adult fiction with drama, sass, and a whole lot of... spice. Emotional and humorous, her books focus on contemporary relationships, inclusive characters, and happily ever afters. Living with her husband in northern Alberta, Canada, Cheryl relies on the heat between her quirky and memorable characters to help keep the gas bill down in the winter.

When she's not writing, Cheryl can be found listening to the same song(s) on repeat for hours at a time, spoiling her pets, keeping way too many house plants alive, and knitting or crocheting.

For more information and to get free books, visit Cheryl's website at **cherylterra.com**

# Also By Cheryl Terra

*Find all of Cheryl's books by visiting* ***cherylterra.com/stories***
*Each series is listed in chronological order*

## Standalone Stories

*One Little Question*
*When It Rains*
*Another Last Call*
*Selfish Love*
*What Happens In Vegas*
*Sore Loser*
*The Happiest I've Ever Been*

## The Unicorn Confessions

*The Unicorn Confessions*
*Unicorn For Sale*
*Death of a Unicorn*

## The Love Across Canada Universe

Theo + Aspen:
*Get Over It*
*More Than Words*

Sean + Rick:
*The Devil Made Me*

Noah + Lacey:
*Runaway*
*Waking Up*
*Finding Home*
*Of Daffodils*

**Collaborations with Jason Caldwell**

*Unseen Love*
*No Strings Attached*
*As You Wish*

# Get Free Books

If you want to be the first to know about new books, upcoming projects, and exclusive freebies, visit **cherylterra.com/freebies** to sign up for Cheryl's mailing list.

www.ingramcontent.com/pod-product-compliance
Lightning Source LLC
Chambersburg PA
CBHW021002260626
47169CB00006B/1896